Good & Evil

D0313068

A former journalist for *Le Parisien*, Eric Giacometti spent several years uncovering some of France's biggest medical scandals. He also spent the end of the 1990s investigating Freemasonry, a subject he then explored in fiction with his writing partner, Jacques Ravenne. Together, they form a bestselling author duo, and have written more than fifteen books together, including the several million-copy bestselling Antoine Marcas series.

GIACOMETTI
RAVENNE

Good & Evil

Translated from the French by
Maren Baudet-Lackner

HODDER

First published in the French language as *La Nuit du mal. Le Cycle du Soleil Noir* by Editions Jean-Claude Lattès in 2019

First published in Great Britain in 2020 by Hodder & Stoughton
An Hachette UK company

This paperback edition published in 2020

1

A CIP catalogue record for this title is available from the British Library

Paperback ISBN 9781529359428
eBook ISBN 9781529359435

Typeset in Plantin Light by Palimpsest Book Production Ltd, Falkirk, Stirlingshire

Printed and bound in Great Britain by Clays Ltd, Elcograf S.p.A.

Hodder & Stoughton policy is to use papers that are natural, renewable and recyclable products and made from wood grown in sustainable forests. The logging and manufacturing processes are expected to conform to the environmental regulations of the country of origin.

Hodder & Stoughton Ltd
Carmelite House
50 Victoria Embankment
London EC4Y 0DZ

www.hodder.co.uk

According to the legend, he who possesses the four swastikas will become master of the world.

Excerpt from the *Thule Borealis Kulten*

Prologue

They've been waiting for this for so long. Since before they were born. Like their fathers before them. And their fathers' fathers. As far back as the village can remember, they've known it would happen.

They didn't know when, or who, but after centuries of waiting, they know the day has come.

Or rather, the night.

A bloody night.

The five farmers slink silently between the olive trees. In the darkness, olive trees look much like people. They are a similar size and a comparable shape, and even if a tree has been bent or broken by the wind, it can still hide a man.

A man must listen. He must listen to the shadows that never fall silent. They whisper to those who listen for them. The same word, again and again:

Xeni!

Xeni!

Xeni!

Invaders.

Warriors from the North, their heads protected by steel helmets, have come to sully their lands and steal the sacred treasure a stranger entrusted to the villagers. A stranger from an ancient boreal nation.

The five farmers are certain that the blond men strutting before their eyes are the barbarians described in the prophecy.

A gentle, fragrant breeze rustles the olive leaves, like a peaceful ancestral melody corrupted by the invaders' presence.

They may not have a name, but the parasites have a sound: the thumping of boots on the earth, of guns jostling in their holsters, the din of imminent war and death. But sometimes death takes another path.

Though still hidden behind the olive trees, the farmers have moved. They need to see now, to know how many invaders there are.

One, two, three.

They see the barrels of the rifles propped up against the wall, the spark of a lighter, and the tiny sizzling circles of cigarettes. They watch as the soldiers become men again. Just in time to die.

The five farmers have been trained to deliver death to anyone who dares defy the rules. Like their fathers before them, and their fathers' fathers.

They are not just farmers, they are Fylaques. Guardians.

All of divine blood. They were born in Crete, the island of honey, the place chosen by Zeus's mother to give birth to the father of the gods.

Fylaques are trained to handle the *kyro*, a dangerous dagger engraved with a red drop of blood, better than any other Cretan. The weapon thirsts for the last ounce of blood in the enemy's body.

From behind the olive trees, the five Fylaques smile as they watch the warriors from the North. The first enemy has just unbuckled his belt and removed his jacket. The heat is stifling. He's not used to it. He and his companions are the children of a cold climate, as cold as their hearts.

Their bodies are pale.

But not for long.

One of the Fylaques steps out of the shadows. He unfolds his *kyro*, the perfectly oiled spring freeing the blade from the horn handle. The metal is coated in charcoal to prevent it from glinting in the light. The others join him, baring their teeth as they prepare to strike.

The invaders have their backs to them. They're working around the well and won't hear a thing. Their ears are focused on the clanging of the bucket against the walls as they retrieve it. They've been thirsty all day and the only thing they can hear is their own cries for water.

They've forgotten they are invaders.

The promise of water drowns out all other sounds.

The first Fylaque emerges further from the darkness.

The head of the pack.

He stands silently, waits for the clang of the bucket against the rim of the well, and attacks.

The *kyro* is so sharp that it slips effortlessly between the enemy's ribs. The pain is so intense that the foreigner doesn't even cry out. He looks up at the stars as if he's never seen them before, then darkness veils his eyes, and he falls silently to the ground. The rest of the soldiers have plunged their hands and mouths into the water. They are deaf to their fate. The blades slide deep into their necks. The last thing they'll notice is the strange taste of the water—the tang of their own blood.

The foreigners are just bodies now. Bodies the Fylaques place around the well in a star shape. They cross themselves, not to ask for forgiveness for what they have done, but for what they are about to do. They turn the corpses over onto their backs.

Each *kyro* pauses just above the victim's sternum, then cuts through the skin, which parts like moist lips.

They plunge their hands inside. Rifle around.

When they stand back up, a bittersweet smell rises from the ground.

Thanatos.

To truly kill an enemy, you must take more than his life.

PART ONE

Before Hitler was, I am.

Aleister Crowley

This idea of himself as the German messiah was the source of his personal power. It enabled him to become the ruler of 80 million people.

Walter Schellenberg, Hitler's
Head of Counter-intelligence.
(From *The Labyrinth*, Harper & Brother, 1956)

I

The horizon disappeared into a lead-coloured sky. A curtain of rain pounded into the silver sea. The Admiralty's forecast was accurate—bad weather always blew in from the southwest. From France. It was only three o'clock in the afternoon, but the harbour master's office had already turned on the safety beacons. The wind was still a breeze, but it would pick up soon.

The port in Southampton—the second largest in the southern part of the country, after Portsmouth—was bustling. Swarms of ships of many different sizes moved in and out of the main docks. Since war had broken out, cargo ships and naval destroyers had replaced the legendary transatlantic cruise ships and luxury yachts. The *Titanic* was but a distant memory. No one embarked on holiday from Southampton anymore—now they went to war.

From the bridge of the *Cornwallis*, Captain Killdare watched the cranes dance over the main deck. It was taking forever to load the last crates. The ship should have got underway hours ago. Killdare wanted to leave the estuary as quickly as possible and get past the Isle of Wight, to avoid a possible Luftwaffe raid. Though the bombings had died down since the end of May— Britain had won the battle for the skies, thanks to its Spitfire squadrons—the Germans didn't let them forget that they were at war, and regularly launched attacks on British military or civilian targets. Southampton and Portsmouth still received their fair share of fire and shrapnel. Stuck at port, the *Cornwallis* was easy prey for Göring's vultures.

Annoyed by the delay, Killdare picked up the receiver and called the officer in charge of the hold.

"Jesus, Matthews, what are your dockers doing? Do you want to keep us here all night?"

"Just one more crate and we're done, Captain. The actuator on one of the cranes got stuck because of that damn synthetic oil."

"Of course, the oil. Why not blame it on Nazi sabotage, while we're at it? If you want my opinion, the dockers are just taking it easy. War or no war, it's all the same to them."

Captain Killdare hung up, even more irked than before. He'd been in a bad mood for a whole week, ever since his meeting at the shipowner's head office. To his great surprise, the manager of maritime operations for the Cunard Line had asked him to captain the *Cornwallis*, a lightweight cruise ship headed for New York.

A cruise ship! Killdare couldn't stand them.

His speciality had always been cargo vessels. He enjoyed an excellent reputation for getting his merchandise—whatever its worth—safely to its destination anywhere in the world. Shipowners had been vying to hire him since he'd rescued a sinking cargo off the coast of Macao, despite half of his crew having jumped ship.

And now they wanted him to captain the *Cornwallis*. It wasn't even a Class A vessel, like the *Queen Mary*. The *Cornwallis* was to transport industrial equipment to the United States as part of a new strategy implemented by the General Staff. An officer from the Atlantic fleet had explained their reasoning: "The German U-boats hunt in packs across the Atlantic, and only go after military convoys and big cargo ships. Their torpedoes are too precious to waste on civilian transport vessels."

The door to the bridge creaked open as a tall man in a stylish camel-coloured raincoat came in. He held his soft felt hat in his hand. Killdare shot him an angry look.

"Hello, Captain. I'm John Brown," the intruder explained calmly. "Lovely to meet you."

The sailor stared suspiciously at Mr. Brown. He'd been warned of his arrival. A bigwig, according to the Cunard management office. The man was in his fifties, with a thin, pale face—a typical

London bureaucrat, from a ministry or a bank. His name was clearly an alias. It all reeked of trouble. The captain mumbled hello and shook his hand, which was firmer than he'd expected.

"What can I do for you?" asked Killdare in the most dismissive tone he could muster.

"When do you plan to leave?"

"In half an hour or less, I'd say."

"Perfect. One of my subordinates will be on board for this crossing. Please do your best to ensure he's comfortable."

The captain shrugged. "You mean the rude, bearded fellow who smells of tobacco and is inseparable from his metal case? The bloke in cabin 35B? He'll be as comfortable as any other passenger on the upper deck. No more, no less. Now, if you don't mind, I have a ship to ready for departure. I'll pass on your recommendations to my second-in-command. Good day."

The captain turned around, terminating the conversation, and began inspecting the pressure gauges on the instrument panel. A few seconds passed, but Mr. Brown didn't budge.

"Captain, I don't think you understand."

Killdare turned his head, and saw a military card bearing Mr. Brown's photo. *Commander James Malorley, Army Strategic Division.*

"You see, that rude, bearded fellow is my deputy. He's on a confidential mission of the utmost importance to the British government, so it would be best for you to make things as easy as possible for him during his stay. Please note that I'm using the conditional only to be polite."

Killdare stood up straight. He'd served four years in the Royal Navy and instinctively grew an inch when confronted with high-ranking officers.

"I apologize, Commander. You should have introduced yourself sooner. I'm a little anxious, with all these Kraut raids. The sooner I'm out of here, the better."

"A network of German spies was uncovered in Portsmouth last week, so I'm wary of lingering ears. I have a letter for you."

Commander Malorley handed him a yellow envelope bearing the Prime Minister's seal. "These are your instructions. Open them when you're at sea. You'll notice that they come directly from the highest authority. Read them carefully. Captain Andrew—the rude bloke, as you call him—will come and explain what it's all about."

"If the mission is so important, isn't it dangerous to get civilians mixed up in it? I have thirty passengers on board. I know we're at war, but using innocent people as a cover isn't very . . . sportsmanlike."

"Do you think Hitler and his friends are sportsmanlike? It's an honourable sentiment, but don't worry about the passengers; they're all professionals who know the risks. Moreover, you'll be escorted by two submarines for the entire crossing. They'll be perfectly discreet, of course, and will join you just outside the port."

A siren sounded twice in the bridge, signalling that the ship was fully loaded.

"I see it's time to go. Good luck," said the commander, staring hard at the captain. "If I told you the outcome of the war is in your hands, would you believe me?"

"Given the look of your deputy, I'd bet you a-hundred-to-one. But anything is possible these days, like talking to a military commander who goes by the name of Mr. Brown, or watching Europe march to the orders of a chap with a Charlie Chaplin moustache. I'll get your precious cargo to its destination, even if I have to cross the Sargasso Sea and confront Neptune himself."

The commander gave the captain a firm pat on the shoulder and left the bridge, tightly buttoning up his raincoat. The temperature had dropped several degrees and the damp found its way into his shirt collar.

As he set foot on the wet wharf, the *Cornwallis*'s siren wailed across the dock. Harbour employees in mustard-coloured overalls untied the mooring lines and threw them to the sailors swarming on the deck.

Commander James Malorley of the Special Operations Executive, aka Mr. Brown, watched the ship's black stern move slowly away from the dock. How curious that the ship chosen to carry the sacred swastika—the first of four such relics; three others were yet to be retrieved by the Allies—bore the name of the head of the British army during the American Revolution, Lord Cornwallis, George Washington's arch-enemy.

The stench of fuel oil filled the air as the vessel spun around to face the harbour's exit. Deep within the hull, machinery whirred softly.

Malorley glanced one last time at the ship, pulled his felt hat down, and turned towards the harbour master's office, where Laure d'Estillac was waiting for him inside the Amilcar.

He didn't want to admit it, but he was relieved to see the swastika leave for the other side of the Atlantic, thousands of miles away. He and his SOE colleagues had risked their lives to keep it from the Nazis, and many lives had been claimed. Jane's face surfaced in his mind. He could still see the surprised, almost childlike expression on the young agent's face as she was brought down by a hail of German bullets. Her blonde hair shone brightly in the enemy searchlights. She had fallen far away, in southern France, near the Pyrenees. In Cathar country in a field at Montségur, at the exact place where the heretics had been burned alive centuries earlier. Unable to save her, he had fled like a coward to keep the relic safe.

Malorley could still feel the kiss she'd given him as they fled the castle. A long kiss, as if the brave young woman had known it would be their last.

Big drops of rain soaked the dock. The commander shivered and tightened the scarf around his neck.

The shower dripped down from his hat, blurring Jane's face, leaving him lost in his thoughts. He was a solitary man who'd given up on a normal life. No wife, no children, not even a dog. He lived to do his duty. Not by choice—fate had decided for him by involving him in the quest for the relics. Malorley knew he was a piece on a chess board, and the game's stakes were unclear. A game of chess that had been going on for thousands of years. He had no idea whether he was a pawn or a king, but he was sure that others before him, people from other times and civilizations, had lost their lives and souls to this adventure.

He hastened his step, so as not to be soaked by the time he reached the car on the other side of the dock.

Suddenly, a strident siren rang out over the port. Malorley's blood began rushing through his veins as the muscles in his legs leapt into action. Since the beginning of the war, the reflex had become an instinct, as it had for most British people. Malorley ran along the dock as fast as he could. He only had a few minutes left. This wasn't a ship siren; it was the anti-aircraft defence system. It meant the German eagle was on the hunt. And its cruel presence promised blood, fire, and death.

2

Karl woke up screaming. He immediately groped for the gun he'd left next to his bed. When he felt the grip against his palm, his pulse began to slow. It put a stop to the unbearable buzzing that filled his ears each time he woke in the middle of the night, his mouth dry and breathing shallow. Fear. Crete was the first place he'd ever truly experienced the indescribable sensation. The fear of death, of the night, of the unknown. He didn't even really know what he feared most anymore. He'd spent most of his life handling shovels and brushes at archaeological excavations, but now the only thing that made him feel better was the gun in his hand. And he was so thirsty. All the time. It was autumn, but the heat was still stifling in Crete. Especially at night. And he was one of the lucky ones—he was staying in a real house that had been requisitioned on the island. For the soldiers, who were staying in tents, sleep was but a distant memory, and it showed in their work.

Karl had alerted Berlin several times, asking for reinforcements, particularly since the excavation site just kept growing. But his boss, Colonel Weistort, had been seriously injured on a mission. And no one in Germany seemed to be interested in Crete anymore. All eyes had been focused on the eastern front since millions of German soldiers had set off to conquer Russia. An indomitable wave was about to crash into Moscow.

Karl Häsner stood up, shaking his head. He wasn't interested in politics, much less war. As for the Nazis, if he was honest, he despised them. He was an intellectual, nothing like those fanatics shouting in stadiums, the SS officers clicking their heels in their black uniforms, or that moustached dwarf with his damn tirades. How had Germany fallen into his hands? Karl plunged his head into the lukewarm water in the sink as if he were trying to wash something away. In fact, he was cheating fate. Thousands of young German men were dying on the eastern front while he delicately handled a brush to reveal the surface of an amphora. Instead of joining the army, he had used his degrees to find a place at Himmler's research institute, the Ahnenerbe. Better to be an archae-ologist for the regime than a corpse out on parole.

Karl began to shake.

He had thought he was escaping death, but this was far worse.

Luckily, work helped soothe his anxiety. Upstairs, the former owner had set up a library with windows as narrow as dungeon arrow slits. It must have been designed to keep out the freezing winter wind and scorching summer sun. For Karl, the room had become a sanctuary. He felt safe as soon as he walked in. The walls covered in books and chests full of artefacts made him feel like he was in a world free of violence and danger. He knew it was an illusion, but he clung to it with all his strength, even if he did keep his gun within arm's reach. Across from the door, stood a long wooden table where Karl gathered the most precious finds from the site.

The Ahnenerbe archaeologists had arrived in Knossos in June, when the German parachutists hadn't yet subdued the entire island, despite ferocious battles. The team had got to work imme-diately. Himmler was obsessed with the legend of the Minotaur and the labyrinth and was determined to find traces of them. Much to Karl's surprise, he was not at all interested in any other Greek archaeological treasures. He wanted specific results, and he wanted them quickly. In just a few weeks, they had made some exceptional discoveries. The rarest pieces were still in the room. He should have sent them to Berlin, but he couldn't bear to part with them. In a world at war, the fragments of frescoes depicting teenagers swimming with dolphins and statues of goddesses with marble breasts, their wrists wrapped in snakes—

all this still, serene beauty—had become absolutely necessary to his survival.

An object was waiting for him on the table. The oval shape featured a delicately carved border. It reminded him of a compact mirror, except that it was made entirely of gold. It was the first artefact made of precious metal that the team had found. They'd uncovered it near a corner of a brick wall, on a bed of ashes, where it seemed to have been purposefully left rather than lost or thrown away. Like an offering. Karl studied the object as it glinted in the light. How long had it been buried? Centuries, undoubtedly, and yet it shone as if it had just left the goldsmith's shop. Karl noticed a carefully drilled hole on the upper edge, probably for a chain. Was it a piece of jewellery a woman had removed from around her neck as tribute for the gods, or a religious relic only worn during sacred ceremonies? Karl sighed. The feeling of oppression that had been with him since waking was beginning to dissipate. Beauty always vanquished fear. Nevertheless, something worried him. The surface of the object wasn't smooth. The goldsmith had engraved it with a symbol. A symbol that was omnipresent in his life.

A swastika.

Karl studied it, fascinated. He resisted the urge to run his finger over it, as if he were afraid of being contaminated by its dark and ancient power. Ridiculous! Häsner shook his head. He was an archaeologist, not a medium. His job was to analyse and interpret, not to explore mad theories. He was still thirsty. He knew he should go down to the kitchen and get a drink, then try to go back to sleep. He knew he shouldn't work so late at night anymore, or he'd start seeing things. And yet, he stayed put, his eyes fixed on the symbol that left him uneasy. Why had a man from thousands of years ago decided to so carefully engrave the object with this symbol? What did it mean? What was it worth? And most importantly, how had this symbol travelled through time to appear in Germany, where it figured at the centre of every flag? That was the real question. Karl had a bad feeling about all of it. A foreboding suspicion that this symbol, forgotten for centuries, hadn't come back for no reason. During its long absence, it had absorbed energy and power, and now it was ready to act.

Karl brought his hand to his forehead. He must be feverish. It was the only explanation. How could he have such irrational ideas? He roughly placed the object back on the table, as if to break a spell. Tomorrow he would send it to Berlin. Himmler would be delighted. The smallest swastika left him jubilant. As for Karl, he was done with these ridiculous ideas and irrational fears. For good.

A fist banged on the front door and the sound echoed upstairs. "Herr Häsner!"

Karl hurried to the window. Through the narrow opening, he saw two soldiers lit by torchlight. Their uniforms were dishevelled and they both held their guns at the ready. Karl returned to the table and carefully placed the artefact in a numbered box, which he slid into a drawer. He locked it inside. Each of his movements was excessively meticulous. Though he didn't dare admit it, he was putting off the inescapable moment when he would have to turn around. What if he wasn't alone in the library? What if there was a shadow between him and the stairs?

"Herr Häsner! Open up! Hurry!"

The wooden door resonated like a drum. He had no choice. He turned around suddenly. The room was empty. He crossed it in three steps, ran down the stairs, and rushed to the entryway. He turned the key in the lock. Two soldiers appeared, their faces filled with terror.

"It happened again!"

The village was not far from the excavation site. Narrow streets full of one-storey houses were dominated by the blue dome of the church. The soldiers stationed there had set up a searchlight to reach even the darkest corners. A wandering dog, startled by the blinding beam, disappeared into an alley. All the town's residents had holed up in their homes, shutters closed tight. The priest was the only one to be seen, kneeling in prayer before a wrinkled canvas. Karl stopped short. The officer on duty came over and grabbed his arm to pull him aside, without so much as a salute.

"Three more!"

"Is this where you found them?"

"No, on the outskirts of town. They were fetching water."

"In the middle of the night?"

"The area is teeming with rebels. We're afraid they're poisoning public wells. So, we go to hidden sources. And never to the same one twice."

Häsner ran his hand over his forehead. He was burning up. To keep the soldier from noticing his dizzy spell, he pointed towards the canvas, hoping his hand wouldn't shake.

"Why didn't you leave them where you found them? There may have been clues, proof . . ."

"The proof is right here! The entire population is complicit. They feed information to the resistance. And this time, they will pay! Dearly!"

Karl imagined the wave of repression that would hit the village. His mission would be definitively compromised.

"How did you find your men?"

The officer, a captain, took a step back.

"It was the dogs. They're starving in this damn place. They must have smelled the blood. They wouldn't stop barking, so a patrol went to have a look."

"I see. Show me."

A guard tapped the priest with the butt of his rifle to get him to move aside. The searchlight shone on the dirty canvas as a soldier pulled it back and turned his head away.

At first, Karl didn't understand. The bodies looked like they had been trampled, hammered, and ripped apart in every direction. He moved closer. Meat. It was already rotting. He couldn't distinguish anything. No joints, no organs. Everything was red, in ragged pieces. Despite his revulsion, Karl bent over. The skull of one of the corpses was broken in several places. Bone fragments had slid down to the face. Karl gestured to the officer to come nearer.

"What happened here?"

The captain cleared his throat.

"When we got there, the dogs had gone crazy, Herr Häsner.

We couldn't retrieve the bodies. So, we had to fire our guns, first into the air, then . . ."

Karl felt around in vain for something to steady himself. ". . . Into the bodies. Transfer them to the military doctor for autopsy. If it's even possible."

The village looked like it was under siege. Every street that led out of town was blocked by a squad of soldiers. Mobile teams kept watch over the houses along the olive orchards. Headlights shone on every home, with the searchlight in the town square focusing on the houses of the village's most notable residents.

"The site is locked down, Captain."

The officer nodded. Now the show could begin.

"What are you going to do?" asked Karl, concerned. "Punish the entire village? We need the locals. How will we find supplies? This excavation is a priority, you know."

The captain pointed to the skull on his uniform collar.

"I'm SS, and three of my men have just been killed. I'm going to do my own excavations. House by house."

"You know that if it was resistance fighters, they're long gone by now. You'll never find them."

"Not them, but we can find their loved ones."

"And do what with them?"

"Take them hostage. A woman and child from each family."

"You can't kill civilians!" protested the archaeologist, his emotions getting the better of him.

"We won't need to. They'll start talking before long."

"You think so?"

"Absolutely. Right after I kill the priest, the mayor, and all the members of the local government."

The field hospital had been set up some distance from the town. It was little more than a group of tents surrounded by barbed wire where a team of doctors and nurses cared for the most recently wounded soldiers, who were awaiting repatriation to Germany. The battles fought by the German parachutists to take control of the island had been remarkably violent, and the cemetery next to the field hospital was full of freshly dug graves. Karl picked up the pace as he caught sight of the many man-sized mounds of earth. He was headed to tent K. That's where they had taken the bodies of the soldiers killed outside Knossos.

"Herr Häsner?" asked a man in a white jacket, his elbows resting on a wooden pillar as he smoked a cigarette, slowly exhaling pale clouds that unravelled in the darkness. "Come in. The bodies are in the tent."

In the light of a storm lantern, the three corpses lay on a long table covered in blood.

"We haven't bothered to clean up around here for a while now," commented the doctor, as if explaining a local tradition.

"How did they die?" asked the archaeologist, though he realized the question was silly.

The doctor dropped his cigarette on the ground and carefully stubbed it out with his foot.

"Impossible to tell. The bodies have been too damaged."

Karl cleared his throat. "Before the dogs got to them, they were . . ."

"Alive, is that what you were going to say? No, they were already dead. If they had been alive, they would have tried to protect their faces. It's an innate reflex, even if you're badly wounded. They have no traces of bites on their hands and forearms."

"Thank God," Karl murmured.

The doctor shrugged. "Now that you've thanked God for letting these poor men be devoured by dogs, why don't you tell me what you're doing here. The soldiers are responsible for security issues, not archaeologists, unless I'm mistaken?"

"Yes, but I'm the one who has to report to Reichsführer Himmler. So, it's either a terrible but relatively straightforward attack by the resistance fighters and I don't bother him with it, or it's something else." Since the doctor remained silent, Karl continued. "Did you notice any unusual lesions, for example?" The doctor put on a pair of gloves and moved towards the bodies. "Or any bullet wounds incompatible with the calibre used by the German army?"

"None of these men were killed by a firearm, I'm sure of it." He gestured to Häsner to come closer. Each body was a bloody pile of flesh. "Look, right here."

Karl leaned in towards an indistinct mass of rotting tissue and shredded organs. The only thing he noticed, beyond the unbearable smell, was a hole that was bigger and deeper than the others.

"And the other two bodies have the same wound. If I were you, I would inform Himmler."

"To tell him what?" asked Karl, annoyed. "That I saw a hole in the middle of a rotting corpse?"

"To tell him someone ripped the livers out of three of his men."

3

Laure turned towards the concrete bunker crowned with a bright-red siren. The screeching stopped at the same time as the rain, which was more fleeting than she had expected. She walked over to the soldier posted at the entrance, who took off his cap shaped like an upside-down plate. "What's going on?"

"Don't worry, Miss. It's just a drill. Everything will be back to normal soon."

An anti-aircraft defence gun, easily recognizable thanks to its long barrel pointed skyward, sat alongside the bunker. The soldier in the turret whistled at her and offered a compliment she didn't understand.

Laure d'Estillac sighed and lit a Morland as she studied the dock that led towards Terminal D, where the *Cornwallis* was docked. Malorley had promised not to spend too long sending the ship off. With the false alert, he'd be back even sooner than planned.

She'd chosen to wait in the car across from the harbour master's office. The foggy atmosphere of the port, the iodine-rich air sullied by the scent of fuel oil, and the sailors who reeked of the rough seas and silt—none of it was her cup of tea. She was a woman of the mountains, raised on pure air and wide-open spaces.

She leaned against the Amilcar's bonnet and breathed in the sweet, almost caramel-flavoured smoke. Her tobacco consumption had skyrocketed since she'd arrived in England, but she'd never felt as strong as she did now. The intense SOE training had sculpted her body and hardened her soul. Four months of suffering, discipline, and deprivation had initiated her into the organization. Laure, the last of the Cathar d'Estillacs, was no more. As a girl on her mountainside, she'd only ever dreamed of beautiful castles, handsome knights, and courtly love. She had fancied herself a princess, but the madness of mankind had turned her into a warrior. At the SOE, they had taught her the twisted arts of destroying, killing, and inflicting suffering of all sorts. The wild young aristocrat was a new woman now. Tougher, surer of herself.

And she had a new name. Matilda. Agent Matilda.

She hated the bland alias and had asked for it to be changed, but the SOE didn't waste its time on such vanities. Laure may have been gone, but Matilda could still feel the need for vengeance running through her veins. Her father was buried at their ancestral home in Montségur, many hundreds of kilometers away. Murdered by Nazis. She had adopted the SOE motto—*Drive iron into German flesh*—as her own. Matilda was impatient to return to France and accomplish the destiny that had been foisted on her.

The sound of heels on a wet pavement rang out. Her boss came into view, his face bright red as he ran.

"No need to hurry, Commander. It was just a drill, like in training," she explained, amused by the situation.

Like many Englishmen, Malorley's pale skin quickly took on a charming flush. Relieved, he slowed down and took off his scarf.

"Did you complete your mission?"

"It's done. God willing, the *Cornwallis* will reach Chesapeake Bay in seven days. The American Coast Guard will retrieve the object and put it who knows where for safekeeping. I really hope this cursed relic will turn the tide in our favour."

"We're not facing Hitler alone anymore. Since he invaded Russia, Stalin has become our new ally."

"Yes, but it's not enough. Last I heard, the Panzers were crushing them. If only the Americans could declare war and join us. Then we would really have a chance."

"Why isn't the *Cornwallis* delivering the relic to New York?"

"Our American friends are prudent. German submarines have been spotted off the coast of Manhattan. And they believe—"

Before he could finish his sentence, the siren sounded again.

"This is getting annoying," said Laure as she watched two guards scramble up the ladder to the anti-aircraft gun.

A man in a beige jacket shot out of the harbour master's office and almost knocked Laure to the ground.

"Hey, you should be more careful," she yelled.

"The Germans are coming! Hide over there, in the shelters inside the fire station."

A muffled buzzing vibrated through the damp air. Laure and Malorley turned towards the entrance to the port and saw a swarm of big black birds in the sky.

"Bloody hell," exclaimed Malorley.

A roar barrelled into them. A Messerschmitt BF 109 was making its way up the canal, heading directly for them. Seconds after they flung themselves to the ground, two bursts of gunfire ripped through the tarmac a few meters from the Amilcar, cutting down the man who had run into them just moments before.

The plane thundered as it passed overhead. It was so low that Laure was able to make out the pilot's white scarf. As they stood up, a huge explosion demolished the harbour master's office. A shower of stone and shards of wood and glass pounded into the ground. Screams rang out all around them. Malorley helped Laure up and noticed a trail of blood running down her cheek from her temple.

"Laure!" he shouted, alarmed.

"It's nothing, just a scratch. I got far worse in training."

A thick cloud of black smoke was spreading over the port, reducing visibility to just a few meters. The smell of burnt oil wafted through the air. The young woman felt like her lungs were about to explode. Above them, the roaring grew louder. Panic raged all around them. Ten meters away, the anti-aircraft guns fired into the sky.

A man in flames staggered out of what had once been a warehouse. He stopped after a few steps and fell to the ground, writhing like a worm. A new explosion boomed in the distance, near the main terminal. A spray of seawater splashed onto their shoes.

Malorley took a pair of binoculars from the glove box and searched for the ship amid the smoke. The charcoal-grey clouds began to clear from one area, and his blood went cold.

"The *Cornwallis*!"

The ship was off kilter, leaning too far starboard, and a thick grey plume rose up from its main chimney. All around, there was nothing but flames and destruction. At the entrance to the harbour, two cargo ships had been hit hard and were now sinking into the port's dark waters. Clusters of sailors were jumping ship here and there. As the vessel regained its balance, a strange whistling ripped through the air.

Two Junkers JU 87 Stukas, with their instantly recognizable wings folded skyward, were dive-bombing the port. Malorley was captivated by the scene. The last time he'd seen these monsters in action was in Madrid, during the Spanish Civil War. Their precision was unparalleled.

"The Trumpets of Jericho," he mumbled.

"Why do you call them that? They're Stukas, I saw them on the news. They showered crowds of civilians with gunfire during the exodus from Paris."

"The Germans installed sirens designed to terrorize their enemies under the landing gear. The Spanish nicknamed them the Trumpets of Jericho. There's no way the *Cornwallis* will make it out of here."

Captain Killdare must have noticed the threat, because the boat was heading straight towards the small space between the two sinking cargo ships that were spewing smoke into the air.

"He's crazy! It's not wide enough," shouted Laure.

"No, I think I know what he's doing. He's trying to hide amid the wreckage."

The Stukas swerved back and forth, flying very low over the terminal. They dropped their bombs on the fuel stores at the end of the dock. The tanks exploded into a giant ball of fire.

Malorley aimed his binoculars back towards the port.

"I can't see anything . . . Wait, there it is! My God, he made it through. Killdare's done it!"

The *Cornwallis*'s siren echoed through the harbour like a victory cry. The ship was speeding towards the last jetty, which separated the port from the estuary.

Just as Malorley put down the binoculars, a shout rang out behind him. He was knocked forward and landed face-down on the pavement. An impact followed by a terrible creaking sound shook the ground. Laure lay on top of him.

"You've got rusty," whispered the young woman in his ear.

She helped him up. As he dusted himself off, he saw a huge, mangled metal hoist on the ground right where he had been standing just seconds before.

"Thank you, Laure. Nice reflexes. That tackle would make any of the players on England's rugby team proud."

"It's all thanks to my training. You taught me to plant bombs, sabotage railways, and kill my enemies at least five different ways—and without a weapon."

Men in blue overalls and white metal helmets bearing the letter "W" came over. Air Raid Protection wardens.

"Quick, follow us to the underground shelter. They say another wave is coming."

Malorley and Laure ran towards a group huddled at the entrance to the fire station. Another explosion rang out from the northernmost part of the port. Orange flames shot up into the black sky. A blast of warm air enveloped them.

"Incendiary bomb!"

Panic ensued. Malorley and Laure were forced down the stairs, like driftwood in a rushing river.

"Calm down!" shouted a loud voice inside. "Wounded to the right."

Several more ARP wardens stood at the bottom of the stairs, doing their best to manage the flood of new arrivals. But in vain. Despite their best efforts, Malorley and Laure ended up in the room with the injured.

"Do you think the *Cornwallis* will make it?" she asked as she watched more and more people arrive on stretchers.

"Yes, as long as she got out of the port. The Germans won't

waste their bombs on a small cruise ship. They'll head for the munitions warehouses north of the city."

"I don't understand how people can still live here."

"Southampton has endured more than three hundred bombardments since the beginning of the war. Three-quarters of the city has been destroyed, but its residents are still here. They rebuild the port again and again. British tenacity."

"We didn't see much of that at Dunkirk," teased Laure.

The sickening smell of burnt flesh reached their noses. Two men brought in a woman on a stretcher whose body was half covered in what looked like charcoal.

"Help me," she pleaded.

Laure moved closer and saw that the two men were heading back out.

"You can't just leave her here!"

"She won't suffer for much longer. Third-degree burns and a shard of glass lodged in her chest. We'll bring her something for the pain, if we find anything."

The poor woman's face was nothing but charred flesh, from which two striking blue eyes emerged. Blood ran from the opening that must have been her mouth.

"But she's in so much pain!"

"God have mercy on her."

The men left hurriedly, abandoning the suffering woman. Laure took her hand, which was still intact. Her skin was soft and supple.

"I . . . beg . . . you. Hurts . . . too . . . much," the woman whispered, struggling to speak.

Malorley came over and held out his gun to Laure.

"We have to put an end to her suffering. Here."

"You're crazy!"

"Didn't they teach you to kill at the training centre?"

"Germans, not British people. I can't just execute her in cold blood."

"What if it was one of your colleagues on a mission? What if you needed to put him out of his misery before he fell into the hands of the Germans, who would surely torture him?"

Laure shook her head, her eyes rimmed with tears. Malorley placed the barrel of the gun against the woman's head, all while staring straight at the Frenchwoman.

"You can watch or look away. If you choose the former, it's all part of the job. If it's the latter, I understand."

"How can you—"

"She won't suffer any longer."

Laure looked away.

A shot rang out and the whimpering stopped.

Malorley put his gun away in his jacket pocket.

"I'm sorry, Laure," he said. "Truly sorry. But you must learn to tame death. It's the only way you'll survive."

"Survive, but in . . . in hell," she replied as she wiped her tears away. "When will this damn war end?"

He sat down next to her and stared into space.

"I don't know. Maybe never."

4

The road to Knossos, Crete
November 1941

The road they had followed since leaving Heraklion was now little
more than a dirt path. The driver slowed to navigate the ruts.
Tristan Marcas looked through the back window at Crete's capital,
which shone bright white in the sun. The Mediterranean was the
only thing that escaped its blinding rays. The sea's deep-blue hue
seemed infinite as it stretched towards the horizon.

"*The sea, forever starting and re-starting,*" recited Tristan when
the line from Valéry's poem popped into his head. A sudden jolt
brought him back to earth. The road was surrounded by another
sea entirely. A sea of olive trees. Donkeys roamed beneath their
branches, scratching their hooves on the dusty ground, hopelessly
searching for a blade of grass. The sun-scorched earth was so
cracked that it looked like it might split apart to reveal dark, swel-
tering depths below. Hell seemed dangerously near. The driver
swerved suddenly to avoid hitting an upended olive tree whose
roots stretched skyward. Tristan noticed that the young man had
just grabbed hold of an enamelled cross under his jacket and
brought it to his lips. He couldn't be more than twenty. The invasion of Crete must have been his first combat experience.

"Superstitious?"

"In Crete, everyone is. If you're not already, you become superstitious. Did you see that uprooted tree on the side of the road?"

"Yes, a gust of wind, I imagine."

"Here people say there's a soul hiding in every tree. A cursed
soul."

Tristan didn't answer. He pretended the conversation didn't interest him, because it was the best way to get the driver to continue.

"Whenever a tree is upended, the soul escapes through the roots. The world below comes to haunt the world above."

Tristan looked at the seat next to him, where Erika had dozed off. In her sleep, her features had softened. She almost looked like a young girl. Her braided hair fell over her shoulder, adding to her youthful appearance. Marcas smiled. Neither war nor death left the face of a woman in love unscathed. And yet . . .

"Did you come from Berlin?" asked the driver.

Tristan nodded. A plane chartered by Himmler himself had just dropped them at the new military airport being used to supply the German troops. Their departure had been decided upon just a few hours ago. The Reichsführer's special orders.

"They must be rejoicing in the capital," continued the driver. "Our troops are being hailed with glory in Russia. They say Moscow will fall before the end of the year."

"They're fighting with as much courage as you are, here in Crete. I hear the fighting has been ferocious."

"Worse than that. The inhabitants of this island are savages. Believe me, don't let yourself be fooled by the beautiful landscapes or the call of the sea. It's all a trick . . ."

The car suddenly braked hard. A roadblock had just appeared before the next turn. Behind an improvised barricade, black silhouettes barred the road.

"They're ours," announced the driver, relieved. "I recognize their uniforms."

Marcas had seen a lot of roadblocks, especially during the Spanish Civil War. He'd learned to be wary of them and to instantly detect any signs of nervousness—white knuckles gripping guns, tense voices, anything that could lead to disaster if ignored.

"Turn off the engine," ordered Tristan.

"But why?"

"Do as I tell you."

Behind the barricade, the soldiers kept their guns aimed at the car. There were no orders, no one moved. They're terrified, thought Tristan. They'll shoot at the slightest provocation. He looked at Erika to see if the excitement had woken her, but she was still asleep. The flight had been exhausting.

The driver began to worry. "I don't understand, shouldn't they ask us to identify ourselves? I have a password."

"Do you recognize their unit?"

The driver leaned over towards the windscreen. "They're too far away for me to see their insignia."

Tristan noticed a glint of light near the checkpoint. He recognized it instantly—the glare of the sun on a lens.

"They're using binoculars to get a better look at us. It must be the commanding officer."

"Why would they do that? We're less than thirty meters away!"

"They want to see our faces. They're scared. The problem is, we don't know what they're afraid of. What's your name?"

"Otto."

Tristan studied the young man's face. His hair was bright orange and his skin was dotted with freckles. He must have been bullied on every playground he'd ever known. Going to war was not the hardest thing he'd ever done.

"You enlisted, right?"

"Yes, but how did you know?"

"That's not important. What matters is that you're a brave man. So, listen up. You're going to—"

Before Marcas could finish, an order rang out, amplified by a loudspeaker. "Knossos is under military lockdown. Nobody can get in. Back up slowly and turn around at the next junction. If you stay there or come closer, you'll be considered hostile and we will open fire without further warning."

"What's going on?" Erika asked, her voice still groggy. Tristan was about to answer when she asked again. He felt her warm breath on his neck with every word.

"Are we there?"

"We're stuck at a roadblock and the soldiers are jumpy. Don't make any sudden moves."

Erika lifted her blonde plait off her sticky neck and pinned it to the crown of her head. She was burning up. The heat was stifling.

"Has someone spoken to them?"

"They're the ones doing the talking, and they've asked us to beat it."

"Or they'll open fire," added Otto. "We have no choice—we have to go back to Heraklion and get them to call the command post in Knossos. They'll send word to the roadblock and—"

"There is no way I'm spending another minute in this oven."

Erika unlocked the door and slid her long legs outside. As they hit the ground, her boots created a fleeting cloud of dust.

The perfect target, thought Tristan. *They'll take her out like it's target practice.*

"Don't come any closer!" shouted a voice from the barricade.

"My name is Erika von Essling, a special envoy commissioned by Reichsführer Heinrich Himmler himself. If you threaten me, you'll end up in military court, and if you place a single finger on the trigger, I'll have you executed."

"Is that true?" asked the driver.

"What do you think?" replied Marcas.

"Now, I'd like to speak to the person in charge here. Come out to meet me. And make it quick; I'm in a hurry."

A figure moved forward, leaving behind the line of soldiers blocking the road.

"Lieutenant Friedrich Horst," he explained. "My orders are clear. No one can enter Knossos, which is under lockdown. Our forces are carrying out a mission."

"Do you really think the people you're looking for are going to queue up in front of this ridiculous barricade?"

"I'm just following orders."

"Well, I'm following the Reichsführer's orders. And there's one I would be delighted to obey: I'm to send anyone who gets in my way to the eastern front! How does that sound to you and your men?"

Tristan leaned towards Otto, whose hands trembled on the steering wheel.

"Slip your head out the window and give them the password. Now."

"I don't know if I can . . ."

"Erika is right in front of you. If they shoot, she'll be the one to die. You don't even have to be brave."

The driver's freckles disappeared in a wave of red as he flushed in shame. He rolled down the window and shouted, *"Ehre und Treue!"*

Lieutenant Horst felt doubt and hostility growing among his men behind him. They had all heard about Himmler's ruthless methods. If this woman was telling the truth, they could all end up in concentration camps. And he'd be the first to go.

"Do you have a written order?"

Tristan got out of the car slowly. The iron cross glinted on his chest.

"The official papers for our mission are in the bottom pocket of my uniform. They've been signed by the Reichsführer himself."

This latest piece of information triumphed over the lieutenant's reluctance. Now all he could do was avoid losing too much face.

"I have no way to reach the command post. The area is crawling with resistance fighters and they cut any lines we install. However, I do have two sidecar motorbikes. They'll escort you to Knossos, where your orders will be properly checked."

Erika hurried back to the car.

"Go, before that idiot changes his mind! I need a bath!"

The car got underway. One of the motorbikes took up a position in front of them, leading the way. Wrapped up in dust-covered overcoats, with thick goggles atop their dark-grey helmets, the driver and his passenger looked like two of the Four Horsemen, escaped from the Apocalypse. As they passed the barricade, Tristan rolled down his window to speak to the officer, who was holstering his gun.

"What's going on here?"

"Keep your eyes on the trees and you'll find out," he replied with an ominous chuckle.

*

The olive orchards were quickly replaced by hillsides blanketed with increasingly dense vegetation. Even in Spain, Tristan hadn't seen brush so thick or tangled. The road had narrowed and was bordered on both sides by slopes covered in wild myrtle bushes. The motorbike in front of them roared at every bump and slowed to avoid obstacles, ruts, and landslides.

"There's no better place for an ambush," affirmed Otto. "If the resistance fighters attack, we'll be sitting ducks."

"They'll kill the soldier in the sidecar first, then the motorbike driver," Erika replied calmly. "That will give us time to figure out where they are and take cover on the opposite side of the car. The slope is gentle, and after that it's endless wilderness. Not even the Devil could find us in there."

"Do you always pay such close attention to your surroundings?" asked the driver, surprised.

"I'm an archaeologist, Otto. I spend my life making the dead speak, and let me tell you, they're not very talkative. So, I've learned to never miss a detail."

Tristan kept quiet. Erika had a gift for defusing tense situations. A savvy blend of calm authority and deadpan humour.

The road grew wider again as it climbed towards a plateau set against blue skies. They were only a few kilometers from Knossos, according to the military map Tristan was studying. He was about to open the detailed plans of the dig site when the motorbike suddenly swerved and came to a sudden stop.

Up ahead, nearly at the top of the hill, the two soldiers had jumped off the motorbike and were now standing silently, as if captivated by something.

"I don't understand," said Otto worriedly. "It looks like they've just seen the Devil."

"The Devil's not real," replied Tristan. "I'll go take a look."

The archaeologist placed her hand on Marcas's shoulder to dissuade him. "Just wait," she said. "They'll move in a second."

One of the soldiers suddenly turned around and stumbled towards the car. A wary Otto unholstered his Luger and placed it on his lap. "I don't like this," he whispered.

Just a few meters from the car, the soldier had to steady himself against the slope. His legs seemed to fail him, and his face was livid. This time, Tristan didn't hesitate. He got out of the vehicle, followed by Erika, took the pistol Otto handed him, and walked over to the motorbike.

"Don't go," mumbled the soldier as he crumpled to the ground and vomited.

Right at the top of the road there was a huge tree. An old oak whose roots had undoubtedly colonized the earth below on their quest for water. It would take four men to reach around its trunk, whose dark-brown bark gleamed like snakeskin in the sunlight.

"The branches," said the motorbike driver.

Tristan looked up. Charred by the heat, the leaves had shrivelled up, but what struck Marcas was a pulsating swarm of wings and beaks hovering around a branch. He cocked the Luger and shot a round into the air. The chaotic flock of crows took to the skies.

But what was left hanging from the tree was not a branch.

It was a body.

Or rather, what was left of a body.

The hands were gone.

The face was an open wound.

The stomach a gaping hole.

A sign hanging from a boot swung back and forth slowly. Tristan felt Erika grab hold of his arm as she translated the bloodstained Greek letters: "*Foreigners, welcome to Knossos!*"

5

Vienna, Austria
October 1908

As he left his opulent-looking building, Professor Wilhemster was already in a terrible mood. Perhaps the rain-coated pavement or the cold shadow cast by the Opera House had left him feeling cross. Whatever it was, he shot a disdainful gaze at everything around him. The sound of a carriage coming up the street renewed his anger, and when he saw an officer walk past, his sword clicking against his boots, the old man smoothed his moustache and looked on in defiance. This morning everything annoyed him. In his black coat, black suit, and black tie, the professor could have been mistaken for an undertaker, except for the shiny top hat carefully placed on his head. The hat was his pride and joy. Every night he brushed it meticulously, and during the day he never took it off. In fact, not one of his students had ever seen him without his "topper", as they called it. Some of them even believed they could tell the professor's mood according to the way he wore his hat. This morning, the top hat sat straight and tall as a tower, letting everyone know that Herr Wilhemster was a force to be reckoned with.

"Good morning, Professor. How are you this morning?" asked the waiter at Café Tannenberg as he held out his arm to receive the old man's cane and coat.

Wilhemster replied with a groan and walked across the café to his favourite seat. He took off his gloves and rapped his fingers on the marble table, then ordered. "A coffee and a plate of Buchteln."

The waiter nodded and made his way towards the kitchen.

"So, Ernst, today's the big day?" asked a patron at the neighbouring table.

Wilhemster just shook his head in despair, as if the man had announced the end of the world. The café regulars all knew October 20 was a dark day for the professor. It was the day he had to decide which of the students in his preparatory class would be admitted to the Vienna Academy of Fine Arts. Very few of them ever got in, since he felt most of his students were talentless.

"Lazy wretches who will never learn the rules of art," raged Wilhemster. "Fools who can't even hold a brush properly."

Luckily, his diatribe was interrupted by the arrival of his Buchteln, from which wafted up the scent of plums and warm pastry.

"I don't even have an appetite! Those ingrates have ruined everything, including my breakfast," he complained, gesturing ostentatiously to the room.

"You'll never guess what one of them did. He painted the portrait of a woman using only geometrical shapes. He calls it cubism . . ."

Whispers of reprobation travelled through the café. This was a bastion of tradition. Values were not to be trifled with. Indeed, a sizable portrait of Franz Josef I hung proudly across from the main door. With his triumphant moustache and penetrating gaze, the Emperor, who had reigned for the past fifty years, was the regulars' idol. A steady rock in a changing world.

"There are too many students!"

"Too many Jews!"

"Too many Hungarians!"

"Too many Slavs!"

The café was on fire. With a rage-filled stab of his fork, the professor tore into his buns. The other patrons' anger echoed through the room and soothed his own. With a glance at Franz Josef, impassive above the fray, he was seized with a mission—to protect true art from all the jealous and angry brushstrokes perpetrated by the degenerates that were his students. He stood up suddenly.

"Are you leaving so soon?" asked the waiter worriedly when he saw the full cup of steaming coffee still on the table.

"Yes, duty cannot wait!"

In the studio, the students had set up easels to display the paintings they had submitted, hoping to gain admission to the Academy of Fine Arts. Some of them had chosen places near the full-length windows to benefit from maximum light exposure, while the cleverer ones had opted for darker corners to hide any failings in their work. All of them feared Wilhemster. Indeed, when the door to the studio slammed shut and the professor's shadow appeared on the wooden floor, they froze behind their paintings. This moment would decide their futures.

There were three categories: landscape, portraiture, and historical. Hoping to attract Wilhemster's good graces, many of the students had chosen to depict an event that glorified the Austro-Hungarian Empire. Large battle scenes filled the easels. The professor stopped in front of a cavalry charge, his expression furious. How could they be so devoid of talent? The riders looked like they were dressed up for a carnival and the horses would have been more at home pulling ploughs. He shrugged disdainfully and the candidate knew instantly that his dream of studying at the Academy of Fine Arts would never be a reality.

"I hope the portraits are better," muttered the professor.

A single glance sufficed for him to conclude that they weren't. Full of despair and exasperation, he turned towards the landscapes. He'd already rejected more than three quarters of the students. He would be even more ruthless now, though he still hoped for a miracle.

In vain.

The first painting was a pastel. A thin rectangular canvas upon which a clumsy brush had tried to depict a farmhouse near a pond. A ball of rage formed in his throat and nearly suffocated Wilhemster. Everything, from the perspective to the colours, was wrong, substandard, just plain bad. Even the people, who looked like garden gnomes fashioned with an axe. How could anyone paint something so hideous and then dare to submit the abomination to *him*, Wilhemster? Furious, he looked up to identify the student who had committed such an outrage.

Suddenly, he understood. With his greasy hair slicked back from his forehead, a feverish gaze, a surly chin, and a bushy moustache, the painter looked much like his work. The professor almost felt sorry for him. He was a poor student, who had escaped his provincial life and believed he had some sort of talent. Vienna was full of people like him. At first, they tried to sell their paintings to gallery owners, then to tourists. In the end, they traded them in the streets for a piece of bread or sausage. When they'd had enough of the humiliation, they went home, happy to find a piece of land to tend. But there was something troubling in this one's eyes. He was obsessive, the professor was sure of it. Unable to accept his lack of talent. A relentless man who would quickly become bitter and aggressive. It was imperative he be rejected once and for all.

But to make sure of that, Wilhemster needed to know his name.

"What's your name, my friend?" asked the professor, stroking the side of his top hat.

A barely audible mumble escaped from under the moustache.

"Speak louder, for heaven's sake!"

"Hitler. Adolf Hitler."

Outside the temperature had dropped. The young painter, without a hat or scarf, doubled over as he walked, to keep out the freezing wind and attempt to soothe the cramps that ravaged his stomach. He hadn't eaten for over a day. But his anger took up more space than the hunger or the cold. He'd never been so humiliated. He'd just been rejected by the Academy of Fine Arts for the second time. The first time had been just before his mother's death, and he hadn't dared tell her the truth. Klara had passed away believing her son's future was bright. But here he was, thrown out again. He'd done everything he could. He'd even changed preparatory classes and enrolled with Wilhemster, hoping someone would finally recognize his talent. But it was all even worse than before. He'd been treated with disdain and contempt.

Adolf pushed back the lock of hair that fell across his forehead. He'd slicked it down that morning with sugar water. Even the cheapest barber in Vienna was too expensive for him. A wave of rage washed over him. Wilhemster! That old bastard! What did that well-to-do fool in a top hat know about painting anyway? When had he painted his last work? Twenty years ago? Thirty? Adolf began gesticulating, alone in the street. He hated the city-dwelling middle classes who bled the people and rural communities dry.

A gust of wind came up through the Burggarten gates and nearly swept him off his feet. He'd become skinnier and skinnier since arriving in Vienna. His roommates said he looked like a hanger wearing a tattered suit. He still cringed when remembering the laughter that the joke had elicited. Since he couldn't afford to rent even the shabbiest of rooms anymore, he was staying in a men's hostel. A rat-infested dump where all of Vienna's down-and-outs washed up. Failed students, the jobless, incorrigible alcoholics, petty criminals looking to stay out of sight . . . Brutes and degenerates who constantly teased him because he still did his best to keep clean.

Exhausted, Adolf stopped at a stall that sold second-hand books and faded prints. He took his painting out from under his thinning coat.

"Do you buy paintings?"

The salesman, an old man with deep-set eyes and an unkempt beard, looked suspiciously at Adolf before examining the work.

"Did you paint this?" he asked.

Hitler swallowed his pride and shook his head. "No, I inherited it from an uncle."

"Well, it would be fair to say he didn't spoil you."

"It must still be worth *something*."

"No, even the canvas it's scribbled on is worthless. A real waste of space."

"Give it back!" shouted Adolf, who felt himself blush in shame.

"My pleasure. And if you want my advice," mocked the salesman, "give up painting!"

Turning his back on this humiliating situation, Hitler found himself facing the National Library. Inspired by baroque art, it looked like a giant, ornate wedding cake sitting in the centre of the city. Intimidated by the stupefying number of columns and statues, he'd never dared go in, afraid he'd be thrown out like a beggar. But it was too cold. He slicked his hair back again, smoothed his threadbare tie, threw his painting into some bushes, and walked up the steps. Much to his surprise, no one bothered him inside. He discreetly made his way towards a long wooden desk where uniformed librarians waited for readers to serve.

"Would you like to consult a volume?"

Hitler was a compulsive reader. He read everything he could get his hands on—brochures handed to him in the street, newspapers left on public benches, books forgotten in train stations. His erudition had spread like an aggressive disease. First, he'd developed an interest in architecture, becoming an expert in totally abstruse subjects overnight. Then he'd moved on to music, determined to write an opera. This plan had never come to fruition, of course, but had earned him the mocking nickname "Wagneribus". History was his real passion. He devoured anything written about the world's great conquerors. Medieval emperors fascinated him the most. He was attracted to the many intellectual journals in Vienna that discussed literature, art, and politics. In fact, he'd just heard about a new one.

"Do you have the journal *Ostara*?"

The librarian's smile dripped with condescension. "You do know you can get it at any newspaper kiosk for a few pennies, don't you?"

"I'd like to consult *all* of the issues."

"Go and sit at desk 621, towards the back of the room on the right. Someone will bring them to you."

As he walked past the room of readers, Adolf quickly came to understand why they had exiled him to the back of the library. The first rows were reserved for professors and researchers, their eyes glued to antique volumes which they revered like the Grail. But the back of the reading room was home to the dregs of Viennese society. Hitler felt sick. Everywhere he went, misery followed. He sat down at his desk, between a drunkard who reeked of bad wine and a toothless old woman mumbling incomprehensibly. They both had unopened books sitting in front of them.

"Hitler, is that right?" asked an employee as she handed him a pile of journals.

The first cover immediately intrigued Adolf. It depicted a castle surrounded by snow, from which a troop of warriors emerged, brandishing axes and swords. The caption was mysterious: *Aryan reconquest*.

Suddenly, Hitler forgot where he was, forgot the humiliations and the hunger pangs. He stared at the dark, isolated castle and saw it as a metaphor for his own life. For years he had been subjected to violence and scorn. Every day since he was a child, he'd had to add a new row of bricks to the wall that protected him from others. He was trapped inside his castle, waiting, hoping that a friend would knock on his door some day, but no one had ever come. The world had continued outside without him, growing increasingly difficult and unjust. He had to accept reality: no one was waiting for Adolf Hitler. If he wanted to find his place in the world, he had to take it, like the noble warriors in the picture, heading out to conquer their destiny.

A bell rang at the door to the reading room. Readers stood up and put on their ragged coats to face the wind and the rain. Hitler stayed seated, his eyes red from the hours he had spent glued to the texts. On the other side of the large windows, it was dark now. He would have to go back to the hostel, but that didn't bother him anymore. He picked up the most recent issue of the journal and quickly flipped through the pages to the table of contents, where he found what he was looking for:

Jörg Lanz, Editor-in-Chief.

He needed to meet that man.

6

The Amilcar zoomed through the countryside. Malorley was a precision driver, who carefully avoided every pothole in the road—and there were many. On either side, flocks of sheep grazed peacefully behind endless fences. Laure hadn't said a word for over an hour, though she had decided to forget the horrific scene in the bunker. She was a professional, after all.

The Amilcar slowed as it neared a village. As they took a turn, they noticed a portly farmer in a cap sitting in front of his barn, smoking a pipe. His glassy eyes watched as the car passed.

"From hell to heaven," said Malorley. "It doesn't seem like the war has had any impact on this place. Maybe that man has never even heard of Hitler. When I retire, I'll come to a remote village like this one."

"You're not that old."

"I know, it's just to convince myself I'll survive this war."

"I'm surprised to hear it. You always seem so . . ."

"Hardened?"

"Sure of yourself. Unshakable, like with that burned woman earlier."

The houses disappeared and the car picked up speed.

"Don't be fooled by appearances. If I listened to my heart, I'd book myself into a hotel in the next village, buy two bottles of whisky, and drink myself to death."

The road straightened out and Malorley reached cruising speed.

"So, you're human after all. I'd better take advantage of this while it lasts. Can I ask you a question about one of your agents?"

"I'm sure I know who you're referring to."

"The double agent you pulled out of your hat at Montségur. He really had me going. An excellent actor."

"Tristan Marcas . . . Good-looking chap, too."

"I don't recall ever having said such a thing."

"That's what women who know him tend to say."

"Well, he had no effect on me. He's not my type. Too pretentious, too full of himself."

Malorley tried not to smile.

"That's how love stories always begin. What else do you want to know? I've told you everything. He worked with me during the Spanish Civil War and now he's hunting swastikas. I should receive a report from him any day now, through one of our networks in Berlin."

"Is he married? Does he have a family?"

"Yes, his wife lives in Normandy and they have five children."

"Really?"

He glanced discreetly at Laure, who had been unable to mask her surprise.

"You should see your face! I'm kidding. He's single and I don't know much about his personal life. The Marcas file is now closed. You'll get nothing more out of me."

"That's fine with me. I'm no more interested in Marcas than in that old grandfather we saw earlier."

"Good. Though I can't say I believe you. Don't forget that I taught psychological tactics at the training centre. I have a sixth sense for detecting lies."

She sighed and looked out the window at the countryside.

"In any case, you'll need to turn your attentions to another man."

"What do you mean? You agreed to send me on a mission. In the field. That was the deal you made to get me to join your relic-hunting, ghost-chasing commando unit."

"It all depends on Marcas. I have no idea where to find the third relic. We're all awaiting his news. For the time being, I need to complete my team. I'd like you to meet with one of the candidates, to get your opinion. He could help me get Rudolf Hess to talk about the swastikas and the *Thule Borealis*. But if my superiors knew I was thinking of using him, they'd sack me on the spot."

The landscape changed suddenly, as the fields made way for industrial sprawl. Rows of brick houses stood on either side of the road. They were entering the suburb of Croydon. London was only half an hour away.

"I'm intrigued. Who is this charming gentleman?"

Malorley turned right onto a main road full of lorries.

"You'll find out by coming with me to my office. I have a meeting with SOE management. While I'm doing that, you can read his file and then we'll visit him tomorrow at his home in London. He's very susceptible to a woman's charms."

"Glad to know you see me as a willing bimbo . . . What about me? Will I enjoy his virile presence?"

"You're from an aristocratic family. That kind of talk doesn't befit a lady."

"Just as well, since I'm not one. Thanks to your school for licensed killers in His Majesty's service. So?"

"Women have always fallen at his feet, despite the fact that he's remarkably ugly."

"He must have other qualities."

"Yes, loads. He's twisted, selfish, immoral, and deviant, as well as a nymphomaniac, megalomaniac, liar, sadist, and probably a murderer."

"Can a single man really tick all those boxes? He sounds like the antichrist."

He turned towards her, his face suddenly as cold as ice. "Precisely. In fact, that's what he likes to be called."

7

Hiding in his library, Karl Häsner feverishly awaited the arrival of Erika and Tristan. The fact that Himmler had chosen to send the head of the Ahnenerbe herself to Knossos was a sign, but he didn't know how to interpret it. He stood in front of one of the windows and watched the road from Heraklion. Since the three mutilated bodies had been discovered, he'd been holed up in his house, shaking like a leaf every time he heard a gunshot. The sentinels had itchy trigger fingers, and firing squads roamed the streets.

The sight of the bodies of the priest and the mayor, ravaged by bullets and on display at the entrance to the village, haunted him constantly. He'd done everything he could to prevent the vengeful act, but the military authorities had been adamant. The village had to be punished, but more importantly, they needed to show the troops that the murder of their comrades had not been taken lightly. The captain had argued that it was the only way to maintain discipline. Since then, Karl had kept his door locked and his windows boarded up, as if he were under attack by invisible forces. He only went out when a military escort came to take him to the church, where the other archaeologists had taken refuge. There was no talk of continuing the dig anymore—everyone was too afraid of an attack. Every time he went out, Karl couldn't help noticing that paranoia was taking hold of more and more of his colleagues. Some of them had even stopped eating, afraid of poison. On his way home from one of these depressing visits, he learned that another soldier was missing. If the troops found his corpse, the retaliation would be brutal. Homicidal rage was on the march and would destroy everything in its path. Karl clasped his hands together. As a child, he'd attended church with his parents. Back then, he'd known how to pray, but what god would hear him now that evil had taken over the world?

The car stopped in the village square. Tristan got out first, to open the door for Erika. Soldiers posted at the windows of a nearby building kept watch over the access points. Just before they'd reached the houses, Tristan had seen two bodies hanging conspicuously from a tree. The first must have been a priest given the pieces of cassock he could still identify. The other was too far gone to tell. Otto had seen them as well but had kept quiet. The first tattered body hanging in the oak tree in the forest had taken its toll.

"I'm Karl Häsner, the head archaeologist."

Tristan nodded. Erika was too taken aback by the dishevelled state of the man to reply. His hair was in knots, his face covered in an unruly beard, and his eyes red from lack of sleep. Häsner was but a shadow of a man, one who could collapse at any moment.

"Aren't there any officers here?" asked Marcas, surprised.

Karl cleared his throat. "The captain is not in any shape to lead. A fever . . ." He shrugged, as if there was nothing more to be said.

"Who has replaced him?"

"You must have passed a roadblock on your way here. The officer there, Lieutenant Horst, will take up command as soon as he's back."

Karl pointed towards a house on a corner of the square. "That's my house. Come with me and I'll try to explain."

They went straight to the library. Otto stayed by the door to keep an eye on all ways in and out. While Erika examined the artefacts on the table, Tristan sat down next to the fireplace, which had been hastily boarded up.

"I doubt anyone could get in through there. It's too narrow."

"Not a man, no," replied Karl as he reached for a half-empty bottle of ouzo, "but we're not fighting men anymore."

"Why don't you start explaining things," Marcas suggested calmly.

The archaeologist grabbed two glasses and filled them to the brim. He looked hesitantly towards Erika, but she was completely absorbed in her thoughts.

"We have been excavating in Knossos since the summer, with protection from an SS company sent here from Heraklion. They run security at the perimeter and watch over our camp. They're strict, but we're used to them."

"Do they manage the locals as well?"

"At first, we agreed that the soldiers wouldn't be in direct contact with the villagers. We negotiated our relationship with them ourselves."

"And, before the recent murders, how were things?"

"The people here are used to foreigners. Archaeological digs have been going on since the turn of the century. For the locals, many of whom are starving, it's a godsend. Some of them work on the dig site, where they're very useful. Others provide supplies, and the women keep the houses tidy. We had a pretty good relationship—until a week ago."

Erika had come closer and was holding the gold artefact engraved with a swastika. Himmler would have paid a fortune to have such an object in his private collection. It was strange that Karl hadn't sent it straight to Berlin. She was full of questions but resisted the urge to interrupt the conversation. Tristan gestured to Häsner to continue.

"The soldiers are stationed in several houses at the entrances to the village, which they turned into fortresses. They filled in the windows on the ground floors and narrowed the ones upstairs to the size of arrow slits. As for the rooftops, they added crenellations."

"Are there any other defences?"

"They placed obstacles outside the houses to prevent suicide collisions. Since the resistance fighters regularly cut our phone lines, they also set up a signalling system on each roof. If there's a problem, each fort can immediately alert the others."

"They left nothing to chance," commented Marcas. "But I suppose that wasn't enough?"

"Last Monday, the captain in charge of site security decided to run a surprise protection exercise at the dig site. The men flooded the zone and fanned out to scan the area, as if looking for rebels. During the exercise, each of the defence posts was guarded by just three men."

"And one of them was attacked?"

Karl served himself another glass. He noticed the artefact Erika had in her hand but said nothing.

"We found three guards, dead, yes."

"What state were the bodies in?"

"They had been decapitated."

Erika fidgeted with the artefact. She followed the lines of the swastika with her index finger. Who had engraved it? A Cretan goldsmith? Or had the object come from far away? Was it pillaged? Traded? From the south or the north? Until its density of pure gold had been measured, there was no way to determine its origin. Instead of asking questions she couldn't answer, Erika decided to join the conversation.

"Were the bodies autopsied? Were the blood-spattered walls analyzed? Did they find the murder weapon?"

Karl shook his head. "The walls were pristine, not a single stain."

"But that's impossible," protested Tristan. "Removing a head with an axe or sword causes multiple, unpredictable spurts of blood."

Erika glanced discreetly at Tristan, a curious look on her face. The degree of precision he'd just used to describe decapitation surprised her. And this wasn't the first time his knowledge had caught her off guard. She suddenly felt like she was seeing a hidden light through a crack in a door.

"It wasn't an axe or a sword," explained the archaeologist. "They were strangled. The attackers used metal wire that easily cuts through flesh. But when you get to the spine, you have to saw through . . ."

Karl made a sawing motion with his hands.

"And often the victim's not completely dead. They may fight, but they would be unable to make a sound. In the end, they drown in their own blood."

"Did you tell the soldiers how their comrades had been murdered?" asked Tristan.

"Of course not," answered Häsner. "But the doctor who did the autopsy got help from a few nurses. They leaked the information. And from there . . ."

Tristan had no trouble imagining the rest. The wildest rumours sparked the worst fears.

"And since then?" asked Erika.

"We found three more bodies yesterday. A patrol unit at a well. This time they were killed with knives, apparently from behind."

"At least they weren't mutilated."

"Right. Oh, except that they ripped the liver out of each of the bodies."

Karl's eyes darted to and fro, as if he were afraid he'd see a ghost if he let them rest. Tristan didn't envy him his sleepless nights filled with nightmares that darkened with each passing day.

"And now a man's been missing since this morning," added the archaeologist.

Erika put a stop to his worrying right away. "We found him. Hanging from a tree. That said, I couldn't tell if his head or liver was missing, given the number of carrion birds that were feasting on him."

Karl shot a terrified glance at Erika. Was she totally devoid of compassion?

"So, to sum things up, three missing heads, three stolen livers, and a corpse hanging from a tree. And no one knows anything?" she asked.

"The soldiers say the resistance fighters are mutilating the bodies to scare us."

"What do the locals say? If they're even talking, since you shot their mayor and priest . . ."

"They say it's the *Abba*."

Erika and Tristan leaned towards the archaeologist at the same time, as if they hadn't heard.

"The *Abba*?"

Otto's voice rose up from downstairs. "Lieutenant Horst wants you to meet him at the dig site immediately."

Karl raised his empty glass to toast his fate.

"You'll know more soon enough."

8

Laure was sitting in a small, impersonal, grey office. A metal filing cabinet, an empty table, a poorly upholstered chair, and a gaudy painting of a fox-hunting scene. English bureaucracy in all its splendour.

Malorley's new secretary knocked and came in without waiting for an answer. She placed a grey box tied shut with green string on the table, and looked suspiciously at Laure. "Here's the file the commander asked me to give you. He also told me to tell you to meet him in front of the British Museum tomorrow morning at half past ten. Don't be late, you know how punctual he is."

"Thank you, Miss Banbridge. I'll put everything on your desk when I leave," replied Laure with a warm smile.

She inspected the box. A white label was glued to the outside, bearing a name in red ink: *Edward Alexander "Aleister" Crowley.*

"These documents are top secret," grumbled the older woman. "I don't understand why the commander has authorized you to consult them. Especially this one—it's not suitable for a nice young woman like yourself. It's full of perversions. You'll be horrified."

"Don't worry. In France, we're pretty open on the topic."

The venerable secretary stared at Laure, an outraged expression on her face, as if the agent had just begun a striptease. Then she turned and left, closing the door behind her. She didn't like the French or the Germans, and she held her nose whenever there was talk of other European nationalities. Only His Majesty's subjects deserved her consideration, and even then, only those born in England. She thoroughly despised the Northern Irish and Scots—ignorant peoples, hardly deserving of their place in the United Kingdom.

"Nutty old witch," whispered Laure as she undid the string around the box. "Let's get a closer look at Malorley's miscreant friend."

She removed the lid, put it aside, and studied the contents. The box contained a long, typewritten report on MI5 letterhead, clippings from English and foreign newspapers, and an open envelope containing photographs. She pulled out the largest of them.

Laure couldn't help but smile as she contemplated the picture. A man of a certain age stared straight at the lens, wild-eyed, with his elbows placed on a table and his fists glued to his cheeks. His features were coarse: a pronounced nose, arched eyebrows, and a wilful mouth. But the strangest thing about the picture was the hat on his head. It was like a big fabric bag shaped like a triangle, embroidered with the Eye of Providence. The sides of the hat fell over his fists, forming a tent shape. To his left, on the table, a richly bound book stood on its side, revealing its spine and an inscription: *Perdurabo.*

Laure sat back in her chair. "I don't know what kind of circus you're in, my dear Edward Alexander 'Aleister' Crowley, but I hope you're not running around in that get-up, or you'll be taken straight to the asylum."

Contrary to what she had assumed, it took her over an hour to go through the files. She could hardly believe what she had learned.

Raised by Protestant bigots, the young Edward had rebelled by studying every possible form of deviance. Driven by his fascination with esotericism, Aleister—as he dubbed himself—began his unusual journey in the world of the occult. After joining the biggest secret societies in England and Europe—Golden Dawn, Theosophy, Freemasonry, and the Templars—he founded his own cult. One that broke with the conventional initiation traditions and replaced them with a blend of sex and magic. The cocktail was a hit in high society. Crowley even opened an S&M brothel in the centre of London, where he openly practised his most scandalous theories.

Laure had spent some time studying a series of erotic sketches of the mage paired with explicit texts, and soon came to understand the secretary's reaction.

When the British press finally revealed his exploits, Crowley moved to India and then on to Egypt. The writer, explorer, journalist, alpinist, medium, and guru attracted the attention of the intelligence services again during the First World War. Suspected of being a German agent, the adventurer had been incarcerated, then released without explanation.

As she continued, Laure encountered so many preposterous escapades all around the globe that she began to feel like she was reading a novel. He was arrested in Paris in 1923, high on opium in a flat in Montmartre, splayed out next to the body of his lover. The man had a voracious appetite for both men and women. He appeared regularly in Germany and Italy. In Cefalú, Sicily, he founded the Abbey of Thelema, where he explored all his vices in the company of a group of followers. When one of them died, Mussolini's government summarily deported him. He turned up next in England, then again in Germany in the 1930s, as Nazism rose to power.

The photographs taken at different points throughout his life were proof of his physical decline. The youthful face he had once possessed had become the mask of a depraved man over the decades.

Laure had read enough. There was something both fascinating and repulsive about the man. The MI5 officer who had followed him over the years seemed to share her opinion. She closed the box and tied the string around the lid. But something Crowley had said that had been printed in a newspaper still had her attention. It had been circled in red by the agent who wrote the report: "*Before Hitler was, I am.*"

A maxim that could be interpreted in many different ways, but which always led to the same conclusion: its author was deranged. She didn't understand how Malorley could use such a man.

Laure checked her watch. Almost seven o'clock, time to go home. The tragic events in Southampton had left her feeling drained.

The desperate blue eyes of the poor woman were still fresh in her mind. As was the disgusting smell of burnt flesh. Laure needed to shower off the scent, which seemed to permeate her nostrils. But that wasn't the only thing that troubled her. She had just witnessed her first ever cold-blooded murder. Her brain understood why Malorley had done what he did, but her heart couldn't comprehend it. She could never shoot an innocent person. She had no problem killing Nazi bastards and their collaborator friends, but that was different. She was impatient to get to work on that account, but she didn't want to become a monster.

Laure shivered and stood up. She grabbed her coat and made her way towards the secretaries' office to return the box. When she got there, she found the room empty. She could hear laughter and voices alongside the sounds of a jazz orchestra on the radio, coming from another room. A little after-work party, she guessed. After all, SOE employees still needed something good in their lives, a way to forget their days spent planning commando operations that sent many men and women to their deaths.

Laure had no desire to join the party. She walked into the office and placed the box on a side table. As she was leaving, she noticed an open filing cabinet, which contained dossiers on all the agents from the France division.

Tristan . . . ? Maybe . . .

Curiosity got the better of her.

Malorley had been right. She was intrigued by the mysterious man who had suddenly burst into her life. She had hated him the first time they'd met. After all, he'd introduced himself as a Nazi collaborator. But then she'd learned he was a double agent. He was a member of the heavenly legions fighting an army of demons. That's how Malorley put it. But Tristan was an unusual archangel. His wings were black, and his forehead bore horns. An archangel disguised as a demon. To better fight evil.

Where did he get the courage to continue operating in the fortress of evil? To risk being unmasked at any moment and suffering terrible consequences? At the training centre, she'd read about the atrocities the Gestapo was wont to commit. Abominations.

Tristan . . . Right there in a file . . .

Laure walked over to the cabinet and contemplated it greedily. Like a hungry child admiring a feast. She had to know. If Malorley didn't want to tell her, she'd find out on her own.

She wouldn't be risking much, compared to what was on the line for the double agent every day. Worst-case scenario, she'd be thrown out of the SOE. Plus, she was a spy now, wasn't she? It was now or never.

Laure leaned in and ran her finger over the labels on the hanging files. She slowed at the letter "M". There were a dozen agent files, all grey or green, each with an ID photo glued to the top of the cover. She rifled quickly through them and stopped at the second-to-last. It was him. The same face, though it was a few years younger. His gaze was kind and penetrating, and his lips curled up in a slight smile—an almost insolent expression.

She looked towards the door. Not a sound in the corridor. If she got caught, her career would be over. Her heart raced. She thought back to her training.

There are two obstacles to overcome when burgling an office. The first is external and very real. The second—fear—is all in your head. It may be the product of your imagination, but it's far more dangerous than the first. Learn to recognize the symptoms: your heart will race for no reason. Train yourself to slow your breath and then . . . believe in your luck.

She took a deep breath, then took the file out of the cabinet and placed it on the table. She peeked out into the deserted corridor, then came back into the office. Her shaking hand opened the folder.

Her eyes opened wide. It was empty. Nothing but a blank piece of paper and a name: *JOHN DEE.*

9

The excavation site was only a few hundred meters from the village. A gentle breeze rustled through the olive leaves as the cicadas chirped incessantly in the scorching heat. In just moments, the land, fresh air, and heat had chased away the thoughts of fear and death from before. At least that's how it felt to Tristan, whose fatigue and anxiety seemed to disappear as he climbed the paved road leading to the first ruins. He could already see the tops of colonnades rising into the hot air.

"Where are the soldiers?" asked Erika, surprised.

"The security perimeter must include the village and the site. The access points and patrols are further out."

"For an art historian, you have a surprising knowledge of military tactics."

"I observe and deduce," explained Marcas.

"You know quite a lot about cutting people's throats, too. Your remark from earlier, about the uncontrollable spurts of blood, seemed accurate."

"I feel like you're studying me as an archaeologist," replied Tristan with a smile. "On the lookout for unexpected details. Speaking of which, what's the *Abba*?"

"Some sort of bogey man, I gather. A creature of the night that haunts memories and legends. Half-imaginary, half-real."

Erika pointed to a column with a series of cracks sloppily repaired with cement—it resembled a tall, thin, grey leper. "It looks like today's Cretan masons aren't quite as gifted as their ancestors," noted Tristan.

"The site first came to light around the turn of the century. At the time, archaeology was in its infancy, and excavations were far from scientific. People just wanted to find artefacts, and quickly. They didn't hesitate to destroy ruins in their quest to find something better underneath. They thought they could always restore them afterwards."

They had stopped under an oak tree to enjoy a bit of shade. The heat was stifling. Tristan handed Erika a canteen. A seemingly endless field of ruins stretched out before them. While the archaeologist studied them as an expert, Tristan simply enjoyed the exhilarating feeling of discovering a new world. The sound of spades on dirt had echoed through the place for decades, but now it was silent. The place men had infused with their dreams was now deserted.

"How was the site discovered?"

"The same way sites are always discovered," explained Erika as she put down the canteen. "Farmers began working new land and hit ruined walls with their plough. They told the mayor and the priest, who mentioned it to another priest. One morning in 1877, Andreas Kalokairinos turned up in Knossos. He was the son of the man who owned the land, which had never produced anything but dust."

"Was he an archaeologist?"

"No, he was a soap salesman. That wasn't surprising at the time, though. You'll remember that Heinrich Schliemann, who discovered the city of Troy, was a grocer."

Tristan had heard the story of the German merchant and great admirer of Homer who had spent his life and fortune proving the existence of the city where Achilles had died.

"So why isn't your soap salesman as well known as Schliemann?"

"Because he encountered certain difficulties during the excavations and—"

Erika stopped short. Lieutenant Horst had just appeared to their left. He looked better than he had at the roadblock, but a deep, interrogative wrinkle still marked his furrowed brow. He welcomed them, then turned towards the village below, where the shutters were all closed and the rooftop terraces were empty.

"They don't want us to keep digging. They're scared."

"Of the *Abba*?" asked Erika mockingly.

The lieutenant sat down on a wall in the shade of an olive tree. The sun shone mercilessly.

"My men used to fear the heat above all else. Now they're afraid of the dark, like the locals, who are terrified by the idea that we might awaken the shadow of this *Abba*."

Erika began twisting a strand of blonde hair—a sure sign she was losing patience.

"So, we have a besieged village, a series of multiple murders, frightened soldiers, and petrified archaeologists, all because of this rumoured ghost?"

The lieutenant pretended he hadn't heard her. The tone Erika had used at the roadblock hadn't sat well with him. He didn't appreciate civilians speaking to him that way, much less women. He ignored her and turned towards Marcas.

"The soldiers weren't murdered by resistance fighters. We know they stay close to their base in the mountains. They never come down this far. Too dangerous."

"Then the villagers must have committed the murders," offered Tristan. "But why would they risk terrible retaliation instead of just letting the dig continue?"

Horst jumped up and turned around, but the only sound came from the stand of pines growing on the slope, blowing in the wind coming off the ocean.

"Did you see a ghost, lieutenant?" asked Erika.

The officer almost replied but held back. Despite her disdain, he had to keep his attitude in check. Going head to head with one of Himmler's Valkyries would be suicidal. It would be better to find a way to work together. He put on a polite smile and continued. "Following the first attack, when three of our men were beheaded, we searched the village house by house, including Kalokairinos's. His family had turned it into a local museum. In the archives, which no one had ever taken the time to organize, we found his notebooks from the original excavations."

The archaeologist gestured for Horst to continue.

"The first thing he found was a series of store-rooms. Since he dreamt of finding something that would make him famous, he quickly tired of excavating ancient pantries!"

Tristan could feel the important piece of information coming. Unlike Erika, who was clearly impatient, he enjoyed the wait before a revelation.

"Kalokairinos had noticed that when the villagers working on the site conducted surveys, they all scrupulously avoided one area: the chapel."

"But there isn't a chapel on the site," affirmed Erika. "It's not on any of the maps."

"At the turn of the century, there was one, dedicated to Saint George. So that's where Kalokairinos decided to focus his efforts."

The lieutenant made his way towards the entrance to the excavation site. A maze of uneven walls led to the ruins of columns that reached nearly as high as the neighbouring pines. Horst walked around the main path, cleared for visitors, and headed towards an area overrun with vegetation. Fragrant thickets hid the ruins. The roots of tall oaks slithered between fallen stones.

"In his notebooks, Kalokairinos drew several maps of the site, including one with the chapel's position. I compared it to the most recent surveys and . . ." He pointed to a pile of grey stones and a trail of broken roof tiles. "This is what's left of it."

Tristan moved closer, as if looking for traces of the chapel.

"There's no point looking. Time has erased everything," said Horst.

"Time and men," affirmed Erika. "Especially if Kalokairinos found something."

Horst took a leather-bound notebook from his jacket pocket, opened it to a page bearing a brown sketch, and held it out to the archaeologist.

"They found it at the back of the chapel, a little over ten meters down."

"It can't be," marvelled Erika.

Tristan grabbed the notebook. The sketch was simple, just a few strokes of the pen. But that was all that was needed to depict the door. A blocked door.

Erika walked over. "Look at the ogival arch. It's definitely a medieval door. But what is it doing under an ancient Greek site?"

Marcas stared at the drawing in disbelief.

"But the day after they found it," continued the lieutenant, "the whole village went to the Turkish authorities, accusing Kalokairinos of waking the demons under the ruins. Afraid of what the locals would do, the Turks immediately put a stop to the excavations and had the door buried."

Tristan looked through the following pages in the notebook. Nothing but a few scattered notes. Kalokairinos's short career as an archaeologist stopped there.

"So, you brought us here to show us the notebook and the chapel?" asked Tristan.

"Have you informed Karl Häsner?" asked Erika. "He's in charge of excavations."

"Well, now you are. As for Häsner, he doesn't live in our world anymore. He's convinced invisible forces are at work in Knossos. He can no longer make responsible decisions."

"And in your opinion, what would the *responsible decision* be?"

The lieutenant walked over to the chapel, then continued a few more steps. He drove his foot down hard into the stones. "We must open the door."

10

Supple bodies squeezed into rigid black corsets. Red leather boots and gloves. Scarlet lips and charcoal-grey eyes. The outfits of the two Amazons running the show in the deep-red salon perfectly matched the Hellfire Club's colours. Red and black. Blood and darkness.

There were many other brothels in the capital, but the Hellfire was the only one that offered its patrons equal shares of pleasure and pain. It was also unique in welcoming women who enjoyed domination.

With a cold expression on her face, the brunette held three naked, hooded men on leads. She studied her reflection in a full-length mirror with a dark-red rim.

"Sit, you mongrels!" she shouted dryly.

They obeyed without question and held out their hands.

On the other side of the room, the blonde was perched on a velvet armchair, driving her heel into the body of a bearded man lying on the stone floor with his legs and hands bound and fastened to steel rings.

"Repeat the sentence I taught you, my little French frog," insisted the woman.

"I'm a backwards man."

"Clearly . . . And the rest?"

She pushed harder with the metal heel of her shoe. The man moaned and then yelped.

"No, that isn't what we agreed."

She increased the pressure further, eliciting a cry of pain.

"All right! When I go home I'll—"

"You'll what, you worm?"

"Aaahh . . . I'll give women the right to vote. Like in England."

The blonde seemed satisfied.

"That's a good boy. But you lack sincerity. You won't be punished."

"No, please! I deserve it."

Behind a two-way mirror, in a neighbouring room, a strange man enjoyed the spectacle before him. A smooth, pale scalp crowned a baby face that had aged prematurely, and bright-blue eyes shone from behind wrinkled lids. His heavy body was wrapped in a black silk robe as he smirked.

"French women can't elect their political representatives . . . Such a strange country. They cut off their king's head over a century ago, but women are still second-class citizens. Who is that, my dear Moira?"

A tall, extraordinarily beautiful red-headed woman stood next to him. Her thick, wavy hair softened her angular features, and her pale skin made her dark-grey eyes and lips stand out. Moira O'Connor, director of the Hellfire, wore her establishment's colours proudly.

"A former French ambassador who came to London after France's defeat," she replied. "I'd be delighted to teach him a lesson to help advance the feminist cause."

"And the dogs?"

"Aleister, you know we only entertain the most elite packs. A Tory MP, a bishop of the Church of England, and I'd bet my life the last one is an eminent member of the royal family. As for the women, they're—"

"No need, I know who they are. The blonde is the wife of a current minister and the brunette conducts one of the largest women's choirs in the city. Poor Frenchman—she's a diehard suffragette."

Moira turned on the light and placed a pile of papers on the desk. "Shall we get down to business?" she asked.

Crowley raised his hand, gesturing for her to wait. He couldn't take his eyes off the scene on the other side of the mirror. The brunette had begun vigorously whipping her pets, who were squealing loudly.

"Such a virtuous change of pace," he mumbled. "In the 18th century, the Hellfire only allowed male domination. Think of all those poor maids tortured by hypocritical gentlemen. They would be proud to see how far we've come. Thanks to the changes I instilled when I took over twenty years ago. I'm telling you, Moira, I'm the biggest feminist in the country."

"So you've said a thousand times," sighed the red-head. "It's beginning to feel like you don't want to sell your shares after all."

"I must! I need the money. And I've taught you well, my sultry fairy. You do an excellent job running this brothel."

"I prefer Scarlet Fairy. Isn't that the nickname you gave me?"

"You're right. My goodness, this show is stirring all my senses."

Moira drew the curtains. "My dear Aleister, you can satisfy all of your vices once the papers are signed."

"You didn't use to speak to me like that. Am I really that old?"

She gave him a look filled with equal measures of compassion and irony.

"Come now, Crowley, you 'initiated' me twenty years ago, and you were already in your prime then. You may be a great mage, but you're still human."

"Your words are like white-hot blades challenging me to a duel. I'll prove my manhood is still intact!"

He forced himself against her and tried to glue his lips to hers. Moira O'Connor deftly pulled a tiny dagger from her corset and placed it against her attacker's throat. She observed him as a feline does its prey—just before devouring it.

"Touch me again and I'll cut your throat. You can have a wank when we've finished our transaction. Sign or get out!"

A drop of blood pearled on Crowley's skin. He retreated pitifully, dabbing at his forehead with a blue silk handkerchief.

"I had forgotten that you always have that witch's dagger on you. Fine, let's finish this."

He took the pen and nervously initialled each page, then signed the last. They left the room just as the lashes and groans from the other side of the mirror were picking up speed. They walked down a long, dark corridor to a bar that could have been in a luxury hotel. The art deco lamps in the corners of the room shed a gentle light on the twenty or so people in various states of undress, who laughed and drank sitting around low tables. A barmaid in a red corset prepared cocktails while two naked waitresses in powdered wigs served. The room was decorated with gildings, tapestries, and suits of armour. Three threatening medieval knights bearing white flags with a red cross in the centre drove their swords into the floor as they guarded the stone wall behind them.

"Do these new decorations have a particular meaning?" asked Crowley.

"Not at all. A simple exchange with one of my regulars, an antiques dealer from Kensington. Five sessions for a suit of armour."

They stopped at the bar. Moira gestured discreetly at the petite, blonde barmaid with a mischievous look about her. She brought over two coupes of champagne.

"To your health, Aleister," said Moira. "Thank you for selling me your shares."

"I live to please," he replied as he cast an insistent glance towards the blonde. "Your queen of cocktails is provocative," he continued.

"Be careful. Banshee knows everything about medicinal plants—those that heal and those that harm. She has mastered the concoctions of the light and those of the dark. I myself taught her the powers of the forest, the wind, and the night. If Pan so wishes, she will replace me someday at the head of our coven."

"It's hard to believe that when I met you, you were little more than an innocent Irish lamb who wholeheartedly believed in the crucified carpenter and his breviary for castrated men and frigid women."

"I thank you for opening my eyes."

"I imagine your barmaid is also your Kamasutra partner?" Crowley enquired lewdly. "I would love to attend your ceremonies."

Moira gave him a disdainful look.

"Our teachings are nothing like your libidinous practices."

"Don't be silly. The phallus and the vulva are the only doors to cosmic understanding."

"Sex is just one dance in the great ball of the universe. And for nymphomaniacs like you, the ultimate pleasure leads to the cemetery. As for me, all I can offer is a *petite mort*. Follow me."

They left the bar and climbed a spiral staircase lit by torches placed at regular intervals. The portly sorcerer had trouble on the stairs. Moira could hear his breathing growing shorter. When they reached the first floor, he stopped to catch his breath. His head was spinning.

"Worn out already, Crowley? You can rest a bit before opening your gift if you like."

"No need. I'm just a little out of shape. Let's go."

When they reached the shiny red door, it was ajar. A young woman in a green silk dress stood before it.

"This is Lei-Ling," said Moira, introducing them. "She's from Shanghai."

"I am your humble servant, Mr. Crowley," said the young woman with a bow. "I've heard much about you."

"Excellent . . . I'm eager to get a taste of this . . . I . . ."

Crowley felt the floor give out beneath him. Moira and the Chinese woman caught him as he fell.

"This is no time to give up, Aleister. I've prepared another surprise, inside."

The red-head pushed the door open with her foot, releasing the strong smell of opium smoke. In the middle of the room stood a four-poster bed. A young woman with golden hair lay atop it. She was on her side, highlighting her full, pale hips against the black satin sheets. Crowley's vision was blurry; he couldn't make out her face.

"This girl is waiting for your offering. Don't disappoint her," whispered Moira.

"I don't know what's happening to me . . ."

Moira and Lei-Ling helped the mage sit up on the bed.

"My head . . . It's spinning."

"Lie down."

The whole room danced around him, but he wasn't scared. Throughout his life he'd temporarily abandoned his soul in many different artificial paradises. Every new experience fascinated him. No matter the risks. He felt his body sink into the welcoming mattress, just next to his gift. His shoulder touched hers.

"Aleister, your new lover wants a kiss . . ." Moira's voice echoed through his mind.

The heady scent of vanilla wafted up from the young woman's body. He turned his head and tried to embrace her, but his arms no longer obeyed his commands. The girl stared at him, her eyes wide. A strange black-and-red necklace stood out on her neck. An image made its way to the foreground in Crowley's mind. He'd seen this necklace before. Long ago, in a wild country whose name he'd forgotten. In a sacrificed village. Men, women, and children lying in the sun, their throats cut.

He tried to stand.

"Moira? She's . . ."

Darkness won out and the face of the beautiful young woman faded away.

II

Crete
November 1941

Tristan had just woken up and was contemplating the dawn light
through the window. That blue was unique to the Mediterranean.
It was the time of day, just after sunrise, when the heat was still
comfortable, and the breeze rustled gently through the bushes as
if this morning were the very first on earth. Marcas felt like he
had been purified, freed of his memories, as if he hadn't existed
before. For a few moments, his difficult past seemed to have
disappeared. But which past? The one he knew, or the one Erika
thought she knew? He closed the window carefully, so as not
to wake her, and made his way towards the bed. Her loose hair
was the only part of her that emerged from the sheets, which
hugged the shape of her body.

What was she dreaming of? Tristan knew so little about her.
She was the only daughter of an industrial family with ties to the
Nazi party and friendly with Himmler and Göring. She was also
one of the few women archaeologists in Germany. Since Weistort
had been wounded, she had become the director of the all-powerful
Ahnenerbe and reported directly to the Reichsführer. Tristan
lowered the sheet to reveal the tops of her shoulders. How could
he know so little about the woman he shared a bed with? What
kind of relationship did she have with her parents, whom she
rarely spoke of? How had she found herself in the most powerful
political circles? Why did Himmler trust her? Erika began to stir
under the sheet, revealing the tops of her breasts. In this room,
lit by the dawn's early light, they looked like a legendary couple,

straight out of Greek myth. But was either of them honest with the other?

"You're awake?" asked Erika's sleepy voice, drawing him out of his thoughts.

"I just got up a few minutes ago, with the rising sun."

"Have the soldiers taken their positions?"

Marcas looked at his watch.

"In half an hour."

The previous day, during their meeting with Lieutenant Horst, they had decided to lock down the village early in the morning and gather all its residents in the central square while they searched every house, one by one. It was a diversion, of course. At the same time, an elite commando unit would surround the excavation site to protect the chapel and begin digging. Horst was very optimistic, certain they would find the door quickly.

Erika got out of bed, rolled up in the sheet which was still warm with the heat from her sleeping body, and sat down at the table covered in the artefacts Karl had discovered.

"Have you seen this swastika?" she asked as she held out the engraved ornament. He spun it around between his fingers. As he felt the precious metal, he tried to imagine the person who had worn it. Had a single woman cherished it? Or had it adorned several bodies? Objects may not have souls, but they have memories. He could almost feel it.

"I was thinking," she continued, "Karl must have marked the place where he found this piece on his site map. Something tells me it was next to the chapel."

"Well, we can't really ask him now. You requisitioned his house and sent him to sleep on the church floor. I doubt he'll be feeling very cooperative."

"No need. The site map is in the left-hand drawer of the dresser in the library. I noticed it during our first meeting."

Marcas didn't look surprised. This wasn't the first time he'd noticed that his lover had professional reflexes that a detective would envy. He spun the artefact around in his hand again. Was it simply a piece of jewellery, or was it a religious symbol designed to honour a divine power?

"What do you think?" he asked.

"The same as you. It's a sign, maybe even proof."

"Do the archaeologists you sent here to Knossos know what the real goal of the excavations is?"

"Of course not. In fact, they're all returning to Berlin tomorrow. The team will be dissolved, and the excavation reports will be made top secret. Each member of the team will be sent to a different site. They'll never see each other again."

"They still might talk. Seven murders in just a few days . . ."

"Well, they would be risking their lives. I will warn them before they leave."

Erika had put on a khaki shirt and canvas trousers with a pair of worn boots. She was tying her hair up in a tidy schoolgirl plait.

"You were wearing the exact same outfit the first time I ever saw you."

"At Montségur, in the castle courtyard. But I didn't see you."

Marcas smiled, then replied. "Did you know what you would be looking for when Himmler sent you to the South of France?"

"No."

Tristan kept quiet. Since he felt compelled to keep his hands busy while thinking, he opened the drawer containing the site map and unfolded it on the table. Karl had been diligent. He had placed each discovery on the map, with the date when it was found. A black dot represented ceramics; a blue triangle metallic objects; and a red star works of art. Marcas ran his fingertip over the map. Most of the artefacts discovered were pieces of amphoras, symbolized by black dots, which were all over the map. The metallic objects were much rarer. As for the red stars, there was only one. Next to it, Karl had noted *swastika* in thin letters.

Erika, who had just gathered her excavation kit—trowel, brushes, and sieves—joined him at the table.

"The chapel is . . ." She leaned over the map and followed a topographical line that indicated the highest point of the site. "Right next to it. Just here."

The red star was only centimeters away. Erika placed a compass on the table and turned the map to make its North coincide with magnetic North.

"The map is too imprecise for me to calculate the exact distance between the chapel and the place where the artefact was found, but at least we know which direction to go. We'll head east from the chapel."

"If we're lucky, we'll find traces of the previous dig."

"Unless the villagers covered them up. After the second series of murders, the site was unguarded for several days."

"According to Karl, they're afraid of the *Abba*. If only we knew why . . ."

Erika had sat down next to the window to enjoy the cool breeze. Her skin had taken on a golden hue. Just a few hours in the sun had tanned her face and softened her strict features. Tristan found her even more attractive this way. She had just opened a dictionary she'd found in the library.

"In ancient Greek, *Abba* means 'Father', but not only in terms of the family. It was also the title used for the head of the religious community in monasteries."

"Which would explain the origins of the words 'abbey' and 'abbot' in English," noted Tristan.

"But the dictionary also says that the word later evolved to mean 'guide' or 'saint'."

"Villages aren't generally terrified of their patron saints, though, are they?"

"Well, that's not entirely true. Medieval saints were feared as much as they were adored because of their ability to pass between the worlds of the living and the dead."

Erika stood up, counted her tools, and put them in a rucksack. The clock in the kitchen downstairs rang out as it struck half past six.

"The soldiers won't be long now—"

Before the archaeologist could finish her sentence, tyres squealed on the main square. The rhythmic sound of boots echoed through the nearby streets. Tristan looked out through one of the small windows. Screams rose up from the houses as men in helmets broke down doors. Without paying the noise any heed, Erika put on her rucksack.

"Time to go," she said casually.

12

The house was deserted, except for two souls—one alive, one dead. They were both in the basement. The first, known as the Scarlet Fairy, was wearing a thick black turtleneck sweater. She was bent over the second, a pair of scissors in hand. Her victim, who had been murdered the day before, was lying naked on a table, her eyes open wide. The cut across her throat was tastefully hidden by a red silk handkerchief. Moira stroked the young woman's cheek, then whispered in her ear, "If it's any consolation, evil actions can lead to good. Thanks to me, you'll be reincarnated. You'll enjoy a better life."

She deftly cut off a strand of hair, along with the nails from both index fingers. She placed them in a matchbox featuring the jovial portrait of a Royal Air Force pilot brandishing the "V for Victory" sign.

Moira O'Connor kissed the corpse's forehead, then held open her right eyelid as she drove the sharp end of the scissors into the orbit. The metal slid easily into the space between the bone and the eye itself. She pressed firmly against the cheekbone with her thumb and popped it right out, then cut the optical nerve. She inserted a ball of cotton wool in its place, then laid the mutilated organ down on a bed of hair and nails.

"In a week, I promise to bury your body in the sacred circle in the New Forest. At the foot of the dolmen erected for our sister and queen, Boudica, whose name shines through the centuries, she who never lay down before the Roman soldiers. We will pray all night to ensure your new incarnation."

The Scarlet Fairy placed the box in a drawer. A shy smile appeared on her drawn face.

"Your soul is safe now. Before handling your body, I must invoke the help of Hecate."

She knelt before an altar where two torches burned. At its centre, on a silver tray, stood a blackened wooden statue of a woman sitting on a throne. In the background, there was a golden crescent moon, its points turned skywards. Two red dots sparkled in the idol's dark face.

"Hecate, goddess of the night, guide me in my carnal mission." Moira brandished a knife with a silver blade and a carved goat's-horn handle before the statuette. "May I wield my athame as your claw. May my mind be your mind. May my will be yours. May all your incarnations manifest through me."

She closed her eyes and breathed deeply. Her consciousness faded to allow the goddess's soul to enter. Though the temperature was only six degrees, drops of sweat beaded on her brow. A hot, intense wave of energy coursed through her veins. Her voice went hoarse.

"Hecate, Durga, Kali, Beyla, Astarte, Bestia, Jarnsawa, Skhmet, Bellone, Ishtar! Give me strength. Give me power!"

Her eyes gleamed. Moira was transformed—a wild expression took possession of her face. She stood up and walked over to the young woman lying on the table.

The Scarlet Fairy placed the tip of her blade just above the girl's belly button and pushed slowly. The silver knife split the tender skin on its path towards the intestines. With a practised gesture, she widened the opening, then used her other hand to pull out the already cold guts. Moira seemed to be in a trance. She didn't even smell the foul odour emanating from the disembowelled body. It took her nearly fifteen minutes to remove the entrails, which she placed in a bucket at the foot of the table. She then inserted a piece of parchment paper, bearing three four-line incantations in Old Gaelic, into the gaping hole. Two of them were curses; the third a blessing. The first aimed to damn Aleister Crowley's soul, the second to torment the King of England, and the third wished good graces upon the man who was renewing the world and who would free Ireland: Adolf Hitler.

It took her another quarter of an hour to sew the girl back up. Next, she cut the hands off the corpse with a saw, then finished her work by tracing a swastika on her forehead. Satisfied, she covered the body with a white sheet, put out the torches, and left the basement feeling calm and soothed.

She walked along a wall of blackened stones—ruins of a structure built before the dawn of time, before the Norman invaders arrived. A light scraping sound accompanied her steps. She recognized it instantly. An honorary escort from her friends the rats. She truly enjoyed the company of the hated rodents. Their numbers had been growing in London since the sewers had been damaged by the bombings. Nevertheless, she forbade them to prowl the upper levels of the building. She couldn't have them scaring away her clientele.

When she reached her office, the rats had disappeared down another path, probably on their way to the Thames. The room was warm. Moira closed the curtains over the two-way mirror, then opened a cupboard full of all sorts of accessories—whips, collars, metal rings, Venetian masks, and more—and pressed the back of it with a click. The panel opened slightly, and Moira pulled out a crate on wheels.

Ten minutes later, the telegraph machine was operational on the desk. She set the frequency to 14 MHz and flipped the power switch. Her watch read eight o'clock. The message from Berlin would arrive in just a few minutes. Satisfied, she opened a drawer and pulled out a thick envelope.

"My poor, dear Aleister. If you only knew . . ."

There were a dozen photographs of Crowley naked, his arms wrapped around the shoulders of the young woman with her throat cut. His fleshy face pressed to the girl's as his left hand held a dagger over her breasts.

Moira O'Connor studied her former mentor with disgust. The braggart never should have told her he'd been approached by British Intelligence. He'd boasted that he was starting a new life in the service of King and Country.

Moira, you must swear you won't tell. An important member of the SOE came to see me. He wants me to help him fight Hitler by using my talents as an occultist. Can you believe it? Me, Aleister Crowley, I'm being recruited by the King to save the country.

They'd asked him to sell off his shares in the Hellfire Club, since His Majesty's services could not employ a brothel owner—even if it was only a tenth of the establishment.

You understand, don't you, Moira? I must devote myself to my sacred mission.

He couldn't help it—old age had ravaged his body, but not his ego.

Moira had gladly accepted his offer and then shared Crowley's ramblings with Berlin. To her surprise, the RHSA was very interested in the information, and had asked her to undertake a blackmail mission.

When the mage had woken up in the red room, the corpse had already been removed. His mind had been addled by the drugs, leaving him with little or no memory of the events of that night. Moira had pushed him into a taxi to take him home.

The light on the telegraph machine began flashing. Moira picked up the receiver and placed it against her ear. When she heard the familiar clicks of Morse code, she grabbed a notebook and began jotting down the message.

13

Lieutenant Horst was waiting for Erika and Tristan at the highest point on the site. He looked out over the ruins of the chapel, attentively watching the soldiers, who were driving long sticks into the ground at regular intervals, then carefully removing them. At least that's what Marcas thought they were doing as he watched them tiptoe through the ruins as if across the back of a dragon they mustn't wake.

"Are they outlining the dig perimeter?" asked the Frenchman.

"Yes. I've asked the bomb squad to find the entrance we're looking for. They have a highly developed sense of hearing."

"Have you got anywhere yet?" Tristan asked Horst.

The lieutenant pointed to a dip in the earth. "The ground was disturbed and then filled in just there. It sounds very different from the surrounding area."

"Can you mark a larger perimeter?" asked Erika, who had just joined the men.

"I'll try."

The most experienced bomb-disposal expert began gently striking the ground, moving along step by step. One of his colleagues followed and drove a wooden post into the ground whenever the first man asked him to. Horst already had a dozen men at the ready with spades and picks. Tristan discreetly brushed Erika's hair aside and whispered in her ear, "You'll be opening the door to hell before long."

*

In under half an hour, they had marked an area of a few square meters. The diggers got to work. The first layer was made up of humus mixed with pine needles and gravel, but they quickly found a pile of hastily dumped rocks and backfill. It hid an entrance that had been dug into the ground. They could now see the side walls, still textured by the spades from the first excavation.

"This is definitely where Karl was digging," announced Erika.

"Right when the murders began," replied Tristan. "We'd better hurry, before the locals get suspicious."

"Look!" said Horst, pointing to two sculpted stones set into an ogival arch. They had found the door.

Erika asked the soldiers to step back. Fascinated, she stroked the perfectly preserved keystones. The door must have been buried just after it was built, protecting it from any sort of wear.

"We need to open it," announced Horst. "And quickly."

"You're clearly not an archaeologist," said von Essling ironically. "The door has been sealed shut with blocks of rubble held in place by mortar for the past six hundred years."

"How long would it take to remove one stone?" asked Tristan.

"If we do it according to the rules of proper archaeological excavation, at least an hour."

"I've got something better."

Erika frowned.

"I found this in Karl's basement this morning," explained Marcas. Tristan put his canvas rucksack down and pulled out a rough wooden box. When he opened the lid, Erika saw three carefully arranged sticks of dynamite. The wicks were still wrapped in oiled paper to prevent the powder from getting damp.

"What do you plan to do with those?" she asked warily.

"Either you take the wall apart stone by stone, and it takes days . . ."

"There's no way I can keep the village under control for that long," affirmed the lieutenant.

"Or we can remove a chunk of rubble, slip in a stick of dynamite, light it, and blow a hole in the wall."

"But the explosion could destroy everything inside!" she protested.

"It doesn't have to," Tristan reassured her. "We can place the stick in such a way that the blast will be directed outwards. There won't be any damage to the inside."

"Get on with it then," decided the archaeologist.

Tristan selected a stone to remove, then took off his shirt and began striking the mortar around it with his chisel.

Erika studied her lover's body. Though she'd explored most of its surface with her hands or mouth, she'd rarely seen it in full daylight. What fascinated her most wasn't the sight of his muscles contending with the stone, or his shoulders at work. It was the number of scars she could see. One of them began on his left shoulder blade and extended all the way down to his elbow. It was particularly impressive, with a cross-hatch pattern of additional scars from irregular stitches. Where on earth had Tristan been butchered like that?

The stone he was working broke free and tumbled loudly to the ground. An acrid smell wafted out of the opening. *The builders didn't bother doubling the wall,* he thought. *As if they were sure no one would ever violate this place. For fear of the* Abba*?* The Frenchman placed the stick of dynamite and struck a match.

"Everyone up top!" ordered the lieutenant.

The blast from the explosion rang out across the site. A dirt wall collapsed, filling the entrance with a cloud of dust. Tristan could just make out the wall through the haze. An entire portion of it had crumbled.

"The hole is big enough for us to get through," shouted Marcas as he jumped down and began making his way across the rubble.

Behind him, Erika blocked the lieutenant's path. "No one but Ahnenerbe personnel inside!"

"You can't give me orders!"

Erika pointed to the breach in the wall Tristan had just slipped through. "If you go past that wall, *you* won't ever give another order."

"That's the second time you've threatened me," raged Horst.

"And the last, because next time there won't be any warning."

The shocked SS lieutenant didn't dare follow as she stepped

through the hole. Inside, Tristan had turned on a lamp, which cast moving shadows on the walls. The ceiling had been damaged by roots but was still intact. As for the floor, it was paved with large, perfectly aligned tiles. Only the far end of the room was still shrouded in darkness. Despite his desire to unveil the mystery, Tristan hesitated to take the few extra steps and raise the lamp. He was in Knossos, after all. The city of King Minos, whose wife Pasiphae had conceived a child that was half-man, half-bull—a being so terrifying, according to the legend, that it had to be locked up in a labyrinth.

"Are you afraid of the Minotaur?" teased Erika.

"I'm afraid of all the follies men have created."

"Well, I'm not."

She grabbed the lamp and shone the light on the far end of the room. Much to their surprise, there was nothing there. Just another wall, identical to the one they had just blasted through. Dumbfounded, the archaeologist walked closer. Just as she was about to touch the stones, Tristan took hold of her arm to stop her.

"Don't move!" he urged.

A long slab had just appeared right in front of her, camouflaged by the chiaroscuro. It was raised above the floor and seemed to float in the darkness. Without touching it, Erika blew on a corner of the slab, revealing a perfectly polished ochre marble surface that sparkled in the light beneath the centuries of dust. It was smooth, without a single inscription, engraving, or image.

"It looks like a tombstone," said Tristan. "And yet . . ."

"What if the corpse inside isn't human?"

"Do you mean the *Abba*?"

"I mean that the villagers have always been scared. From the Minotaur to the *Abba*. Scared enough to kill . . ."

This was the first time Marcas had ever seen Erika troubled by an unexplained phenomenon, the first time a mystery had seemed beyond her. Was it just the tension that had been mounting over the past few hours, or an irrational fear of the moment when they would learn the truth?

"There's only one way to find out," affirmed Tristan.

He left the room momentarily to get a sledgehammer. As he returned, he noticed a dark vein in the marble slab, snaking from left to right. Marcas followed it to the centre of the slab.

"If I hit it here, the vein might be weak enough for the marble to crack."

"Are you sure?"

Tristan replied by slamming the tool into the spot he'd chosen. The sound of the impact echoed through the vaulted room. *If the* Abba *was asleep*, thought Marcas, *he's definitely awake now.* The slab had broken, and the right side had dropped suddenly into the space below.

Erika hurried over, the lamp in hand.

There was no body.

No swastika.

Nothing.

"This doesn't make sense. Everything lined up. Kalokairinos's excavations, Karl's . . ." Von Essling stood stock still, the useless lamp dangling from her fingers.

"What did all those people die for? To protect an empty hole?" Marcas wondered aloud.

The faint light bounced off the walls of the rectangular space in vain, until Tristan noticed a reflection cast on the bottom of the chasm. As if the light were hitting a piece of mirror. He bent down next to the edge.

"What are you doing?" she asked.

"Bring the light down here."

Just beneath the part of the slab that was still in place, something flashed intermittently. Tristan reached out his arm and felt cold metal beneath his fingers. He pulled hard. The left side of the slab, destabilized by the movement, fell inward. Marcas had just enough time to save his arm, raising the treasure he had found towards Erika.

A sword.

14

It was nearly dusk in Bloomsbury. The British Museum had been closed ever since August 1939 and looked eerie without the usual hustle and bustle of visitors. Sitting on a bench facing the columns at the front of the Museum, Laure couldn't stop thinking about Tristan's ghost file that she'd found the day before at SOE headquarters. She'd barely had the time to put it back in the filing cabinet before the secretary turned up. The file was empty except for a single name: *John Dee*. Another alias. Maybe his status as a double agent meant his real file was kept under lock and key somewhere else. She looked at her watch. Commander Malorley—punctuality incarnate, according to his reputation—was half an hour late.

"Don't ever sit with your back exposed. I could have stabbed you in seconds." Malorley's voice was as neutral and precise as ever. Laure refused to gratify him by turning around.

"Bloomsbury isn't exactly hostile territory."

"In our profession, the entire world is hostile. If you haven't figured that out, you're already dead."

She stood up slowly and smiled ironically. "Charming," she said. "I think I just might prefer the company of your libidinous mage to your own. He must be fun, at least."

Malorley ignored the joke and hurried over to a narrow street that led towards Holborn.

"What did you think of his file?"

"He's clearly deranged and depraved—an unscrupulous charlatan. And a pimp at the head of a brothel that caters for perverts, to boot. My God, who knew the English were so corrupt . . ."

Malorley slowed his pace. "Despite all his perversions, I believe him to be a devoted patriot. Ah, here we are."

They stopped in front of an esoteric bookshop called Atlantis. The display window featured an array of books on astrology, magic, and sorcery. Treatises on Kabbalism sat next to works on theosophy and spiritualism. Large reproductions of tarot-card illustrations decorated shelves filled with silver bracelets and necklaces. A central display case featured Crowley's books and his photograph in a large gilt frame.

"Looks like he's the star author," commented Laure.

"How astute . . . In the basement they sometimes host magical ceremonies."

"Black masses?"

"No, not that I know of. For that, you'd have to visit far shadier parts of London."

Malorley didn't open the door to the bookshop. Instead, he stopped in front of the building next to it, where he rang the bell—decorated with a demon's grimacing face—three times. The door opened and an elderly Asian man stuck his head through the half-open doorway.

"Your master is expecting us," announced Malorley.

"Indeed. Please come in."

The SOE agents entered the foyer, whose walls were covered in purple velvet. The servant, dressed in a black silk robe, took their coats and gestured towards the only door to the rest of the house. They walked down a hallway lined with paintings of couples in the most erotic positions imaginable. The man—conspicuously bald—was always the same, but the female partners changed. Laure smiled as she noticed Malorley's awkward expression.

"Wait here, please," requested the servant with a bow. "My master is just concluding another meeting."

A door opened at the other end of the hallway and a tall, thin, red-haired woman came out. She was wearing a beige trenchcoat and a large brimmed hat that hid part of her face. A frigid smile on her lips, she walked towards Laure and Malorley. The Commander watched until she was out of sight.

"You seem to have a thing for red-heads," offered Laure mischievously.

"Not in the slightest. But I'm sure I've seen that face before. I must have met that woman somewhere."

"With fiery hair like that, it must be hard to go unnoticed. She reminds me of the actress from *Jamaica Inn*—I saw it at Leicester Square. It's by a very talented director: Hitchcock. Have you heard of him?"

"I don't have time to go to the cinema," Malorley replied dryly.

The servant gestured at them to come into the sitting room. Once they were inside, the strong smell of incense tickled their nostrils. A man with a shiny scalp had his back to them. His massive body was wrapped up in a long mauve toga that went down to his ankles. He was standing in front of a floor-length window that looked out over a garden of box bushes.

"Please forgive me, but I was tied up with the young woman you just saw leaving," said their host as he turned around.

He had to be well into his sixties. His face looked swollen and his cheeks sagged. His round, smooth head was dotted with red splotches, his lips were shapeless, and his large, broad nose sat below two bulbous eyes. Unmoving, penetrating eyes. Aleister Crowley no longer looked much like the man in the pictures Laure had seen in his file.

"Who is she?" asked Malorley.

Crowley placed a finger on his mouth. "Come now, it isn't proper to reveal the name of a woman leaving a meeting, particularly a meeting with a man like me."

"Oh, knock it off. If you want to work for me, there can't be any secrets between us."

The mage looked up. "Moira O'Connor. She runs the establishment I used to have some shares in, and is also its majority owner. Since you asked me to sell my interests, she brought over a copy of the final sale document. Would you like to see it?"

"No. Moira O'Connor . . ."

Crowley opened his arms wide. "Forget about her. Welcome to my home," he articulated enthusiastically. "Enter freely. Go safely, and leave something of the happiness you bring."

"I'm not quite sure how to take that invitation, Aleister," replied Malorley. "Isn't that Count Dracula's line to his future victim?"

"I'm pleased to see that even secret agents have a modicum of literary culture. Bram Stoker was a friend of mine. Who is this charming person you have brought along?" he asked, staring intensely at the young woman.

"Matilda. Just Matilda," replied the Frenchwoman.

"Simplicity is often most beautiful." He took Laure's arm and showed her three drawings on an easel. "Look, aren't they exquisite? The Fool, the Star, and the Devil! Lady Frieda Harris, one of my disciples, has just sent over these illustrations for my tarot deck." He paused, as if speaking only to himself, then leaned closer to Laure. "But how terribly rude of me, my dear. I must introduce myself. I am the Mage of Thelema, the grand Tau Mega Thirion, the Perdurabo, the beast of the apocalypse, or 666. I am he who was, is, and will be."

"We'll stick with your legal name. George Alexander Crowley, also known as Aleister Crowley," replied Malorley. "Since last we met, I've gone over your files, and I must say your reputation reaches the heights of detestability. But when it comes to fighting Hitler, I've found it's best not to be fussy."

Crowley chuckled. "Ah, the Nazis. Such a fascinating movement. The Führer has stolen from me shamelessly."

"What do you mean?" asked Laure.

"He has applied my motto—*Do what you please!*—to the letter. That said, I admit he's taken things a bit too far. I was wondering, my dear Malorley, how will I be paid?"

"We'll attend to your fees after you've proven yourself on a mission. Didn't you just sell your shares in the Hellfire?"

A fleeting shadow veiled Crowley's face. "Yes, but 'Money makes the world go round', as they say. Tell me more about this mission."

"You'll be meeting with a man you knew in Germany in 1931, according to your MI5 file. A certain Rudolf Hess."

Crowley closed his eyes as if he'd suddenly nodded off, then opened them as his lips curled into a jovial smile. "Mm, yes, of course. Hess the rabbi! The eminent Talmud specialist."

Laure and Malorley exchanged confused glances.

"I don't think we're talking about the same man," said Malorley. "I'm talking about Hess, Hitler's former right-hand man, who landed in Scotland in May. You must have read about it in the papers."

The mage looked hurt. "I've made no mistake. I did meet that man in Germany, and discovering his secret almost got me killed."

PART TWO

Hitler was so driven by the forces of evil that he stopped living a normal life with a woman. The ecstasy of power in all its forms was enough.

Walter Schellenberg, Hitler's
Head of Counter-intelligence.
(From *The Labyrinth*, Harper & Brother, 1956)

15

The Viennese were wary of the Margareten neighbourhood. An obvious though invisible barrier had existed for some time between the notorious area and the rich, elegant city centre. People crossed it—in either direction—with reluctance, convinced that they were entering hostile territory on the other side. For the middle classes, Margareten and its dilapidated buildings were home to the dangerous elements of society: workers from the factories on the outskirts of the city, jobless peasants fleeing the countryside, Hungarians, and Slavs. All of the Empire's down-and-outs ended up in the neighbourhood, whose shade of dismal grey sprawled all the way to the dreary suburbs. Hitler himself was quite surprised to see that *Ostara*'s offices were located in the heart of Margareten. But that didn't deter him from his goal of meeting Jörg Lanz, the man behind the journal. His curiosity had been further heightened when he learned that Lanz was a former Cistercian monk. That order had been founded in the Middle Ages by Saint Bernard, who had inspired the Crusades and founded the Templar Knights, and who had fascinated Hitler for many years.

He had just asked for directions for the third time, but the foreigners he kept encountering spoke such poor German that they were no help. Though he'd been born in Austria, Adolf hated the Empire. The mosaic of different countries, languages, and cultures disgusted him. In his eyes, a nation should be united and homogeneous, like Germany, their superb neighbour, which served as his model of political perfection. He continued wandering the

sordid streets, certain he was just steps from *Ostara*. He crossed
the road to get a better handle on his surroundings, and finally
caught sight of two slate-grey towers, behind a block of residential
buildings. He instantly recognized them and delighted in his
discovery. They featured in an illustration on the journal's back
cover.

He immediately walked back across the street and around the
residential buildings, until he reached the journal's headquarters,
which were as incongruous as they were provocative. The architect
had clearly delighted in combining and parodying different styles.
While the towers evoked those of a medieval castle, the façade
featured Venetian windows, and the gabled windows resembled
those of a charming English country manor house. Hitler couldn't
help but wonder how a feat of such architectural whimsy could
have come to be here, in the middle of Margareten. Adolf stepped
up to the monumental gate, which seemed to open onto a mysterious and forgotten estate.

"Are you looking for something or someone?" asked a young
man smoking a cigarette in the garden.

He wasn't any older than Hitler, but his face already featured
a scar that began on his cheek and ended under his thin moustache.

"Before you ask, it was a swordfight. A duel at university . . .
and the end of my brief time as a student. But I have every intention of finishing my studies once the grass has grown thick on my
adversary's grave. I'm Weistort. What's your name?"

"Hitler," said Adolf, who had just noticed an engraved copper
sign at the top-right corner of the gate. *Ostara*, it read in dark
letters. "And I would like to meet Herr Lanz."

"After you."

Weistort pulled one side of the gate open, then gestured towards
the stairs. "*Ostara*'s offices are on the first floor. Knock and go
in."

"Just like that?" asked Hitler, surprised.

Weistort stared at the other young man. "I know a soul on a
quest for destiny when I see one."

★

The main room was empty. The only sound—of a single typewriter clicking away—came from behind a glass door. Adolf moved closer. His shadow must have betrayed him, because a high-pitched voice invited him in before he'd even knocked. This other room resembled a den. The windows were blocked by piles of books, and the wooden floor had disappeared under heaps of boxes. Behind a desk, in the middle of this paper kingdom, a man sat comfortably, protected like a bee larva in its honeycomb. Hitler was struck by his long, thin, incredibly white hands. It was like the blood no longer circulated in them. His face was of an equally unreal and unsettling pallor. Without a word, the man stood up to examine his visitor. He seemed to be holding an invisible compass.

"Less than five foot nine. No muscles to speak of. Not even seventy kilos. Olive skin. Excessively hairy. Your moustache gives it away. Southern Italy, I would venture. Somewhere along the Mediterranean, in any case," guessed Lanz.

"I was born in Austria," protested Adolf.

"That means nothing. On the other hand, your eyes. Grey, pale grey. That's a good sign. You have some Germanic heritage in you, and it speaks through your eyes. What do you want?"

"I—I'm a reader of *Ostara* . . ." stammered Hitler.

"Yes, otherwise you wouldn't be here. What else?"

"I wanted to tell you how much I admire you."

The compliment did not have the effect he'd hoped for.

Lanz took a step back. "Who sent you? Jews or Freemasons?"

"I thought they were one and the same," mumbled Adolf, surprised.

"Think again! You can recognize Jews—smell them, even. But Freemasons are like you and me—undetectable. That's what makes them the most dangerous of all. But soon enough a time will come when the servants of the Leviathan will pay for their crimes. And the tears of their blood will usher in a new era. Have you met Weistort?"

"Yes, the young man at the entrance."

"He's my secretary. You saw him, his features? His broad

shoulders? His golden hair? He is the picture of the new Man, of renewal, as the Book says." Lanz pointed to a Bible on the desk. "The true divine word, but only for those who know how to read it. The Jews corrupted everything with their ignorance. A nomadic people who thought they could understand the will of the Almighty. They distorted, twisted, and hid the truth. But the hour of revelation is near."

Hitler had always had an innate disgust for religion, but what he hated most of all was the sanctimonious morality of priests and pastors. The absurd dishonesty of loving your neighbour! It was a despicable farce that protected the interests of the powerful and kept everyone else in servitude. As a child, nothing had made him as angry as watching his mother bow to the important people in town. Hypocrites who drank the blood of Christ on Sunday and sucked every last drop out of the people the rest of the week.

"Do you know the Book of Genesis?" asked Lanz.

Adolf nodded.

"Then you know that Eve was tempted by the snake, which led mankind to sin. But what is the snake, do you think?"

"A symbol for evil?"

Lanz smiled. "That's what I thought for a long time, but it's wrong. The snake isn't a symbol; it's a metaphor. The Jews made Eve's temptation an embodiment of the Devil, but it's a trick to hide the truth. Pure manipulation."

Hitler's expression had changed. His lips were still as he observed Lanz, a feverish look in his eyes. Deep down, he had always known that everything he'd been taught was a lie. Society was a rigged performance that benefited secret forces, who used it to satisfy their desire for power and domination. How else could he explain the fact that he'd known nothing but misery and rejection for years, that every door had been shut in his face?

"The snake never really existed. The story of Genesis is really about something else entirely. It tells the secret history of our world."

The glass door opened and Weistort sat down on a corner of the desk.

Lanz continued. "Yes, mankind fell from grace, but it wasn't because of a woman or a lowly snake."

"In the beginning," explained Weistort, "a single race reigned over the world. White men with pale hair and eyes. They came from the North and had conquered everything in their path. That's where your grey, almost blue eyes come from. They're proof you are Aryan."

"But what happened?" asked Hitler.

"To find out, all you have to do is properly interpret the myth of the Garden of Eden. Little by little, the men from the North grew lazy and stopped conquering lands, hunting, and fighting. Their skin darkened from the climate, giving rise to the dark, idle, and corrupt race."

"Which sullied the world, then mixed with the original race, reducing its worth and finally destroying it," explained Weistort.

"The real meaning of the story of Eve seduced by the snake is the contamination of the superior race by inferior blood."

Hitler was dumbfounded. He'd never heard anything like this before. He didn't fully understand it yet, but he now knew he was Aryan. That's why others hated him so much—they were all of inferior race.

"So, to restore the original race," affirmed Lanz, "we have to get rid of the degenerates and enforce *racial purification* by forbidding impure marriages. The only women who will be allowed to procreate will be those with pure racial heritage. We will found fertility convents where they will only be fertilized by true Aryan men."

Adolf felt like he'd just seen the light for the first time, but his critical thinking nevertheless surfaced. "But how do you plan to reverse the process? How can we go back in time?"

"I was right about his eyes," said Lanz to Weistort. "He has ancient blood in his veins." Then he turned to Adolf. "What do you do for a living, Mr. . . . ?"

"His name is Hitler."

"I study art and paint. I—"

"You mean you have nothing but yourself. No resources or friends—correct?"

Hitler paled. The unbearable rejection he had suffered yesterday resurfaced.

"I'm not surprised. The dark race is everywhere and, as soon as they identify an Aryan, they persecute him. No help, no work. They prefer to bring in tens of thousands of nit-ridden Slavs and thieving Hungarians. Or worse, Jews."

"Did you know they have their own neighbourhood in Vienna now? And that it's impossible to get in, because there are so many of them?" asked Weistort.

Adolf nodded silently, though he didn't actually know a single Jew.

"And do you know why they proliferate so quickly? Why there are more of them?" asked Lanz. "It's because they stick together, unlike us. We have nothing in common anymore—no history, nor family, nor religion. The dark race has made us rootless in our own country." *Ostara*'s editor-in-chief stood up and placed his hand on Hitler's shoulder. "Would you like to find your real family? Would you like to find yourself?"

16

The Asian servant had brought in a tray of tea and cakes. Crowley dismissed him and served his guests himself. He poured the amber liquid into Laure's cup, gazing intently at her all the while.

"Sugar?" he asked.

"No thank you," replied Laure, uncomfortable.

"I admit I don't understand. Hess isn't Jewish. That's absurd," said Malorley.

Crowley had sat down in his armchair and ceremoniously placed his hands on the armrests. His expression changed completely, as if he'd been replaced by another man. He exuded authority and his voice deepened.

"Listen carefully, your reports are wrong. It wasn't 1931; I met him in October 1932, at an intimate dinner party in Berlin, hosted by Hanussen, Germany's most famous clairvoyant. Adolf Hitler wasn't in power yet and was terribly depressed. He no longer believed he was the chosen one. He'd sent Hess to mingle in all the occultist and astrology circles, on a hunt for positive signs. Hanussen was the only one to foretell his future victory, when the political commentators believed Nazism had lost its appeal. Hess and Hanussen became friends. They shared the same passion for the science of the stars. We had a lovely dinner that night, though unfortunately no women were in attendance. Hess didn't make a very good impression. A closed-minded man with set beliefs. His diatribes on National Socialism and the superiority of the Aryan

race were beginning to put us all to sleep, when I got the idea of
offering to hypnotize the guests."

"Did you hypnotize Hess?"

Crowley placed his hands over his eyes and pulled his lids to
the sides, massaging them. Then he sighed contentedly. Like a cat.
A fat, vicious cat.

"Oh yes. I do have that talent," he replied. "After dinner, the
conversation had drifted to the topic of reincarnation. A doctrine
in which Hess and many other Nazi officials believed wholeheartedly. He was sure he had been a great Viking king at the beginning
of the 7th century, so I offered to take him through a temporal
regression, but something very strange happened. Just after he'd
gone under, he started speaking Yiddish! He said he was a rabbi
who had lived in Nuremberg in the Middle Ages. A Talmudic
scholar. You can imagine our surprise. Hitler's right-hand man, who
brandished his anti-Semitism like a flag, was engaged in a passionate
monologue about the Torah and other sacred Jewish books!"

"Are you serious?" asked Laure, sceptical.

"Always, when speaking about reincarnation," replied Crowley
without a pause. "I'll let you imagine the expressions on the faces
of Hanussen and the other guests. Half of them were laughing
hysterically, the other half were terrified. If Hess discovered that
he'd been a Jew and not a Viking, he would have sent a troop of
Brownshirts to do away with all the guests within the hour."

"How did you get out of that one?"

"I relied on my talent for inception. I implanted false memories
that were more in line with his fantasies. Thanks to me, he saw
himself as a ferocious Swedish lord who became a priest in the
5th century. When he woke up, he was delighted and told us he
had truly enjoyed his extraordinary mystical experience. Obviously,
no one said anything about the rabbi.

To conclude, I must also tell you that there was an unexpected
side effect. A week later, Hess came to see me. He was thrilled
and wanted to thank me. He told me he had started hearing the
voice of a Nordic god named Baldr. A kind of guardian angel with
a horned helmet, who gave him advice now and again. Hess was

so enthusiastic that he even wanted me to hypnotize Hitler and record the session for the annals of history. I cautiously declined."

"Why?"

"What if Hitler had been a Jewish carpenter in Palestine or a black slave in the United States? At the end of the session, they would have shot me in the head. The next day, I left Berlin to come back to England. But I kept a list of Nazis who believe in reincarnation. I always document my travels in my notebooks. I must have at least fifty names."

"Could you share them with us?"

Crowley was visibly annoyed. "I'll have to find them. They must be in a box in the attic somewhere. It'll take some time, and I haven't proven myself yet . . . Let's see how things go with Hess, and if you're satisfied, we'll both have found something to occupy our time."

"Meaning?"

"I'll dig through my archives, and you can have a little chat with the SOE accountant and bring me a nice fat envelope of pounds."

Laure kept quiet. She had changed her mind about Crowley—madmen sometimes had a knack for politics, but rarely for business.

Malorley stood up. "All right. At least Hess will have a good memory of you. That will make things easier. I hope he'll recognize you when you visit him. I want you to get as much out of him as you can."

"On what topic?"

"I'll tell you when I come to fetch you tomorrow, late afternoon."

"Where is he being held?"

"In our most prestigious prison, of course. One that has seen many a crowned head lopped off its shoulders. In fact, he's the only person being held in the Tower of London at the moment."

Malorley seemed preoccupied when they left the mage's residence. He took Laure's arm. "I'm going to give you a mission."

"Right this minute?"

"Yes. I know where I saw that woman we crossed paths with. She's Irish and a supporter of Mosley's Blackshirts."

"I thought they were only in Italy."

"No, we had some here, too. Fascists who admire Hitler and Mussolini. The party is run by a blue-blooded aristocrat: Oswald Mosley. He even paraded thousands of partisans through the streets of London before the war."

"And they're allowed to continue their activities?" asked Laure, surprised.

"No. When war broke out, the party was dissolved. Mosley and the other leaders are rotting in prison. I met Moira O'Connor in 1938 at a party celebrating the signature of the Munich Agreement, signed with Hitler and Mussolini. She made no secret of her admiration for the Führer and, like Mosley, she was also in favour of Irish independence. Her relationship with Crowley worries me. You're going to tail her and report on all her comings and goings."

17

It was dark in the library. None of the institute's researchers had reported for work yet at this early hour. The offices were empty, the corridors silent, the building still asleep. Tristan was sitting near the French doors that led out to the terrace. The sun would soon rise over the tops of the trees in the surrounding grounds, but for now Tristan was enveloped in a soothing darkness that left him feeling particularly serene. He enjoyed the last hour of night, when daybreak was still but a dream. He felt like he was wrapped in an invisible blanket that kept him safe and warm. He took his coffee cup between his two hands, like a silent prayer, and rested his head against the thick leather armchair. Erika was still sleeping upstairs. Tristan was totally alone. Even if someone came into the library, they wouldn't notice anything in the darkness except the dozen or so books open on the desk, which were all about Crete. There were antique maps, travellers' logs, and accounts of the island's history. Tristan had surrendered to a nocturnal urge to learn as much as he could.

Alongside the books lay an empty notebook. Despite all he had read, the Frenchman hadn't come across anything to help explain what he'd found in the underground room. Nothing that could explain the empty tomb and the anonymous sword. He and Erika needed to find a viable explanation quickly. The Reichsführer wanted answers, not questions.

"You're up early," said Erika as she entered the library, wrapped in a blanket she wore like a toga.

Tristan stood up and pushed the armchair over to her. She sank down into it and got comfortable.

"I slept on the plane," explained Marcas. "Since I couldn't get back to sleep, I took advantage of the time to do some research."

"Did you find anything?" asked the archaeologist as she used her foot to pull over a chair to rest her legs on.

"Nothing, except that Crete has been invaded repeatedly throughout history. Romans, Byzantines, Franks, Arabs, Venetians, Ottomans . . ."

"Who was there when the room was built?"

"The Venetians."

Erika pulled the cover up to her knees. A first ray of sunlight made its way in through the top of the window and shone on her ankle.

"Venice," mused the archaeologist. "Have you ever been?"

Tristan shook his head.

"Did you travel a lot before we met?"

"You already know I was in Spain."

"Actually, I know very little about you. For example, that scar on your left shoulder. Whoever sewed you up wasn't the best surgeon."

"He wasn't a surgeon at all."

Erika pulled the blanket up a few inches higher, revealing part of her thighs. "Every time you share something interesting with me, I'll pull the blanket up a little more."

"What do you want to know?"

"What were you doing in Spain?"

"Didn't Colonel Weistort tell you?"

"He didn't have time. A bullet to the chest tends to slow conversation. And since he's still in a coma . . . So?"

"I was in Spain to oversee the transfer of an art collection, but its owner died before I could finish."

The archaeologist dragged the edge of the blanket higher up her legs.

"But how did you end up in Montségur in a German uniform?"

"After shedding the Republican uniform. That's the problem

with civil wars that go international—the only uniform that keeps you safe is the one that's winning."

The blanket moved higher.

"So, you're an opportunist?"

"No more than you. After all, Weistort's coma comes in handy for you. You're the head of the Ahnenerbe while we wait for him to wake up. That said, I'm not complaining about the situation. Your predecessor would most certainly have got rid of me after Crete, now that I've outlived my usefulness. I'm happy for him to keep sleeping until the end of days."

"Be quiet," said Erika as she covered herself completely with the blanket. "People are always listening. Hitler would be furious if he knew you'd said that."

"Why?"

"He and Weistort met as young men in Vienna, before the Great War. They crossed paths at the headquarters of a journal, *Ostara*, whose founder, Jörg Lanz, developed the ideas that blossomed into National Socialism. Himmler once told me that Lanz and Weistort had played a pivotal role in the Führer's ideological transformation."

A voice sounded suddenly at the door. "Everything's ready, Madam. What time would you like to leave?"

Erika jumped up on her bare feet, still wrapped in the blanket. "In two hours," she said.

"You're leaving?" asked Tristan, surprised.

"*We're* leaving."

"Where are we going?"

"To Wewelsburg Castle."

The Ahnenerbe's headquarters were located in the suburbs of Berlin, where noble families had built their mansions to be close to the seat of power while maintaining a safe distance from the masses in the city's poor neighbourhoods. Nestled at the centre of vast grounds and protected from view by thick curtains of mature trees, it felt like it was in the middle of the countryside. That was probably why Himmler chose it—he wanted privacy for his most confidential research. While Erika got ready for the trip to Wewelsburg, Tristan took a walk through the grounds. After the arid landscapes in Crete, walking through shaded undergrowth and listening to the flutter of a bird's wings and the sound of an unseen animal scurrying through a thicket did him a world of good. The paths had narrowed and were covered in dead leaves. It seemed no one ever came out this way. The Ahnenerbe's scientists took their short strolls close to the buildings. Tristan turned around. He could see the columns and the entrance, and above them the terrace with its French doors. Behind one of them, Erika was getting ready.

He felt a sudden surge of desire. Their time in the library had been interrupted too soon. She must be thinking about it as well. Unless she was still wondering about his past . . . Tristan turned back towards the path to listen to the sounds around him. The woods were full of noises, making it easy to follow someone undetected. He left the trail and made his way through the trees. In seconds, he had disappeared into the foliage. Erika's questions had made him wary, especially today.

The grounds were surrounded by a wall that protected them from view. Tristan followed it for about ten meters, then stopped at a door whose lock, recently oiled by security services, didn't hold up for long against his lock-picking talents. He stepped through the door and immediately closed it without a sound, then made his way down the cobblestone road that ran alongside the estate. From there, he could already see the grey roofs of the houses in town. Once he'd passed the first façades, the Frenchman turned towards the central square. At this time of day, the only people there were the few parishioners who had attended the first mass. Tristan waited for them to disappear, then entered the church.

The smell of incense filled the air. Near the altar, a choirboy was folding a chasuble. Tristan waited until he took it to the sacristy, then walked towards the chapel, where the confessionals were located. Shy rays of daylight entered through greying stained-glass windows. The sanctuary was visibly neglected, and the floor had not been swept. Since Nazism had come to power, Catholics had been discreet. In his speeches, Himmler regularly criticized them now. Many of them wondered if they would be the regime's next scapegoats, after the Jews. Tristan sat down on the wooden bench in the confessional, closed the door, and leaned towards the latticed window.

"Bless me Father, for I have sinned, as it says in the great book."

With those last words, which were not part of the ritual, the shadow on the other side of the confessional replied, surprised, "We are all sinners, my son."

"Some more than others, as it says in Isaiah."

"I'm afraid I don't remember that verse, my son."

"Chapter 33, verse 11."

A relieved sigh escaped from the confessional. "It's you!"

"I have very little time. Can you transmit a message for me?"

"If it's short enough, yes. One of our friends can get it out right away. It will be broadcast today, in a public Swiss radio programme."

Tristan looked at his watch. He had to get back to Erika before she began looking for him.

"How short?"

"No more than twenty words. The radio stations of neutral countries are under constant scrutiny. We can't draw attention."

The Frenchman remained silent. The fact that this priest knew about the whole transmission process was much more dangerous than a hypothetical interception by the Reich's intelligence services.

"How does your friend who's leaving for Switzerland contact you?"

"He doesn't. I leave the message in the charity box at the entrance to the church. I never lock it, since no one ever donates anymore anyway."

"Do you write the messages?"

"Yes, but I disguise my handwriting," explained the priest.

"All right. Do you have pen and paper?"

"I always have my notebook on me."

"The Minotaur's home is no longer the way of the cross but the way of the sword," dictated Tristan. Then he left the confessional, followed by the priest. He was a frail, hunched man, who seemed too small for his cassock. He showed Tristan the message.

"I'll put it in the box right away. I don't like to keep them on me."

The choirboy came out of the sacristy. He'd removed his liturgical clothes and was now wearing the uniform of the Hitler Youth. A band bearing a swastika was wrapped around his left arm.

"You can go home now, Adrian. The next mass isn't until eleven," announced the priest.

But the teenager didn't move. He was fascinated by Tristan's Iron Cross.

"Where did you get it? On the eastern front?"

The Frenchman nodded.

"As soon as I'm seventeen, I'm going to join the SS too, so I can kill communists," said the boy, joining his two hands to fire an imaginary machine gun.

The priest sighed. "Adrian, this is not the place for such words. I've told you before. You can't be a good Christian *and* want to kill your neighbour."

The choirboy looked up, confused: "But why not? Jews and communists aren't even human."

The priest was about to reply, but Tristan stopped him.

"Thank you for your spiritual comfort, Father. It's a great help before returning to the front. Will you give me your blessing?"

Surprised, the priest placed his middle finger on the Frenchman's forehead. His roughly hewn nails marked the skin. As Tristan was about to leave, Adrian let out a booming "*Heil Hitler!*" that echoed through the vaults. Tristan replied with a click of his heels.

As he made his way out the door, he turned around.

The priest in his black cassock stood near the teenager with his blood-red armband. The Frenchman had a strange feeling that only one of them would survive.

18

The Tower of London
November 1941

Freezing rain pounded unrelentingly into the dark fortress located on the banks of the Thames. An unsettling monument that reminded all Londoners of the dark side of British royalty. Here, for over a thousand years, they had imprisoned, tortured, judged, hanged, and decapitated enemies of the Crown—often innocents who had simply displeased the king or queen in power. Plantagenet, York, Tudor, Stuart, Saxe-Cobourg—most of the reigning dynasties had used or abused the services provided in this place. The latest royal family, the Windsors, were the first ones who seemed to be free of this unhealthy passion for the sinister building. There was only one prisoner there now—a foreigner, a German who had fallen from the sky. And even that was on the Prime Minister's personal orders.

Sitting in an office on the second floor of the west wing, Malorley, Crowley, and the Tower's director were chatting over three mugs of hot chocolate.

"How is the prisoner?" asked the commander.

"Good. He eats all his meals and walks in the courtyard for an hour each day. But your colleagues from MI5 can't get anything out of him. He reads a bit and sometimes talks to the guards, but . . ."

"What?"

"Sometimes he hears voices. And he does some strange things."

Malorley didn't display any emotion. He had to concentrate on the meeting with Hess. But the message Tristan had sent via Swiss radio, just before he'd left the office, kept coming to the fore of his mind. The hunt was on again.

They were back in the race for the swastikas.

Sitting by his side, Crowley kept quiet, simply jotting things down in a notebook. He had swapped his toga for a brown three-piece suit with a purple silk pocket square.

The warden cleaned his glasses with a handkerchief, which he folded carefully before continuing. "For example, he asks us to bring him insects. And then he eats them. He says they're a source of vitality."

"How extraordinary! It's Renfield to a tee," commented Crowley.

"Renfield? I don't understand. Is that a behavioural disorder?"

"Of course, one that's described in great detail in *Dracula*. Renfield, the notary and servant to the count, ends up in prison, where he consumes flies and cockroaches. To regenerate. Haven't you read the masterpiece?"

"I did, a long time ago. A good novel, but I—"

"A novel? You're wrong there, my friend. It's a first-hand account of vampirism. I knew its author, Bram Stoker, quite well. He was a member of a secret society called Golden Dawn, of which I was a grand master. Stoker didn't make anything up, you can take it from me. Except for a bit of nonsense on the power of crucifixes."

The warden frowned. "Uh, could you remind me again exactly who you are?"

Malorley stood up and interrupted the mage. "This is Dr. Kenneth Andrews, a behaviouralist. Please excuse us, though, we're in a bit of a hurry."

The warden verified the papers Malorley had provided one more time. "Do you mind if I make a call, Commander? Just to be sure. You can wait in the entryway."

Malorley and Crowley left the office for a gloomy corridor.

"Don't ever do that again," scolded Malorley. "This is no time for humour."

"I was serious."

The warden joined them again a few minutes later and gestured to a guard. "Take them to cell 3."

He gave the papers back to Malorley as he said goodbye and cast one last inquisitive look at Crowley. "I feel like I've seen you before. I ran a few other prisons before the war. Maybe you came to interrogate one of the prisoners?"

"I'm sure that can't be," Malorley replied before Crowley could speak. "Thank you for your help."

The walk was short. They went down a narrow staircase to a damp corridor that led to an octagonal room with a vaulted ceiling featuring ogival arches. There were seven wooden doors, all painted green.

The guard put a heavy key into one of the locks. An ominous creaking echoed against the walls. As the two men stepped inside, the strong smell of mould barrelled into them. It looked like the cell hadn't changed since the 12th century. Blackened stone walls, a cobblestone floor, and a roughly cut gap in the stone for a window, protected by thick iron bars. The cell was truly medieval. The prison administration had nevertheless granted a few modern concessions, like a proper bed, an electric lightbulb that cast a yellowish gleam, and a toilet that would have been perfectly at home in a Shoreditch hovel.

The visitors stopped at the centre of the cell. Rudolf Hess was sitting on his bed, where he had placed a book face down, to gape at them in surprise. The contrast between his pale eyes and black eyebrows was striking. He had grown thin and seemed to have aged ten years since the photos that had been published in the press. He blinked again and again, like an owl.

"We're delighted to make your acquaintance, Herr Hess."

"Are you MI5 or MI6? I can't keep all your acronyms straight."

"Neither. We're here at the behest of Prime Minister Churchill."

Hess's face suddenly lit up. "Better late than never! I was unable to convince those idiots from the intelligence services. I suppose you're finally here to get me out of this terrible place. At long last! Strange things happen here, you know."

"Well, we would like to clarify a few things," continued Malorley.

"*Nein!* I am sick of this!" shouted Hess as he shot up, his face red with disdain. "Another interrogation! You English are so stupid.

I confronted so many perils to bring you peace, and in exchange you torment me. Is this how you treat diplomats in your country?"

"If you'll remember, Hitler has disavowed you and—"

"You don't know anything about the Führer's intentions. Nothing! Leave me alone. I won't answer any of your idiotic questions until I've been released from this place to see Churchill."

"That's exactly what we're suggesting. During your first meeting with the Prime Minister, you alluded to sacred swastikas found in Tibet and in southern France."

"I won't tell you anything! Get out," said Hess, folding his arms defiantly across his chest.

Crowley leaned towards Malorley and whispered, "Let me." Then he walked over to the Nazi dignitary. "Rudolf, don't you remember me? Aleister Crowley. We met at that dinner at Hanussen's in Berlin. I put you in touch with Baldr. The god Baldr . . ."

Hess studied Crowley from head to toe before answering. "Yes, yes, the English mage. But you aren't like I remember you! You've gained some weight, my friend. That's not healthy."

Aleister took him by the shoulders. "My appearance isn't important. My soul is what counts, you know. We have the same spiritual values. How is Baldr?"

"He's angry and hasn't spoken to me since I've been stuck in this damn prison. Tortured spirits haunt the place and keep him from appearing to me."

"What spirits, Rudolf?"

"Terrible things have happened here. They locked up noble prisoners to execute them. Anne Boleyn and Catherine Howard were shut away in this very cell, until Henry VIII had them beheaded! I hear them screaming at night. That's why I eat insects— they don't like it, so they leave me alone."

He stopped and glanced warily at Malorley. "What about him? He looks like he might be of the race of David. I won't tell him anything about the swastikas."

"No, he's a pure Aryan. Don't worry, Rudolf. I'm here to help you," said Aleister, placing a hand on Hess's shoulder. "Would you like me to hypnotize you? Like at Hanussen's? That way, I could speak directly to Baldr. The ghosts can't touch me—I have a protective talisman."

"You would do that for me?"

"Of course! We're friends, aren't we? Just sit back against the wall and relax."

19

The village tavern contained just a handful of locals who banged on the counter as they downed small glasses of schnapps. Himmler, who had restored the castle to create a spiritual fortress for the SS, had probably never been through the village or met its residents. There were no tall Aryans with blue eyes here. Just sturdy farmers, their faces tanned by work in the field and covered in rough black beards beneath faded charcoal-grey eyes. Germans who looked nothing like the images of the Nordic superman celebrated in Nazi propaganda.

Sitting nearby, Tristan listened carefully to their conversation. He and Erika had come to the tavern because she wanted to read the various reports from the Ahnenerbe mission to Crete. On Tristan's advice, they were both in civilian clothes, which made them nearly invisible to the regulars, who thought they were a couple of sales representatives. Moreover, Tristan had been feigning sleep for some time now with his mouth agape. No one is ever wary of a man who snores in public.

"I'm telling you, my cousin says they hear strange noises at night. And that the women who work there don't want to go to the tower anymore," explained a voice.

"Your cousin's full of it! No one can enter the tower anyway. The SS soldiers keep it all under lock and key."

"But why?"

"To protect Hitler's tomb. That's where they'll put him when he kicks the bucket. And in the meantime . . ." said the voice, getting quieter, "they hold ceremonies and perform rituals to prolong the Führer's life."

"Shut up! The walls have ears."

The conversation suddenly stopped, and Tristan could no longer hear anything other than the regular sound of cards falling on the table. He could wake up now, but he waited for Erika to shake him.

"Did you fall asleep?"

"I guess I did," said the Frenchman. "I dreamt of you."

A labyrinth of narrow, twisting streets led up to Himmler's new Camelot. As they neared the entrance to the castle, whose restored walls blended into the ash-grey sky, Tristan asked his lover, "What were the regulars at the tavern talking about?"

"No idea, I was focused on my reading. Why are you interested?"

"Just curious. It seemed like a lively discussion. What's up next?"

"We have an appointment with Professor Waldenberg. He's a specialist in medieval weaponry. But first, we're going to visit the swastikas."

At these words, the Frenchman stopped short, surprising Erika.

"Don't you want to see the relic you saved in Montségur?" she asked.

"I do, but I thought it was off limits."

"The Reichsführer has issued special orders."

As they passed through the security checkpoints, Tristan thought back to the conversation at the tavern. It wasn't surprising that the locals had imaginative stories about a place they could no longer visit. Especially since the castle was Himmler's personal property—a fact that evoked all sorts of fantastical ideas. People said he worshipped pagan gods in secret and that he was obsessed with collecting books on witchcraft, but Tristan had never heard any rumours that he was conducting magical rituals or ceremonies, certainly not to extend Hitler's life. How had such an idea got into the heads of the men at the tavern? What exactly *was* Himmler doing with his condemned souls and the swastikas?

They had just walked through the main courtyard, decorated

with black banners bearing the SS runes, and were now climbing the stairs to the tower.

"Have you been here before?" asked Tristan when Erika stopped in front of a door on the first landing.

"Yes, Himmler took me to visit the swastikas when we got back from Montségur."

An officer opened the door, bowing to the archaeologist and gesturing towards a narrow stone corridor. Without a word, von Essling stepped in, followed by the Frenchman. The door shut immediately behind them.

"I expected to see more guards."

"Keep quiet."

They had just entered a round room with stone walls. Four projectors hidden in the floor came on, shining vertical light on the vault and illuminating the entire room. Four swastika-shaped alcoves carved into the stone marked the four cardinal directions.

"To the east, you'll see the swastika found in Tibet," explained Erika. "To the south, the one from Montségur."

Tristan walked over to each of them in turn. They were identical, except that one bore a series of large brown stains. Suddenly, Marcas felt like he was in a sacrificial temple dedicated to unspeakable divinities. He looked up at the vault and noticed an opening.

"What's up there?"

"In the Middle Ages, this was the dungeon. Since the corridor we came through didn't exist back then, they lowered prisoners down through that opening."

"What's there now?" Tristan probed.

"Hitler's bedroom."

As they walked back through the corridor that led to the rest of the castle, Marcas did his best to hide the urgent questions in his mind. Himmler had been using an expression more and more often over the past few months, and he couldn't help but think of it. *We're building a Thousand-Year Reich.* What if the real goal of the swastikas wasn't just victory over Churchill's Britain and Stalin's Russia, but immortality? Hitler's immortality.

"Here we are," said Erika as she turned the handles on a pair of double doors that opened onto a huge room filled with floor-to-ceiling bookcases. A few windows, dimmed by curtains, lit the room with wan light. On the wooden floor stood long, varnished oak tables, which were covered in piles of books. On each table stood a copper placard bearing a name. All of the names were preceded by the honorific "Professor".

"They're the names of the teachers who train the SS officers at the castle's seminary."

"I thought that in Germany you used the title 'Doctor' rather than 'Professor'."

"When the person in question has a doctorate from a university, yes. But some of the people who teach here have never set foot in a university. So, to avoid upsetting anyone, we give everyone the title 'Professor'. Himmler selected a few teachers with rather marginal, if not heretical, ideas."

They had just reached a table where they saw globes instead of books. Tristan moved closer. He had always been fascinated by antique globes. Especially those inscribed with the magical words *Terra Incognita* to name parts of the world that hadn't yet been discovered.

"This is Professor Hörbiger's desk. He has some deliciously eccentric views about the earth. He believes we live on the *inside* of a giant, hollow planet, like on the stone of a fruit."

"Are you joking?"

"Not at all. And when we look up at the sky, it's not infinite space that we're contemplating, but the inside of the fruit's skin."

"What about the stars?"

"A simple optical illusion due to the diffraction of light."

Marcas was speechless.

"But Hörbiger also wonders if perhaps the fruit, whose stone we live on, is bathed in an ocean of light. In that case, the sparkling of the stars would be due to the light passing through the skin of the fruit in areas where it is thinner or damaged."

"Good thing Professor Hörbiger is living in this century. In the Middle Ages, he would have been burned at the stake. I can't believe the Reichsführer is interested in such nonsense."

"Himmler is only interested in the military implications of the theory. If there's a wall, membrane, or whatever you want to call it above the earth, and you shine a very powerful ray of light on it, the ray will be reflected. And if you calculate the angle properly, you can hit any part of the globe that is currently out of range for your bombers."

"Like the United States," exclaimed Marcas, who finally understood. "But for that to work, you would need an incredibly powerful energy source."

"Yes, but we'll soon have the four swastikas."

When they finally reached the centre of the library, they stood before a stone altar, which must have been stolen from a church. A wooden lectern protected by a glass pyramid sat upon the stone.

"Heinrich Himmler's private collection," announced the archaeologist.

"I recognize his exquisite taste in the juxtaposition of a Romanesque altar with a baroque lectern."

"Come closer."

There was a book on the lectern. The red leather binding bore a title in gothic letters. As he studied the spine of the book, Tristan noticed that the pages were of different sizes. It wasn't a printed book, but an antique manuscript.

"This is the *Thule Borealis Kulten*."

Marcas jumped. This was the book that had led Weistort to kidnap him in Spain, fake his death, and bring him along on his murderous quest to Montségur.

"What is really inside? All I know is that it was written at the end of the 13th century."

"Our specialists have studied it in detail. It was most likely written by a monk in the scriptorium of an abbey. That's what analysis of the parchment and writing revealed."

"Do we know what part of Europe it's from?"

"By comparing it with other manuscripts from the time, we've determined it was written in southern Germany."

"Are there many monasteries there?"

"Not really, but what makes things more complicated is that

the person who wrote it had historical and geographical knowledge far beyond that of religious communities at the time."

The Frenchman shrugged in surprise.

"Maybe it wasn't a monk, but a traveller passing through," suggested Erika.

"How did you come by the manuscript?"

"Weistort got it from a Jewish bookseller."

Tristan didn't bother asking exactly *how* Weistort had got it. It was unlikely the former head of the Ahnenerbe had made a fair trade.

"Can we look at it?"

"Himmler has the only key," explained Erika, pointing to the lock on the glass pyramid.

"Do you know what it's about?"

"Yes. It tells the story of the first men. The Hyperboreans, who split up into four migratory groups following a climate disaster. Each group carried a swastika. The text gives clues to where they left their relics."

"But there wasn't anything in Knossos."

"There was the sword," said Von Essling as she turned towards the far end of the library, where a lamp shone in the half-light. "And I know someone who can help us."

20

Malorley watched incredulously as the Nazi obeyed like a child.

The mage took a small red prism from his jacket pocket, wiped it off with a handkerchief, then let it shine in the yellow light that fell from the ceiling. "The ruby of Cytorak. A gift from the Maharajah of Rashpur. It enables the beholder to attain a state of hypnosis without any effort."

Malorley didn't believe a single thing Crowley said, but Hess seemed convinced. That was the important thing. Crowley moved the prism back and forth in front of the prisoner's eyes for a moment. "Look at the ruby and listen to my voice. Only my voice. You are safe. The light of Cytorak brings you infinite peace. Your breathing is slowing, your heart is beating regularly. Inhale and exhale slowly, very slowly. We are far, far from here. In Germany, in your comfortable home in Berlin."

Hess seemed relaxed.

"You go inside and make your way straight to the lounge. It's warm and welcoming. Now, sit down in your armchair. What do you see?"

"The garden. It's full of flowers."

"What kind of flowers?"

"Beautiful red roses. My wife, Ilse, is an excellent gardener."

"Good. Now, focus on the roses while I call Baldr."

Crowley stood up and walked over to Malorley.

"He's in a deep state of hypnosis. I imagine you want him to talk about the swastikas and the book you mentioned. What was it called again?"

"The *Thule Borealis Kulten*."

"Given what happened during our previous session in Berlin, I can't guarantee results, and have no control over the consequences."

"It doesn't matter. Hess will be back under the supervision of MI5. They'll handle any side effects."

"As you wish."

Crowley went back to sit down next to Hess, who looked particularly serene.

"It's me, Baldr," mumbled the mage in a strangely melodious voice. "Do you recognize me?"

Hess's face lit up with pure joy. "You're back at last! I had a terrible nightmare that I was locked up in a prison. In a tower in London. I don't know why, but there were headless women there who stared at me."

"A bad dream, nothing more. I need you. Will you help me?"

"Yes, but I must see the Führer as soon as possible. Göring and the other snakes want to push him to invade England. I must prevent him from committing such a mistake. We aren't invincible yet. We haven't found all the sacred swastikas."

"Speaking of which, could you tell me where the one found in Tibet is located?"

Hess tensed. "It's in Himmler's castle, where they will all be reunited. Himmler is my only ally. He has to help me convince Hitler."

"Describe the castle to me."

"Wewelsburg . . . It's the cathedral of the Black Order. A place inhabited by spirits. But you already know it. You spoke to me there."

"Of course, that's right. But tell me, the book, the *Thule Borealis Kulten*, is it there, too?"

"Yes, in a library. I studied it. It's a dangerous text."

"Take my hand, Rudi. Let's leave your home so you can remember the place. We're in the castle. Do you see it?"

"Yes. There are torches all around. It's dark. Himmler is here, showing me the *Thule* on a lectern. The red cover bears the symbol of our party."

"Open it."

"One of the pages depicts a burning witch. There's a warning. It says that those who are unworthy to read it will burn. There's a drawing of a demon, but I can't see any more. It's all going dark."

The German writhed on his bed, his face tense. His breathing grew choppy. Despite the cold air in the room, he was sweating profusely.

"Keep reading, I'll protect you."

"I . . . I . . . I can't. The demon has come out of the book and he's whispering in the darkness. No . . . Let me be!"

Crowley glanced at Malorley. "We have to stop the session."

"No! Ask him where the third swastika is!"

"As you wish."

The mage turned back to Hess. "Look through the pages, Rudi. Nothing can hurt you. The demon is no match for a god from Valhalla."

"I can't. Himmler has put it away."

"Where?"

"The witch . . . She keeps . . . Oh no! The demon has seen me."

"What witch?"

Suddenly the Nazi started screaming. He went stiff as his eyes opened wide. "He's devouring me! Please . . ."

The door to the cell burst open as the guard came in brandishing a truncheon. "What on earth is going on in here?"

Crowley was twirling the ruby before Hess's mad eyes while Malorley held the prisoner down.

"Wake up!" shouted Crowley. "I chased the demon away. You're safe now."

"No! He's entered my body!"

Hess screamed louder and louder, saliva frothing at the corners of his mouth.

"Looks like a seizure. Call a doctor!" ordered Malorley.

The guard walked over to the bed. "Jesus!"

"You can call on your god later," mumbled Crowley disdainfully.

Two other guards arrived, followed by the warden, who glared at Crowley. "Now I remember where I met you! At the prison in Leeds, where you were incarcerated. Convicted of public indecency, and you had the nerve to organize the sale of pornography in my establishment! Get the hell out of here before I have you locked up!"

21

Heiligenkreuz Abbey
October 1908

A fine layer of snow had just fallen on the cobblestone road that led to the monastery's main gate. Resting his back against a tree, Hitler stared at the steeple, which sparkled in the moonlight. There were fields on either side of the road. To the left, there was also a rise crowned with a tower. *Most likely a watchtower,* thought Adolf, *but it didn't do much good.* Everyone in Austria knew that Heiligenkreuz Abbey had been pillaged and burned by the Turks in 1683. A symbolic date when Vienna had almost become Muslim— and the rest of Europe would most likely have fallen with her. Adolf turned up the collar of his coat and blew into his hands. He had received a message from Lanz inviting him to come to the monastery just after dark, but he now wondered if it had been a good idea to accept. He'd read all the issues of *Ostara* at the national library, and while he shared most of its editor's ideas, he still couldn't understand how Lanz planned to implement his plan to restore the Aryan race and its supremacy. Hitler shrugged. An hour-long walk through Vienna was enough to confirm that the city had become very cosmopolitan. As for the Viennese, they were obsessed with acquiring the new marvels of modern technology: telephones and cars. Lanz's ideas only found listeners among ostracized citizens, a group to which Adolf had to admit he belonged.

"Herr Hitler?"

Weistort had just appeared, a lantern in hand. He gestured towards the monumental entrance to the abbey, barred by tall gates. "There's a service entrance off to the side. Follow me," he said.

They walked quickly across the snow-covered courtyard, then turned left towards the church. Light shone through the stained-glass windows. They heard a bell ring, calling the monks to prayer.

"Where are we going?" asked Hitler, intrigued by their clandestine stroll.

"Definitely not to pray with the monks."

They walked alongside a chapel, which Adolf guessed must be much older than the rest of the buildings. Flying buttresses surrounded it, protecting it from the tests of time. It seemed to be abandoned. As they passed the apse, Weistort stopped and handed the lamp to his companion. He pulled a key out of his pocket and plunged it into the snow. "The lock is rusty," he explained. "The key makes less noise when it's a little wet."

The pallid light from the lantern shone on a low door that seemed to lead to a passage between the tall, thick walls, whose grey stones shimmered with frost. Adolf went in first. The stone floor of the chapel was covered with bird droppings. When Weistort lifted the lantern to get his bearings, a group of bats shrieked and flew out of a broken window. A close, musty scent clung to the walls.

"The smell of the Catholic church," joked Weistort, "as it agonizes and decomposes. The smell of a slow death. It's hard to believe thousands of Cistercian monks fought as crusaders to conquer the Orient . . . Such degeneration!"

Hitler wasn't listening. He was taking in his surroundings. A holy font lay on the floor alongside a headless statue. The walls were covered in thick layers of saltpetre. He hadn't touched a brush for weeks, but he suddenly felt compelled to paint. He imagined the dismal, ghostly effects he could create with such a place. His hand involuntarily mimed a brush stroke. But what was the point? No one wanted his paintings. His rejection from the Academy of Fine Arts had left him wiser. He felt he had finally come to understand something crucial—it was useless trying to transform real life into an ideal. Art was an illusion and the greatest artists were skilled manipulators. They depicted the world as colourful to make it more bearable. But it was all lies and imposture. He knew now that he no longer wanted to magnify reality—he wanted to change it. And that required action.

"You came," said a voice, as Lanz's silhouette came into view between two columns. He stood still, observing Hitler, as if he feared the young man might not really be there. "You've answered the call of destiny. This is why you're here," he explained, pointing to a blackened wooden panel sitting on the floor just in front of the dilapidated altar. "Pick it up."

Adolf did as he was told. The black abyss of a well appeared, exhaling a frozen gust.

"This is the sacred source that our ancestors worshipped before the laws of Christ ran the world. This is where Celtic, then Germanic temples stood, temples the monks quickly annexed and converted. In the places where they had celebrated the strength and power of the earth, they were forced to prostrate themselves before the crucified god who turned the other cheek," recounted Lanz, his voice growing deeper as it echoed through the chapel. "But nothing is ever truly lost; everything reappears after a time. Have you heard of the Templar Knights?"

"The men who protected pilgrims on their way to the Holy Land?"

"Precisely. There were just a handful of them at first, but they became the armed hand of God on earth, fighting the infidels wherever they may be. From the Black Sea to the banks of the Nile, from Spain to Jerusalem. They were feared by their enemies and their friends alike."

Lanz took off his thinly rimmed round glasses and ran a hand over his scalp, then continued. "The Templars were destroyed in a show of fire and blood. A tragedy orchestrated by the Pope and the King of France to hide their true mission."

Adolf's interest was piqued.

"Their brutal demise created a myth. Libraries around the world are full of books that claim to reveal their secrets. People dig through archives looking for the source of their power and excavate old sites on a hunt for their treasure, but they're all after a legend. They're in denial."

"Denial of what?" asked Hitler.

"Of Truth."

The church bell sounded, signalling the end of evening prayers. The monks headed back to their rooms. Weistort threw his coat over the lantern. The chapel suddenly went dark, until they could see again in the moonlight that shone through the tall windows. Weistort had silently padded over to the door, to keep a lookout.

As for Lanz, he hadn't moved. He stared straight at Hitler and asked, "Do you want to know the truth?"

The truth? He already knew the truth. A violent father he hated, a mother who'd died too soon, failed studies, a lack of talent . . . That was the truth. The only one that mattered.

"Yes," he replied. Surprised by his own answer, Hitler almost turned around to see if someone else had spoken for him, but Lanz grabbed his arm.

"Come then, it's time to go down to the crypt."

It was the first time Adolf had visited the underground world. As he descended the unstable steps, he felt like he was making his way down into hell. And yet, when Hitler walked into the dark, vaulted room below, he had no negative feelings. On the contrary, the darkness, silence, and heavy stones unexpectedly made him feel safe. No one could get him here—the injustice and disdain that had plagued him for so long had stayed up at the surface. He was so focused on his impressions that he hadn't yet noticed the shadows standing in a half-circle before him. When he looked up, Weistort had just placed the lantern at their feet. Hitler felt like he was facing a tribunal. Six men in black suits stood around Lanz.

"Come forward."

Adolf took a step and froze. He couldn't see the participants' faces, hidden in the darkness. He, however, was perfectly visible. What were they thinking? Why were they staring at him like that? Maybe it was a test? He bit his lip behind his moustache. To hide his impatience, he looked at the floor. One of the stones was lighter and longer than the others. It seemed to be engraved with something. A tomb, maybe, but this crypt had to be full of them.

"Do you know why you're here?"

Just as Adolf was about to reply, voices rang out in unison.

"To see and to know."

"Then let him see."

In front of Lanz, who had just spoken, Weistort raised the lamp, revealing the chiselled stone of an ancient altar.

"Do you know why the stone is uncovered?"

This time Hitler knew not to answer. This game of questions and answers was childish. This wasn't what he'd come for.

"To study and learn."

"Then let him learn."

Weistort intervened again, carefully placing a book on the altar. Adolf immediately noticed the red cover and that the pages weren't all the same size. It wasn't a bible, as he had expected, but an old book. Very old. Most likely a manuscript.

"Do you know why the book is closed?"

"To confuse and mislead."

Lanz turned towards Hitler, who still hadn't moved. "Whoever opens this book will know the truth. The hidden truth that bursts forth. The real story of Man and the world. Are you ready?"

"What must I do?" asked Adolf, who was growing impatient with the silly ritual.

Weistort took him by the arm and led him to the altar. At the same time, Lanz's companions lit candelabras at the far end of the crypt. The stone floor disappeared, replaced by sand that glimmered in the light.

"Open the book."

Hitler lifted the cover, revealing a blank page, followed by another filled with tiny writing. In the right-hand margin, two knights on a single horse rode into battle, swords in hand.

"The truth speaks through images. Do you know what those riders represent?"

Adolf shook his head. He was tired of riddles.

"They're Templar Knights. They're always depicted in pairs to symbolize their brotherhood. Templar Knights never go into battle alone. That's their strength," replied Hitler.

Each of the participants held out a hand to touch the edge of the book, as if to share in its mysterious knowledge.

"May we be as one," said Lanz.

Hitler waited a few moments, then interrupted their silent meditation. "Could you tell me why I'm here, instead of going on about the Templar Knights?"

Ostara's editor-in-chief stared at the young man for a minute before answering. "As you know, the dark race has conquered the world, diluting pure Aryan blood, nearly annihilating it. But throughout history there have always been times when the blood speaks again. In the Middle Ages, it was through the Templar Knights."

"I don't understand."

"Don't you see that in the Middle Ages, as Christianity imposed obedience, social order, and guilt, the Templars embodied the spirit of conquest and the vital need for violence? They are the visceral reaction of the Aryan spirit to any form of enslavement. That is why we celebrate their memory."

Hitler thought for a moment. So even scattered, beaten peoples could have bursts of energy. He thought of Vienna and its mongrel mix of nationalities, races, and religions. Could the city still be home to a spark that could set the ancient Germanic people on fire?

"Bring the Light," ordered Lanz.

Each of the participants chose a candelabra, then they formed a triangle of light that pointed towards the darkness at the far end of the crypt.

"Walk," said the leader to Adolf.

The arrow of light stopped a few feet from a black sheet that hung like a theatre curtain. Hitler had a feeling of déjà vu.

"Darkness and ignorance have veiled the earth. Our destiny, our past, and our strength have been stolen from us. They have made us men without futures, without hope . . ."

Everything went quiet.

"But not without knowledge."

Lanz turned towards the sheet, which hid the rest of the crypt from view. "Let the truth be known!" he exclaimed.

One side of the curtain opened, revealing a wall engraved with a unique cross. A cross whose branches were all bent at right angles. Hitler had never seen anything like it.

"This symbol comes to us from the depths of time. It has been the Aryan emblem throughout the ages and all over the globe. It gave them the strength to conquer the world and vanquish the darkness. Its power brought the light that illuminated the planet."

"All hail the swastika!" shouted Lanz's followers.

"Thanks to this symbol, mankind has attained the highest knowledge and wisdom passed on by our ancestors. With this symbol, we are their heirs. With this symbol, we will conquer the world again."

"All hail the swastika!"

Hitler turned discreetly towards Weistort, whose face remained impassive. Did he believe in all this? That a symbol had enabled a superior race to conquer and civilize the globe? A symbol whose meaning was lost to the superior race, until the Templars found it again? Before he could finish contemplating his questions, Lanz took him by the arm and led him to the engraved swastika.

"Take a good look, Adolf Hitler. Fill yourself with the mystical power of the swastika, because it will soon regenerate the world."

He didn't know if it was the hunger he'd been fighting for days or the occult power of the symbol, but the young painter felt his legs begin to tremble. When he reached his hand towards the swastika, it began to grow and spin, prepared to devour everything in its path.

He opened his mouth to call for help, but it was too late.

An unknown power overwhelmed him and carried him away.

He collapsed onto the floor.

22

Professor Waldenberg had left the world of the living long ago. When he had taught at the university, his absent-mindedness had been legendary. It was a well-known fact that he could enter the wrong auditorium and give an entire lecture to an audience of students captivated by his knowledge of the Middle Ages, despite the fact that they had been expecting a class on fluid mechanics. As he floated through his ocean of erudition, his colleagues seemed little more than tiny, faraway islands. His passion for history consumed him and he felt more comfortable in the company of an 11th-century knight than with members of his own family. His knowledge was infallible and his logic so remarkable that he had quickly attracted the attention of the Reichsführer, who offered him room and board at Wewelsburg. Within the comfort of the thick walls he never left, the Professor lived for his research.

"And this is the man who's going to help us?" asked Tristan, surprised.

"He's the best specialist in medieval weaponry in all of Germany. I sent him the sword as soon as we landed in Berlin. He must already have information to give us."

The Frenchman followed the archaeologist through the labyrinth of books, but his mind was elsewhere. He wondered if his message had reached Malorley in London. The priest who passed on the messages didn't exactly inspire confidence. It wasn't his loyalty Marcas questioned, but his ability to keep quiet under interrogation. Faith in God did nothing to ease the pain of torture. And if the priest talked, how long would it take for them to find him? A day? Two? How long would *he* resist torture?

"There he is," whispered Erika.

The Professor sat smoking a cigarette behind a table as he waited for them. It surprised Tristan, since he knew how much Himmler hated the faintest smell of tobacco. Waldenberg looked nothing like the man Marcas had imagined from the descriptions he'd heard. He was elegantly dressed in a black suit with his hair slicked carefully back. Tristan had imagined a dishevelled researcher with foggy eyes, but he found a dandy with a penetrating gaze who looked ready to attend a fancy party.

"Frau von Essling, I imagine?"

Erika nodded. The sword from Knossos sat on the table. It had been carefully cleaned and shone brightly in the wavering light from the nearby candles.

"So, you're the one who found the sword in Crete," continued the historian. "A surprising discovery, since it was most certainly made elsewhere."

"Have you already analyzed the alloy?" asked Erika, surprised.

Waldenberg tapped the sword with his index finger. An unexpected sound rang out, then faded. "With an experienced ear, you can accurately estimate the proportions of iron, copper and tin. It's just as reliable as performing a series of chemical analyses and is much faster. And, since each European kingdom had different mining resources in the Middle Ages, they also all had their own techniques for forging swords."

"So, you can tell us where it was made?" asked Tristan.

"In the south of medieval Germany. The area that corresponds to the present-day region between Munich and Vienna."

"But how did this sword end up in Crete?" Erika asked urgently.

"During the Crusades, the island was a strategic location and an economic crossroads," explained Waldenberg. "The ships heading east stopped for supplies, while those returning home sold rare oriental goods. There were many Europeans there. One of them was the bearer of this sword."

"A crusader?"

"Perhaps. Or a merchant or a monk. Everyone carried weapons in that region. It was a question of survival."

The archaeologist placed her hand on the pommel, still wrapped in leather.

"As I'm sure you know better than me, some swords were more intricate than others. Can you draw any sort of indication of the owner's social status from the sword?" she asked.

"No, it's a simple, unadorned pommel. A battle sword, not a ceremonial one."

"Are there any figures, symbols or signs engraved on the blade?"

Waldenberg gently stubbed out his cigarette. His hands were long, with bony knuckles. "If you're looking for clues, there aren't any. No motto, no crest, nothing. The sword is thoroughly anonymous and will remain so."

The meeting was over. Tristan suddenly understood that Erika's portrait of the Professor was accurate. The historian had just left them. Though he was physically present, he was already elsewhere, and the smile on his lips was like the wake of a ship about to disappear over the horizon.

"He's like an oracle," commented Marcas as they walked back across the library.

"Except that he's never wrong. This sword won't get us anywhere."

"But then why hide it in a crypt?"

Erika stopped short. "Because we made a mistake," said Erika, her voice full of anger and disappointment. "That crypt was never a tomb. It was a cenotaph, and I'm an idiot for not realizing it sooner."

"I don't understand."

"It's a custom from the Crusades. If a pilgrim died in the Holy Land, they didn't bring his body back. It took too long and was too expensive. So, when the family learned of their loved one's death, they would build an empty funerary monument to celebrate his memory."

"But where does the sword fit in?"

"The tradition dictated that the family leave an object that belonged to the deceased in the cenotaph."

As they neared the entrance to the library, an officer approached them. "Frau Essling, a telegram from Berlin has arrived for you."

Erika opened it immediately. "Goebbels is having a party tomorrow night. Himmler wants us to attend." She thanked the messenger with a nod, then took hold of her lover's arm.

"We didn't find anything in Knossos, and we've found nothing here. The Reichsführer is growing impatient. I'm sure he wants to make an announcement at the party."

"What kind of announcement?" asked Marcas as he placed a discreet kiss on her neck.

"When Hess fled to England, Himmler lost an ally. Goebbels is taking advantage of the situation."

"So, Himmler needs to regain the upper hand by announcing that he's found the swastika," concluded Tristan.

The archaeologist confirmed his suspicion with a stiff smile. This was the first time the Frenchman had seen her in the throes of doubt. She wasn't the same Erika, the woman who was arrogant and sure of herself, who threatened officers in Crete. Tristan wondered if her promotion to head of the Ahnenerbe was more important to her than she let on. A form of revenge? On her own family, perhaps. Now *she* was the von Essling who sat closest to power. A privileged status she didn't want to lose.

"What will happen if you don't find the relic?"

"You mean, if *we* don't find it?" corrected Erika. "I'll go back to being an archaeologist. As for you, I'm not sure."

"Did you notice that Waldenberg said the sword was from the south of medieval Germany? That's the same place you told me the *Thule Borealis Kulten* was written. The book that tells where to find the swastikas."

"And?"

"What if the same person left the sword in Crete and then wrote the book in Germany?"

"A knight turned monk?"

The couple had stopped near a table topped with a collection of hourglasses. Tristan turned one upside down, and the grains of sand began streaming through the neck. Nothing was ever definitive—a hunch could change everything.

"Listen, if we can connect the sword to a monastery located between Munich and Vienna, we just might have a solid clue to give your Reichsführer."

"But the sword doesn't present any clues!"

"Because the sword *is* the clue."

Waldenberg was surprised to see them again, but Tristan's very precise question didn't give him any trouble.

"How many important monasteries were there in medieval times in the area where this sword would have been made?"

"Seven."

The professor was as quick as his knowledge was limitless.

"How many of them were active at the end of the 13th century?"

That was when Erika said the *Thule Borealis Kulten* had been written.

"Two of the seven were built after that time."

"So, five," interrupted Tristan.

He grabbed the sword and watched it shine in the light. "Where in an abbey would they have kept a sword? In the church? On a statue? Saint George, for example, is always depicted with a lance or sword as he slays the dragon."

"And Saint George was the patron saint of the chapel we found the sword in," remarked Erika.

"In the Middle Ages, statues of saints inside churches were always small. There's no way one of them could accommodate a full-size sword," Waldenberg countered immediately. There seemed to be no question he couldn't answer.

"Where then? In the dormitory? The canteen? The scriptorium? The cloister?"

"None of those places."

Erika stamped her feet in frustration. She'd wasted enough time. "This is pointless. Let's go back to Berlin."

The Professor stopped them. "There's only one place you could find a sword in an abbey. On a tomb."

Tristan placed both palms flat on the table, as if preparing to pounce. "Tell us, quickly."

"You must look for a recumbent statue. A sculpture representing the person buried beneath. When it's a clergyman, there's often a cross on the tomb, but when it's a knight . . ."

"His sword," finished Erika.

"That's why the man we're looking for left his sword in Knossos. To lead us to his tomb!"

Her eyes bright with excitement, von Essling asked the question on the tip of all their tongues. "Of the five abbeys present in the 13th century, how many of them contain recumbent statues?"

"None of them."

The Frenchman clenched his fists in annoyance. He was sure they were on the right path.

"However, one of them has a funereal slab. The stone is covered in engravings. One of them represents a knight and has a place for a sword."

"Where?" Erika asked weakly, as if all the twists and turns had left her doubting his reply.

"At Heiligenkreuz, south of Vienna."

23

Tower Hamlets cemetery, London
November 1941

The gravestones changed colour with a supernatural regularity. They went from pure, silvery white to dark, dirty grey, and the engravings sparkled in the night, as if the dead were sending signals to remind the living of their presence.

Moira O'Connor was sitting on a slab, her back resting against a headstone, as she contemplated the battle taking place in the sky. Snowflake-filled squadrons passed rapidly in front of the moon, which disappeared and reappeared, depending on the wind.

Every time the heavenly body came out victorious, it filled the cemetery with an otherworldly light and the Scarlet Fairy closed her eyes. She could feel the benefits of its rays deep within. It was like a gentle, soothing bath. A moon bath. A ritual from the depths of time, when men communed with nature and respected its power. A time when women were not servants. A time when the moon had been the equal of her daytime twin.

The delightful sensation faded. She didn't have to open her eyes to know a cloud had triumphed over the sphere of light.

She gently lifted her eyelids, stood up, and raised her arms in silent prayer. The tombs all around her had been plunged back into near darkness. She turned up the collar of her coat. A cool wind ran up the row of graves, which followed a troubled path amid twisted oaks and wild bushes. A strong, damp smell wafted between the decaying tombs and abandoned headstones.

Moira knew the paths of the Magnificent Seven—a group of large cemeteries that ringed the city of London—by heart. After

Highgate, Tower Hamlets was her favourite. Lush and calm, wild and harmonious, it was the perfect location for Moira and her sisters to practise their rituals. And the dead of Tower Hamlets enjoyed their company.

She turned towards the neighbouring tomb, crowned by a winged statue. A dark shape lay on the stone. The shape of a body.

A flood of silver light appeared, as if by enchantment, to reveal the body's identity. It was a young woman with golden hair. Her arms and legs, spread wide, were missing hands and feet. The naked victim studied the sky with a single, dead eye. An ancient symbol now reviled throughout Europe had been carved into her head. Above her, a black marble archangel held out a stump that must once have been his protective arm. Moira had chosen the place for the body carefully.

Suddenly, the sound of crushed leaves reached her ears from behind one of the tombs. Moira looked in that direction and noticed the silhouette of a man walking swiftly towards her. He was on time, as usual.

He nodded upon reaching her, without removing his hat. The Abwehr agent was an average-sized man with a full, grey face and round glasses on a tiny nose. He was even less expressive than the stones in the cemetery. His unremarkable face helped make him a highly effective spy. He gave the girl's body a disgusted look, then stared coldly at the Scarlet Fairy.

"Good evening, Miss O'Connor. Why did you choose this suburban cemetery for your sinister plot?"

The man's English was perfect, without any trace of German accent.

"I would have chosen Highgate, but Tower Hamlets is closer to the Hellfire, and its popularity ensures someone will find the body tomorrow morning. It'll be sure to make the headlines!"

"If you say so. I don't have your talents for macabre stage direction."

His irony was but thinly veiled. Moira had hated the man since the first time they'd met. A man who looked down on women and made it very clear. She would have liked to throw him to her

Amazons at the Hellfire for obedience lessons, but Berlin wouldn't have liked that. She had to make do; he was her only contact.

"Your superiors in Berlin asked me to do this," she replied.

The man shook his head. "Make no mistake! I work for the army's intelligence services, not for the SS. My job is to transmit military information and to plan sabotage missions—in short, to help win the war for Germany while risking capture, torture, and execution on a daily basis. So, believe me when I say that I have no time to waste on a chat in a cemetery next to the dead body of a poor girl. But Reinhard Heydrich, Himmler's second-in-command, asked me personally to assist you. I'm just following orders."

"You're less difficult when I'm feeding you information on the vices of the upper classes. Do you have the money?"

The Abwehr man pulled an envelope out of his coat. "It's the promised amount. I suppose it will end up in the hands of your Irish friends?"

"Indeed, it will."

"A witch who's funding the IRA, whose members are fervent Catholics. Strange alliance, don't you think?"

"There are sacred causes that go beyond religious differences. My parents were murdered by the English during the Easter Rising and my brother was sent to an orphanage, where he died of malnutrition. I would kiss the Pope's feet if it would get rid of the damned English!"

"If you say so . . . What's the next step of your mission for the SS?"

He had uttered the name "SS" with unmasked disdain.

The Scarlet Fairy placed the toe of her boot on her victim's naked stomach and burst into laughter. "To make the Antichrist sing!"

Just ten meters from there, hidden behind a plaster statue of the Virgin Mary covered in moss, Laure watched the two protagonists. The long hours on O'Connor's trail had paid off. Laure had almost missed the madam's departure from the Hellfire aboard a lorry.

Luckily, she'd caught up with her at the cemetery gates, where one of her accomplices was dragging what looked like a lifeless body.

From her hiding place, Laure couldn't hear the conversation between the redhead and the mysterious man. Frustration boiled up inside her. What could they be talking about in the middle of the night with a corpse at their feet?

As they walked away, she stealthily made her way between the headstones to reach the tomb where the body lay. The moon covered the corpse in immaculate white light.

Laure resisted the urge to vomit and looked away. She watched the two silhouettes walk towards the gates.

She had to stay focused and make a decision. Quickly. Follow the redhead as Malorley had ordered, or try to figure out who the man was.

Don't leave her side for even a minute.

Laure hesitated for a few seconds. Should she go with her orders or her intuition?

She made her decision and forgot all about her boss.

24

Since Germany had invaded and annexed Austria in 1938, Austrians—at least those not in exile or prison—seemed immensely pleased to be citizens of the great Reich. Their joy shone at every street corner, if you believed the impressive number of Nazi flags hanging from the windows. However, Tristan couldn't help but wonder if the mothers of the young men sent to the front shared that enthusiasm. As for the children, they didn't seem to have any reservations. They ran through the streets happily saluting adults with a "*Heil Hitler!*", which the adults obligingly returned. Marcas was tired of constantly raising his arm like a robot. It seemed that Nazism strengthened the muscles of one's arm but atrophied one's brain.

When they finally reached the abbey, there wasn't a swastika in sight. Not on the steeple, nor on the façade. The fervour for National Socialism seemed to diminish as they neared the house of God.

"The monks don't seem to be the Führer's leading fans," commented Tristan.

Erika ran her hands over the long, dark-grey, ankle-length dress she was wearing. The most suitable thing she could find for visiting a monastery. The garment's gloomy hue seemed to have affected her mood as well.

"The Catholics are realizing that Nazism isn't just an ideology or a party, but a new religion, which, once it's got rid of the Jews, won't tolerate Christian competition much longer. Speaking of which, just look at the young monk waiting to greet us. He's already glanced disdainfully at your Iron Cross."

With both hands hidden in his cassock, the monk bowed and announced that the abbot was waiting for them in the entrance hall. They walked across the pristine gravel courtyard. Tristan was fascinated by the diversity of architectural styles that coexisted within the abbey. From the baroque gate to the oriental dome of the steeple, the centuries seemed to have been brought together haphazardly. There was even a Romanesque chapel in the stylistic mix.

The abbot stood waiting for them in front of a monumental staircase that must have led to the monastery's private areas.

"The local party head told me you'd be coming and asked me to answer your questions. The next mass is in half an hour, so it would be best if we could make this quick. We're not used to receiving impromptu visitors."

"How many monks live in the abbey today?" Erika asked calmly.

"Fifty-seven."

"I see that since Austria was annexed, your numbers have nearly doubled. The power of the Holy Spirit, no doubt?"

Marcas realized Erika had prepared for the visit.

"The Lord works in mysterious ways," replied the abbot dryly.

"So, none of these sudden vocations were kindled by the fact that joining a monastery means they don't have to fight on the eastern front?"

"How dare you!"

"I believe you're hiding deserters, traitors to the Fatherland and enemies of the Reich. I'll have to ask the Gestapo to interrogate all of the brothers under the age of thirty to assess their spiritual commitments. I'm sure that the two of us will have a few conversations with them as well."

It was time for Tristan to intervene.

"As for me, I'm sure the abbot doesn't need any more martyrs in his abbey, and that he'll happily help us, out of Christian kindness."

"What do you want?"

"To visit a tomb. The tomb of a knight," answered Tristan.

The abbot couldn't believe it. They had threatened to send in the Gestapo, and all for a simple grave?

"You want to see Brother Amalrich's tomb?"

"So he was a monk?"

"Yes, a knight turned monk," explained the abbot. "They say he first went to Jerusalem, then came to spend the rest of his life in our monastery. They also say he was a Templar Knight, but since the order was dissolved, that might just be a legend."

A detail troubled Marcas.

"Why was he buried dressed as a knight when he was a monk?"

"I don't know, but that's not the only unique aspect of his tomb. I'll show you. It's in the oldest part of the monastery, the medieval chapel."

The abbot's attitude had totally changed. He seemed almost enthusiastic about giving them a tour of the abbey. If Erika could keep her cool, he might reveal much more than they had hoped.

"You've been running this monastery for many years. It can't have many secrets left for you," ventured Tristan.

"It's true, I spend a lot of time in the archives. That's how I identified Brother Amalrich's tomb. Speaking of which, we're here."

The door to the chapel looked its age. And yet, not a single wrinkle scarred the masterfully carved stones that formed the ogival arch above. As he did every time he entered an ancient building, Tristan wondered how many anonymous people had passed before him.

"We know from a period text that Brother Amalrich requested to be buried in the crypt. Let's go down. We had the stairs re-done."

The passage of time had left the stone floor disjointed, but a paler stone that seemed to have been placed haphazardly stood out. Unlike the tombstone at Knossos, this one was covered in engravings. It featured the silhouette of a knight, his face hidden by his helmet, hands joined on his chest. To his right was a place for the sword. Marcas didn't need to measure it to know it was a perfect match for the shape and size of the sword found in Knossos.

"You told us this tomb was unique," said von Essling, "but I don't see how."

"Because you're missing the details," replied the abbot. "Look at what's around his neck."

A very thin stole, like those that priests wore during mass, fell over each shoulder.

"Was it to remind us that he had also become a monk?" asked Tristan.

"Look closer."

Tristan knelt. There was a swastika, level with Amalrich's heart, delicately engraved in the stole.

"It's very unusual," commented the abbot. "There's something even more remarkable at the east end of this crypt."

There, another swastika had been carved into the stone. Its large size made it stand out in the confined space. But what struck Marcas was the object underneath it.

A bust of Adolf Hitler.

Just as surprised, Erika had moved closer to read the copper plaque.

"When Austria became German, this is the first place the Führer came, even before Vienna," she paraphrased.

"An honour for our community," said the abbot, out of obligation.

"Is the symbol on the wall from the Middle Ages as well?" she asked.

"Yes, and it's what brought the Führer here. It's incredibly rare to find a swastika in a Christian sanctuary from that time."

Erika was growing impatient. She returned to the tombstone and examined its edges as she ran a finger over them, noting the chips and other marks left by the passage of time.

"We'll need to open it, but carefully. I'll have an Ahnenerbe team dispatched from Berlin immediately. They can be here in—"

"That won't be necessary," interrupted the abbot. "The tomb was fully excavated when we restored the monastery forty years ago. A full, official report was drafted. There was a complete skeleton—undoubtedly Amalrich's—and nothing else."

Erika walked over to Tristan, who was still examining Hitler's bust. "There's nothing special about this," she said. "They put up statues and plaques everywhere the man goes. We have more important things to do. There's nothing to find in this crypt. No relic and no clues to help us find it. I'll go over the report, but I'm certain we won't learn anything new."

The abbot walked over to the Frenchman as well. "If you'd like to know more about the Führer's visit, we have a monk who's become rather obsessed with it. He'll tell you everything in detail, if you like."

"Thank you, I would like to meet him," said Tristan.

"He's very old and spends most of his time in the infirmary. You'll see, he's very talkative, but don't take everything he says for the truth. His imagination gets carried away sometimes. The poor man had a stroke."

"You're just leaving me here?" exclaimed von Essling.

"You don't need me to study the excavation report, so I might as well do something. Don't forget to take a picture of the tombstone, though. It could turn out to be useful."

From the dirty look she gave him, the Frenchman knew it wouldn't be easy to make this up to her.

A few minutes later, he found himself in the room used as an infirmary. The term seemed rather pretentious, given the austerity of the place. There was a rickety bookcase full of bottles containing dark, mysterious contents, a half-open chest of drawers full of greying sheets, and a box of medicines in faded containers. Three old metal beds took up the rest of the space.

An old man lay under a dark blanket reading a bible. He regularly opened his mouth as if he were mumbling prayers.

Tristan walked slowly towards him.

Up close, the monk's bald scalp seemed to be cracked like overcooked pottery, but bright, pale eyes sat behind thin, round glasses in the middle of his wrinkled face. The right half of his face hung limp like a wet rag. An invisible line seemed to divide his face into two parts: one alive, the other dead.

"Hello, Brother," Tristan said softly.

The monk reluctantly put down his reading to offer Tristan an inquisitive look. "Who are you?" he asked.

"A researcher."

"We're all searching for something. Did *he* send you?"

"He who?"

The monk chuckled from the functioning side of his mouth. "The Führer. You're clearly not German."

"French. No one is perfect."

The brother rolled his one mobile eye to the heavens. The other continued to stare at Tristan. "Ah, the French . . . Hitler doesn't like you very much. I met him, you know. Did they tell you?"

Tristan nodded. "Yes, they say you like to tell stories. I'd love to hear some about this monastery."

The monk seemed disappointed. "Oh . . . You don't want me to tell you about the Führer's visit?"

"Not especially."

The old man looked left, then right, then lowered his voice. "You're wrong, little Frenchman. Many things have happened here . . ."

"Really?"

"Yes, I've seen strange things, and voices share many secrets with me. This abbey is the only one of its kind in the world. Unique. I can tell you the story of the sparrow and the Christmas pig . . ."

Tristan shook his head. He wasn't going to get anything out this poor man. His brain was as limp as his face. "Another time. I have to go."

The monk grabbed Tristan's arm, a desperate look in his eyes. "Please, don't leave me. No one here listens to me anymore . . ."

The vesper bell had just sounded, and the November night was beginning to make its way into the church through the stained-glass windows. To combat the darkness, the monks were lighting dripping candelabras here and there. The abbot stood tall next to von Essling. They had waited half an hour for the photographer from the nearest town to arrive, then another hour before they could take the picture, because it was too dark in the crypt. They had to find and hook up a spotlight. When Tristan joined the archaeologist, she was clearly frustrated.

"We're going back to Berlin," she announced. "I hope your visit to the infirmary was useful."

"More than you might think. The poor old man was so happy to have someone to talk to that I couldn't stop him."

"You French are so good at wasting time . . ."

Tristan shrugged. "You wouldn't understand. For you Nazis, good deeds are about as useful as a bouquet of roses in a Panzer."

Von Essling rolled her eyes. She couldn't stand it when her lover made jokes at her expense. With Tristan, she never really knew if he was kidding or not

"Who is this monk?" she asked the abbot.

"A problem. As I mentioned, he's been slowly but surely losing his mind for the past several months."

"*The Lord gave and the Lord hath taken away*," recited Marcas. "That's from Job, right, Father?"

The abbot nodded, shocked that Tristan was reciting the word of God in such a situation. But von Essling felt reassured. As usual, Tristan was perfectly incapable of keeping his repartee in check.

25

Boodle's wasn't the oldest nor the most prestigious gentlemen's club in the capital, but it provided tranquillity, comfort, and exquisite service for its members. The bar featured a full range of excellent spirits, though the war had unfortunately dried up the club's sources for cognac and Armagnac. As for the restaurant, it had lost its head chef—requisitioned to run an officers' mess—but he had been replaced by his sous-chef, who made particularly delicious stews.

Malorley left his hat and coat in the cloakroom and made his way towards the welcome desk, where the receptionist was a former sergeant in the Indian Army.

"Commander Malorley, what a lovely surprise! People were starting to think you were dead!"

"Not this time, Tommy. The army's logistics department isn't particularly dangerous, you know. It wasn't Hitler who had me bedridden, just a bad bout of flu."

"That's what I said. A respectable man like you would have had an obituary published in *The Standard* or *The Times*."

"Thank you, Tommy. Is it busy tonight?"

"Not very, unfortunately. As in all the London clubs, our numbers keep dropping because of that damned Führer. He's such a repugnant character. He'll soon destroy social life as we know it!"

"May God and the King protect us."

Malorley just wanted to sit quietly in his favourite armchair sipping a twelve-year single malt to forget his work for an hour or two. He needed a little break. A chance to think rationally.

Between Hess's hypnosis session, which had ended badly, and Laure's disturbing report from the cemetery, he felt he deserved to fall back into the comfort of his routine.

The young Frenchwoman had disobeyed his orders, but the results had been worth it. The mysterious visitor in the cemetery had returned to his home in Pimlico. Laure had jotted down the address and the name on the mailbox, and brought them triumphantly back to SOE headquarters. Half an hour later, Malorley had passed the information on to MI6. The commander had a hunch it was something big. He hadn't shared that with his colleagues, though. After all, it was above their pay grade. However, he had every intention of interrogating Crowley about this madam who left mutilated bodies in cemeteries.

But for the moment, Malorley felt a pressing need to relax. Fighting Nazism was becoming an obsession. Though he would never admit it, he was fascinated by the way Hitler had catapulted to power. How had a marginalized, nearly homeless man become the most powerful ruler in the world in just twenty years? Political and psychological reports and analyses on the Führer could have filled an entire library. And yet, the man was still a mystery. Malorley was convinced that the dictator's power was intimately tied to the possession of the relics. And he'd shared this conviction with a number of people, affirming that Nazism was mystical in nature and that the way the Germans worshipped their messiah in brown was the result of mass enchantment. The Thule Society hadn't chosen Hitler in Munich on a whim. Malorley was certain that something had happened during the future chancellor's youth. Something had radically transformed him. That was where the answers to the mystery lay.

He made his way through the half-empty grand salon, where wrinkled, grey-haired members of the club engaged in whispered discussions. It had been six months since he'd returned from France, but he hadn't found the time to come to Boodle's even once. He regretted it. The club was more than just a sanctuary—

even in wartime, it embodied the indestructible permanence of British values. It had come to feel like home to him since his wife had left him for another man, four years earlier. A happier, younger man in better shape, as she had said the day she ended things between them.

A waiter of Indian origin came over.

"Good evening, sir. Shall I pour you a glass of your usual Mortlach?"

"Yes, please, Sadhu. I'll take it in the library."

The waiter had been working at the club for a year, but every time Malorley saw him, he wondered if someday Boodle's would accept members from the Empire's colonies. He'd spoken about it one day with an acquaintance, a renowned professor of medicine, who had burst into laughter. "An Indian! You've lost your mind, my friend. Why not a woman, while you're at it? We already began allowing Jews to join, before the war."

Nevertheless, Boodle's was one of the most liberal clubs in London. Bankers, lawyers, doctors, judges, newspaper owners, and military men, whose fathers had all been members before them, still accounted for the majority of members. Yet, more and more "unconventional" people were gaining admission, causing the most conservative members to grumble. First there had been a writer, then an opera singer, and finally a racing-car driver better known for his multitude of mistresses than for his victories. But admissions continued, since many of the oldest members needed new audiences to regale with their tales.

Malorley entered a smaller room, which served as both a library and a smoking room. As he stepped around the billiards table, he noticed one of the newer members sitting reading the *Daily Telegraph*. Archibald Meyer, a lawyer with a Jewish mother and a Welsh father, worked for a group of American companies with subsidiaries in England. His admission had caused five men—whose families had been anti-Semites for generations—to leave the club. Malorley walked over to greet him.

"Hello, Archie. It's been ages since we've seen each other. Shall we have a drink?"

The lawyer looked up from his paper and gave Malorley a friendly smile. "Of course, sit down. You must be very busy in your department, with the war effort and such . . ."

"Yes, alas. Paperwork. There's never a shortage of paperwork," joked Malorley. "But I interrupted your reading."

"I was finishing a frightful article on the discovery of a mutilated corpse in Tower Hamlets cemetery. Her hands and feet were cut off."

"Just terrible," Malorley agreed gravely.

"And that's not all!" continued the lawyer. "Her murderer also carved a swastika into her forehead and opened her stomach to fill it with witchcraft incantations. I hope Jack the Ripper hasn't come back to life as a Nazi butcher!"

"I hate to contradict you, Archie, but Jack is definitely out there."

"What do you mean?"

"He has a ridiculous little moustache and must have already killed hundreds of thousands of victims by now."

The lawyer frowned. "You're right, and I'm afraid of what he'll do to the Jews. I've just returned from the Isle of Man, where I was devastated by what I saw."

"Really? Bombing victims?"

"No, that's where they're keeping Jews from Germany and central Europe. They fled certain death in Germany and now Britain is crowding them into shacks, for lack of a better idea."

"The sad life of refugees."

"But they tell horrific stories of the persecutions they've experienced. They say the Nazis are massacring people on the eastern front. SS units are exterminating men, women, and children after the army moves on."

"What are you doing for them?"

"I'm trying to get them out of the camps, but it's difficult. Since most of them speak German, they're seen as potential spies."

The lawyer paused as the waiter placed a glass of whisky down next to Malorley.

"I didn't know," explained the SOE agent. "Are there many of them?"

"Nearly twenty-five thousand people in all of the United

Kingdom. The biggest camp is on the Isle of Man. The worst bit is that they've been mixed with the Germans who were arrested in England after the declaration of war—most of whom are real Nazis. I've been trying to get a meeting with one of the Prime Minister's advisers to plead their cause, but in vain."

"Do you have support?"

"Some. There are organizations that welcome refugees. The Quakers are the most active among them. They're working tirelessly to help the Jews."

Malorley felt uncomfortable as he listened. He could easily have secured a meeting with a member of Churchill's cabinet, but doing so would reveal that he was more than a mere cog in the military bureaucracy.

The lawyer stood up. "I'm afraid I must go. I have a lot of work to get through tonight."

The club's concierge suddenly appeared, an alarmed look on his face. "Commander, there's a woman looking for you at the front door. She says she works with you."

"Show her in."

"You know I can't do that, sir. The club is not open to the fairer sex. The by-laws . . . You understand, don't you?"

"No, and I plan to suggest to the committee that we change the by-laws to include women." Then Malorley turned to the lawyer. "I do hope you'll support me."

Archibald laughed out loud. "So they can say a Jew ruined the venerable Boodle's? No, thank you. I don't want to awaken any latent anti-Semitism. Find some goy supporters first, then we'll talk."

Malorley smiled broadly at the lawyer and made his way towards reception. Much to his surprise, he found Laure standing at the desk. She seemed to be on edge.

"Perhaps you weren't aware, but I hate to be disturbed when I'm not on the clock," he declared.

"Sorry, but it's an emergency. We called, but we couldn't get through."

The concierge rolled his eyes. "All our lines have been cut for a week because of the latest bombing. And the telephone repair services are overworked as it is."

"I was at the office when the news hit," continued Laure, "and I wanted to come and tell you right away. The relic from Montségur is working. It's a miracle! Hitler's just been assassinated by a Wehrmacht general."

"What? Hitler is dead?" asked Malorley, who looked like he'd been struck by lightning.

The young woman remained silent for a few moments, then burst into laughter. "I can't believe you bought that!"

"Really? That wasn't funny at all."

"So, you really do believe in the power of all these talismans. You're a strange man, Commander."

Malorley grabbed her arm. "So that's not why you bothered me here?"

"No. Crowley has been trying to reach you. He was panicked on the phone."

"What's going on?"

"He wants to see you immediately. He's terrified of the red-headed woman you asked me to follow and the body in the cemetery."

26

Decorated from top to bottom, the Ministry of Propaganda attracted all eyes to the centre of Wilhelmplatz. Spotlights borrowed from anti-aircraft defence sent columns of light up into the autumn sky as guards in dress uniform escorted high-ranking officials and celebrity guests. At the top of the steps stood Magda Goebbels in a silver sheath dress, welcoming people with her famous laugh. Every German knew Magda, whose beauty featured on the covers of magazines and even graced the front pages of newspapers when she joined Hitler at official events. Though the Führer was officially single, to keep his relationship with Eva Braun secret, he had made Magda the Reich's First Lady and a model for all German women.

"Look at her," grumbled Goebbels. "As if *she* were tonight's host!"

The butler, who had been at the ministry for years, nodded quietly. He was used to his boss's monologues. Goebbels was watching the guests arrive through a peep-hole in the attic. He had set up a secret room there to meditate. The old service staircase, reserved for his own personal use, also facilitated his trysts with young actresses—a clandestine source of stress relief that Magda didn't need to know about.

"She would probably go to the Führer again," complained the minister.

Just remembering the scene caused Goebbels to break out in a cold sweat. In the summer of 1938, Magda had stormed into the Berghof to tell Hitler about her husband's affair with a twenty-two-year-old actress. To add insult to injury, she was Czech! Of course, Uncle Adolf, as the couple's children called him, ordered his minister to put an end to the shameful relationship immediately.

"Ever since, she's felt all-powerful because she has the Führer's ear, but she's wrong."

Goebbels poured himself a second glass and turned away from Wilhelmplatz. He had no desire to see his wife welcome Himmler with a smile on her face. Since Hess's disappearance, the Reichsführer had become his main adversary—the one man who could outrank him in the Führer's esteem.

"Don't you worry, Chicken Man. I'll put you back in your place. I'll put you all in your places."

The minister pushed himself out of his armchair. His right leg was terribly heavy, a handicap he'd had since the age of four. Goebbels had always been a short, skinny man with a limp—the kind of man people underestimated. That was a foolish mistake, for the Dwarf had more than one trick up his sleeve. Tonight he would show them all.

The great hall was so full of people jockeying to reach an acquaintance or the buffet that it looked more like a train station. The women moved more slowly. After greeting the ravishing Magda, they all wanted a chance to be admired as well.

In a strapless black dress, with her back against a column, Erika waited for the Reichsführer, casually waving to guests she had met at her parents' house. Over the past few years, traditional high society had lost its appeal. Now people were desperate to attend Göring's hunts and Goebbels's parties, which had become the new markers of social status.

"In your opinion, how many of the people here are true Nazis?" asked Himmler as he approached Erika.

With a smile, the archaeologist counted on her fingers and stopped at the first hand. The Reichsführer burst into laughter.

"I see your time in Crete did you some good. It's a shame you were unable to complete your mission."

"You know I never give up."

"And you know I have the utmost faith in you."

"I'm glad to hear it."

Himmler nodded. Their meeting was over. Magda had just walked in, surrounded by a crowd of admirers. The head of the SS clicked his heels as she passed by. The Dwarf's wife replied with a radiant smile. Himmler regularly sent her an updated list of her husband's mistresses. It was an investment that cost him nothing and could someday pay big dividends.

Erika found Tristan in the smoking room contemplating a photograph from Goebbels's wedding. Farmers and their families stood along the edges of a snow-covered path, holding their arms out straight to salute the couple. The picture was fascinating, but the most interesting part was the dark shadow behind the young couple.

"Did you know that Hitler was the best man at the Goebbelses' wedding?"

"No, and I don't care. I didn't even have time to talk to Himmler about our visit to Heiligenkreuz Abbey," complained the archaeologist. "Much less to show him the photograph of Amalrich's tomb!"

A waiter entered the smoking room and cleared the glasses, then announced that the minister was about to make his grand entrance. All guests were to assemble in the great hall.

"The Dwarf has really done it this time," commented von Essling. "All of Berlin is here. He'll be sure to make the front page of all the papers. Himmler will be furious to have been made a simple spectator."

Whispered rumours and questions filled the hall. Relegated to a corner, Magda no longer seemed to exist. With a pinched smile on her face, she tried her best to look happy, but she kept glancing restlessly up towards the balcony that dominated the room, where a technician was readying a microphone. Suddenly, Goebbels appeared, provoking a thunderous wave of applause. He was wearing the sandy-brown uniform that was synonymous with the party of victory and power.

"He looks taller," remarked Tristan.

"They must have him on a pedestal to keep his chin off the podium," joked Erika.

"My friends, today is an important day. A moment that will go down in history. And you will be able to say you were there."

The audience suddenly went silent. Everyone was holding their breath.

"Our troops have reached the outskirts of Moscow. The Kremlin is only a few subway stations away!"

An ovation filled the hall, which echoed like a drum. As all experienced public speakers do, Goebbels let the din die down on its own. Once the room was quiet again, he continued. "Our Führer orchestrated this victory and changed the face of the earth in just a few months. Germany has conquered all of Europe, up to the border with Asia."

A giant map was rolled out just behind Goebbels. In bright red, Germany spread like a bloodstain from Norway to Crete and from France to Russia. A continuous bout of applause hailed the new world order.

"During this offensive, our Führer fought tirelessly, devoting all his time and energy to the success of the campaign, which is unique in human history. For months, from the Chancellery to the Berghof, he worked without stopping, without rest, to ensure that Germany accomplished its destiny. It is now time for our steadfast leader to emerge from the shadows and take his place in the spotlight."

Arms rose up instantly, like a tsunami rushing through the crowd, as waves of "*Heil Hitler!*" shook the chandeliers.

"I am thus delighted to announce that some of you will have the chance to accompany the Führer amid these extraordinary circumstances. A week from today, Chancellor Hitler will meet with Mussolini in Venice."

Erika looked at Himmler. She could read the stupefaction on his face. He was responsible for Hitler's safety, and yet he hadn't been told. Up on the balcony, Goebbels delighted in his triumph. The Dwarf had the upper hand again, but he hadn't even played all his cards yet.

"Over the next few days, I will draft a list of those who will have the honour of travelling with the Führer to Italy, but I can already give you one name . . ." he said as he turned towards the far end of the room, his hand on his heart. "Magda, you will be among them."

A concert of exclamations sounded around Goebbels's wife, who broke into tears as an orchestra began playing the party anthem, "Horst Wessel Lied", which the entire audience sang in chorus.

"We have to get to the Reichsführer right away," urged von Essling. "He must be furious."

But Tristan didn't react. He stood stock still, his eyes glued to the balcony, where the minister had just spoken.

"What's wrong? Did Goebbels cast a spell on you?"

Marcas still didn't move. Erika took his hands in hers. "Are you all right? Are you too hot?"

"Do you have the photograph of Amalrich's tomb with you?" he finally asked.

The archaeologist took it from her clutch and handed it to him. Tristan grabbed it hurriedly. When he looked up, his eyes were feverish.

"I know where to find the swastika!"

27

Bloomsbury, London
November 1941

A ray of sunshine brightened the lounge, but Crowley's mind was full of darkness. Moira O'Connor sat across from him at the broad table, where she had lined up five photographs for him to see. All of them showed the mage lying in the four-poster bed at the Hellfire with the dead young woman. She hadn't been mutilated yet, and she could have been sleeping if it weren't for the red wound across her neck.

"Photographs can be doctored nowadays. They don't prove anything," said Crowley.

"You're right, but the reporters will still be delighted to publish them alongside your name on the front page. Don't forget that your reputation as a depraved sorcerer is well established. I doubt I need to remind you of all the sensational articles published about you before the war. Imagine the headlines: *Crowley Sacrifices Young Woman to Satan and Hitler*, or better yet, *Homicidal Mage Works for SOE*. I'm not sure your current employer would be pleased."

Aleister was devastated. "I've known plenty of whores in my time, but you top the list of heartless bitches! I can't believe you would do this after I pulled you out of your Irish gutter!"

She slapped him as hard as she could. "You would do well to adopt a different tone, you idiot! You took advantage of me when I was still basically a child. My parents had been murdered and I was working as a maid for your English friends. You seduced me with promises of a better life. It was easy for a man like you to impress a poor, fragile girl."

"You ungrateful shrew! I brought you to London and made you my partner. I took care of you, introduced you to a world of infinite pleasure."

"Of course—by handing me off to your depraved friends. I learned a lot about men, thanks to you. Luckily, I discovered witchcraft and true knowledge along the way, otherwise I would have become just another harlot in your personal harem. But let's forget the past."

She pushed one of the photographs towards him. In it, the mage held a knife to the victim's throat.

"I really like this one," she mused.

"It's disgusting. Let's get this over with. What exactly do you want?"

"The negatives will stay locked up in my safe if you bring me information about your new job with the SOE."

"That's it?"

"Of course not. This is just the beginning of a new and fruitful relationship between us. One based on my talents as a photographer. I'll leave you these prints for your personal collection. I seem to remember you enjoy pornography."

"Aren't you ashamed to betray your country? To be serving the Nazis?"

The Scarlet Fairy stood up and collected her things. "England is not my country and I couldn't care less about Hitler. I follow my own best interests. Oh, and don't bother telling your boss at the SOE about me, or you'll see your perverted face on the front page of the *Daily Mail* tomorrow."

Moira O'Connor's taxi turned the corner and disappeared. On the second floor, Malorley drew the curtains and left the room to join Crowley and Laure, who were sitting in the lounge. The young woman was looking through the photos. The mage downed a second glass of gin. He raised his devastated face towards the Commander as he entered the room.

"That bitch has really got me over a barrel. It's over."

"No, you did well to tell me the truth," said Malorley as he poured himself a glass.

"You'll arrest her, won't you? You have more than enough proof, don't you? You can get the negatives from her safe!"

The SOE man shook his head, an enigmatic smile on his lips. "We won't do anything of the sort."

"What?"

"You'll do exactly as she asks. First, give her a full report on Hess without omitting a single detail. Then, continue to give her any information she asks for. I'll make it as easy for you as possible."

"I don't understand," replied the mage.

Laure pushed the photos away, a disgusted look on her face. "The Commander is trying to explain that we're going to turn the situation to our advantage. Feed her false information."

"Precisely," confirmed Malorley. "And you, Crowley, will be the poisoned well."

"Congratulations," offered Laure as she patted Aleister's arm. "You're now officially a double agent."

28

Wervicq, northern France
October 13, 1918

"I've been on the front line for four years. Four years and not a scratch!" boasted Sergeant Extelman to his soldiers in the trenches. "Look! I fought at the Marne, at Verdun, the Chemin des Dames, all the big battles, but nothing. Not a single bullet in this chest!"

Leaning against the trench's mud wall, the men listened to their sergeant without a word. Many of them remembered that he'd given a similar speech before the last offensive, so they were less than thrilled.

"So, who's on guard duty tonight?"

Four soldiers stepped up. Their greatcoats were in tatters, their boots covered in mud, and their beards unkempt. They didn't even have guns. Extelman pretended not to notice. During the last attack, the company had lost more than two-thirds of its men in less than a quarter of an hour. As for the survivors, most of them were now deaf and racked with convulsions from the sheer terror of the bombardments. Given the conditions, it was better not to ask them how they'd lost their rifles. After sending the sentinels to their posts, the sergeant turned to his men. "Did you notice I've doubled the guards tonight? We're likely to have a visit."

Fear flashed across the soldiers' faces.

"No, no, there's no French attack planned! It's higher-ups from headquarters, for an inspection."

A groan rang out. The men in the trenches didn't care for high-ranking officers in grand uniforms, their chests covered in decorations, though most of them had never come near a battle.

"I know how you feel . . . Pen-pushers who make themselves look good at the expense of enlisted men, and you're absolutely right. The problem is, I can't welcome them with unarmed sentinels!"

"Guns aren't exactly in short supply," suggested one of the men. "You just have to go and get them."

In the last attack, the German troops had only advanced a few hundred meters before being slaughtered, covering the ground with thousands of corpses and rifles. It was an open-air armoury out there.

"Are *you* going to leave the trench to get the guns?" shouted another man. "I swear, if I'm chosen ."

Extelman understood the danger. He was perilously close to having a mutiny on his hands.

"No one will go into no man's land! No one from the company, I swear."

One of the oldest members nodded in thanks. He was a farmer from Wurttemberg. A short, stocky man who had managed to make it through the war by taking the minimum amount of risk every step of the way.

"Good decision, Sergeant. But we still have the same problem. We can't let the higher-ups know we only have one gun left. That would be bad for you."

The sergeant lost his cool. "What do you expect me to do? I can't go out there myself!"

"Of course not," replied the farmer ironically. "And neither can the rest of us. However . . ."

Intrigued, Extelman moved closer to the man.

"A courier arrived this morning with orders, but couldn't leave again due to the bombardment of the rear lines. I think he must be getting very bored waiting around. Maybe we should find him something to do."

"Where is he?"

"In the shelter. He's drawing."

*

A wooden parapet just above the trench marked the entrance to the tunnel. Extelman walked into a corridor supported by rickety posts, which led to a square room where the men took cover during bombardments. Sitting in a corner, under a lamp hanging from a hook, the courier was carefully sketching a geometric shape in his notebook.

"Attention!"

The soldier jumped up and saluted.

"Corporal Hitler, Sergeant."

Extelman was surprised by how thin the young man was. It looked like he'd shrunk under his uniform. As for his emaciated face, it almost disappeared under his moustache. _This one doesn't have much longer,_ thought the sergeant, and he suddenly felt less guilty about sending him to his death.

"Corporal, I need a brave man, and since I see that . . ."

Extelman had just noticed the shiny black decoration on Hitler's chest. _How did this scrawny kid earn a first-class Iron Cross?_

"Corporal, I need to get some of the rifles that were lost in no man's land. It's a difficult mission, and—"

"I'll do it."

Extelman tried to hide his surprise. "Good . . . I'll . . ."

"When do you need me to go?"

The sergeant contemplated the man he was sending to certain death once more. "Where are you from, Corporal?"

"Vienna, but I enlisted in Munich."

"Have you fought the whole war?"

"Since day one."

A madman, thought Extelman. _What kind of person comes all the way from Austria to get shot to pieces in this damp hell?_

"It will be dark in two hours. There is no moon. We'll light flares to guide you. Any questions?"

"No," answered Hitler as he returned to his sketchbook.

Intrigued, Extelman moved closer. Both pages of the book were covered in a design, repeated again and again with slight variations. It looked like a cross that the artist had spun to the right and to which he had added four perpendicular lines. The sergeant shrugged. It didn't matter—in a few hours the notebook and its owner would be no more.

Adolf Hitler refused the helmet the men had offered him. The light from the flares would make the reflective surface a target. Two soldiers placed a ladder against the side of the trench.

"The enemy lines are two hundred meters away. You won't find any good weapons until you get pretty close," added the sergeant. "During the last attack the French waited to fire until our men were just steps from their trenches. In other words . . ."

Hitler nodded. He understood. If he wanted to find working rifles, he'd need to get as close to the enemy lines as possible. He placed his foot on the first rung of the ladder.

"Corporal Hitler," Extelman called out, about to begin another pompous speech.

But Adolf had already jumped over the side of the trench.

Once he'd left the German line, Hitler decided to head left. He climbed out of a hole left by a shell, then ducked and moved slowly forward. The ground was uneven. He knew if he broke an ankle, it was over. No one would come out to save him.

Adolf had always feared that kind of anonymous death, without a hint of glory. He stopped to catch his breath. How long had he been walking? He still couldn't see the enemy lines, fortified by their barbed-wire walls. However, there was a smell he could identify—death.

He had to be close. A gust of wind carried a high-pitched tinkling sound with it. The men on the front lines had told him about this. To protect themselves from night-time attacks, the French hung pieces of scrap metal from the bushes and barbed wire. The sound alerted them to any intruders. He smiled. He was lucky it was windy. He had to find working rifles, and to do that, he'd have to cock them. The sound was easily recognizable but would be covered by the dance of the metallic objects.

Suddenly, the sky lit up. A flare had just exploded above the French lines, illuminating all of no man's land. Hitler caught sight of a group of soldiers lying flat on their backs, their chests riddled with shrapnel. He began crawling towards them, taking cover behind a muddy ridge. When a second flare shot up, he was only a few meters away. A wave of gunfire rang out, angrily tilling the ground. Then it stopped suddenly. Adolf had just grabbed a rifle. He cocked it. It worked. He reached out and grabbed the leather strap of another gun. The second flare swerved to and fro as it made its way to the ground. Then everything went dark again. He had accomplished the first part of his mission. Now he just had to make it back alive.

Adolf strapped the guns to his back to keep his hands free. He was terrified the enemy might launch their own flares. He would become a target in seconds.

He lay down in the mud and made his way along a line of raised earth peppered with bullet impacts. When he reached the end, Adolf did his best to calm his racing pulse. The wind had died down, and he could no longer hear the metallic clinking from the barbed wire. He continued on his hands and knees, feeling the ground with his fingers. In theory, he was only a few meters from his own lines. At this distance, enemy bullets couldn't reach him anymore. He could have stood up and walked normally, except that then he might be shot by friendly fire. Extelman had warned him to identify himself.

Suddenly, he heard a whistle. Too high-pitched to be a large shell. Then a second whistle, followed by a muffled sound, but no explosion. He hurried.

In the trench up ahead, he heard shouting.

"Gas! Gas!"

Hitler opened his mouth to say the code word, but a terrible smell invaded his nostrils. He rolled to the ground and into the trench. A hand grabbed him by the hair and placed a rag over his mouth.

"To the shelter!"

Carried by the flood of panicked soldiers, he found himself pushed up against a wall as they took the guns from him.

"Bring a light. He may be wounded!"

Adolf opened his eyes to terrible pain.

"Hitler! Hitler!"

He recognized Extelman's voice, but not his face. He ran his hand past his eyes and saw nothing but darkness. He screamed. He was blind.

29

"You clearly want to hasten England's demise!"

"No, Prime Minister, the United States remains your most loyal ally against the Nazi threat. Our arms deliveries have doubled since last month and—"

Winston Churchill slammed his fist onto the table. "That's enough! It's five minutes to midnight on the Doomsday Clock. You heard the reports from the General and the Admiral. Operation Barbarossa is a brilliant success. The Panzers have reached the outskirts of Moscow. Stalin won't be able to hold out much longer. And if that communist bastard falls, the Germans will get their hands on an enormous arsenal. Once it's finished with Russia, Germany will swallow us whole in a matter of weeks. America must enter the war!"

The two high-ranking British military officials watched as the Prime Minister and the American ambassador sparred. Since they'd delivered their pessimistic forecasts for the conflict in Russia, Churchill had been furious. He had summoned Ambassador Winant to the meeting so he could hear the conclusions directly from the mouths of the officers.

The American diplomat sat up straight in his armchair. "Listen, Winston, you know that I am constantly pleading your case with President Roosevelt. I'm nothing like my predecessor."

"Yes, well, no one could be as bad as bloody Joseph Kennedy," mumbled Churchill. "That anti-Semitic Irishman admired the Führer and even broke out the champagne when the Munich Agreement was signed."

"That's why the President named me as his replacement. I fervently believe my country should enter the war at your side, as does the President, but . . ."

"I know, I know," replied Churchill. "Public opinion isn't on your side."

"Exactly. The United States isn't a dictatorship. The President can't decide, of his own accord, to declare war on Germany."

Churchill stood up and walked over to the General and the Admiral, who remained silent.

"Well then, strategists, what needs to happen for the Americans to join the war?"

The officers glanced cautiously at each other. The Admiral spoke up. "German U-boats would need to attack American merchant ships."

"Hitler isn't stupid enough for that," replied Churchill. "He'd never take such a risk."

"Well, if not him, then one of the other Axis powers. We can forget about Mussolini, who has no contact with the United States, so we're left with Japan. They have plans to conquer the Pacific, which they think of as their territorial waters, a bit like the Germans with Eastern Europe. I'm sure that the Emperor and Prime Minister Tojo dream nightly of dropping bombs on the American Pacific territory nearest the Empire of the Rising Sun."

The American ambassador coughed. "You can't really want the Japs to attack us. I'm going to pretend I never heard any of this."

Winston Churchill leaned in towards Winant, placing his hands on the ambassador's armrests. "John, I would sell my soul and my daughter's virtue to the Devil to get you into this war. If, one morning, they wake me up to tell me the bloody Japs have vaporized—I don't know, let's say Hawaii—well, I would share my finest cigars with all my employees and get incredibly drunk."

The ambassador tensed and stood up.

"You're daydreaming, Prime Minister. The majority of our Pacific fleet is stationed there. We have more than eighty vessels—destroyers, battleships, cruisers, and subs—stationed at a naval air base. The Japanese will never risk attacking the largest military port in the Pacific. They don't have the means."

The antechamber outside the Prime Minister's office was decorated in an equestrian theme. Paintings of hunt scenes were set amidst riding accessories, from harnesses to spurs. The décor was a far cry from that of the underground bunker where Malorley had first met Churchill. The SOE officer studied a Stubbs canvas of a horse rearing up before an arrogant-looking king. He could hear a regular staccato clicking coming from the next room, where two secretaries worked on typewriters. He looked at his watch for the fifth time. He'd been waiting for two hours. Since he'd brought back the relic from Montségur, he'd had a standing monthly appointment with Churchill. The Prime Minister generally rushed him out in less than fifteen minutes, but this time Malorley had news. Tristan had a promising lead. They may need to send another commando unit anywhere in Europe at the drop of a hat. And to do so, the SOE officer needed the green light from the head of the government.

Churchill's door suddenly opened as two officers and a man he recognized as the American ambassador stepped out. They continued their discussion, visibly unconcerned about his presence. The diplomat waved to the military men and left quickly as they were still gathering their coats.

The General's face was familiar. It took Malorley a few seconds to place him at the Gordon Circle meeting, where he'd given his speech about the occult aspects of Nazism.

The General gave him a quick glance and leaned closer to his colleague. "I'll see you back at headquarters. I need to have a word with an acquaintance."

The Admiral gave Malorley a suspicious look. "Who is this able young civilian and why isn't he in uniform?" he asked rudely.

"He's SOE . . ."

The Admiral pulled his cap down on his head and mumbled, "In the last war, we didn't need his lot to destroy our enemies. They're honourless, with no respect for the codes of war. Yet another sign of the Empire's decadence."

"My dear Andrew, do you really believe the little Austrian corporal follows the rules? Times have changed, and the Empire has had to change along with them."

The two men parted ways. Malorley had heard bits of the conversation but had stayed out of it. Since the SOE had been founded, extravagant rumours—mostly spread by MI6 and Naval Intelligence—had circulated about its methods.

The General walked over to Malorley and shook his hand energetically. "Commander Malorley, congratulations on the success of your operation at Montségur. You impressed a lot of people. So, why don't you tell me where you keep the relic?"

30

When Erika woke up, daylight had been streaming through the shutters for some time. She reached her arm out, but Tristan's half of the bed was empty. The night before, when they'd come back from Goebbels's party, he had refused to explain himself—he needed to confirm his hunch first. The archaeologist had let it go, having experienced her own feverish moments of passion before a discovery. Tristan seemed to be on to something big, and she had no intention of getting in his way. She pulled up the covers to keep warm and thought back through the evening at the Ministry.

She quickly filtered out the social aspect to focus on Goebbels's announcement. The Führer hated travelling, so why was he going to meet Mussolini in Venice? Did Hitler now have his sights set on the Mediterranean and the Orient, to hit England via its commercial empire? But Erika wasn't particularly interested in geopolitics. What worried her was that Goebbels had made the announcement. Everyone knew the Dwarf was gifted in the art of propaganda. So, if he had organized this meeting in Venice, it must be a useful show of power. The whole world would suddenly learn that Germany had triumphed over Russia, sending Churchill into despair and convincing the Americans not to enter the war.

A masterful move.

Except that he'd left Himmler out. The Reichsführer was no longer a member of the inner circle. Hitler was making decisions without him.

Von Essling felt her throat tighten. She had to find the swastika.

She jumped out of bed. Tristan had better find something, and quickly.

The archives room at the Ahnenerbe was one of the largest in the building. It contained an ever-expanding collection of manuscripts—mostly medieval—and rare documents from all over the world. It was where they had prepared for the mission to Tibet to find the first swastika.

Tristan had taken a pile of old papers and books with worn bindings out of the reserve. When Erika came in, he was annotating an old map which he was studying with a magnifying glass. She began flipping through a dry, dusty register of coats of arms to avoid disturbing him. The photograph of Amalrich's tomb sat folded in half in the middle of the table.

"Did you notice that he didn't have a surname?" asked the Frenchman as he put down his pencil. "It suddenly came to me when Goebbels kept mentioning Hitler last night."

"And?"

"While you were taking pictures of the tombstone in the chapel, I had my little chat with the old monk in the infirmary. He wasn't only interested in Hitler's visit. He also knew a lot about the knight buried in the chapel—including his name. Amalrich's surname was Mecuplus."

"That sounds very Latin, but other than that . . ."

"It's not a real name," he explained, gesturing towards the pile of books. "I looked through all the genealogies and registers of coats of arms."

Intrigued, von Essling grabbed a piece of paper and wrote out the letters: *M E C U . . .*

Tristan stopped her. "I had the same idea!"

"An anagram?"

"Yes, and there's only one: *speculum.*"

"Mirror," Erika translated from the Latin. "But that doesn't make any sense!"

"Except that, when you look in a mirror, your right side becomes your left and vice versa. So, I looked at the tomb like a reflection."

As Erika watched in disbelief, Tristan showed her the black-and-white picture of the tombstone. "I cut the image in half vertically, then traced each half, and placed them on top of each other . . ."

The Frenchman held the tracings out to Erika, who lined them up.

"Shoulder to shoulder, leg to leg, everything is perfectly symmetrical. Foot to foot . . ."

"The spurs don't line up!"

Despite his sleepless night, Tristan smiled. "And now, look closely. When you put them on top of each other, the spikes of the spurs make letters. First a B, then an R, an A . . ."

"Just tell me the word!"

"It's BRAGADIN."

Erika seemed disappointed. "It's not a common noun. It's a name, of a place or a family. How can we find out more?"

Tristan smiled again.

"If Bragadin is a proper noun, then wouldn't the easiest thing be to look in a dictionary?" he asked as he pushed the huge volume across the table. A dagger-shaped bookmark poked out from the worn pages.

"Don't tell me you've already found it?"

"The Bragadins are a very old family. Depending on the generation, they were wealthy merchants, ambitious politicians, or famous military leaders. One of them even served as governor of Crete."

Erika's excitement grew as she listened to Tristan. Though she occasionally doubted her love for him, she now knew she hadn't made a mistake. He'd just saved her. She finally had a real lead for Himmler.

"Their success enabled them to build a palace, where they lived for centuries."

"Where?"

Tristan offered her the magnifying glass. She placed it in front of her eye and saw a street lined with black rectangles that symbolized houses. One of them was circled in pencil, with a name above it in italics:

Bragadin.

She instantly recognized the city she was studying, which looked like a fish in water. She glanced meaningfully at Tristan.

Venice.

The archives room was buzzing like a hive when Tristan slipped his head in. The morning calm had disappeared, replaced by the frenzy of the researchers' quests, like bees after pollen. Some of them explored shelves that had been forgotten for years while others flipped through old books, and still more quickly drafted notes that Erika—their demanding queen—accepted or refused.

"I want everything on the Bragadin family. Their origins, their history, their disappearance. Everything. Same goes for the Castello neighbourhood where their villa is located. Maps, history, anecdotes. Everything."

"I see you haven't wasted any time," remarked the Frenchman.

"We have a meeting with the Reichsführer in two hours. I want to be ready. Especially since Heydrich, the head of the SD, will be there as well."

"Head of the SD and the Gestapo," added Marcas. "If we're meeting with that man, I'm going for a little walk to prepare myself," he said as he leaned in to kiss her, but she was already lost in her notes again.

Fog and frost covered the village when Tristan reached the square in front of the church. He'd stopped in front of a greengrocer's, using the reflective shop window to ensure no one was following him. The streets were deserted, but he still wasn't reassured. He closed his eyes to better distinguish the echo of furtive steps or the halting sound of breathing, but all was quiet. He couldn't wait any longer anyway. He only had a few minutes before he had to leave.

The door to the church opened silently. The nave seemed even greyer than the last time. This sanctuary exuded despair. Even Christ on his cross, his head hanging on his chest, seemed like he was about to die a second time. The sacristy was open, and Tristan was about to step in when the sound of chairs being knocked to the ground stopped him in his tracks. He pressed his back against the wall and looked cautiously through the space between the door and its hinges. The priest was lying on the floor, trying to pull himself up. Marcas hurried to his side. Apart from the two of them, the sacristy was empty.

"Who did this to you?" asked Tristan as the pool of blood on the floor grew larger.

"The choirboy informed on me. The Gestapo came. A man. He beat me."

"Did you talk?"

The priest's face suddenly lit up. "I didn't have time. A haemorrhage. Our gracious Lord saved me from the pain."

"Where is the man now?"

"Searching the presbytery."

Marcas couldn't help but cling tightly to the message he had prepared. Malorley absolutely needed to know that he was going to Venice after the relic. And that Hitler and Mussolini would be there as well. It was vital information for the outcome of the war.

The priest grabbed his arm. "I changed mailboxes. It's not the donations box anymore. Go to the cemetery, the Stifter family tomb. Under the bronze crucifix. Someone comes every day to pick up your messages and drop off orders from London. Now go. Go!"

"I can't leave you like this!"

"Let God handle my fate. I'll pray for you."

The Frenchman stood up as a mumbled *Pater Noster* escaped the priest's lips. The cemetery was right next to the church. There had to be a door. Tristan struggled to get his bearings in the nave. The left-hand wall, that's where he had to look. He ran over but found nothing but statues of saints lit by a few votive candles. No door.

"Where are you going?" asked a voice as he reached Christ on the cross. Marcas turned around slowly, as if he had nothing to fear. The Gestapo man wearing a leather jacket held a crowbar in his hands. "Did you see the priest?"

Tristan nodded.

"Well then, you've seen too much," replied Heydrich's man as he drew closer, brandishing the metal bar.

"I'm nice and warmed up now, thanks to the priest. I'll do an even better job with you."

"Would you really kill a man beneath Christ on the cross?"

"I don't give a shit about your Lord. He was just another dirty Jew!"

The Frenchman moved closer to the cross, took hold and knocked it to the floor. Jesus came off the wood and crashed to the ground. A nail rolled under a chair and the crown of thorns bounced with a clang.

"Do you really think you can stop me with your broken Jesus?"

The Gestapo thug raised the crowbar overhead with both hands, leaving his face unprotected. The moment Tristan had been waiting for. He grabbed the rusty crown and drove it into the man's throat.

"I hope you got your tetanus jab . . ."

His eyes filled with disbelief, Marcas's adversary stared at the blood spurting from his neck. His hands went towards the crown.

"If you remove it, you'll die."

The priest's murderer hesitated.

"If you leave it, you'll die, too. So, have a good think about the way you prefer to expire."

As Tristan left the church on his way to the cemetery, he walked past a blackened painting of the Devil accompanying a group of souls to hell. The Frenchman smiled knowingly. "I've just sent you a new charge."

31

10 *Downing Street, London*
November 1941

Malorley raised an eyebrow. The General shouldn't have had that information. "I don't know what you're talking about," he replied.

The military official winked. "Ah, you and your damn secrets. But no matter, I'm very glad our talk with the Prime Minister was fruitful."

"So it was *you?*"

After making his presentation to the elite members of British society at the Gordon Circle, he'd always wondered who among them had championed his cause.

"No, an eminent member's emissary. Speaking of which, I really hope that bloody talisman changes the tide. Things aren't easy at the moment."

"That bad?"

"I'm afraid so. Though we've basically won the war in the skies over this country, the Fritzes are on the offensive everywhere else. They're giving the communists a thrashing, and if they keep on this way, they'll have Stalin by the short hairs before Christmas. Rommel's damn Afrika Korps is having a ball in Libya, and everyone in the Balkans is doing the Nazi salute these days. As for the Middle East, the Abwehr is sending guns to the Arab nationalist movements to help them throw us out."

"There is still some good news, though. I heard the Americans are sending more supplies."

"Yes, but we're just buying time, and I—"

Churchill's personal secretary approached the two men.

"Commander Malorley, the Prime Minister will see you now. I must warn you that you only have ten minutes. He's needed at Buckingham Palace."

"I'll leave you with the Bulldog," said the General. "Come see me sometime. We'll have dinner and I'll introduce you to some friends. Your vision of Nazism opened my eyes."

"I'll try, but I don't make it to headquarters often."

"Who said anything about headquarters?"

He held out his hand, but this time the grip was different, particularly the position of the index finger.

"Newton Lodge," whispered the General.

"Green Devil," Malorley replied with a smile. The General, who patted his shoulder as he left, was a Freemason like himself.

The SOE officer entered the Prime Minister's office. The décor was simple—nothing like the flamboyant equestrian exploits of the antechamber. A flag, a portrait of the King, an operations map. A single painting—of the Battle of Trafalgar—offered a moment's distraction. Churchill seemed to be in a bad mood. Before Malorley could open his mouth, he launched into a tirade.

"So, Commander, you've been playing up again, I hear? I received a complaint from the prison warden at the Tower of London. He wants your head and that of your suspicious colleague on pikes. That bastard Hess has lost his mind because of you. They had to take him to an asylum. The head of MI5 keeps asking me to airdrop you into France without a parachute. Your department of sorcerers and fortune tellers won't make it through the winter if things continue like this."

"We tried a hypnosis session, which ended badly. I'm truly sorry."

"Not as sorry as I am. That said . . ." Churchill paused to light a cigar as thick as his thumb. "That said, you've got me out of a tight spot. They were never able to get anything out of him at MI5, and the man was clearly disturbed before your visit. I think this is the one and only time I will ever agree with Hitler—the man is away with the fairies."

A weight lifted from Malorley's shoulders.

"So," continued Churchill, "has your relic been sent to our friends on the other side of the Atlantic?"

"Yes, aboard the *Cornwallis*, escorted by two Typhoon submarines. If all goes to plan, they'll collect it from the rendezvous point in two days."

"If only it could convince Roosevelt to declare war on Germany . . . That would make me the happiest of men."

"The American ambassador didn't seem to share your point of view."

"He's not a bad chap, really. I have the utmost confidence in him. John is almost part of the family. He's my daughter Sarah's official lover."

Malorley's eyes opened wide as he wondered if the Prime Minister was making one of his famous jokes. Churchill sneered and stubbed out his cigar in an ashtray shaped like an upside-down bowler hat.

"Bloody hell, another doctored cigar! Can't anyone get their hands on a decent Romeo y Julieta for me? Anyway, if I remember correctly, there are still two more blasted swastikas out there. Where are we on that?"

"I've had some news from our agent embedded in Himmler's entourage. Things are on the move. John Dee has a new lead. We must be ready to send a commando unit. With your authorization, of course."

"Granted. Given where we stand, I'd French kiss Stalin if it would help. How did your agent contact you?"

"He sends and receives messages via a network of German Catholic resistance fighters."

"Perfect. One last thing. I learned that you hired the depraved old Crowley and used him to interrogate Hess. You have to get rid of him."

"Why?" asked Malorley, intrigued.

"Good God! Don't you know that idiot has claimed all over town that he gave me the idea of 'V for Victory'?"

"I didn't know you knew each other."

"I've met him twice, and let me tell you, I still remember each time vividly. A disgusting reptile. Don't tell me you've really added the Devil's sidekick to your team."

"I have, and I know all about his lack of morality. But men like him aren't exactly ten a penny. He went to Germany and Italy many times before the war and has quite a few contacts in occultist circles there, particularly among the Reich's high-ranking officials. He could be very useful."

Malorley decided to keep quiet about Moira O'Connor's attempt to blackmail Crowley and their plans to feed the German spies false information.

"I know all about his networks! Throughout the country, and even among those closest to me. Did he show you his tarot cards when you went to see him?"

"He did."

"Well, some of the drawings were done by Lady Frieda Harris, the wife of my personal adviser, Percy Harris. I warned him, but Percy enjoys the mage's company. He even gave him a tour of Parliament. If Crowley weren't so old, I would have thought Frieda was his mistress."

"You clearly dislike him in any case . . ."

The Prime Minister stood up from his armchair, joined his hands behind his back and paced the room. "And yet, there is a certain logic to having Crowley work for the Crown."

"I don't understand," said Malorley.

Churchill stopped right in front of the SOE man. "Despite his scandalous conduct, I'm thoroughly convinced that Crowley has been protected for decades. Protected by . . ." Churchill looked towards the framed portrait above his desk.

Malorley tensed. "The King?"

"Not the King, but his family. George VI was still in primary school when Crowley began enjoying favours from the Windsors."

"But why?"

"I've never known. Maybe he has something on them. But if you repeat any of what I've just said, I'll have you hanged."

32

Pasewalk military hospital
November 11, 1918

The wind was king in the attic at Pasewalk, where breezes and gusts alternated, depending on the season. The old mansion had been converted into an asylum at the turn of the century, but the madmen who had lived there had been unable to stand the constant gales. To prevent an epidemic of murders and suicides, the institution had been closed.

But the war had re-opened it. Tens of thousands of gassed German soldiers needed fresh air to rejuvenate their lungs, and the incessant winds of Pomerania became a miracle cure. Every day a new truckload of wounded men turned up. Lorries covered in tarpaulins dropped off broken men with trembling hands who were doing their best to hold on to what little life was left in them.

"Watch out, there's a grave to your left. You could trip on the freshly tilled earth."

The morose voice of the nurse who took Hitler on his morning walks annoyed him. He couldn't stand her weary tone or the musty smell of her hair anymore. Since he'd lost his sight, his sense of smell had become his main link to reality, and the odours around him were not to his liking. From the dormitory, which reeked of urine, to the rotten smell of the meals they were hastily served, everything disgusted him. And what he heard was hardly better. The wounded men who arrived from the western front, crossing all of Germany, spoke of a country devastated by poverty and hunger. Hitler hadn't seen any of that. He'd made the trip in a dirty livestock trailer, surrounded by filth, terrible smells, and darkness. He had received a diagnosis at Pasewalk. He was totally blind. The doctor had suggested he pray to God to restore his sight. Hitler mistrusted God and felt he would never see again.

"Come, we're going back in. Be careful when you turn around."

"Have the newspapers arrived?" asked Adolf. "I'd like someone to read them to me, at least the headlines."

"The papers? No. There's nothing but bad news anyway."

"What's happened?"

"Germany is defeated. We've asked for an armistice!"

Hitler lay down on his narrow cot, compulsively fiddling with the sheet. He had been through a lot. Hunger, poverty, shame. But the country's downfall was too much. This time, he wouldn't be able to get back up. Without the war, which had given meaning to his useless life, without the army, which had given him a family, he was nothing. Nothing but an eternal loser. He was blind. Blind and out of options. He reached for his jacket and pulled out his sketchbook. He didn't dare open it. He felt like his chest was in a vice—like Germany itself, caught between the Allies to the west and the communist revolution to the east.

Despite his shaking hands, Adolf finally opened his notebook. The last page was dog-eared. He ran his index finger over the paper but didn't need to feel the texture to know what he had drawn. A swastika. A wave of emotion washed over him as he remembered himself in Vienna, compulsively reading all the issues of *Ostara* at the national library and meeting Lanz. Then that night at Heiligenkreuz, which had left him intrigued. He counted on his fingers. Ten years already. What had he done in ten years? Nothing—except lose his sight.

"Get up, lazy bones!"

An angry hand pulled the sheet off him. He smelled alcohol on the orderly's breath. He knew him. Everyone knew he was a coward who had cut off his own index finger—needed to pull a trigger—to avoid being sent to the front. And he was known to spread revolutionary ideas. People said he was a communist and that he had a portrait of Lenin hidden in his room.

"I've brought you some company. Another poor idiot like you."

He listened as the orderly left, then heard the springs of the bed next to his creak.

"Hitler!" said a voice made raspy by the gas. "It must be destiny for us to find each other again."

Adolf was captivated. Despite the hoarseness, he recognized the voice. But from where? The trenches? Munich, where he enlisted?

"Keep looking," continued the voice, as if the person knew what Hitler was thinking. "Vienna, in Margareten. I was smoking a cigarette."

"Impossible," cried Adolf. "You're . . ."

"Weistort."

"It can't be. You can't be real."

"Unfortunately, I am, my friend. What happened to you?"

Just as Hitler was about to reply, a nurse interrupted. "The doctor is waiting for you. I'll take you to him," she announced as she made her way to Hitler's bed.

"We'll talk later," offered Weistort.

The nurse took hold of Hitler's shoulder and helped him walk haltingly in his shroud-like pyjamas. As he watched his old friend leave, Weistort thought he looked like Germany herself. Battered and unsteady. He wouldn't last much longer.

As they made their way down the corridor towards the doctor's office, the agitation was palpable, even for a blind man. People were running here and there as doors slammed and shouts rang out. Hitler even thought he heard "The Internationale".

"Hug the wall," whispered the terrified nurse. "They could knock you over."

The sound of broken glass filled the air.

"My God, they've gone mad!"

"What's going on?" asked Hitler.

"The armistice, comrade. The armistice! The war is over!" yelled a moving voice.

A gunshot sounded outside. Hitler held out his right hand. The nurse had gone. He leaned against the wall and went back the way he had come. He knew there were no obstacles, just doors. He had to get back to the dormitory, and quickly. He moved like a spider, glued to the wall, his hands on the wainscoting and the tips of his toes against the skirting board. People were running and shouting all around him now. He tightened the waist of his trousers, which were threatening to fall down, and trudged on.

"Hitler!" cried Weistort. "Get in here."

From the smell, Adolf recognized the storeroom where they kept the cleaning products. Weistort closed the door. Hitler heard him move a cupboard.

"What are you doing?"

"I'm saving our lives, or at least trying," replied Weistort. "The war ended at eleven o'clock this morning. It's a total defeat. Our troops are abandoning our positions, leaving artillery and all means of transportation behind. In other words, Germany no longer has an army to defend itself. But the worst is yet to come. The country has been paralyzed by strikes. Communist activists have already seized certain cities. The revolution has begun. Here, too."

"What do you mean?"

"Well, half of the nurses and orderlies have gone down to the cellar to get drunk, and the other half have disarmed and imprisoned the guards, relieved the hospital management, and proclaimed a communist rebellion. If you leave this storeroom, you'd better call the orderlies 'comrade', or you'll get into trouble."

Adolf was speechless.

"To make matters worse, you're a decorated veteran, and the proletariat doesn't like medals. They go against their concept of equality. If I were them, I'd shoot you."

"How can you joke at a time like this? Aren't you scared?"

Weistort placed his hand on Hitler's bony shoulder. "The darker the night, the brighter the day."

"I doubt I'll ever see the light of day again," replied Adolf ironically.

Weistort stood up, ran the tap, and adjusted the hair that fell across his forehead. His mastery of his fear, despite the surrounding chaos, impressed Hitler.

"You underestimate your mind's resources," said Weistort. "That's where the light and darkness reside."

Hitler's moustache shook with disappointment. How could a man as educated as his friend offer such platitudes?

"After all, your life is loathsome," he continued. "No job, no friends, no future. Why would you want to open your eyes to such despair?"

"Are you suggesting that I'm still blind because I'm afraid? That I'm responsible for my own misfortune, because I'm weak, a failure?" said Adolf, his anger intensifying. He couldn't accept such a verdict.

"I'm suggesting that you're not living up to your life or your situation. There's chaos all around us. Go and face it."

"I'm blind," groaned Hitler.

"Then you always will be."

Weistort opened the door. The din of shouting and shattering glass was overwhelming.

"It's time to face yourself."

Hitler went pale, but replied, "You don't believe I can do it, do you?"

"Only you can prove it. If you're brave enough."

Adolf hesitated for a few seconds, then went out into the anarchy. He felt Weistort hold him back. "Do you still have the swastika Lanz gave you?"

Hitler nodded.

"Then may its power be with you," he said as he closed the door of the storeroom.

The corporal found himself alone with the orderlies.

"That's enough!" Hitler's voice rose above the bedlam.

"Who is this clown in pyjamas?"

"And why is he holding his arms out like that?"

Adolf knew people were coming closer, driven by unkind curiosity. The sensation wasn't new. He remembered it from his school days, when packs of bullies would surround and humiliate him.

"A blind man giving orders!"

"Corporal Adolf Hitler, List Regiment, decorated with the Iron Cross, First Class."

The entire corridor burst into laughter, and one of the orderlies grabbed him by the collar. "Listen up, little man, there are no corporals here, no medals, no nothing. There are no more privileges—that's all over. So, we'll give you a bucket and a mop and let you clean up the piss in the dormitory. We've done it long enough. It's your turn now."

Hitler tightened his fist around the swastika, pushing it into his flesh.

"No," he replied.

"As you wish!" chuckled the orderly.

The blow hit him hard. He felt the skin above his eyebrow split as he fell to the floor. He tried to get up, but his face was covered in blood. The tip of a boot hit his chin next, followed by a kick, which broke his ribs. He screamed, but kept his hands clenched into fists.

"Let's give him a lesson to remember!"

They were all about to jump on him when a gunshot rang out in the courtyard, followed by a scream.

"Quick, the prisoners are escaping!"

The corridor was suddenly empty, as if by magic. Weistort came out of the storeroom and turned over the body lying on the floor. His pyjamas were stained with blood and his face was covered in cuts and bruises.

"Don't talk. Your lips are ripped to pieces and one of your cheeks is split to the bone. That'll make a nice scar."

"Like yours."

Weistort stared incredulously at his friend, who had just pointed at his scar.

"Adolf, how can you see my scar?"

Hitler opened his hands and brought them to his face. The swastika fell to the floor.

"A mirror, get me a mirror."

Weistort hurried back to the storeroom, broke the mirror

hanging on the wall, and brought back a piece of it, which Hitler eagerly held to his face.

With a single glance, he understood.

He could see again.

33

Malorley stood facing the large map of Venice he'd found in a specialist shop in South Kensington and pinned to his office wall. The commander allowed his gaze to wander through the tangled mass of streets and canals. It was a labyrinth he knew fairly well, since he'd stayed in the city before the war, with an Italian friend.

Since he'd received Tristan's message, he had been champing at the bit. Once he'd obtained Churchill's authorization, he had spent hours organizing Operation Doge, down to the last detail. He was tired, but two good nights of sleep would recharge his batteries.

His secretary came in without knocking and placed an envelope bearing the navy seal on his desk.

"You're to call the Prime Minister's office immediately after reading this," she said.

"Really?" he asked, surprised. "I have other priorities at the moment . . ."

Annoyed, he opened the envelope and pulled out a typed page stamped by Naval Intelligence, as well as a file featuring a photograph of a young naval officer. His face flushed as he read. He felt like the rug had been pulled out from under him.

"Bloody hell! This can't be right!"

The secretary had never seen him in such a state.

"What's the matter, Commander?"

"They've taken me off the Venice operation! Replaced me with someone from Naval Intelligence! They won't get away with this!"

He picked up the phone and dialled Churchill's office. After a few rings, the Prime Minister picked up. The Bulldog's voice shook the receiver, despite the tight grip that Malorley had on it.

"Malorley . . . You must be fuming. I understand."

"Prime Minister, your decision is unfair. I have every qualification required for this mission."

"I know, but I can't afford to risk an officer of your rank. It's too dangerous. The navy is sending you one of its best men to lead the group in your place. You will, of course, still run Operation Doge from London."

"I suppose you are wary of me because of what happened at the Tower of London with Crowley?"

"That will be all, Commander. Good day."

Churchill had hung up. Their conversation had lasted less than a minute.

Malorley was dumbfounded. He'd been replaced just two days before the mission was scheduled to begin. He didn't know what, but something had gone wrong during his meeting with the Prime Minister. Thank goodness the commando unit was still made up of SOE agents, including Laure. The Commander opened the Naval Intelligence file on the man who would take his place. He barely had half an hour to digest his disappointment and put on a happy face before the briefing with the team.

The room was dark. Malorley placed a slide of the Mediterranean into the projector. Laure and three other SOE agents stared at the screen.

"This is your flight plan," said the commander. "Tomorrow you will take off from Baybridge on a Lockheed Hudson that's been refitted for parachute drops. It will take you to Malta, to a military base north of Valletta."

"The home of the Knights of Malta," commented one of the men. "I've always dreamt of visiting Santa Maria Assunta in Mosta, which has a magnificent dome from the—"

"I'm afraid you won't be a tourist this time. In Malta, you'll be transferred to the port, where a submarine will be waiting to take you to Venice."

Laure raised her hand. "To get to Malta, the plane will fly over occupied France. What if we're shot down?"

"You'll have the standard survival kit, a pistol with a box of thirty rounds to kill as many Germans as possible, and three hundred francs."

"And how will we get back to England?" asked the oldest among them.

"We haven't planned for that. We cannot share the information with our French network. If you crash in Frogland, you'll have to count on Laure here to get you home safely."

"It's in your best interests to make sure I survive . . . But, let's say that, thanks to divine intervention, we do make it to the Duce. What then?"

"The SOE set up a network of resistance fighters in the Veneto six months ago. I don't want to give you false hope, but it should be less dangerous than parachuting into France. The Italians aren't as vigilant as the Germans."

"That still doesn't tell us what we'll be doing in Venice," insisted Laure.

Malorley smiled. "You'll know soon enough. Now, for the more practical aspects. You'll be given equipment and a procedure briefing tomorrow morning at eleven o'clock with Major Lanchester in the armoury."

The lights in the room were then switched on. The four members of the commando unit blinked and stood up slowly.

"You're scheduled to leave tomorrow at two o'clock. A lorry will take you to the airfield, and I'll come along to introduce you to your mission leader. He knows Italy, and Venice in particular, quite well. In the meantime, I suggest you get some rest or have some fun. The next few days will be difficult."

Once the other members of the commando unit had left, Laure walked over to Malorley. "How are things with Crowley?"

"He gave the Irish woman the information and she seems satisfied. According to MI6, her contact is a high-ranking German agent, one they've been after for quite some time. Our counter-intelligence teams are delighted. We'll work together to determine what to feed them via Crowley."

"I wanted to tell you that . . ."

"Yes?"

"That I'm sorry you aren't coming with us."

"Believe me, I'm more disappointed than you are."

Malorley turned off the projector. Laure was still standing right in front of him.

"Is there something else?"

"So, we'll be seeing Tristan again."

"I was wondering when you'd say something. I thought you couldn't care less about him."

"Let's just say I'm eager to cross paths with him again—"

Malorley cut her off. "There's something you should know. He's very close with the German archaeologist who ran the excavations at Montségur. I imagine you remember her."

Laure couldn't hide her surprise. "A member of the SS? Strange choice of mistress." Her tone was harsher than she'd intended.

Malorley pretended he hadn't noticed. "It seems to be more than a little complicated."

Laure was halfway out the door by the time he'd finished his sentence.

"No matter. I'm going to follow your advice and have some fun. Oh, before I go—what's the name of our mission leader?"

"He's a young Naval Intelligence officer. Ian Fleming."

34

Erika and Tristan had been sitting on a sofa as grey as the sky outside, waiting for the Reichsführer to see them, for quite some time. People said he hated tardiness, but the head of the SS seemed to have lost his sense of punctuality. His secretary hurried in and out of his office, her arms laden with files. She kept forgetting to close the door. Though Erika was so absorbed by her report that she heard nothing, Marcas hadn't missed a single word of the discussion taking place next door.

"Hitler has agreed for the SS to manage his safety during the trip to Venice. We need to ready a team of bodyguards as soon as possible."

The Frenchman recognized Himmler's unusually high-pitched voice.

"Did he give you any sort of explanation for this meeting with Mussolini?"

Reinhard Heydrich, guessed Tristan.

"You know the Führer. Now that Moscow is about to fall, he's euphoric. Goebbels must have told him that if he strengthened his alliance with Mussolini, he could be master of the Mediterranean as well."

Tristan heard pages rustle.

"This surprise trip creates unnecessary risks," affirmed Heydrich. "It's a golden opportunity for the British or the Russians to make an attempt on the Führer's life."

"For the moment, they don't know about it."

"Given Goebbels's spectacular announcement, you can be sure it's only a matter of hours or days. And the Italians will shout it from the rooftops as well."

Himmler took his time to digest the information.

"The Führer has given us full responsibility for his safety. We must live up to his expectations. What do you suggest?"

"I recommend we avoid planes. The risks of accident or interception are too high."

"Yes, travelling by train seems safer. We can make sure the route is clear and provide bodyguards."

"I was thinking three trains, to leave from different stations, at different times, following different routes. You'll take one, Goebbels another—"

"And the Führer the third. That's quite clever, Reinhard. Good work. This strategy will stack the odds in our favour."

"Thank you, Reichsführer, but I believe we can still optimize security."

When she left, the secretary distractedly pushed the door closed, leaving only a thin gap. As if to distract himself from the wait, Tristan stood up and went to the window. It was perfectly in line with the remaining opening in the door.

"Three days before the Führer's departure, we'll organize a leak about the trip."

"That's a huge risk!"

Heydrich's voice remained steady. "We'll say which train Hitler will be in . . ."

Dumbfounded, the Reichsführer didn't reply.

"But it will really be Goebbels's train."

Tristan barely had enough time to return to the sofa. He would have loved to send what he'd just heard to London, but it was too dangerous: there was no way of reaching the drop at the cemetery. On the day of the priest's murder, he'd left a message about the trip to Venice. To his great relief, someone had left a reply for him from Malorley the next day. Tristan felt less alone in the wolves' den.

As soon as Heydrich had stamped conspicuously through the antechamber, the secretary took Erika and Marcas to the

Reichsführer. Himmler's office was extremely understated. A single photo graced the pristine white walls: an aerial view of Wewelsburg Castle. There weren't any books either—except for a first edition of *Mein Kampf*, which sat on the desk. Tristan was sure it was signed. For the moment, he stood directly behind Erika, who had been invited to sit. Himmler contemplated the report the archaeologist had given him, his hands joined in front of his mouth.

"So, you have a lead?" he asked.

"Yes, Reichsführer."

"Sum things up for me."

Von Essling knew how her boss worked. He interrogated his people first, then read the report afterward, looking for inconsistencies. A police officer's instinct.

"As you know, it was my predecessor, Colonel Weistort, who decided to send a research team to Knossos, based on clues found in the *Thule Borealis Kulten*. Unfortunately, the information provided on the swastika's hiding place was incomplete, so we combined it with the notes of the first Greek archaeologist who excavated the site, and our specialists' knowledge of the terrain."

"Has the whole team returned from Crete?" interrupted the Reichsführer.

"Yes, and I made sure they were all sent to different digs."

"You did well. What happened next?"

"We found an underground room built during the Middle Ages and excavated it. It contained what we thought was a tomb, but inside there was only a sword."

Himmler's eyes sparkled behind his round glasses at the sound of this word. He'd always been fascinated by the age of chivalry and dreamt of making the SS a new order of soldier-monks destined to conquer the world.

"Where was the sword from?"

"We had Professor Waldenberg examine it. It's German."

"That's no surprise," affirmed the Reichsführer. "The Germans were the best blacksmiths in medieval Europe."

"Unfortunately, it bears no identifiable markings to link it to its owner."

Marcas had been watching Himmler since the beginning of the conversation. He was the second most-feared man in Europe after Hitler, but he didn't look it. He lacked the Führer's magnetic gaze and the stark, narrow features of Heydrich. He was near-sighted and his eyebrows were thinning. Nothing about him said, *murderous monster*.

"Tristan had an idea to compile several data sets, which in the end led us to an abbey in Austria," continued Erika.

"In Germany," corrected the Reichsführer with a brief glance at the Frenchman. "Austria is now part of the Reich."

Von Essling accepted the remark impassively. Hitler's conquest of neighbouring countries had never interested her. She continued in the same tone. "We now know who the sword belonged to, as well as his biography. His name was Amalrich, a knight who travelled to the Holy Land and stayed in Knossos before withdrawing to the monastery for the rest of his life. He's buried in the chapel."

"Which abbey?"

"Heiligenkreuz, near—"

"I know where it is."

Himmler stared at the Iron Cross on the Frenchman's chest. "How did you link the anonymous shield to Heiligenkreuz Abbey?" he asked.

"I hypothesized that the knight who had embarked on the quest for the swastika was also the monk who wrote the *Thule Borealis Kulten.* To corroborate my theory, we needed to find an abbey that fitted three criteria: active at the beginning of the 14th century, located in southern Germany, and linked to the sword. It didn't take Professor Waldenberg long to find it."

The Reichsführer was silent for a moment, then turned back to Erika. "Did you visit the place?"

"Yes, we found the knight's tomb. It contained a coded message. Once we found the key, it led us to a name."

Strangely, Himmler didn't ask a single question about how they'd broken the code. He gestured to the archaeologist to continue.

"The name is Bragadin. A well-known family since the Middle

Ages. They also travelled to the Holy Land and Crete. Yet, despite our research, we haven't found a link to Amalrich."

"But the name isn't just the name of the family," added Tristan. "It's also the name of their palace. In Venice."

Himmler didn't believe in coincidences. There was always a hidden meaning, the hand of fate. It had to be so. How else could he explain that he had risen from the utmost anonymity to the highest levels of government? He had a sacred mission to fulfil. Suddenly Hitler's surprise meeting with Mussolini in Venice took on new importance. Goebbels might have orchestrated a diplomatic success for the Führer, but *he* would give him total victory.

"You're coming with me to Venice. We'll accompany the Führer, who's going to meet with the Duce. Once there, you will find the swastika. Whatever the costs."

Back in the antechamber, Erika was stunned. The idea of joining Hitler on his official trip seemed unbelievable. As they walked towards the stairs, Heydrich stepped out of his office.

"Frau von Essling, you're running the Ahnenerbe, aren't you?"

"Yes, Gruppenführer."

Himmler's right-hand man, who had never participated in a single battle, was very proud of his title as a general.

"I'll be sending you a Gestapo unit to handle security at your headquarters."

"Why?"

"One of my men has just been murdered in the village neighbouring the Ahnenerbe estate. He was keeping an eye on a priest accused of spying for the British."

The archaeologist tensed. "Do you have any suspects?"

"Everyone's a suspect in my book, Frau von Essling, but don't let that keep you up at night," he said with a toothy grin. "My men will be watching you from now on."

35

The Ritz's orchestra was making its way through a frenzied bolero, sending the dancers below spiralling this way and that. The war seemed so far away. Laure sat on a stool at the bar, drinking her second gin and tonic. She'd accepted an invitation from an SOE secretary with whom she was friendly. Carried away by their own tempo, the musicians let loose. The music picked up even more speed, setting the whole room on fire, as if there was no tomorrow. The luxury hotel's ballroom looked remarkably like Versailles' Hall of Mirrors. The Louis XIV style was everywhere: on the walls, which featured a profusion of gilt sculptures and mirrors; on the ceiling, where a crystal chandelier sparkled like fireworks; and even under the dancers' feet, where the polished wooden floor shone like a mirror.

Laure met her reflection in one of the mirrors and smiled awkwardly. She wasn't used to wearing evening gowns. Especially not in bright red, and with such a dramatic décolletage. She had rented it from a pawn shop near SOE headquarters. Three shillings for the night—a steal.

Laure would have liked to dance, but her talents in that area were nearly non-existent. She watched attentively as her English friend spun this way and that in the arms of a frigate captain. Laure's entire generation had been scarred by sacrifice and misfortune. War had crushed her innocence like a boot crushes an ant. She longed to make circles on the dance floor and forget about the next day. Suddenly, the music stopped, and her breathless colleague slumped down next to her.

"What an amazing orchestra! Why aren't you dancing? Have a little fun. Don't just sit here at the bar. There are plenty of handsome men here."

Laure smiled. Helen was right. The room was full of young men whose zest for life made them almost as attractive as they were energetic.

"Don't tell me you don't know how to dance!"

The Frenchwoman shrugged. She'd learned many things since she'd moved to England, but the swing and the waltz were not among them.

"Good evening, Miss. May I have this dance?"

She looked up to see a tall, blond young man in a captain's uniform standing in front of her. She didn't know what to say. Her friend elbowed her. "Go on!"

"I'm French," replied Laure. "I'm afraid I don't really know these dances."

The aviator gave her a ravishing smile. "Not to worry," he said "Britain supports General de Gaulle, so I'm sure we can also manage dance lessons for his charming citizens. I'm Bradley Cox. Captain Bradley Cox. What's your name?"

"Matilda. We'll see about a surname later."

She let him take her to the dance floor. He placed one hand on her shoulder and the other on her waist and began leading firmly but gracefully. It wasn't so difficult. Much easier than setting bombs or learning combat techniques. Cox picked up the pace in time to the music. She felt herself let go, intoxicated.

When the music stopped, he took her back to her table and struck up a conversation.

"What are you doing in London?"

"I can't tell you, it's top secret."

He moved closer and whispered in her ear. "I won't tell. Heart crossed, hope to die."

"All right. I spend my nights exhuming bodies in cemeteries. And tomorrow I'm off on a commando mission to find a talisman that will help us win the war. Nothing special . . ."

He stared in surprise, then burst into laughter. "Oh, I love French humour. But what do you really do?" he asked.

"I'm a secretary at the transport administration."

"I fly bombers. I'm leaving on a mission to Germany tomorrow. But I'm delighted to have met the most beautiful woman in the world before taking off—this could be my last night on earth."

"I imagine you use that line on all the women you meet."

"I don't, actually. I'm quite sincere."

She gulped down her drink and looked at him more carefully. He really was attractive, and he'd achieved a major feat—he'd made her forget about Tristan.

She accepted a furtive kiss after their third dance, then indulged in a second, much more passionate embrace in the corridor that led to the exit. Laure wasn't drunk; she just wanted to enjoy life. This could be the last time for her as well.

Bradley had suggested they have a nightcap at his house, and she'd accepted immediately. There was a war on, after all.

As they were about to leave the Ritz, the porter stood in their way. "I'm sorry, but protesters are blocking the entrance to the hotel on Piccadilly Street. You'll have to wait for the police to arrive."

"What do they want?"

"To close the hotel. They say the rich should have to face the same hardships as the rest of the population. King Zog of Albania, who's in the royal suite with his wife, ordered thirty jars of caviar for his guests. That really set them off."

"I think we can defend ourselves. And I doubt they'll confuse me with the King of Albania, given my uniform."

The porter shrugged. "As you wish. But don't go out the main doors. I'll open the one on the side for you."

Once in the street, they saw a growing crowd. Shouts and insults rang out all around.

"My car is parked a little further up the street. We can either cut through the crowd or go around them via Nelson Street."

"Let's take the most direct route."

The protesters shouted angrily and hurled tins of paint at the façade. Red, yellow, and green splotches stained the ground floor. Two particularly worked-up men were trying to rip a street sign out of the pavement.

"This will end badly!" said Cox.

Police car bells rang out. The crowd replied with an angry roar. A rumbling suddenly rang out at the end of the street. Officers on horseback were charging the protesters, who were throwing cobblestones and bottles.

"We have no choice. We have to go back inside," shouted Bradley.

Three minutes later, they were back in the hall. A window suddenly exploded with an ear-splitting crash. Shards scattered every which way. A metal street sign lay across the plush red carpet. Protesters rushed into the building as the hotel's security team tried to push them back, truncheons in hand. The lobby of the prestigious hotel quickly became a battlefield.

Bradley took Laure's hand and guided her towards the grand staircase, which led to the floors above. No one paid them any attention. They climbed the stairs quickly, with the Frenchwoman leading the way. The scene was so unreal that she couldn't help but laugh as she took the stairs four at a time, thanks to her daily training. Behind her, the pilot was slowing. He stopped at the deserted third floor.

"Matilda! You didn't tell me you were an athlete!" he said as he finally reached her, out of breath. She let him kiss her.

"Too bad we don't have the keys to a room," he whispered.

"Who needs a key?" she asked mischievously.

She pulled away and walked over to one of the doors. She quickly took a hairpin from her purse and easily triumphed over the simple lock. She'd learned to handle much more complex ones.

"Are you a burglar, too?"

"Perhaps."

They pushed clumsily into the room. The pilot let out an exclamation when he saw what was inside. "It's fit for a king!" he said.

A carved bed covered in green silk seemed to disappear under a pile of satin cushions. The oval mirror above it featured a gilt frame and reflected the view from the balcony, which looked out over all of London. Laure was amazed as she contemplated the capital's monuments—at least, those that Göring's planes hadn't destroyed.

"That's Saint Paul's. That's . . ."

Bradley moved closer and took her in his arms. His lips brushed against her neck. She felt herself letting go. A hand slipped under the bodice of her dress, and she let it.

"Do you want to?" he asked.

"Yes," she replied emphatically.

Suddenly, sirens rang out. Searchlights shot up vertically from the nearby park, cutting through the dark sky.

"Those bloody Nazis," grumbled the pilot. "I'll get them back tomorrow. Far worse!"

Dark shapes emerged in the sky. An explosion boomed and a ball of fire lit up the night, just on the other side of the park.

"They'll get their total war—"

Bradley didn't have time to finish his thought. Laure pulled him close and pushed him onto the bed. She straddled him confidently and removed the straps that kept her dress on. Her pale breasts heaved over the top of her white bra. Bradley reached out a hand that got lost in layers of lace, encouraged by the husky voice near his neck. Laure knew there was no going back. She raised her dress and pushed her body against his with the urgency of a rushing river. She gently brushed past his crotch and, pleased with what she found there, whispered in his ear, "Who gives a shit about the war?"

36

Munich
April 21, 1919

The first barricade stood at the intersection of Maillingerstrasse and Rotkreuzplatz. It was a jumbled pile of cobblestones ripped from the street, upended wardrobes still full of clothes, and a large wagon, whose handle they lifted to let people through. The joyous chaos could have been fun, if it weren't for the black barrel of a machine gun atop it all, which threatened the entire neighbourhood. The street signs had been vandalized and replaced by graffiti praising Lenin. Red flags hung from the windows. Activists in armbands featuring the scythe and the hammer glued posters to the shuttered buildings declaring that Munich was now a red dictatorship. In one corner of the square, under a decapitated statue, volunteers unloaded crates of munitions from a lorry while singing "The Internationale".

"Halt!"

Two men appeared at the entrance to the barricade, trigger fingers at the ready.

"Identify yourself!"

"Soldier Hitler."

Once the city had fallen to the communists in November, Adolf had quickly learned that ranks and medals were things of the past. He had removed his epaulettes and his Iron Cross from his uniform.

"Come closer. Have you been demobilized?"

"No, I was assigned to guard a prison camp through the beginning of this month."

One of the men came over, suspicious. "What nationality are the prisoners?"

"Russian."

"Ah, our comrades!"

Hitler didn't bother correcting them, despite the fact that he'd not seen any fervent partisans of the revolution in the camp. They were just starving prisoners who knew they'd never be strong enough to go home. Corpses on parole.

"And what are you doing now?"

"Guarding official buildings."

Ex-corporal Hitler didn't reveal that the last building he'd been assigned to was now a pile of ruins following a raid by communist activists, who had burned it to the ground.

"Where are you going?"

Adolf had always hated being asked too many questions, particularly with a gun pointed at him. But he didn't get angry. He smiled, in fact. Since he'd regained his sight, he knew he could handle anything life threw at him.

"I live in a hostel for soldiers at the corner of Rotkreuzplatz."

"It's called Leninplatz now," the guard corrected as he opened the barricade. "You'd do well to remember that next time."

"Thanks for the advice."

The hostel was full of soldiers waiting to be demobilized. It was little more than a few tiny rooms in a building that had been hit hard with machine-gun fire during the revolution. There were no doors or windows, but there was still a building manager, who had miraculously survived the fighting in the streets. Just a few years earlier, he'd worked in Munich's finest luxury hotels, but his uncontrollable love of the bottle had packed him off to the unkempt office of this building in ruins. His past life had left him bitter, with a need to talk about his former glory, and a hearty disdain for the proletarians that reigned over the city. He'd nonetheless shaved off his moustache—associated with the military—and wore a worker's cap to ensure he went unnoticed. Better safe than sorry. But at night, when he was alone behind his locked door, he pulled out a portrait of the former Emperor Wilhelm, placed it on his kitchen table, and drank a glass of schnapps to his health. When he saw Hitler, the building manager unlocked his door and called out to the young man.

"Corporal?"

Adolf gestured at him to keep quiet. The building was full of snitches who would denounce anyone to the communists for a bit of food. Everyone was a suspect.

"There's a letter for you," he said, holding out an envelope bearing several postmarks. It seemed the letter had been following him around the country for weeks. "Have you heard the news?" he asked.

Intrigued by his unexpected mail, Hitler shook his head distractedly.

"They say several regiments are marching on Munich. The regular army. They'll take the city back. Apparently, there's already fighting . . ."

The building manager rubbed his hands together gleefully. Tomorrow he would be the one denouncing people—denouncing Reds. Adolf made his way to the stairs without answering. He couldn't wait to open the letter. Once he reached his room, he lit a candle and threw himself onto the bed. The windows were all broken, and the temperatures were very low despite the arrival of spring. In Munich, more people were dying of hunger and cold than from communist bullets. The young man wrapped himself up in a thin blanket, then opened the envelope. He didn't recognize the small, tight handwriting. He turned the page and looked for the signature. The name made him jump.

Weistort was back.

April 7, 1919
Pasewalk Military Hospital

Dear Adolf,

I'm still at Pasewalk, where things have returned to normal. The proletarians, who began the revolution by nationalizing the wine cellar, did not put up much of a fight when the military police came to restore order. Most of them are locked up. I doubt the justice system will be clement—firing squads are working overtime in Germany at the moment. The various attempts at revolution that took place in the northern and eastern parts of the country have all been thwarted. Munich is the only place where the communist revolution is still in full swing. You must have a front-seat view to hear them singing "The Internationale" and watch them brandish red flags. But the songs will be followed by bullets. The new government and the army cannot tolerate such a rebellious enclave of sedition. Repression will soon reach Munich, and the colour red will move from the flags to the blood that will flow in the streets.

That's why I'm writing to you now.

Ten years ago, in Vienna, we met, thanks to Jörg Lanz. The ideas he spread through the journal Ostara *made their way beyond the Austrian borders, reaching many fans in Germany, and particularly in Bavaria. Indeed, I made several trips to Munich to meet with readers. Many of them felt that the ideas propagated by the journal needed to find expression in the political realm. So, they created a group—the Thule Society—whose members aim to infiltrate and influence political parties. Today the Thule is the leading clandestine force working against the red dictatorship in Munich. And if the army soon takes back the city, as I believe it will, the Thule Society will be at the helm. As such, it seems crucial to me that you join them. They are the future of Germany. They defend the purity of the Aryan race and fight for the swastika. You'll be right at home—their ideas and symbols are the same as those from* Ostara!

And they need someone like you. Hundreds of thousands of soldiers have been demobilized all over the country, left hopeless and penniless. They are the ideal prey for the communists, who will try to win the upcoming elections in the wake of their failed coup. They were unable to win power through combat, so they will attempt to do it via the ballot box. The Thule Society doesn't need a politician to talk to the men who responded to the discipline and solidarity of the trenches throughout the war—they need a soldier like you, someone who has first-hand experience of their suffering. In Munich, you can be the man of the hour. You've wondered about your destiny for so long, and now it's knocking at your door.

I've told our friends in Munich about you. They're eager to meet you. One of them in particular. His name is Rudolf Hess, a former soldier, like you. An aviator. He will introduce you to the others.

The Thule Society meets on the last Monday of each month at nine o'clock in the evening at the Vier Jahreszeiten Hotel, Maximilian Strasse, 17. It is led by Count Rudolf von Sebottendorf.

I'm certain you still have the swastika. Show it to them to gain entry.

Warmest wishes,
Weistort

Hitler quickly folded the letter and placed it over the candle flame. As it burned, he carefully studied the envelope. It didn't appear to have been opened. The triangular edge was perfectly smooth. There were no bubbles, so it couldn't have been steamed open. Neither the army nor the post services had intercepted Weistort's message.

While checking the envelope, he had been thinking. Though his faith in his friend Weistort remained strong, the myths and neo-Templar rituals of *Ostara* seemed outdated now. His return from the trenches had opened his eyes once and for all. Something had to be done to get rid of the traitors who were killing Germany. Not the communists—the army would take care of them—but all of those who had stabbed the country in the back and forced it to lose the war and submit to a humiliating peace. The corrupt bankers, greedy merchants, and slave-driving industrialists were the real enemies. Alongside the bourgeois opportunists, the degenerate aristocrats, and the rapacious Jews—a whole family of criminals that must be eradicated.

That's why meeting in a grand hotel with what was left of the dominant class didn't tempt him. He hadn't survived the trenches to help save the same old-world order that benefited the rich and profiteers. But Adolf had learned to be wary of his own antipathies. He knew he was strong enough now to use others without being used. Maybe these old conspirators could help him after all. One name—von Sebottendorf—intrigued him. And he knew where he could find out more.

"Is there a problem, Herr Hitler?" asked the surprised building manager, holding out his candle as if he had trouble recognizing his tenant.

"You said you used to work in the finest hotels in Munich, didn't you?"

"Quite right, and if circumstances outside my control hadn't—" Hitler cut him off.

"Do you know the Vier Jahreszeiten?"

"Do I know it? It's the best hotel in Munich, where the cream of the crop are regulars. Nothing but high-society types. Fortunes as solid as rock, families that date back to the Crusades—"

"Speaking of which, do you know Count von Sebottendorf?"

"The Turk? Of course!" exclaimed the building manager. "He divided his time between the Vier Jahreszeiten and the Four Seasons. And he rented a full apartment every time."

"Why do you call him the Turk?"

"They say he lived in Turkey for a long time, where he studied the history of religions. In any case, he didn't have to work. Money flowed from his hands, but he used it all to buy books. His servants spent all their time building bookcases!"

"Did he fight in the war?" asked Hitler.

The building manager smiled knowingly. "People like him don't fight in wars, Herr Hitler. Others fight for them. With his contacts in Turkey, he was a precious asset for the government. He had many official visitors, and . . ."

Adolf drew closer.

"Well, he's a Freemason. High-ranking. He often rented rooms at the hotel for their ceremonies. And believe me, the attendees were a smart set!"

Hitler didn't react to the word "Freemason". He had enough political savvy to know that there were many different kinds of "brothers". The real question lay elsewhere.

"And politically?"

The building manager tensed and straightened as if he were coming to attention. "Von Sebottendorf? A pure nationalist. A true German!"

Hitler walked over to the calendar hanging on the door of the office. *The last Monday of each month.* He ran his fingers over the dates. 26, 27, 28. He stopped. The 28th. That was the night he would meet the Thule Society.

PART THREE

To understand the very essence of Nazism, you must first hate reason.

Colonel Karl Weistort

37

"What are you doing?"

"I'm making you a toy, sweetheart."

The little girl moved closer to her father, who had his back to her. He was busy at his workbench. The banging of the hammer and the smell of damp wood chips and paint filled the air. She liked the scent. It was soothing.

"Can I see it?" she asked.

"Aren't you curious!"

She walked around the hunched silhouette and stood on her tiptoes.

"What is it?" she asked impatiently.

"A surprise."

She focused on the table, where she saw a strange object. A wooden sculpture about the size of a phonograph. Her father was dipping a brush in a pot of bright-red paint and slathering the viscous liquid on the sides.

The brush waved to and fro over the sculpture, leaving it the colour of a crushed tomato. A swarm of tiny drops gushed through the air, staining the pine board from which the tools were hanging.

"Be careful, Papa. You're getting it everywhere."

Her father wasn't listening. He kept slathering the paint on the object without a care in the world. The little girl even got some on her face. Annoyed, she pulled on his trouser leg. "Stop it, I'm covered in paint."

"It's all right, I've finished."

Her father turned around to the light and brandished the toy before him. She screamed in horror. His face was covered in a red film dotted with a host of black pustules. As if someone had ripped his skin off. In his hands, he held a huge swastika dripping with warm blood.

"Look, Princess," he laughed. "Here is your present! The third swastika. The blood swastika. The heart of power. With it, you can conquer the world."

The terrified little girl huddled at the back of the room.

"Please, Papa. I don't want—"

"You can't refuse, or humanity will perish!"

Laure woke with a start. She blinked several times at the malevolent red eye above her. It took her a few seconds to realize that it was a lamp bolted to the inside of the Lockheed Hudson. The deafening roar of the Pratt & Whitney engines finally brought her consciousness up to speed.

It was just a nightmare. But the evil swastika had seemed so real.

Drops of sweat beaded on her forehead. Her mouth was dry, and her lips were cracked, as if she hadn't had anything to drink in days. The young woman sat up with difficulty. Her back was sore all over. Like the rest of the team, she'd lain down in a sleeping bag on a thin mattress directly on the metal floor.

"The Royal Air Force seems to put little thought into comfort for its guests. A total lack of *savoir-vivre*, don't you think?"

Laure turned her head to see the new mission leader sitting to her right, holding out a silver flask.

"Go on. It's my own personal blend of Scotch, Portuguese ale, Spanish lemon juice, and acacia honey. A guaranteed pick-me-up, as long as you don't drink too much."

"No, thank you. I'd rather have some water."

"Whatever you say, Matilda," said Captain Fleming as he took a canteen from his bag and poured some water into the lid.

Laure watched him as she gulped the liquid down. When Malorley had introduced him to the team before they boarded the plane, she hadn't been the only one who was perplexed by their new leader's profile. He was an attractive man in his thirties, rather thin, with bright, mischievous eyes. His hair was longer than the usual navy cut, and the corners of his lips curled into a seemingly permanent smirk. He looked nothing like the tough guys that made up most SOE and SAS commando units. She found it easier to imagine him as a member of England's high society, enjoying casino tables and private clubs. His perfect manners were proof of a meticulous education—certainly not the kind dispensed in the barracks.

"Bad dream?" asked the officer. "You seemed agitated."

"You could say that. Are we far from Malta?"

"No, we should be there soon."

She looked out the window to see a full, white moon sparkling in the sky, reflected by silver foam on the sea. The scene was better suited to a honeymoon than a war. She closed her eyes, and the soft, handsome face of her lover at the Ritz appeared. It had been a magical night. Unbelievable. No one had noticed them. The morning after, they'd gone their separate ways, promising to see each other again. He'd left her an army address to write to him. That is, if they both survived their missions. Unlikely.

She chased Bradley's face from her mind, then turned towards Fleming. "Can I ask you a question, Captain?"

"Go ahead."

"Why did they put you in charge of this mission?"

He smiled enigmatically. "I like Italy, and Venice in particular. I have wonderful memories of the place, of Carnival. You'll never get lost in the labyrinth of canals and winding streets with me. Plus, I speak decent Italian . . ."

He clasped his hands under his chin, leaned his head to the right and slowly intoned, "*Vanno spavalde, nude, disarmate, armate solo dei loro vestitini per espugnare una loro remota Gerusalemme celeste.*"

"In English?"

"It's a passage from a poem by Elio Pagliarani. *They walk naked, unarmed, armed with nothing but their little dresses to conquer a faraway celestial Jerusalem.* A bit like you, right?"

"I don't think so, Captain. And you didn't answer my question. I doubt they chose a poetry lover to lead this mission."

"You're right. But you won't get anything else out of me. For the moment—"

A siren sounded in the cabin. The door to the cockpit jerked open. An RAF pilot in a sheepskin flying jacket emerged and shouted, "Hang on! Enemy planes! A lot of them. An Italian squadron."

The four other members of the commando unit had also got up. The turbulence was terrible, as if the Hudson was being guided by a drunk aviator.

"And we don't even have a machine gun set up in the rear!" continued the pilot worriedly.

Laure held tightly to a handle hanging from the cabin ceiling and glued her face to the window. Outside, the moon shone on the Hudson's right wing.

"Are we far from Valletta?" yelled Fleming.

"No," replied the pilot. "But the landing gear is—"

Before he could reply, a barrage of bullets tore through the fuselage. His head exploded like a dropped egg. Bits of his brain splattered onto Laure and Fleming. A cry rang out to Laure's right. One of the SOE agents lay on the floor bathed in his own blood. Just as she was about to tend to him, a second wave of gunfire ripped through the plane. A muffled explosion then sent it into a nosedive. The passengers who hadn't grabbed onto handles banged into the sides of the cabin. Their bags flew wildly this way and that. Only the chest of weapons remained strapped in place.

"Don't let go!" shouted Fleming.

Laure clutched the handle as best she could as her body hung towards the back of the plane. Through the window, she saw that the engine under the right wing had turned into a ball of fire.

The Hudson went into a spin, then back into a nosedive, roaring in pain.

Laure's handle broke. She was thrown to the back of the aircraft as if an invisible hand had pulled her down by her ankles, and found herself pressed against the body of a man who seemed to be glued to the cabin wall. The last thing she saw before passing out was the pilot's maimed face and his bloody lips, far too close to hers.

38

Tristan had got comfortable in the library, which was bathed in darkness at this hour, enhancing its mysterious atmosphere. As a child, he'd often wondered what books did when no one was around. Did they stay obediently on their shelves, or did they jump to the floor to dance the night away? Before falling asleep, he imagined the books sitting side by side, reading each other. During his solitary reading sessions, he even wondered if the books ever exchanged pages to create a collective work, the book of books, which no one would ever read. Life had forced him to forget his childhood dreams, but he still secretly hoped that one day, in a library, he would discover something that other people had never even dared to imagine.

Tristan had just reached the maps department. It was one of the library's most comprehensive collections. There were heavy atlases and hand-drawn maps scribbled down hastily by eager explorers delighted by their discoveries. It was a real El Dorado for specialists, as long as they didn't preoccupy themselves with the origin of certain works, which came directly from the SS's systematic pillaging of occupied territories. Maps were one of Himmler's great passions. He would spend long evenings dreaming about faraway lands, where his imagination could run wild. Since the German army had invaded the USSR, he had been frantically studying maps of the former Russian empire, breaking it apart like a greedy child as he created new imaginary German states one after another, all the way to Asia. It was a passion he shared with Hitler. *It's best not to trust men who believe that putting their dreams down on paper makes them reality,* thought Tristan.

The Frenchman opened a long drawer and pulled out a map of Venice, which he laid out on the neighbouring table. Despite the centuries, the vellum was like new. Tristan closed his eyes to savour the scent of damp ink. When he opened them, Venice shone brightly beneath his eyes. The city, nicknamed La Serenissima, was depicted at the centre of the lagoon, surrounded by a string of islands, which looked like a handful of stones thrown carelessly into a puddle. He placed his finger on San Michele Island—the city's cemetery, where all of Venice was buried—to get his bearings. Just across from it sat Fondamente Nove, the long stone dock that bordered the entire Castello neighbourhood. That was where he and Erika would arrive; it was just two streets from the Bragadin Palace. Now he needed a more detailed map to study all entry points: both streets and canals. In Venice, any property worth the name had two entrances—one on land, the other on water. Given the stakes, Tristan took the time to master the details.

As he stood up to consult the index, he wondered if an SOE agent in London was also studying up on Venice. Maybe Laure was in a plane somewhere over France, winding her finger through the streets that led to the Bragadin villa. Maybe . . . Shouts suddenly sounded below one of the windows.

Fog was slowly coating the park outside in an impenetrable blanket, which made the presence of the agitated black silhouettes among the trees and undergrowth even more surprising. Inside, though the sun had set, several researchers were still there, watching the tumult through the windows. They heard orders, barked at regular intervals by a hoarse, aggressive voice. The crows alone replied, in a foreboding tone, annoyed by the disturbance.

Rumours circulated throughout the building. A gardener had killed his wife and they were looking for the body on the grounds. A high-ranking official was expected, and they were securing the area . . . Tristan had advised Erika not to explain why Heydrich's men were there. For the moment, it was better to let her employees imagine what they would. They would learn soon enough that a priest and a police officer had been murdered in the neighbouring village, and that the Gestapo suspected the killer worked for the Ahnenerbe.

Tristan had already noticed that Heydrich's henchmen were focusing their attention on the estate's outer wall. They must have found the door and inspected the lock by now. Could specialists tell if it had been used recently? The Frenchman couldn't answer his question, but the risk was high enough that he had to act. He left the window and made his way down to the sorting room—a former ballroom where the artefacts found at the various dig sites around the globe were gathered and organized. Erika didn't say much about these foreign missions, most of which had been launched by her predecessor, Weistort. In the corridors, people whispered that the Ahnenerbe was conducting excavations in South America and near the Arctic Circle, but nothing was ever confirmed. When Tristan entered the room, workers were still opening wooden chests and carefully placing their contents on a long glass table, despite the late hour. Von Essling was checking their registration numbers and descriptions in a notebook that bore the Ahnenerbe seal.

"I see the objects from Crete have arrived," said Tristan when he recognized a fragment from a fresco of leaping dolphins.

Absorbed in her work, Erika simply nodded. The Gestapo's presence made her nervous as well. While she was certain the murders in the village had nothing to do with any of her researchers, she had doubts about Heydrich's motives. If there was an area in which Himmler excelled, it was manipulation. After all, he'd taken down the Minister of War, General von Blomberg, by revealing, just after his wedding, that his new wife had been a prostitute. His sudden interest in the Ahnenerbe was suspicious. It was a risk she needed to mitigate quickly, before it became a threat.

Tristan noticed the gold pendant engraved with a swastika, which they had found near Amalrich's empty tomb, sitting off to the side. It seemed to be even shinier than it had been in Knossos, as if its precious metal had been moulded the day before. Not a single dent or scratch marked its surface. It seemed more like a ritual object than a simple necklace.

"You put it aside?" asked the Frenchman.

"Yes, as a gift for the Reichsführer."

"A thousand-year-old swastika—who could say no?"

Tristan moved a lamp closer, to shine the electric light directly on the artefact. The symbol carved into the gold was surprisingly perfect. Each angle was superb, each line precise down to the millimeter.

"It's a bit like a mould," suggested the Frenchman. "Maybe they used it to create a very small swastika."

"You're clearly not an archaeologist," corrected von Essling. "Look at the hole at the top, obviously for a chain to wear it around the neck. It's a pendant, nothing more."

The Frenchman threw up his hands in a sign of surrender. There was no point arguing with Erika on her own turf. However, he could provoke her in other areas.

"So, does Himmler have a mistress? You'll be making her very happy. I'm sure the Reichsführer's lover will be delighted to wear an age-old swastika."

"You'll have to talk to Heydrich if you want to hear about the Reich's sex scandals. You know, the head of the Gestapo, with his sharp features and narrow face. The man whose men are conducting an investigation right under our windows . . ."

Such a discussion would be difficult, to say the least.

"Listen," Erika continued, "we're flying out of Tempelhof tomorrow. By night, to maximize secrecy. We'll land discreetly on the edge of Venice's lagoon. Then a boat with an escort will drop us off near the Bragadin Palace. I hope you're sure about this, because this time there's no room for error."

39

Malta
November 1941

"Wake up!"

"Huh?"

Laure blinked. Red flashes danced in the jet-black sky. A blurry face floated above her. She tried to get up but stumbled.

"Wait, I'll help you up," said the male voice. "Let me."

She felt her body rise. The back of her head throbbed as she tried to stand up straight. She reeled, but two strong hands kept her from losing her balance completely. Captain Fleming's face became clearer, with the smoking wreck of the Lockheed Hudson and its smashed wings in the background. An officer was shouting orders at British soldiers who were working with extinguishers to put out the fire.

The world around her danced; none of it seemed real.

"Where are we?" mumbled Laure, her mouth dry.

"In Malta, at Luqa Airfield, where RAF squadrons 267 and 268 are stationed. I don't know how the co-pilot did it, but he managed to put us down on the runway."

The terrible smell of burnt rubber filled the air.

"It looks like your time's not up yet," said Captain Fleming. "You do have a magnificent bump, though."

"And the others?"

He moved aside. Four bodies covered in black tarpaulins were lined up in front of a jeep with its bonnet open.

"We're the only survivors," he explained. "Not even the co-pilot made it. End of the line for our team members. They're sending replacements, who will meet us at the port. How do you feel?"

"Pretty out of it."

"I can ask headquarters to replace you . . ."

She stepped back and shook her head.

"No need. We're wasting time."

"Up to you. Wait for me here."

Fleming walked over to the officer overseeing the firefighting unit. They talked for a moment, then he came back to Laure, his thumb raised.

"We're good to go. Our saviours put our gear in the jeep," he announced as he checked his watch. "We have four hours to spare. Not enough time to play tourists in Valletta, but definitely enough for a nice long shower at the military port before getting into the submarine for Venice. Follow me. They're lending us a Willys MB. Running a priority mission has its advantages."

He opened the passenger door of the covered jeep, then walked around to the driver's side. As soon as Laure had climbed in, Fleming set off swiftly, the engine roaring. The young woman found herself glued to the back of her seat.

"I thought we had plenty of time," Laure protested.

"Speed is like a vice—once you've experienced it, there's no turning back," replied Fleming enthusiastically.

The jeep sped down the runway past a row of Spitfires and old Gloster Gladiator biplanes, then slalomed between two bombed-out hangars. Soldiers swarmed around a huge smoking crater. Fleming nearly ran over two of them, who shouted a few well-chosen words after him.

"Are you trying to kill more British men than the Italian Air Force has, Captain?" asked Laure.

"Quite the contrary—I'm honing their reflexes. A slow soldier is a dead soldier."

He braked hard at the guard tower at the exit. A tired-looking soldier in an unbuttoned jacket checked their papers and opened the gate. "The main road is blocked," he said. "You'll have to go around, heading south, then get on the main road near the port. There are detour signs. Be careful—we've had reports of lorries on fire."

"Thank you, soldier. And do your uniform up properly. You represent His Majesty!"

Before the guard could reply, the jeep was hurtling down the road.

Laure frowned. "I heard that Malta is under constant siege from enemy bombings. That poor man probably has other priorities than his uniform."

"I disagree. Appearance is directly linked to self-esteem. In difficult times, it is of utmost importance. When my brother and I had the flu, my mother always made us wear our finest suits. It worked every time."

Laure sat up straight. The worn, grey tarmac twisted between hills covered in pines and carobs, whose trunks looked like stone sculptures.

"Please don't go too fast. I didn't survive that plane crash to die in this jeep," pleaded Laure.

The captain slowed the vehicle imperceptibly.

"American engine, sturdy mechanics, a little clumsy. I've never driven this model before. I would have put in an Amherst-Villiers compressor to give it a little more power, but not everyone can make a Bentley."

An orange glow appeared from behind the hill ahead. Fleming took the hairpin turns with his hands tight on the wheel.

"Can I ask you a question, Captain?"

"Please."

"Do you know the aim of our mission?"

"Yes, to get our hands on the third magical swastika that could change the course of the war. When my boss, Admiral John Godfrey, told me about it, I found it all so exciting. Like something out of a John Buchan novel."

"Do you have all the details?"

"Yes, your boss drafted a fascinating report. I spent quite some time studying the operation at Montségur, and what happened before in Tibet and at Montserrat. The double-agent art historian intrigues me. I'm eager to meet him in Venice."

"Tristan Marcas . . ."

"I think of him as John Dee. At least that's the name Malorley provided."

Laure looked away. That was the name she had found in Tristan's file when she'd searched the archives in the secretary's office.

"A very English-sounding alias," she said. "But Tristan is as French as I am."

Fleming smiled.

"You don't understand. John Dee was a famous British secret agent who worked for Queen Elizabeth I in the 16th century. He was a mathematician, an astronomer, and an astrologer interested in the occult. Thanks to his multiple talents, he spent time at all of the European courts. Before he died, he invented a language for speaking to angels and claimed he had found the philosopher's stone. So now you see why Malorley chose his name to be Tristan's alias. He's also a secret agent on an esoteric quest, at the behest of powerful leaders."

The jeep climbed over the top of the hill and braked hard. A long line of cars and lorries sat waiting on the road, engines idling.

"Jesus!" swore Fleming. "Good thing they checked the brakes."

Laure thanked God she had been gripping the door handle so tightly.

The officer cut the motor and held out his silver cigarette case to Laure. She took one for herself and lit Fleming's.

"Malorley should have led this mission, as he did the one at Montségur," said the young woman. "Why has Naval Intelligence stuck its nose into our business? I don't, for one second, believe Churchill's claim that the Admiralty is in charge of secret operations around the Mediterranean."

The officer exhaled a column of smoke. "You're right. I'll give you the real reason: the SOE is the one who elbowed its way into *our* interest in National Socialism and the occult."

Laure's eyes opened wide in surprise.

"We at Naval Intelligence were the first to open the door to the Nazis' haunted house."

40

Munich
April 28, 1919

Located in the most elegant street in Munich, the Vier Jahreszeiten Hotel was a mystery. How could such a place still exist in a city run by a proletarian dictatorship? The revolution seemed to have come to a screeching halt at the foot of the building. Porters decorated like generals hurried to the doors of luxury cars from which emerged women in high heels and men in tuxedos. A carriage drawn by two impatient horses awaited passengers, just as it would have done at the height of the German Empire. Though most of Munich was preoccupied with famine and arrests, the Vier Jahreszeiten seemed to be an island of abundance and safety.

Hitler was stunned into immobility outside the entrance. *This* was where the Thule Society met? He didn't dare try to enter the building in his heavily mended coat and worn shoes. He wasn't worried about what others thought of him—no one really noticed him. The problem was how he saw himself. His poverty and mediocrity were blinding. Nothing had changed since Vienna. Ten years had gone by, and he was still little more than a beggar. The confidence he had developed since regaining his sight at Pasewalk seemed to have suddenly disappeared. He clutched the swastika Lanz had given him tightly. How many more times would he have to face humiliation? Would shame always well up in his throat? He felt like an anonymous knight constantly facing trials without even a sliver of hope. He was angry at himself for being so weak— he couldn't cross the street, climb the steps, and speak to the doorman. He had survived four years under a hail of bullets and shells, but now he was terrified by the idea that the porters might cast disdainful glances his way.

"Herr Hitler?"

Surprised, Adolf swivelled around. A young man leaning on a cane stood before him. His dishevelled hair crowned a large, flat forehead that seemed to continue all the way down to his chin. His face looked like a hastily drawn rectangle with terribly thin lips and unsettling eyes. But the most surprising thing about him was his dark, messy eyebrows, which made him look like a gnome who had only just emerged from the darkness.

"You look exactly as our friend Weistort described you. I'm Rudolf Hess."

Relieved, Adolf held out his hand. "You're a pilot, aren't you?"

"I was. I'm demobilized now and . . ." He studied Hitler's suit. "In need of a kind seamstress to keep my coat together."

For the first time in months, Adolf laughed. Finally, a former soldier like him, who wasn't afraid to joke about his own misfortune. He pointed to the pristine façade of the hotel. They could hear the sounds of music and dancing coming from inside.

"We'll never get in wearing these rags."

This time Hess chuckled. "You'd be surprised. It's like in the old legends: in the heart of the dark and dangerous forest, the castle of promises seems forbidden, unless you know the guard at the door."

"Do you know him?"

"Yes. Do you have the talisman?" asked Rudolf, revealing a swastika hooked to the back of his buttonhole.

Hitler opened his fingers to show his, nestled in the palm of his hand.

"Then the doors will open."

They made their way towards the entrance. A furious porter approached, to chase them away.

"We are guests of Count von Sebottendorf," Hess said confidently.

Clearly impressed, the employee bowed deeply. "Welcome, the Count is waiting in the red room."

★

The hotel lobby was crowned with a stained-glass dome that made it look like a cathedral. The illusion was quickly dashed when Hitler saw the strange company he had fallen into. He'd barely reached the lounge when a young woman in a sparkly evening gown and stilettos asked if he wanted to buy some cheap jewellery. When Hitler compulsively slicked a strand of hair back from his forehead, she burst into laughter and danced away. In a corridor, two men with thick necks and ruddy faces exchanged wrinkled envelopes, then disappeared like shadows. The entire room seemed to be a stage where actors were putting on a comedy of secrets and betrayals. Adolf felt like he was going to be sick—he hated these dodgy people. How could his new friend bear the company of such degenerates? Before he could ask the question, a piano suddenly came to life in a dark corner of the room. Focused on the keys, a grey-haired man played note after note, like a secretary typing away at a machine. It was an unfamiliar noise without any recognizable rhythm or melody.

"It's jazz," explained Rudolf. "It's from the United States."

"But who came up with such nonsense?" asked Hitler, who swore by Beethoven's sonatas.

"Negroes," replied Hess.

A pair of young women with short hair walked past kissing, then erupted into laughter. One of them had slipped her hand into the other's back pocket. It was the first time Adolf had ever seen a woman wearing trousers.

"Gomorrah," he mumbled in disgust.

"Sodom is this way," commented Hess as he pointed towards a window frame, where a soldier in uniform was vigorously embracing a man wearing lipstick.

They stepped up to the bar, where conversations were taking place in several languages. Two impeccably dressed foreigners with perfectly manicured moustaches were chatting alternately in Italian and English as an Asian man looked on, constantly wiping his brow.

"And here is Babel," added Rudolf.

"Why are you putting me through this? Is it some sort of test?

A joke? Are you making fun of me?" asked Hitler, clutching the swastika even more tightly in his right hand.

Before Hess could answer, one of the bartenders approached and welcomed them as he would his regulars. "Might you gentlemen be interested in foreign spirits? We have everything you could dream of: French cognac, Scotch . . . And most of them are over ten years old."

Adolf almost choked. He never drank and found those who overindulged repulsive. He grabbed his neighbour by the sleeve.

"Let's leave this place! Take me to where the Thule Society meets."

Rudolf made a calming gesture. "I'll have a cognac. A Rémy Martin."

"Excellent choice, sir. Why don't you have a seat in the armchairs near the fireplace? I'm certain the two men already sitting there will appreciate your company."

Hitler followed reluctantly as Hess said hello and sat down.

"Do you fancy a good cigar?" asked one of the strangers. "Despite the shortages, we still have a nice collection. Havana or Dominican, your choice."

Adolf spoke. He'd had enough of these slights. "I can't stand tobacco. I would appreciate it if you could abstain."

"This place doesn't seem to agree with you."

Hitler stared at the man. His face was heavy, swollen, with red cheeks, his chin hidden in folds of fat, his eyelids drooping. In a few years, the thick, gelatinous flesh would cover everything. Only his light-grey eyes, like something from a faraway land, pierced through it all.

"This place is full of abundance and excess when the people are dying of hunger," said Hitler, annoyed. "It seems to be home to the vilest corruption, shameful debauchery, and odious prostitution."

"All very useful things in times of crisis. Do you really believe wars are won with guns alone?"

Disgusted, Adolf turned to Hess. "You promised to introduce me to the Thule Society."

"And I have done."

Dumbfounded, Hitler returned his gaze to the heavy man, who nodded ironically. "I am Count Rudolf von Sebottendorf, and this is the realm of the Thule Society."

The syncopated rhythms of the piano had been replaced by a languid melody played by a string ensemble. Couples were making their way to the dancefloor.

"Most people only ever see the whirlwind that events leave in their wake," explained von Sebottendorf. "It all moves too fast, reaches too far. Now the world has picked up its pace and no longer reflects an image we recognize. That has made people scared and aggressive."

Despite his initial surprise, Hitler listened attentively. The Thule leader's words resonated with him. He perfectly expressed what an entire sacrificed generation felt deep down. German society had fallen apart, suddenly carried away in the current of defeat and ravaged by the swell of revolution. Millions of people had been left behind, alone amidst the debris, lost, terrified, and angry.

"It's a mistake to believe that you can stop history when it's only speeding up. It has its own rhythms. Fighting them is useless. On the contrary—"

"You mean we must keep pace? Follow along? Fall into decadence and corruption?" interrupted Hitler.

"Not at all. History is like a tornado—if you're in the eye, you're safe. If you place yourself at the unmoving centre of events, you become the pivot point."

Von Sebottendorf gestured towards the dancing couples. "Where do you think you are? In a shady club where what's left of the aristocracy, the rich middle classes, crooks, and whores forget about their troubles, thanks to alcohol and music? No, you're in the Thule's kingdom, where we bury the past and resuscitate the future."

Hitler wondered if he'd made a mistake. Maybe the count was just another illusionist, an opportunistic con man.

"Haven't you wondered how it is that this place is still standing, despite the red revolution?" the count continued.

Adolf's eyes confirmed that he had.

"Because this is the only unmoving point in the chaos that is Munich."

"Everything can be bought, sold, and traded here," Hess broke in. "That's why the communists haven't shut it down. They know that although this place seems to be a den of pleasures, it's really Munich's stock market. And they need it."

"But why?"

"Because this is where you come to bribe an army driver who delivers arms; this is where you can pay a girl to sleep with and spy on a high-ranking officer . . ."

"That's disgusting," exclaimed Hitler.

In a slow, measured tone, von Sebottendorf replied, "Corruption is just politics through other means. The communists believe they're taking advantage of it, but nothing guarantees that we're delivering accurate information or weapons in working order."

"The government is sending troops to the city," explained Hess. "Fighting will begin soon, but the military fears it may turn into street fighting. From barricade to barricade and building to building. Munich wouldn't survive. That's why the Thule Society has infiltrated this place—to weaken the communists and pave the way for the German army."

Von Sebottendorf pulled out a swastika identical to Hitler's and Hess's and placed it on the table. "This symbol has fascinated civilizations since the dawn of time. You find it in Central Asia and Northern Europe, in Tibetan religion and Catholic churches. Ethnologists say it represents the path of the sun." The count slowly spun the swastika to the left, then continued, "For our friend Lanz, it's the symbol of the Aryan people and of *Ostara*."

"And for you?" asked Hitler.

Von Sebottendorf spun the swastika again, but clockwise this time. "The symbol isn't the important part—it's who's spinning it. The invisible spot in the middle, the secret pivot, and the hand that drives it are what matters."

"The Thule Society," whispered Adolf.

"Today, yes, but we need to begin thinking about tomorrow.

Beyond Munich, to all of Germany . . ." The Count nudged the swastika into a faster spin. "The whole world will join in."

Hess was about to speak when the bartender approached the Count. "Sir, they say the government troops have entered the suburbs. The fighting has been extremely violent. The communists are arresting huge groups of people in the city."

Von Sebottendorf stared at the spinning swastika. "Who knows when it will stop now?" he mumbled. Then he turned to Hess and Hitler. "Gentlemen, I think it's time for you to go."

Adolf stood up first but couldn't hold back his question. "The army is attacking, and the Reds will fight back. What will the Thule Society do?"

The Count seized the young man's hands. "We're going to write history—and this time, in blood."

41

London
November 1941

The Green Lion was one of the few pubs east of Kilburn High
Road where regulars could still get a beer late at night without
worrying about being fleeced when they stumbled out. It didn't
look like much—the yellowed windows set into the greenish cement
walls were far from inviting.

This Irish bastion in North London was like a second home to
the heads of the local mob and Irish Republicans, who tolerated
zero violence. It was full of gangsters, IRA members, recently freed
prisoners looking for jobs, and people who were simply nostalgic
for their native Eire. Every last one of them was Irish. Not a single
police officer, snitch, or private detective would dare enter this
venerable institution. The owner —a pure Irishman in his sixties,
who had spent more than twenty years in His Majesty's prisons—
had an eye for intruders. No one knew his real name; everyone
called him Old Uncle, and none of his customers would be stupid
enough to ask why. He'd been placed at the head of the establishment by a neighbourhood boss long ago.

When a fat bald man pushed through the door, Old Uncle
studied him warily. The trespasser didn't look Irish at all. His
affected, feminine appearance spoke volumes. Aleister Crowley
disinterestedly scanned the room. He'd visited much more
dangerous places over the course of his life. He walked over to
the bar with its green, white, and orange Irish flag. On a pillar
next to the tap, there was a caricature of John Bull getting his arse
kicked by a laughing green donkey.

"You have a fine establishment here, sir. You must be very proud of it."

Old Uncle shrugged. The man's accent was indefinable, but it definitely wasn't local. "Either you drink, or you leave."

"Perfect, I'm thirsty. Give me a glass of your best wine."

The bartender couldn't help but smile. One of the customers sitting on a stool chuckled.

"Hey Uncle, this loafer thinks he's real funny, dun' he. Wine . . . Why not champagne, while you're at it?"

"We don't serve wine here. You should look elsewhere. Turn left outside, then head straight for the Thames, where you can catch a boat to France."

Laughter sounded throughout the bar. Crowley smiled.

"Ah, I see, you have a limited selection. All jokes aside, I have an appointment with Moira. Is she here?"

The owner nodded and gestured towards a door at the far end of the room.

"Thank you kindly, friend," said Crowley. "Bring me a beer, one that won't burn a hole in my stomach. A Kilkenny will do nicely."

The mage crossed the bar without paying any attention to the insistent stares. He found himself in another room full of booths. He quickly recognized Moira's red hair. She was reading a newspaper as she sipped a Beamish Stout that was as dark as her soul.

"Twenty minutes late, Aleister," she said, looking up from her paper. "I was beginning to think you weren't coming."

"I'm sorry. I'm not used to visiting this part of the capital. My cabby almost made me walk the rest of the way."

The owner came in and placed a large glass of beer in front of Crowley. He spoke to Moira in Gaelic, leaving the mage in the dark.

"It's all right, my guest is a good Englishman."

"There's no such thing. You should know that," grumbled Old Uncle as he turned to leave. "The only thing they're good for is hanging."

"Ah, the legendary Irish hospitality," chortled Aleister.

Moira spread the paper out on the table. "Look," she said. "This should interest you. An article on the cemetery at Tower Hamlets. The police have just found the body of a poor girl. The details are horrific. The victim was mutilated."

Crowley took the paper in his hands as if it were a venomous snake. He easily recognized the young woman he'd crossed paths with at the Hellfire. The article went on for two pages and included interviews with the cemetery guards. Apparently, the police had been unable to identify the victim.

"How dreadful," mumbled Crowley. "Did you really have to chop her into pieces like that?"

"Her soul is safe, if that's any consolation. Just like the photographs of you with her. Do you have any information for me?"

Crowley pulled an envelope out of his coat and slid it across the table. She reached out to take it, but he left his big hand on top. "When will you give me the negatives?" he asked.

"Move your hand, Aleister."

He did as he was told, and she opened the envelope to browse a dozen pieces of paper, which she studied carefully before looking up again. "Not much here. We already know where the SOE training sites are, what listening equipment they use, and how the hierarchy works. I'm afraid you won't be useful after all. The reporters will be thrilled to have a new chapter in the macabre Tower Hamlets series. You'll need to find a good barrister . . ."

"Do you really think it's that easy? I can't just show up at SOE headquarters and take what I want. And you didn't look closely enough. Read the second half of the seventh page."

She picked it up again and read more slowly. "Operation Dusk 1 Retrieval aborted . . . *Thule Borealis*. Interrogation of Rudolf Hess . . . I don't understand any of this."

"It's about a mission planned by my superior, which took place in the south of France. At Montségur Castle. The operation apparently failed, and a new mission is underway, but Malorley seems nervous about it all. The operation is somehow linked to the interrogation of Hess."

"You told me he was completely mad."

"If you don't want my information . . ."

"I always feel like you're hiding something, Aleister."

Three men in caps entered the room and sat down in the first booth. The Hellfire Club owner lowered her voice. "I'll send all of this to Berlin, and we'll see what they say. You'll be hearing from me soon."

Crowley stood up without touching his beer. "Do you even know what your good friends the Germans are doing in Europe?"

She looked coldly at him. "Fighting the Russians?"

"Not only. They're doing terrible things. To Jews."

"Just like the English did to the Irish when they rebelled. Like the Inquisition did to witches. Nothing new under the sun of human cruelty."

"You're wrong. It's extreme. They say they're exterminating an entire people."

"I don't have anything against the Jews, and I'm sorry to hear they're suffering, but they're not going to help me free my country from England's clutches."

"Oh, come off it, you stupid Paddy. You got your independence. Ireland is even officially neutral in the war, and Dublin still has a German embassy."

"Not totally neutral. Too many Irishmen still support England, for my taste. They volunteer to fight with your countrymen. And what about Northern Ireland? Our friends in Belfast are still under the Tommies' heels. As long as our island is divided, the fight will continue."

"You choose some strange allies."

"Germany has always defended the idea of an independent Irish Republic. The Kaiser funded our uprising in the last war, and the Führer is supporting us now. He's our friend. It's that simple. And don't think you can give me lessons in morality— you've been invoking the Devil and his court of demons for decades."

Crowley shook his head and made his way towards the exit. As he pushed through the door, he turned back towards Moira. "In this war, Satan has found someone much worse than himself. Much worse."

"Who?"

"Mankind."

Tempelhof Airport, Berlin
At the same time, November 1941

A gust of wind filled the hangar where the mechanics were working on the aircraft. To disguise the Messerschmitt, they were quickly painting over the swastikas that decorated its wings and tail. Erika stood with her back against a corrugated wall, watching the mechanics. One of them was checking the tyre pressure while another was hunting leaks in the hydraulics system. When she thought of the innumerable parts and pieces that had to work together to make a plane fly, she wondered how people ever managed to trust them enough to get on board. For Erika, courage had replaced trust long ago. It was an easier feeling to count on, since it meant she depended only on herself, whereas trust . . .

"The weather might be a problem," announced Tristan. "Especially over the Alps."

Erika looked up, her eyes full of determination. "We can't wait. We have to take off for Venice."

"The pilot will want to talk to you about it."

She stared at her lover for a moment, looking for a shadow of fear or doubt, but she found nothing. If she decided to go, he would climb into the plane with a joke and a smile. But for him, it wasn't courage or trust—it was something else entirely, something she couldn't quite put her finger on. She smiled. She had to admit that, trust or no trust, she loved the man.

"Tell the pilot we're taking off."

42

Stuck in traffic, Laure and Fleming got out of the jeep to smoke their cigarettes as they contemplated the arid landscape. The starry night had enveloped the surrounding countryside. A cool breeze announced the arrival of winter in the Mediterranean.

"It's so peaceful," said Fleming. "It's hard to believe the island is under siege by the Italians and Germans, that the whole world is overrun by fire and blood."

"We're in the eye of the storm, but not for long . . . You didn't finish explaining how British Naval Intelligence became interested in the Nazis' penchant for esotericism."

"It all started in May 1940. A week before the German offensive moved into France, Belgium, and the Netherlands, Goebbels, the head of Nazi propaganda, had hundreds of thousands of tracts bearing quatrains by Nostradamus printed. The prophecies alluded to an Allied defeat and Germany's triumph. The texts, in French and Dutch, were air-dropped on the population to demoralize them. After Germany's victory, Goebbels openly bragged about the operation."

"Don't tell me people believed those predictions!"

"They did. We watched huge groups of refugees flee south, because the prophecies said the south would be protected from bombings. As a result, our intelligence services began taking it seriously—not the predictions themselves, but their psychological impact. Naval Intelligence has been a pioneer in terms of psychological warfare. Moreover, my superior, Admiral Godfrey, has always had a personal interest in secret societies, astrology, and the occult. So, he ordered a report on the affair, and I was chosen to oversee things."

Laure decided not to ask why he had been chosen. She would keep that question for later.

"Thanks to several sources," explained Fleming, "I was stunned to learn that German astrologers had been hired by Goebbels to develop this evil propaganda. Two of my colleagues got interested as well and began studying the occultist networks linked to major Nazi officials like Hess, Himmler, and Rosenberg. And to get a better handle on what our adversaries were thinking, we turned to a German astrologer exiled to England, Louis de Wohl. A charming man, though a bit too nutty for me. And we did all of that with the greatest discretion, of course. Unlike the SOE . . ."

"What do you mean?"

"When Malorley went to interrogate Hess at the Tower of London with his colourful friend Aleister Crowley, it set off alarms at the highest levels. That's how my boss learned about the creation of your little group of sorcerers at the SOE and about the quest for the relics."

Laure cut in, annoyed by Fleming's haughty tone. "That still doesn't explain what you're doing here!"

"It's quite simple. My boss went to see Churchill to tell him we had been working on this topic for longer, and, since the Prime Minister can't say no to Admiral Godfrey—a long-time friend of his—they found a compromise and decided to send me into the field. As for Malorley, he's still running the operation. In short, everyone's happy."

"But I imagine you'll send your report to Naval Intelligence?"

"Of course."

The Frenchwoman carefully stubbed out her cigarette. The dry undergrowth around them could easily catch fire. "So, to sum things up, we've got an admiral who's interested in the occult and works with an astrologer, and a secret service devoted to hunting mystical relics. Oh, and a Prime Minister who sends a commando unit to retrieve another magical swastika . . . The British will never cease to amaze me. I have a hard time imagining France's Deuxième Bureau wasting its time on clairvoyants and other fortune tellers."

Fleming exhaled slowly. "Why are you so doggedly rational? All of the great legends and esoteric figures come from your country. Nostradamus, the Cathars, the Templar Knights, spiritualism, the alchemist Nicolas Flamel, the Grail . . . Though for the last one, I think Chrétien de Troyes stole a Celtic legend."

"Nothing but fables!"

"You don't understand, Laure. It doesn't matter whether or not these things really existed. What matters is why our enemies believe in them. Once we know, we can exploit their weaknesses to predict their behaviour."

Engines began to roar, followed by a concert of honking. The road was open again. Fleming gestured to Laure. They got back in the jeep, which took off noisily.

"Could you be more specific, Captain?"

"Take, for example, the invasion of the Soviet Union. Don't you think it's strange that Hitler declared war on Stalin on the 22nd of June?"

"I don't see—"

"Surprising for a Frenchwoman. It's exactly one year, to the day, after Germany signed the armistice with your country. In the Compiègne Wagon. On the 22nd of June 1940."

"And?"

"Exactly one year after total victory over his adversaries to the west, he launches the largest invasion of all time against those to the east! And that's not all. There's also Napoleon."

"What does Napoleon have to do with any of this?"

"Your emperor also invaded Russia on the 22nd of June. The 22nd of June 1812, the day after the summer solstice, the longest day of the year. The Corsican eagle also mobilized the largest army the world had ever seen, exactly like Hitler. Admit it's strange, won't you?"

"A coincidence."

"What you believe is up to you, but pagan lore holds that the day after the summer solstice, the sun's forces go down into the world of darkness to purify it. Once they've accomplished their mission, they return to the surface victorious, for the winter solstice, on the 21st of December. Put yourself in the shoes of a Nazi with all sorts of Nordic beliefs, who is convinced he's on the side of light, then replace the darkness by communists, and you have to admit the symbolism is troubling."

Laure was beginning to understand why Fleming had been chosen for this mission. He was just as passionate about occult coincidences and secret revelations as Malorley.

"Did you know that Himmler celebrates both solstices at Wewelsburg Castle with his entire general staff?" asked the Englishman. "He lights a bonfire that can be seen for miles around."

"Okay . . ."

The jeep kept moving, avoiding the chaos on the road. They could see the lights of Valletta in the distance.

"And I haven't finished with Napoleon and Hitler either. The Führer attacked Russia one hundred and twenty-nine years after your emperor. That number, one hundred and twenty-nine, links the two tyrants in strange ways. Bonaparte was crowned in 1804, Hitler was named Chancellor in 1933. One hundred and twenty-nine years later. Napoleon defeated Austria in 1809, Hitler annexed the same country in 1938. Do the maths . . . It's still the same number."

"What did you do for a living before the war? Expert in coincidences?"

"No, but I've always been fascinated by numbers and I'm exceptionally inquisitive."

"So does one hundred and twenty-nine mean something special?"

"The eternal cycle! One of my friends, a numerology specialist, explained that if you take the Pythagorean sum of one hundred and twenty-nine, you get one plus two plus nine, which equals twelve. Twelve is the number of time and renewal. The same twelve hours that tick past again and again on your watch, the twelve months of the year . . . You see the symbolism. Hitler is an avatar of Napoleon, who has returned after a cycle of twelve symbolic units."

Laure shook her head. "Only an Englishman could come up with something so far-fetched! Napoleon was a great conqueror, not a monster. He didn't invent the Gestapo, and he wasn't anti-Semitic."

"And only a Frenchwoman would say such a thing. He conquered much of Europe, yes, but he was also responsible for millions of deaths. Go and ask the Spanish, the Russians, or the Germans how they feel about him. And let's not forget that he reinstated slavery. But the past is the past. This method can help predict future events. You left your own country to join us, so what do you want to know? Something you care deeply about."

"When will the Germans be ousted from France?"

"Apply the method."

"If I remember correctly, Napoleon left France for Saint Helena just after his defeat at Waterloo in 1815. Which, if we add one hundred and twenty-nine, would give us 1944."

"In 1944, the Germans will have left France, but that doesn't mean Hitler will leave the scene that year."

"We'll have to wait another three years . . . To hell with your stupid figures!"

"That's a shame. I could point out other similarities on the revolutionary side. Stalin came to power in the Soviet Union in 1922, in Lenin's shadow, and rolled out a reign of communist terror. And one hundred and twenty-nine years earlier, it was 1793. The year of the Terror organized by Robespierre in France. And that's not all. There's another link between Stalin and Robespierre. They were born one hundred and twenty years apart."

"But not one hundred and twenty-nine, thank goodness."

"Not so fast. One hundred and twenty is one hundred and twenty-nine's mathematical twin in numerology. If you don't separate the first two digits of the first, it's twelve plus zero, which equals twelve—just like one plus two plus nine. And there are also one hundred and twenty years between the birthdates of Napoleon and Hitler. History has come full circle."

"You have a gift for landing on your feet with your implausible calculations."

"I think there really is a hidden harmony of numbers behind

our perception of reality. I'm sure of it. Look at the intelligence community—it's all about numbers. We communicate using secret codes to obtain information, which is often just a succession of numbers. Coordinates for a bombardment, the quantity of war materials held by our adversaries, the date of an upcoming military operation, the number of a unit on patrol, the speed of a cruiser, a factory's production capacity . . ."

Laure stared at Fleming. She feared he would never run out of examples.

"And the Germans were the first to become obsessed with numbers. You know how far they've taken it? Right up to the executions of their enemies. I've seen terrifying reports on mass murders of Jews carried out by special Einsatzgruppen commando units as they make their way east through Russia. They have precise quotas for the number of people they must kill. The Nazi reaper handles maths with disturbing dexterity."

The car slowed to take a road that wound along the coast.

"We'll reach the port soon. In fifteen minutes at most, if the bloody Italians don't bomb us first," said Fleming.

Laure let her gaze soften on the view before her eyes. She realized that in a few hours she would be under that beautiful sea. She had fled France aboard a submarine, and now another one would take her to meet her enemies once more.

"Why are you so fascinated by numbers?" she asked without looking at him.

"Not only numbers. I'm interested in anything that can influence our adversaries' thinking."

43

Munich
September 7, 1919

Hitler watched as a covered lorry parked in the courtyard outside the barracks. This was the fifth one he'd seen since he'd been waiting in Captain Mayr's office. It was the same ritual every time. Soldiers lifted the cover and pushed and shouted until the men and women inside got out, hands in the air. They were communist suspects who would be methodically interrogated in the building's overpopulated basement.

"Hello, Corporal," said Captain Mayr as he stepped into the room, his monocle in place in front of his left eye and his riding boots gleaming. He was an archetypal *Junker*, an aristocratic officer who made it seem like the German Empire had never been defeated or dissolved. He walked over to the window and lit a short cigar. Hitler refrained from revealing his distaste for tobacco. Captain Mayr ran the Grukko—army intelligence in Munich—and wasn't known for his tolerance of dissent.

"Since the city fell at the end of April, we've arrested nearly fifty people a day. Most of them via denunciations. How many of them do you suppose are simply victims of jealous husbands or spiteful neighbours?"

"I don't know, Captain."

"According to our statistics, almost half. But, you see, the ends justify the means, because these innocent people are so scared of being found guilty that they begin to denounce others in turn. In just a few more weeks, thanks to their reluctant help, we'll have rid Munich of its communist leprosy."

Mayr sat down at his desk, opened a locked drawer, and pulled out a file bearing a red band and the word *CONFIDENTIAL*.

"Sit down, Corporal. I'd like to show you some photographs. Look closely."

When he saw the first picture, Hitler instinctively pulled away. A man was slumped on the ground, his shirt ripped, an anonymous hand holding his head up by the hair like a hunting trophy. Once he'd recovered from his surprise, Adolf leaned in for a better look. He realized the shirt wasn't ripped but riddled with dark holes.

"Dannehl Franz, executed at Luitpold-Gymnasium. Does his face or name mean anything to you?"

"No," replied Hitler.

Mayr slid a new photo across the table. This time, the body was naked on a stretcher. The face was hidden in the shadows, but a milky-white arm hung down towards the tiled floor. Probably a morgue.

"Deike Walter, also executed at Luitpold-Gymnasium. Look closely at his hand."

Adolf brought the image closer but couldn't make out anything particular because of the dim lighting in the photograph.

"His finger was amputated to remove his signet ring. We don't know if he was mutilated before or after he died. Do you recognize him?"

"No, Captain. Why are you asking me these questions?"

"Because you crossed paths with each of these victims just hours before they died. Now, look at this last photograph."

This time, Hitler's expression changed. He tried to minimize it by quickly slicking his hair back. It was a woman collapsed against a wall full of bullet holes. Her murderers had shot her in her evening gown. One of her shoes had rolled across the floor. Adolf recognized her. It was the young woman who had offered to sell him some jewellery at the Vier Jahreszeiten Hotel.

"Heila von Westarp, also shot at the Luitpold-Gymnasium. She was thirty-three years old."

Hitler decided it was best to answer before the Captain asked the question. "I saw this woman in a hotel in the centre of Munich, one evening last April. I suppose these men were there as well."

"Indeed. They were among a group of seven people arrested by the communists at the Vier Jahreszeiten Hotel on the night of the 28th of April, then executed."

"I knew, from the papers, that the communists had executed several people as the army entered the city, but I didn't know the victims had been arrested at the Vier Jahreszeiten."

"What were you doing there?" asked Mayr. "It's not the kind of place for a simple corporal. Or a demobilized pilot, like your friend Rudolf Hess."

"We were guests."

"Of this man?"

Hitler answered without even glancing at the photo. "Of Count von Sebottendorf, yes."

"He's the man the communists were after. They captured and killed seven of his friends as a condolence prize. A very symbolic number, don't you think?"

"I don't know."

"I bet you don't know where to find von Sebottendorf, either?"

Adolf kept quiet as he felt an invisible rope tighten around his neck.

"You're a strange man, Corporal Hitler. With strange friends. Do you have anything to tell me?"

"No, Captain."

"Stand up and go to the window."

In the courtyard, prisoners who had been interrogated were waiting to be transferred. Soldiers divided them into two groups, according to the instructions of an officer who closely studied each prisoner's face.

"Do you know how we identified the executed members of the Thule Society? Thanks to lists, including arrest locations. The communists love bureaucracy. That's a mistake. It's better not to leave records behind," said Mayr as he pointed to a group of prisoners climbing into a lorry. "The Grukko doesn't make lists. We write nothing down," he continued. "We use physiognomists, who take note of the prisoners selected during interrogation, then recognize them when they come out and discreetly sort them into groups."

"I don't understand," ventured Hitler.

"The men you see getting into the lorry will be facing a firing squad in less than an hour. Their bodies will never be found."

Adolf nervously fiddled with his moustache.

"Many of them are former soldiers. Their families are far away, they have no friends. They're much like you, really. So, I'll ask one last time: Do you have anything to tell me about that evening at the Vier Jahreszeiten, Corporal Hitler?"

"No."

Mayr pulled a swastika out of his jacket pocket, placed it on the table, and casually set it spinning.

"Don't ask any questions. Just know that Jörg Lanz, myself, and von Sebottendorf have shared interests, invisible though they may be."

Terrified, Hitler stared at the swastika, which had just gone still.

"I've been a member of the Thule Society since it was founded, and if you had revealed anything about your meeting at the Vier Jahreszeiten, I would have had you shot. Do you know exactly what the Grukko does?"

"It monitors and infiltrates communist movements, their members and leaders, I think."

The lorry's engine started up outside.

"We also crush them. But the Grukko doesn't only fight subversive ideologies—we now also work to prevent them from spreading. And to do that, we need to become political, to engage in preventive politics."

Adolf agreed. Since the spring, he'd been responsible for new recruits' ideological training in his regiment, and he'd been shocked by their lack of understanding when it came to social issues.

"We need an effective propaganda machine," continued the Captain, "to convince the masses, who have been left confused and impoverished by the defeat."

Hitler nodded mechanically as he watched the lorry leave,

carrying the prisoners to a death that he had narrowly escaped. Why hadn't he shared the content of his meeting with von Sebottendorf? Out of loyalty? Vanity? No, his instinct had guided him. Just as it had from Vienna to the trenches and from Pasewalk to Munich.

"To defeat communism, we need to fight it on its own ground— social ideas—and create a rival political movement," explained the Captain. "We have to focus on men out of work, former soldiers, and war widows, to give them hope and restore their dignity."

"If I may, Captain, the Reds are much better than us at spreading their ideas. They have a structured, hierarchical party, proven logistics, and plenty of volunteer activists."

"We don't have the time or the means to create a new structure, so we're going to take a lesson from the cuckoo, which lays its eggs in other birds' nests. Are you familiar with the *völkisch* parties?"

Many political splinter groups had emerged in Germany since the end of the war. All of them wanted to help the country rise up, get revenge on France, and find a scapegoat responsible for their defeat. Most of them were little more than a few raving hotheads. Some of them wanted to bring back to life the Holy Roman Empire from the Middle Ages. Others wanted to reinstate the Teutonic Knights, replace the Latin alphabet with Viking runes, or worship the old gods of Germania and get rid of the Catholic church. The groups were so diverse that they were unable to come together to form a serious and effective political movement.

"We've identified sixty-three *völkisch* groups, but the number is always changing. Schisms are a regular occurrence, and some-times groups simply disappear after a few months. Nevertheless, they are part of a subtle trend with a growing number of followers. The wind is picking up, and we need to make sure it reaches all of Germany."

Hitler thought for a moment. Though he shared many of the *völkisch* groups' ideas, he had nothing but disdain for the way their members spent their time meeting in bars, drinking beer, and barking nationalist slogans. They were disorganized, with no hier-archy or financial resources, and their members were mostly just rabble-rousers. Loudmouths who could barely manage to beat up a starving Jew. He didn't really understand how Mayr planned to use people like that.

"We need to bring these groups together and give them some political weight and media presence. And we need to do it here, in Munich, where most of them are based."

"You do know, don't you, that most of these *völkisch* partisans don't have any political savvy or vision?" asked Hitler.

"Stop thinking like an art student, who believes that, because he's holding a brush, he's better than everyone else, better than those with calloused hands!"

Hitler joined his hands behind his back to hide their unwanted trembling. He hated it when people alluded to his youth.

"These men you belittle will change the course of history. All we have to do is set things in motion."

"How?"

"The country is a body. A body that is suffering because it can't express itself. It needs a voice. And we're going to give it one."

"A voice?"

"Yes, yours."

Given Adolf's silent surprise, Mayr explained. "We've been watching you for a long time, since Lanz in Vienna. Even then you had that mute frustration and blind anger that is now shared by all of Germany."

"Is that why Lanz took me to Heiligenkreuz Abbey?" asked Hitler. "Why did he have me participate in that ritual?"

"Because a voice isn't enough to make the people rise up—you need a strong symbol as well, a magnet to draw them in. That's why Lanz revealed the swastika to you."

Hitler thought about the number of times the symbol had played a role in his life. At Pasewalk when he'd stood up to the revolutionaries. In Munich when he'd met von Sebottendorf, and now here.

"But frustration and anger, even combined with a powerful symbol, won't be enough to bring out the crowds. The man who hopes to embody the people must first face difficult trials."

"The war," mumbled Adolf.

"Yes, the trenches were a crucible: men died there or emerged purified and prepared to meet their destiny."

"Or blind."

"There is always light in the deepest darkness," replied the Captain. "Have you found it?"

Hitler hesitated. Since he'd regained his sight, he had become more and more certain that he could accomplish great things. The one thing that held him back was his lack of faith—not in himself, but in others. Lanz and his occult ceremonies, von Sebottendorf with his secret society, Mayr with his intelligence service. They all roused his innate distrust and awakened his deep fear of being used and manipulated. The war may have been a crucible, but Adolf's paranoia had survived the trenches unscathed. Magnified, even.

He stared at Mayr. This man needed *him*. Not the other way around. That much was certain. So he decided to go along with it. But as soon as he'd figured out the rules of the game, he would be the master of his own future. "Tell me what I have to do," he said.

The officer placed a collection of tracts in front of Hitler. "Here are the names of several different *völkisch* parties. Choose whichever one you like. The German Ring, Wotan's Hammer, The Silver Shield . . . But, if I were in your shoes, I'd opt for the German Workers' Party, founded by the Thule Society."

"The German Workers' Party? Not a great name!"

"True. To reach the people, it's best to speak their language. German Socialist Party has a much nicer ring to it," suggested Mayr.

"If we want to attract millions of jobless men and former soldiers that our defeat has left poor and hopeless, 'national' is the most important word to use," countered Hitler.

The captain held out the tract. "Go and explain it to them. Their next meeting is five days from now, on the 12th of September at the Sterneckerbräu brewery. You have a date with destiny."

44

The military airfield where they'd just landed was located directly on the lagoon. Both pilots were busy readying the plane, which was heading straight back to Berlin. A Wehrmacht unit responsible for Tristan and Erika's safety awaited their orders to board the Italian motorboat. Despite the darkness, the Frenchman was trying to get a good look at the channels that crisscrossed the lagoon, which formed a protective labyrinth around La Serenissima.

"It will take an hour to reach Venice," announced von Essling. "I've sent word to the city's monuments manager. He'll be waiting for us on the dock, to take us directly to the Bragadin Palace."

"You don't want to stop by the hotel first?" asked Tristan, surprised.

"Hitler will be here tomorrow."

Marcas needed no further explanation. Himmler wanted to please his master. The soldiers climbed aboard the boat in their helmets and boots. Erika had a hard time hiding her annoyance. Since Crete and the pile of dead bodies they'd left there, she felt that soldiers only made things worse in delicate situations.

"As soon as we arrive, I'll get rid of these incompetents," she continued.

Tristan remained impassive. His lover had been increasingly quiet of late, as if constantly plunged deep in thought. And when she came out of it, she was in a bad mood. She was under a lot of pressure, of course, but she usually faced it with insolence and a good sense of humour. This change in her behaviour had him on high alert. He placed his hand on her shoulder and pulled her close. She let him but didn't return his affectionate gesture. She kept her gaze focused on the space in front of the boat, which had just entered a larger channel marked by rows of stakes where noisy gulls landed periodically. At the far end, pale lights shimmered like a promise. Venice was about to emerge from the dark waters.

A cool breeze swept across Ospedale dock. Silence reigned over the City of Doges. Across the way, they watched the stocky shape of San Michele island disappear into the fog. The motorboat reached the dock as a handful of mesmerized Venetians looked on. The squad of German soldiers hurried off the boat, jostling the Italians out of the way to form a guard of honour on the floating wooden platform that led to the dock.

Tristan and Erika left the boat next and quickly made their way to the dock. Two rats wove between their legs on their way to seek refuge in a dark alleyway.

"What I love most about you Germans is your sense of romance and discretion," joked Tristan. "The only thing missing is a fanfare! Silly me, I thought we might take a quiet stroll through the city, ride in a gondola . . ."

"We don't have time. We have to find the relic before the Führer gets here. Speaking of which, there's our guide."

A short man in a black coat and shirt waved energetically at them from the entrance to a narrow street that ran perpendicular to the dock. Followed by an assistant carrying a lantern, he hurried towards them. "I'm Matteo Deonazzo, the fascist Grand Council's head of monuments in Venice. Such an honour to meet one of the Reich's most famous archaeologists, even at this late hour!" he said as he feigned a kiss on Erika's hand, then vigorously shook Tristan's. "The Bragadin villa is only a few minutes' walk from here. Follow me, please."

The commander of the Wehrmacht troops gestured to his men, but Erika shook her head. "No, we'll be fine, Lieutenant. Stay here. I'll contact you if we need anything."

"But Miss, I have orders!"

"And now you have new ones. We're just going for a little walk. The neighbourhood is secured, with police officers on every street corner."

"As you wish," said the lieutenant, impressed by von Essling's confidence.

Tristan and Erika followed their guide, who was heading up a narrow street bordered by tall brick walls damaged by humidity. The Frenchman couldn't believe how quickly they'd reached Venice. Barely four hours from Tempelhof Airport. Himmler had lent them one of the fastest Messerschmitt transport planes in his personal fleet. Now more than ever, he was counting on them to regain the Führer's trust. This meeting with Mussolini, which Himmler had found out about at the public announcement, felt like a personal slight. He needed to score some points—whatever the price. Tristan wondered if the Allies knew what a viper's nest Hitler's inner circle really was. Göring would do anything to maintain his position as the Führer's favourite; Goebbels used his wife as bait; and Himmler was using the SS to infiltrate the entire Reich. The fight to be Hitler's successor had already begun.

"I'm very impressed," exclaimed Deonazzo. "You've only just arrived and here you both are, hard at work. And in the middle of the night!"

"The Reich cannot wait," explained Erika. "Is it much further?"

"Just a few hundred meters. Would you like me to give you a tour of a few other palaces? The neighbourhood is full of sumptuous estates with incredible pasts. We'd have to wake the owners, but—"

"No, just the Bragadin Palace," interrupted Erika.

They turned right into a slightly larger street, which led deeper into the Castello neighbourhood. The only sound was the clicking of their boots on the pavement as they walked. The street was deserted. The local businesses had been closed for hours. Light escaped from the poorly closed door of one shop.

"He's risking a fine," sighed Deonazzo, "but how do you keep Venetians from getting together to chat? Especially since they've heard your Führer is coming to visit. Did you know the entire

Santa Lucia train station has been secured? They say the Duce will welcome Hitler on the platform."

Tristan stopped. He'd just recognized the entrance to the palace. A stone archway barred by a heavy door. The pediment bore a sculpted medallion featuring a face of stone.

"One of the many Bragadins who contributed to the history of our city," began Deonazzo as he pointed towards the medallion. "This one—"

"No need for a history lecture," Erika said, cutting him off again. "Who lives here?"

"Well, the palace belongs to a French family. The Montronds. But they're not here, of course."

Tristan was about to ask a question when he noticed Erika's impatience growing.

The historian, who was now afraid of the archaeologist, rang the bell.

"We contacted the caretaker. Since the owners had left him a set of keys, he's readied everything for us, turned on the lights."

A sleepy Italian man with a greying beard slowly opened one side of the massive door, revealing a long garden. Trees that hadn't been pruned in years towered almost as high as the building's façade, the top of which was invisible in the darkness. An impressive wrought-iron gate seemed to disappear into the night. Just above it, a window with a loose shutter was lit by a collection of candles. Tristan felt like he was stepping into the past—with no clear path back to the present.

"Welcome to the Bragadin Palace."

45

HMS Triumph's diesel engines purred quietly. The metal monster was floating peacefully on the calm, black water. The only sound was the lapping of tiny waves against the beast's metallic skin. Fleming stood in the tower taking deep breaths of salty air. He told himself he was purifying his lungs, contaminated by the close air and the smell of oil and sweat during his time in the submarine. Nevertheless, the secret agent was desperate for a cigarette. But all sources of light were strictly forbidden by the *Triumph*'s captain, who was standing at Fleming's side watching the coast through a pair of binoculars.

They had reached their rendezvous point—somewhere southeast of Venice, about fifteen kilometers from the entrance to the lagoon two hours early. The captain had been able to navigate above water for most of the night, gaining speed and recharging the accumulators. The ship had made its way up the Adriatic without any trouble, diving just once, off the coast of Brindisi, when an Italian squadron neared, probably on its way to Libya.

Fleming looked down. Laure was sitting on the main deck with the three new members of the commando unit who had been sent to replace the victims of the Malta crash. They were from the elite Special Air Service, diverted from rejoining their regiment stationed in Egypt. Fleming had briefed them on the mission, without revealing the ultimate goal. They were all wearing fishermen's clothes, including Fleming, who sported waterproof grey trousers, a thick grey woollen jumper, and a navy-blue woollen hat. Three dinghies were attached to the flanks of the *Triumph*, with the commando unit's equipment carefully strapped into the last one.

Suddenly, the captain tensed and pointed towards the lagoon. Flashes, short then long, appeared in the night. He easily deciphered the Morse code and said softly: "*The Doge is sleeping in his palace.* That's the agreed signal—perfect."

He put down his binoculars and touched the shoulder of the sailor leaning over the transmission device. "Transmit: *His children are back.*" The sailor did as he was told, and a series of flashes escaped from the tower.

The captain turned towards Fleming. "Our Italian friends are here. Get your men ready to go."

"Don't take this the wrong way, but I will be delighted to set foot on dry land again. I couldn't have lasted another minute in your tin can. Your no-smoking rule drove me crazy."

"It was only twenty-four hours! We'll be back in four days. I've always wanted to visit Venice with my wife, but I'm not jealous of your stay here now. There must be more policemen and fascists in the streets than tourist couples. Good luck."

"Thank you, Captain. I'll bring back a souvenir for your wife."

Fleming quickly climbed down to the deck, then into one of the dinghies, which shifted under his weight.

"Can't we just go directly to Venice in the submarine?" asked Laure as she helped him get settled in the back of the boat.

"We could, but only if we want to spend the rest of our days as fish food at the bottom of the lagoon. Venice is one of the Italian navy's main bases. And Trieste, just north of here, is one of Italy's most strategic ports. The area is littered with underwater mines and motorboat patrols armed to the teeth."

A muffled purr bounced off the surface of the sea as a fishing boat suddenly emerged from the darkness. The boat was impressively large, with a massive rust-coloured dredger—a feature unique to the trawlers working in this part of the Adriatic—positioned over its bow.

The members of the commando unit plunged their short oars into the freezing water. It took them a little over ten minutes to reach the sides of the fishing boat, where sailors helped them climb aboard. A short man, around sixty years old, wearing a weathered cap, welcomed Fleming and glanced at Laure with surprise.

"Welcome to the Veneto," said the man with a strong Italian accent. "I won't give you my name. I don't want the fascists to find me if they catch you and make you talk."

"Same here."

"We'll put you in the hold," explained the Italian. "I apologize for the smell of fish, *signora*."

He quickly inspected the two agents, then turned the folds of their hats up on the right side of their faces. "That's a bit better, but I doubt it would fool any real fishermen. We don't wear trousers or jumpers like that in these parts. You look like you bought them at a costume shop."

"You speak our language well for . . ." replied Fleming, who stopped mid-sentence.

"For a little Venetian fisherman? Of course I do! I run a salting and exporting company, and before the war, I worked quite a lot with your compatriots. Let's go up to the bridge. 'Let's get moving', as our beloved Duce likes to say."

Laure and Fleming followed the captain to the bridge, where the Italian took the helm and activated a lever on his left. The engine made the entire hull vibrate as the strong smell of diesel fuel filled the little room. The boat took off so quickly that Laure and Fleming almost fell backwards as the captain smirked.

"She's got an Isotta Fraschini engine. It could take us to the ends of the earth. Or almost."

"Where will you leave us in Venice?"

The fisherman shook his head. "We've had a change of plans, my friend. With Hitler and Mussolini in town from tomorrow, the authorities have doubled patrols. All ships are being searched before docking in the city. We'll be making a little detour on an island in the lagoon. An island I would have preferred to avoid . . ." He concluded by spitting on the ground and swearing in Italian.

"He doesn't seem pleased," whispered Laure.

"Could you be a little more specific, Captain?" asked Fleming.

"We're going to Poveglia. It's an island Venetians believe is cursed. Lepers were sent there to die in the Middle Ages. Later it was used as a prison. And now it's an asylum. They say ghosts will haunt the island forever."

"Charming. And then what?"

"The fascists and *carabinieri* won't go near Poveglia. The head of the establishment is a friend to our cause. He's found a clever way to get you into Venice."

"How?"

"He's going to kill you," the captain replied without the slightest hint of irony.

46

The blanket of clouds suddenly disappeared as the plane dived down into a sea of light. Göring's plump finger pointed to the rays of sunshine, which sparkled like liquid gold on the Junker's wings. Hitler leaned towards the window for a moment, then returned to the comforting darkness of his seat. He didn't like the light. He gestured to his secretary, who was at the ready with a notebook.

"Take this down. For the leaders of the Hitler Youth. Limit members' exposure to the sun. It's very bad for their health."

Hess, who was sitting a row back, nodded. As usual, the Führer was right. Preserving the new Germany's human capital was essential. A true Nazi had to lead an exemplary life. Like Hitler, who drank nothing but water, despised tobacco, and ate a vegetarian diet. Not like Göring, whose enormous stomach hung over his belt and whose breath reeked of cigars.

"And this. For today. Schedule an open hour when I arrive in Nuremberg. I want to see Himmler," continued Hitler.

Goebbels's worried voice echoed through the cabin. He was sitting in the back of the plane writing Hitler's closing remarks for the Nazi party convention. The first since Hitler had been elected Chancellor in April. "But, *mein Führer*, you have meetings with the local party officials, followed by a session with the mayor . . ."

"Don't worry, Joseph, we'll just push them back a little. I believe Magda's already in Nuremberg?"

"Yes, she's organizing the day for the ladies of the party."

"Ah, Joseph, you have such an exceptional wife!"

Goebbels forced a smile. Three days earlier, he and Magda had hurled vases and plates around their Berlin home. His "exceptional wife" seriously lacked empathy when it came to her husband's need to meet with young actresses, to convince them to star in propaganda films for the glory of the Reich.

"We're about to begin our descent towards Nuremberg," announced Göring. "The city will appear to the left. I've asked the pilot to fly low."

Hitler didn't answer. Comfortably ensconced in his seat, he watched as the city slowly took shape. First the outer suburbs, then the medieval city with its maze of streets and old houses. Huge Nazi banners covered the towers of the cathedral, from the steeples to the foundations. Now even the Church had recognized Nazi supremacy. Hitler savoured his victory. In a handful of years, he had established the reign of the swastika—which he wore in his buttonhole—over all of Germany. The pilot took the plane lower still. Party members were practising marching in a tree-lined street. Tomorrow there would be hundreds of thousands of them from all over the country, here to celebrate his rise to power. Germany and Adolf Hitler were now one and the same.

Hess studied the Führer. Who would have thought the nobody he'd met fifteen years earlier in Munich could become the beloved leader of the Reich? It was like he'd been anointed, blessed with some unknown grace.

"Rudolf!"

"Yes, *mein Führer*," replied Hess as he sat down next to Hitler under Goebbels's and Göring's watchful eyes.

"Tell me, Rudolf, do you ever think of the past?"

"I was just thinking about Munich. That's where we met for the first time."

Hitler remained impassive. He also remembered Munich, the civil war, the poverty, and so much more. As they flew over Nuremberg, where his supporters were preparing to cheer for him, he could truly measure the strides he had made, from those difficult years in Vienna up to the Chancellery in Berlin. But now he only wanted to remember the destination, symbolized by the huge esplanade that had just appeared below, the *Reichsparteitagsgelände*, where the party would celebrate his victory.

"Whatever happened to the Thule Society?" asked Hitler.

"It no longer exists. Its members have scattered."

"And von Sebottendorf?"

"He lived in Turkey for many years. He can live out his days there."

Hitler gently tapped Hess's hand. They understood each other perfectly. Himmler would take care of the rest. The fuselage shook as the pilot lowered the landing gear.

"*Mein Führer . . .*" announced Göring.

"I know, Hermann," interrupted Hitler. "We're here."

Crowds pressed against the barricades, guarded by SS soldiers in black uniforms, all along the Führer's route. Standing in the Mercedes which had been specially modified for the parade, Hitler saluted, raising his arm to fervent cheering. The driver compulsively checked the passenger-side mirror so he wouldn't miss the German leader's signal. If Hitler placed his hand on his belt after a salute, the driver was to slow down. He didn't have to wait long for the sign. A mother hoisted a child above her head, a bouquet clutched in his tiny hand. The car stopped. The movie camera in the second vehicle didn't miss a moment of the scene. Hitler holding the child, kissing his cheeks. Hitler taking the tearful mother in his arms. The images would be seen all over Germany.

The crowds grew increasingly dense as they neared the city centre. Hitler had sat down and was now simply raising his arm mechanically at every crossroads. He had to save his energy. By his side, Hess was intoxicated by all the cheering, which was growing louder and stronger. "Such passion, *mein Führer*, such passion! The people are enchanted!"

The Mercedes stopped in front of the town hall. After quickly greeting the officials who had been standing there waiting for him for hours, Hitler made his way into the secured building.

"Is Himmler here?" asked the Führer, sending an SS officer scurrying down the corridor to alert his boss.

Before Hitler could shut himself away in the drawing room, Goebbels stopped him. "*Mein Führer*, you must salute the crowds from the balcony. The foreign journalists have just arrived, and they must see how the population rejoices in your presence."

Hitler let his propaganda minister lead him to a window. Goebbels was a compulsive philanderer and a bad husband, but he was the one who had made Hitler a household name throughout the country. He had elevated propaganda to an art form.

The balcony was bathed in sunlight. Blinded by the brightness, Adolf couldn't see anything, but he could hear the sea of people thundering his name. He took off his cap, smiled, and saluted the crowd. He didn't mind not seeing. He had got used to it at Pasewalk. It made it easier to really feel the people's fervour, which filled him with unbridled energy.

"Turn a bit to the left, *mein Führer*. That's where the journalists are."

Once the window had closed, Hitler headed back to the drawing room, where Himmler was waiting, absorbed by a file he was reading. When the Führer stepped in, the head of the SS stood.

"Please sit, Heinrich."

Himmler closed his file and slid it across the table to Hitler. "I have a project I'd like to submit. You know how much the academic community hates us, silent though they may be."

Hitler shrugged. "Emasculated thinkers! Paper-pushers! Useless lumps whose ideas weaken the German nation and corrupt our young people!"

"Precisely. That's why I would like to create a new academic institute entirely devoted to our cause."

"Tell me more."

"I want to recruit all those who have resisted the call of Marxism and democracy and give them a mission: to prove the supremacy of the Aryan race to the entire world."

"Do you have a name for this institute?"

"Ahnenerbe, the Institute for Ancestral Heritage. To affirm our superiority, we must find and prove the existence of our line throughout the ages. I will need archaeologists, ethnologists, anthropologists—"

The Führer raised his hand. "Granted, Heinrich. You can begin recruiting on the SS budget. But do you have someone in mind to run this institute?"

"I'll submit a list of names and—"

"I have a name for you."

Behind his round metal glasses, Himmler's eyes revealed a glimmer of surprise. Hitler wasn't usually one to recommend people.

"Weistort. Karl Weistort."

Himmler had never heard of the man. He would begin investigating him immediately. Heydrich, whom he'd just named head of SS intelligence, would make it a priority. "An excellent choice, I'm sure, *mein Führer*," he said simply.

"Heinrich," asked Hitler, as if he could read Himmler's thoughts, "do your intelligence services have any contacts in Austria?"

"Of course. There are many supporters of our cause there. And quite a few high-ranking officials who feed us information."

"I'd like you to find a man for me. A man named Jörg Lanz. A former monk."

There was a timid knock on the door, followed by Goebbels's voice. "*Mein Führer*, tens of thousands of party members await. They're arriving from every direction and we're having a hard time keeping order. The city will be overrun . . ."

Hitler stood up. Himmler followed suit.

"As soon as I've found him, I'll let you know," replied the head of the SS.

"Don't let me know. Just make sure he goes back to his monastery. For good."

47

The trawler had carefully moored in the island's tiny artificial harbour. A huge, austere, 18th-century building rose up in front of them. Ivy covered the crumbling outer walls. Behind them, further inland, they could see a belfry which looked even older.

Laure and Fleming got off the ship behind the three new members of the commando unit, who were all carrying big canvas bags. They followed the captain's gesture and made their way up a rocky path that ran along the side of the building.

"Hurry up, no dawdling," said the captain.

"I thought we were safe here."

"Yes, but we don't want to disturb the residents of this fine establishment," said the captain as he pointed towards the rectangular façade.

Laure looked up to see a woman with long grey hair in a white coat who seemed to float in a first-floor window. She stared at Laure as she drew something on the pane. Her eyes were open wide, as if she no longer had eyelids. Laure pulled on Fleming's sleeve to point her out to him, but by the time he looked up, she was gone.

"Did you see a ghost?" joked Fleming.

"Very funny. I think she must be a resident here. What did the captain mean when he said the director of the asylum was going to kill us?"

"I don't know. Maybe it's a Venetian joke."

"Back in the Middle Ages, when the black plague struck, they built a hospital here to quarantine those who had been contaminated," explained the captain as he walked briskly. "The same building was later renovated and turned into an asylum. Nearly a hundred and sixty thousand people killed by the epidemic were buried here. You're walking on graves."

A long scream suddenly came from a window with half-open wooden shutters.

"Such showmanship! It sounds like they're cutting people's throats up there," commented Fleming in a less assured tone than he'd intended.

"My God, what was that?!" asked one of the SAS men out in front.

The captain stopped before a heavy iron door, which let out a terrifying creak as he opened it and ordered them all through.

"Don't worry about them. They're Dr. Giamballo's patients. Quickly, inside."

The SAS men looked around warily. "This place gives me the creeps, Captain," said one of them to Fleming.

"Come now, it's just an asylum for the insane. We don't have time for these childish fears," replied the Naval Intelligence officer as he went in first, followed by Laure, who raised an eyebrow at the three hesitant soldiers as she passed.

"If you're too scared to come in, help the fishermen clean the fish," she said. "At least you'll be good for something that way."

The men grumbled, then followed.

A few minutes later, the commando unit and the trawler's captain found themselves in a whitewashed room stacked high with light wooden boards. The only thing on the walls was a dingy painting of the Virgin Mary, a stricken look on her face. Just as they were about to put down their bags, a voice came from a half-open door.

"No, don't bother. We have very little time," said a man in a doctor's coat with pale skin and dark circles under his eyes, partially veiled by small round glasses. Despite being out of breath, he greeted the captain warmly, then shook Fleming's hand. "I'm Dr. Gianni Giamballo, the director of Santa Maria di Poveglia. I'm sorry for the lack of comfort, but this is just a storage area."

Another scream echoed through the building. The doctor smiled, as if it was all perfectly normal.

"Who do you treat here?" asked Laure.

"People with mental—or social—issues. The fascists no longer want to see anything but happy, healthy Italians in the streets. Antisocial behaviours or a lack of productivity are now seen as madness. The authorities send us everyone they see as deviants. We even had one of the Duce's former mistresses for a time. An exquisite woman, though a bit deranged."

"I can imagine . . . Sleeping with a man like Mussolini must be a pretty traumatic experience," commented Laure sarcastically.

"In any case, thank you for your help," said Fleming.

"Of course. I see this regime and its policies as an expression of true folly. Italy—the cradle of art, culture and beauty—doesn't deserve this fate. Many of us are unhappy with what's happening here. You'll meet the head of our network soon. A great man. He's the one who convinced me to join the anti-fascist resistance. Please follow me."

He stepped back through the door, followed by the small group. They walked down a corridor to a chapel with immaculate walls. Five coffins were lined up in front of the altar. The doctor gestured towards them. "I had them made big. I hope you won't be too cramped inside."

The three SAS soldiers immediately trained their Sten guns on Giamballo.

"Is this some sort of trap?" asked one of them. "Do you really think I'm going to let you put me in one of those bloody coffins?"

Laure and Fleming shared a knowing glance. "Now I see what the captain meant," said Laure.

"Put your guns down and let me explain," replied the doctor. "Our establishment no longer receives any financial support from the government, and the amount the families pay isn't enough to keep us open. So, our healthiest patients work in our carpentry workshop making inexpensive coffins. A business which, unfortunately, is always steady. We send the coffins to the centre of Venice by boat. Once in the city, they are sent to the various undertakers.

The *carabinieri* and the Blackshirts won't dare open them, out of superstition, since they come from the cursed island of Poveglia."

Laure stepped over to the first coffin and looked it over in disgust. "How kind, they've put cushions inside," she remarked.

"We've also pierced several discreet breathing holes," added the doctor. "Once you're on the boat, it will take about two hours to reach Venice. Once there, you'll meet the head of our network."

"There is no way I'm getting in one of those bloody boxes," said one of the SAS men as he crossed himself. "I signed up to fight a war, not to play dead." He was sweating and was clearly worked up. He kept his index finger firmly on the trigger of his sub-machine gun.

"I'm afraid we don't have a choice, soldier," said Fleming as he placed a hand on the man's shoulder.

The man pulled away. Fear was written all over his face. He kept looking at the coffins as if they really contained dead bodies. "I won't," he said. "Get away from me."

Fleming pulled a matt, black Browning out of its case and glued it to the soldier's temple. He cocked the pistol. "Put your gun down immediately. Disobeying a direct order in time of war is desertion. I can shoot you right here to protect the mission. Your body can join those of the people who died from the plague. So, choose now: the coffin or the island's mass grave."

The man remained quiet, still sweating profusely as he shook his head.

Another SAS man came over to Fleming. "Captain, I'm afraid it's not that easy . . ."

"Explain."

"Douglas spent a whole night in a grave full of dead members of his regiment during the fighting in France, near Abbeville. He managed to escape in the wee hours, but it left him claustrophobic."

"I'll go anywhere, to hell and back, but not in those damn boxes!"

Fleming turned to Laure, who shrugged. There was nothing to be done.

The Italian doctor intervened. "Captain," he said, "I've treated patients with this phobia, and I don't think he's faking it. Leave him here and we'll see if we can find another way to smuggle him into the city."

Though dissatisfied, Fleming holstered his gun. "Down another man. I'm beginning to think this mission really is cursed," he grumbled.

48

The Bragadin Palace, Venice
December 1941

A black gondola was gliding down the narrow canal. There was
no one inside, and it seemed to be guided by an invisible force.
Or maybe a ghost. Anything was possible in Venice, after all—even
a ghost enjoying a ride in a gondola. Leaning against the railing
of the stone balcony that overlooked the water, Tristan wondered
if the boat might manage to turn at the next junction.

He looked back inside, where he saw Erika perched on a table.
She was studying the details of the painted ceiling, which was
peeling in several places. It depicted a host of *putti*—plump little
angels—as well as baskets of exotic fruit. In one corner, a bundle
of lances sat forgotten against a tree trunk, seemingly suggesting
that after war came heaven on earth. An allegory of Venice, whose
wealth was the result of not only its merchant savvy, but also its
military victories.

They had spent hours inspecting the palace with their guide,
Deonazzo, but had found nothing relevant to their quest. They
had both become experts in the building's history. The famous
womanizer Casanova had lived there for a time after saving the
owner's life. To finance his sexual exploits, the adventurer had
organized seances, and courses on kabbalah, taking advantage of
the gullibility of the owner and his friends to coax large sums of
money out of them. Deonazzo had told them many other intriguing
anecdotes, including one about the French ambassador, who had
had trysts with a young nun in the palace.

While Tristan had let himself enjoy their guide's talents as a storyteller, Erika had continued to display her annoyance and disappointment. Nothing in the history of the Bragadin Palace seemed to be linked to their quest for the swastika. This time, Tristan admitted he couldn't make the pieces fit.

Shouts rang out along the edge of the canal that ran past the foot of the palace. Tristan turned around and saw two men on a jetty trying to lasso the gondola, which had overturned upon hitting the decaying wall of a building that had seen better days. It almost looked like the boat was alive, rearing up furiously as the apprentice cowboys tried to capture it. Tristan smiled at the surreal scene, secretly praying the gondola would make its escape and pursue its poetic journey through the labyrinth of La Serenissima.

The sound of familiar footsteps echoed against the stone. Erika stuck her head through the opening in the French doors to the balcony. "Come on, Tristan!" she said.

He moved regretfully away from the attempt to tame the gondola.

The archaeologist stood across from him, her hands on her hips, a frigid expression on her face. "We're stuck. There's only one explanation: you made a mistake bringing us here."

"I may have," conceded the Frenchman.

"I can't believe you're so nonchalant about it."

Tristan walked over, wrapped his arms around her waist and kissed her. "Maybe, for once, we could see the positive side of things. We're in Venice, which is considerably more romantic than Heiligenkreuz Abbey. We could take advantage and allow ourselves to . . . let off a little steam?" he suggested, slipping his hand under her top to stroke the small of her back.

"No. I need your other talents at the moment."

He hugged her closer. "I saw a plush bed upstairs. There's a staircase just behind this door . . ."

"How on earth can you be thinking about that right now?" she asked, annoyed, though she closed her eyes to enjoy his embrace for a moment before pulling away. "Time is of the essence. We have to get back to work. Even if we don't find anything conclusive, I want to have something for Himmler before his visit with the Führer. We'll start all over again. I—"

Tristan shook his head. "No, I've had enough," he said firmly. "We haven't stopped to breathe for days. I'm exhausted. As soon as we landed we headed straight here without a moment's rest. I'm not German; I'm not a machine. Do you really think barking orders will magically solve the mystery?"

She took a step back, surprised by her lover's reaction.

Deonazzo burst into the room upon hearing raised voices. "Is everything all right, *signora* von Essling?"

Tristan took the Italian man by the shoulder and led him back to the door. "The *signora* and I are in desperate need of some privacy. Please excuse us," he said as he slammed the door.

"You're losing it, Tristan."

"No, I'm just exhausted. I need to spend a whole night sleeping. I need to rest my brain and take advantage of being in Venice. I can't solve mysteries twenty-four hours a day." The archaeologist listened without a word as he continued, his voice filled with exasperation. "And, between us, I don't give a shit about your Führer. As for your damn sacred swastika, you can shove it! After all, it might be better for me if you didn't find the relic, and the Reich finally took a good beating."

The Frenchman collapsed onto a sofa and crossed his arms defiantly. Erika couldn't hide her astonishment.

"You know talking like that could put you in front of a firing squad, don't you?"

"*Me ne frego!*"

"I'm sorry?"

"It's your fascist friends' motto. 'I don't care.' If I'm going to be killed, it might as well be here. Don't they say, 'See Venice and die'?"

She sat down next to him and stroked his cheek. "For your own good, I'm going to forget what you've just said. You're right, maybe I overestimated our ability to go without sleep. I'm tired, too. But before we go to the hotel . . ." she said as she kissed him and straddled him. "You're so attractive when you're angry," she whispered.

"Why don't we go upstairs?" he suggested.

"Don't be so conventional," she replied, forcing him back against the sofa. "Who needs a bed?"

49

Saint Mark's Square was deserted, haunted by groups of pigeons flying in tight formations around the bell tower. Hitler had forgone his usual lie-in to visit the Doge's Palace with Himmler. The Italian police and two SS detachments had blocked all access points, and the lagoon was being closely watched by the navy. The most famous square in the world hadn't been this empty for decades. It was so quiet that Hitler and the head of the SS could hear the tide receding from inside the covered alleyway where they walked.

"They say Mussolini doesn't like Venice," remarked Hitler. "Which doesn't surprise me. He's a country boy from Romagna, incapable of appreciating all this beauty."

"Of course, *mein Führer*," agreed Himmler.

"When you think about it, Venice is nothing like Italy. What do u half-blood from Naples and the people who built this marble city on the water have in common?"

"Nothing. In fact, I'm certain Venice was built by people with Germanic roots," added Heinrich. "As soon as we get back, I'll have our best Ahnenerbe researchers prove it."

Hitler stopped in front of the main door to the Doge's Palace, tracing the shape of the ornate archway with his finger. "Look at that, pure gothic style! Speaking of which, do you know how long Venice remained under Austrian rule? Nearly a century! Maybe I should ask Mussolini to give the Veneto back to us!"

Despite the usual ease with which he hid his feelings, Himmler suddenly panicked. He imagined how the Duce would react when faced with Hitler's demands. "The Toad", as Hitler liked to call him, would be furious.

"Do you plan to talk territory with Mussolini, *mein Führer*?"

Hitler had stopped at the centre of the inner courtyard to admire the immaculate lace of the façades. "I know what you're worried about, Heinrich, but I'm here to discuss something else entirely with the Duce. This isn't just a propaganda trip, as Goebbels believes. Now that we're about to finish off the Russians, we must look elsewhere. To the south."

The naturally suspicious Himmler was surprised. "We're already in Greece and the Balkans, and our troops led by Rommel are fighting in Libya alongside the Italians. You know I have always been against our presence on the other side of the Mediterranean."

"Oh, Heinrich. You'll understand in just a few minutes."

They had just climbed the monumental staircase to the first floor. Hitler didn't bother looking up at the richly decorated ceiling—he hated excessively busy architecture. "I bet Jews worked on the decorations here. So gaudy! Come, I want to show you something."

Himmler felt his heart begin to race. He was always so flattered when Hitler took the time to share his private life, despite his overwhelming responsibilities. It made him feel like he was entering the holiest of holies, the secret place where the Führer was his real self.

"While I was in prison, I spent entire nights devouring books on Venice, imagining this city, this palace. I can't even count the number of times I wandered through its streets in my dreams!"

"You've devoted your life to Germany. You're a saint for the Fatherland!" said Himmler sincerely. Nearly fifteen years had passed between when Hitler joined the future Nazi party and his rise to power. Years of constant battles, during which he had given his time and energy without a second thought. And during the months he had spent behind bars, writing *Mein Kampf* and reorganizing the party from his cell, he had also found the time and energy to study Venice!

"Look!" said the Führer as he opened a door to reveal a room that seemed to have been forgotten by visitors. The air was thick with the smell of old wax. Heinrich raised the blinds on the windows. What he saw amazed him. He had expected to find portraits of wrinkled old doges or of the Virgin Mary, but instead the entire world was before his eyes.

"This is the Maps Room," explained Hitler. "Forget about the sculpted angels and painted ceilings. Forget about the state rooms and all the gold designed to impress and blind visitors. This is the secret heart of Venice. This is where ambition coalesced to become politics."

The globe was spread out all over the wall. Heinrich recognized the Adriatic Coast, dotted with La Serenissima's possessions, then Crete with its unassailable fortresses. Further still, mysterious Africa with its caravans full of gold and ivory. Hitler pointed to Europe.

"Look at what we have already conquered. Even Venice, at the height of its power, didn't reach as far! And we won't stop there!"

The head of the SS studied the Mediterranean. The entire northern shore belonged to the Reich and its allies, Spain and Italy. Suddenly, he understood Hitler's plan. What if the Führer had sent an expeditionary force to Libya not to help his ally Mussolini, but to take hold of the Middle East and destroy Britain's colonial empire piece by piece? All the way to India.

"You're a visionary!"

"Now do you see why I need Mussolini? He already has troops on the ground there, though not enough."

"According to our soldiers, the Italians aren't very good fighters . . ." ventured Himmler.

"They're Italian. They haven't known how to fight since the fall of the Roman Empire. However, we still need them for logistics: transport, supplies, and such. Those things are crucial in the desert."

Hitler gestured towards the Nile. "First, we'll take Egypt. Then the rest will fall like dominoes. Palestine, Syria, Lebanon, then Iraq and Arabia, where we'll have access to their huge oil reserves. I will awaken the power and dreams of the Arab world . . . I'll free the Indian continent."

The India drawn on the wall was nothing but a coastline. The Venetians' knowledge and ambitions had been limited—the Führer's were not.

"Beginning next spring, I'll send new troops to Russia and we'll head for the Caucasus. There too, all of those who have been oppressed by the Russians will rise up to join us. Millions of people will owe us their freedom—at least, those we deem fit to serve us."

Though Himmler never drank, he felt intoxicated. Nazi Germany was going to write a new chapter in the history of the world. A chapter that didn't stop at the Caucasus or India. Napoleon had stopped in Jordan, Alexander the Great at the Indus River. Hitler would go much further. To the edge of the Pacific.

"*Mein Führer*," said Himmler, his voice tinged with emotion, "I can't think of a better moment to give you this."

Surprised, Hitler took the box the Reichsführer held out and opened it.

"The Ahnenerbe found it in Knossos. It's undoubtedly one of the oldest swastikas in Europe. It was carved into the gold over a thousand years ago."

The Führer removed the artefact from its case and examined it silently. Hitler had short, thick fingers, but he handled objects very delicately.

"I'm certain the craftsman who engraved the symbol was Aryan. The lines are perfect . . . Your own swastika would fit almost perfectly in it," said Himmler, pointing to the gold swastika Hitler wore in the buttonhole of his jacket.

Hitler instinctively placed his hand over his lucky talisman. He was never without it. "Thank you, Heinrich. This is a wonderful gift. Even more than you know."

Hitler's eyes stared at a map that depicted the Atlantic Coast, from Brittany to Gibraltar. The ocean seemed to go on forever.

"America didn't exist back then," said Hitler. "Now it's a rising power. We will have to face it someday."

The Führer stroked his swastika pin.

"Mark my words, Heinrich, as long as I am who I am, America will not declare war on Germany."

50

"My friends, before we enjoy our coffee and conclude this dinner, may I offer a toast to the glory of the man we so admire!"

"To the Duce!" shouted the guests in unison. The men, in immaculate white dress uniforms, and their wives in evening gowns, had all stood to toast.

The man who led them was greying at the temples, with an aquiline nose and penetrating eyes. His angular face and elegant figure gave him an aura of natural authority. Something about him reminded people of the condottieri mercenaries of old. He brought his glass to his lips, studied his guests with a satisfied look on his face, then gulped down his glass of Barbaresco in a single swallow. Count Galeazzo Di Stella was dressed in the full uniform of high-ranking regime officials, with the golden fasces insignia sewn onto his lapel and a full row of multicoloured ribbons and medals from the Great War. All of them were for valour in battle, including the prestigious Cross of the Order of Savoy. None of the other men around the table had as many military decorations. In fact, most had only honorific medals awarded by the fascist party or earned in Abyssinia. The Count, a descendant of one of the oldest Venetian families, placed his glass back down on the table.

"Thank you, all of you. Our Supreme Guide needs your energy and unshakeable loyalty. Might I suggest we make our way to the sitting room for a glass of excellent grappa, which is sure to fortify our fascist passions?"

His guests laughed heartily as the servants zigzagged between them to clear the table. A naval officer with a pronounced forehead beneath carefully parted black hair made his way towards the host.

"My dear Count, I don't know where you get your supplies, but that meal was absolutely divine. The veal would have been fit for the Duce's table."

"Thank you, Prince Borghese. Will you stay a few days, or are you scheduled to lead your brave men on a new mission?"

"Top secret, I'm afraid!"

"I assumed as much."

"No, I'm joking. I was supposed to head out for a mission, but they asked me to attend the banquet that's been organized for the Führer and the Duce tomorrow night. Will you be there?"

"Of course. But I don't understand why the event is shrouded in such mystery. No official speeches, no guided tour. It's nothing like the 1934 summit."

The officer looked around warily, then moved closer to the Count. "Can we speak openly?" he asked.

"Please do."

"What do you think of this unexpected visit from Hitler?"

"It's a great honour," replied the Count enthusiastically.

"Of course, but I meant the reason behind it."

Count Di Stella held out a cigarillo, which the officer politely refused. "They must need to talk face-to-face about the eastern front. The Russian campaign has been a huge success, but Moscow still hasn't fallen, and the Axis troops will have to survive the winter. We sent over two hundred thousand expeditionary troops to help the Germans. I don't envy our men who will have to face the Siberian climate."

"The Russian campaign, yes, that's what I thought, but I wonder if there might be something else."

"What do you mean?" asked the Count as he lit his cigarillo.

"North Africa . . . Rommel isn't holding his lines anymore, the siege of Tobruk harbour failed, and our troops led by General Bastico are retreating in Libya. Malta is still resisting. I don't like any of it . . ."

"Come now, it's only a temporary change in the tide. Our forces are stronger than those of our enemies."

"Yes, but this is the first time we've ever lost so many men. And don't forget that the Libyan coast is closer to Rome than the banks of the Volga."

The Count raised his eyebrows. "Don't be defeatist. Not you, the black Prince, Junio Valerio Borghese, the proud leader of the elite Decima MAS commandos!"

The naval officer heard the irony in the Count's voice but chose to ignore it.

"I'm not being defeatist. I'm being strategic. The Mediterranean is Italy's *mare nostrum*, our territory, like the plains of Eastern Europe are Germany's. It's our main sphere of influence. If Britain acts up any more, we'll need to strengthen our presence there. Otherwise, we might lose Libya and Tunisia, just like we were pushed out of Abyssinia this year."

A servant interrupted them to whisper in his master's ear. The Count nodded, then waved the man away in annoyance.

"Mussolini must negotiate with the Führer to obtain more troops for the Afrika Korps in Libya," continued Borghese. "It's critical that we attack Egypt and the British again."

The Count exhaled a large cloud of smoke and stared into the naval officer's eyes. "You must be joking, Borghese!" he scolded. "We've already asked the Germans for help with our failed invasion of Greece. And Hitler has to concentrate all his forces to defeat the Reds! We can't humiliate ourselves a second time."

"This isn't about our egos. If the Americans enter the war alongside the British, you don't have to be a seer to know they'll invade North Africa. And that will be the beginning of the end . . ."

Count Di Stella placed his hand firmly on Borghese's shoulder. "This discussion is over. Our glorious army is capable of magnificent feats, and it will do its duty, in Africa and in Russia. I don't want to hear another defeatist word uttered under my roof. That kind of talk is unfit for a distinguished officer like you. Get a hold of yourself immediately!"

Borghese blushed and puffed up his chest. "My deepest apologies, Count."

"Fascists never apologize. They know only two verbs: obey and act!"

"Yes, of course!"

The man with the greying temples smiled. "Thank goodness. Now, I'm going to forget this conversation immediately. Why don't you go and enjoy some of my famous grappa and drink to the health of our beloved Duce?"

"I would love to. Will you join me?"

"I have an urgent issue to attend to first. I'll join you in a moment."

The naval officer nodded and walked into the neighbouring room as the Count watched. He waited for his guest to disappear before turning in the other direction and making his way towards a door at the far end of the dining room. A servant in livery bowed and opened it.

"If anyone comes looking for me, I'll be back in ten minutes."

"Yes, sir."

The aristocrat hurried down the stairs to a room with damp-eaten walls. A group of eight men in black shirts stood facing four coffins placed side by side. They came to attention as the Count entered.

"Where did you find them?"

"In the harbour master's office, in the agreed warehouse."

"Open them!"

One by one, the members of the British commando unit got out of their coffins, worried by the presence of the men who had just freed them. Fleming and Laure were the last to emerge. The others already had their hands in the air.

Count Di Stella studied them silently for a few moments. His gaze was penetrating and authoritarian—the gaze of a man who was used to being obeyed. When he spoke, his voice was curt. "I know you are British spies sent to carry out a mission in Venice, though I don't know exactly what that mission entails. You'll need to share that information immediately."

None of the commando members opened their mouths. Laure felt her pulse begin to race—they must have been betrayed by the fishermen or the doctor on Poveglia. She ran her tongue over the molar which contained the small capsule of poison. All she had to do was bite down hard, and it would all be over in less than a minute.

The Count grabbed a rifle off one of his men and shoved the barrel into Fleming's stomach. "According to my information, you're their leader."

"I really don't understand what you're talking about. We're American tourists. I have no idea how we ended up in these coffins. It must be some sort of Venetian welcome tradition!"

The Count was silent for a moment, then burst into laughter. "Tourists with Sten guns. Right! Only an Englishman is capable of that brand of humour. You can put your hands down. I'm Count Di Stella, and I'm sorry for this little show, but some of Heydrich's men tried to infiltrate our network recently by pretending to be British agents."

"You were very convincing," said Fleming.

Laure relaxed her jaw in relief. The idea of dying in a fit of convulsions receded. At least temporarily.

"There's something I don't understand. Why are you wearing a fascist dress uniform?"

"Because I'm the head of the organization of aristocratic fascists. At this very moment, I'm hosting an official dinner for the highest-ranking fascists in the city. They're all upstairs, just over your heads, in the smoking room. This would be the very last place anyone would look for a British commando unit, don't you think?"

51

Holborn, London
December 1941

"Good God, man, have you got jelly for brains?"

"I'm sorry . . . Truly, I am."

Malorley pushed Crowley back against the wall, his hand pulling the mage's collar tighter and tighter around his neck. "You're the craziest person in the world, after Hitler. Next time, I'll let you rot in jail." The SOE man had kept his anger in check until they'd turned the corner and were out of sight of the Holborn police station and the bobby on guard duty outside. "You put my department in danger with your nonsense."

"You're hurting me . . . I . . . I can't breathe," whined the fat man, whose face had turned bright red.

"I can do much worse. You'd be surprised how much we know about suffering at the SOE."

Malorley let go of Crowley, who seemed to liquefy as he collapsed to the ground. The Amilcar appeared at the end of the street and parked beside them. The driver got out to open the doors.

"Get in!" Malorley ordered curtly.

As soon as both men were seated, the car took off with a squeal. The commander pulled out a stack of typewritten pages and threw them in Aleister's direction.

"Assaulting a prostitute, drug use, animal sacrifice, exhibitionism, and insulting a police officer. The worst part is that you had the balls to tell them you worked for the SOE."

"Please, let me explain," yelped Crowley. "I asked a . . . professional to participate in a magic ritual. I incorrectly dosed the hallucinogenic mushroom tea, and the woman had a bad reaction. I swear. The police turned up because the neighbours heard her screaming. As for the rooster, I just needed a little of his blood. I never would have killed him. When the police found us, I was naked. But I had to be, to let the energy circulate freely."

"Magic! For Christ's sake, what were you thinking?"

"You don't understand. It's like a drug. If I can't communicate with the spirits, I get weak. Magic keeps me alive."

"Rubbish!"

Crowley sat up straight and wiped his face with an embroidered handkerchief, then looked defiantly at Malorley. "Really? But believing in magical swastikas that can change the outcome of the war *isn't* rubbish?"

The SOE officer kept quiet. The powerful purr of the Amilcar's engine made the back seat vibrate. Outside, the buildings gradually changed in style. Sumptuous Victorian mansions made way for more austere, functional structures. Wealth faded behind them as they drove. Malorley turned towards Crowley. "Luckily, I was able to get my hands on the report covering your exploits. One advantage of working for the secret service is that you can count on the police to cooperate."

"Thank you."

"But the next time you mess up, I will handle you myself. For good. Do you understand?"

"Yes."

The car quickly made its way north along Eversholt Street. The cityscape was still scarred by the previous year's bombings. Hollowed-out buildings sat alongside boarded-up, abandoned shops.

"Excellent. Now, I'm going to drop you off at your friend Moira O'Connor's so you can give her these documents," said Malorley as he handed Aleister a grey envelope bearing the SOE seal.

"What's inside?"

"The names of three saboteurs working for the Germans in Coventry, Manchester, and Cardiff respectively. They're all British, former Blackshirts of Mosley's. MI5 has been watching them for months."

"I don't understand. Why don't you arrest them?"

"They're small fish. If they pack up and leave, we'll know that Berlin is taking your friend the Scarlet Fairy's information seriously, and we can use her to feed them whatever we like."

Di Stella Palace, Venice
At the same time, December 1941

The members of the commando unit were finishing the exquisite meal provided by their host. Aubergine, tomato, and onion caponata, tender prime rib à la Florentine, Pecorino Romano and Valtellina Casera cheeses, and to top it all off, a delicious spiced-almond panforte drizzled with honey. Count Di Stella had called upon his personal chef to honour his British guests. They'd waited for the reception to end, then made their way to a small dining room.

"I haven't eaten this well since the beginning of the war," said Fleming contentedly. "From now on I'll volunteer for any mission in Italy."

"Running the Veneto's organization of aristocratic fascists has its privileges when it comes to supplies," replied the Count as his eagle eyes studied his guests.

Laure politely refused a glass of wine and wiped her lips with the fine cloth napkin. "Why are you, the head of a fascist organization, helping British spies, enemies of your country?" she asked.

The aristocrat sat up straight in his chair at the head of the table and held his glass up to the light to contemplate the colour of his wine. "Don't misunderstand, Miss, I don't think of myself as a traitor to my country. I marched on Rome with Mussolini in 1922. I truly believed Fascism was the only way to get the country back on its feet and combat the Reds. But then there was the war in Abyssinia, where I lost my oldest son, Bartolomeo. He was thirty-two years old. And after that, the invasion of Greece, which cost me my younger son, Livio, who was twenty-eight. The Duce's folly robbed me of my children. The Di Stella line will end with me."

"I'm sorry," replied Laure, "I—"

"Don't be," the Count interrupted. "I'm responsible, at least in part, for my sons' deaths, since I helped put that madman in power. And that's not all. I also lost my loyal secretary and friend, Samuel—a Jew whose family had lived in Venice for three generations. He fled in 1938, because of the anti-Semitic laws. The worst part of it all is that he was a fascist, too!"

"There were fascist Jews?" asked Fleming, intrigued.

"Of course. Up until he aligned us with Hitler, Mussolini had nothing against Jews. There were even some in his inner circle. But he was corrupted by the German *diavolo*, whose power is based on lies: the superiority of an Aryan pseudo-race, the Jewish conspiracy, and the sanctity of German blood. And the people love lies—especially those that flatter their egos. The roots of National Socialism run deep in ignorant lands. Lands that Hitler continuously fertilizes with hatred. But many Italians are ashamed of what's happening here."

"How did you find yourself at the head of this network?"

"Before the war," said the Count as he gulped down his entire glass, "I had many British friends, including Malorley, at the SOE. It's important to remember that we were on the same side during the Great War. And, of course, nobility has always transcended borders. As for my men, it may surprise you, but many of them are former socialists and communists."

"I'm not surprised," replied Fleming with a nod. "It's the same in many resistance networks throughout Europe. After all, we're allied with the Soviet Union now. So, how do we proceed?"

"One of you will meet your double agent embedded with the Germans tomorrow. Malorley told me he'll be at the top of Saint Mark's Campanile at precisely four o'clock in the afternoon. I only know his code name: John Dee. I'll also give you the password."

Laure tensed. Fleming noticed her reaction and spoke. "Our friend here will go. She's crossed paths with him before. We'll determine what's next after their meeting."

"You are going to collect an important object thanks to this man—is that correct?" asked the Count.

"Yes."

"I hope it's worth it. We're taking a big risk."

The Hellfire Club, London
At the same time, December 1941

Moira O'Connor lay naked on the stone floor, her arms and legs spread. Her hands and forehead were caked in blood. Her limbs and head traced a five-pointed star painted on the floor. A woman in a hooded black cape knelt at each point. The Scarlet Fairy suddenly opened her eyes and spoke an incantation that emerged from the depths of time: "*Diolco to dea Herecura genatan nemi ac diaras ac carantian dumni. Esi inter dumnei ac diara ac nemei.*" The ritual was over. The group had spent two hours invoking the great mother goddess, as they did at every full moon. The woody scent of incense filled the vaulted cellar, partly masking the smell of damp that dripped down the saltpetre-stained walls.

Moira stood up slowly, followed by the five other women. One of them handed her a wet towel to clean her hands and forehead. Another placed a jet-black silk robe over her shoulders. Moira was in a heightened state of well-being. The ritual purified her and filled her with a deep, gentle energy. Just as she was about to embrace her sisters, there was a knock on the door. Moira frowned. No one at the Hellfire was allowed to disturb her during the red moon ritual. Their punishment for doing so would be terrible. Annoyed, she opened the door. The club's butler, a Scot whose face was covered in syphilitic scars, bowed low. "Mistress, I'm sorry to bother you, but Aleister Crowley is asking to see you. He says it's urgent."

Di Stella Palace, Venice
At the same time, December 1941

Captain Fleming exhaled a cloud of smoke from the excellent Cuban cigar the Count had offered him, then continued his story.

"And that's how my incredible mission in Portugal ended with a memorable game of baccarat at the Estoril casino. A few Germans took me for all I was worth, but since I was, as they say, 'Unlucky at cards, lucky in love', I met a charming Italo-Bulgarian countess, Vesper Di Alexandra, and we spent a torrid night together."

The Count smiled. This Fleming had a flair for recounting his adventures, though he suspected the Englishman might be embellishing reality here and there. "I played at the tables in Estoril as well," said the aristocrat, "but it was before the war. It was *the* place to be at the time. All of high society was there. I hear it's become a den of spies these days. Traditions are so easily lost."

The two men had been chatting for over a quarter of an hour in the Count's office, savouring an Abruzzian grappa. Fleming had wanted to talk to him alone. The other members of the commando unit had gone to bed in a far wing of the palace. Laure had been pleasantly surprised to find herself in a room with a bathtub and hadn't hesitated to use it.

The Count stood up and walked over to a painting depicting a man in Renaissance armour, his hand resting on the pommel of his sheathed sword. The proud warrior had arrogant eyes and the same hawk-like profile as the Count. "My dear Captain Fleming, may I introduce Sigismondo Di Stella, one of my ancestors. He was a mercenary as a young man, but settled down once he met his wife, a young beauty descended from Venetian nobility. His motto was *Non decipimur specie* — 'Don't be deceived by appearances.'"

"And?"

Di Stella moved closer to Fleming and placed his hand on his shoulder. "You haven't told me everything about your mission. I don't believe for one second that there's an object out there worth putting together a mission like this one. Am I wrong?"

"No. I was waiting to be alone with you to talk about it."

"I'm listening."

"It's a dual mission. The first part is to retrieve an object of utmost importance, but I won't go into details because you'd think me a madman."

"And the second part? The more crucial part, I imagine?"

Fleming stood up. His eyes hardened as he stubbed out his cigar in the marble ashtray. "To end this war by killing Hitler and Mussolini."

PART FOUR

If I wasn't a devil myself, I'd give me up to the Devil this very minute.

Faust, Goethe

52

Hitler's visit of the Doge's Palace was over, and Saint Mark's Square was bustling once again. Laure slowed as she walked past Caffè Florian. Despite the cold, damp weather, the terrace was full of customers—and not just any customers. German officers in their grey-green uniforms occupied a dozen tables. They smiled blissfully as they delighted in the café orchestra's rendition of "Blue Danube". Laure shuddered. The last time she'd seen greyish uniforms, it was in France, on her ancestral land. The same colour worn by those who had killed her father.

She hid behind an archway to study them more closely.

The enemy. Right there in front of her again. A wave of pure hatred washed over her like a lava flow rushing down the sides of a volcano, scorching everything in its path.

She wished she had her Sten gun so she could kill them all. She wanted to see puddles of blood dripping off the tables, flooding the whole square. She wanted to see their faces ripped to pieces, their stomachs riddled with bullets, and their limbs torn from their bodies. More than anything, though, she wanted to hear them scream loud enough to cover the sounds of the orchestra's trumpets and violins. And when the final soldier took his last breath, she'd put her feet—still covered in blood and warm bits of flesh—up on a table and would drink a glass of chianti to her father's memory. Avenged at last.

A hand landed on her shoulder and a disturbingly guttural voice echoed in her ear. "*Scusi, signora!*"

A chill ran down her spine. The words were Italian, but the accent was from further north. From Germany. Her heart jumped, as if it might escape her chest. She instinctively reached for the little Browning pistol she had hidden in her raincoat. Then she turned around slowly.

An SS officer was standing in front of her. He seemed enormous and was at least twenty centimeters taller than her.

She'd been spotted.

Her mind churned at top speed. What had she done wrong? How had she betrayed herself? She never should have stopped to watch the military men in the café.

Then the man smiled as if they were old friends. He took out a map of the city and placed his finger on Saint Mark's Square.

"*Dov'è il palazzo del Duce?*"

Laure had learned a few key Italian phrases for the mission, but nothing came to her.

She froze.

"*Dov'è?*" he asked again, jovially.

She took a deep breath and replied calmly in her native tongue, all with a charming smile. "I don't know, I'm French."

The German looked at her more closely, curiosity in his eyes.

"Do you speak my language?" she asked.

"A little . . . I was stationed in Paris. What are you doing here, Mademoiselle?"

"I'm the daughter of the Vichy ambassador, on a cultural visit of the city."

The lie had come to her almost instinctively. One of her instructors at the SOE always told them that creativity was to lying like sap was to a tree.

As the SS officer was about to reply, a whistle blew at the other end of the square. The German sighed. "I'm sorry, I must get back. Where are you staying? Perhaps we'll meet again?"

"I'm sorry, but you mustn't ask a young woman such questions. I hope we'll meet again."

She hurried off under his watchful eye. As she put more and more distance between them, her heart beat faster and faster. She crossed the rest of the square without turning around a single time. When she reached the bell tower, she contemplated the famous red brick façade—the glory of Venice. At the entrance, she handed a twenty-lira bill to the guard and began climbing the legendary stairs. Standing nearly a hundred meters tall, Saint Mark's Campanile had triumphed over the knees and courage of thousands of visitors before her. It took Laure ten long minutes to reach the top. Once there, her cheeks on fire, she looked around. There were a few tourists, two Italian families, a German soldier, and a priest with two nuns. No sign of the man she was here to meet, but the walkway wrapped around the top of the bell tower. She made her way to the railing. The view of the square was breath-taking.

Venice looked like a forest. A stone forest over which soared tall marble steeples and the glistening roofs of the palaces, above the still water in the canals and the complex labyrinth of winding streets.

Suddenly she saw him.

Tristan.

He was there. Across from her, his back against a stone pillar, a cigarette tucked into the corner of his lips. He was wearing a dark three-piece suit and his face was partially hidden by a soft felt hat. He watched as she came closer.

"Venice is much colder than Rome this time of year," he whispered.

"But not as cold as Turin," she replied dryly.

"How's that for a surprise? The great Laure d'Estillac. So, Malorley recruited you for his extraordinary circus. Where is the commander? Not here with you?"

"He had to stay in London. Are you sad not to see him?"

"Not at all. I get to see you this way. If memory serves, our last encounter was rather tumultuous. You didn't seem to like me very much."

"A Frenchman eagerly serving the worst kind of Nazis doesn't exactly incite fraternization. Hats off for your acting, Monsieur Marcas. Or should I say, John Dee. I can't keep your aliases straight."

Tristan frowned unintentionally. "You know my name?" he asked, surprised.

"Yes. Is Tristan your real first name?"

"Who knows?"

A German soldier taking pictures of the square came closer. Marcas took Laure by the arm and they began walking.

"How many men do you have?"

"There are four of us, including my superior, plus Count Di Stella's men. That should make about a dozen."

"A dozen . . . Such irony. The city is crawling with fascists and Nazis on every street corner! Even Mussolini and Hitler—the biggest criminals in Europe—are here with their packs of rabid followers! And we have to go up against all that with twelve men? I must be out of my mind."

"But it's worth it, isn't it? You committed yourself fully at Montségur, after all."

"Speaking of which," asked Tristan, "where is the relic?"

"Safe . . . Very far from here."

"Good."

Annoyed by Tristan's banal reaction, Laure couldn't help but voice her scepticism. "It doesn't seem like it's changed anything in the war."

"The Germans invaded Russia, didn't they? Opening a second front, which leaves the British some much-needed breathing room."

"So, you believe in its power, too? You're all completely nuts."

Tristan tightened his grip on her arm. "There are forces beyond your comprehension at work in this. Beyond anyone's comprehension. People have died to keep that relic out of the Nazis' hands. Like your father! He believed in its power."

She abruptly pulled her arm away. This meeting wasn't going anywhere near as well as she'd hoped.

"Thanks, no need to remind me. I paid in blood."

"I'm sorry," said Tristan in a gentler tone, "but our mission cannot wait. So, listen closely. I know where to find the third relic. And I know how to get our hands on it. But there's no way we'll survive."

She stared at him, dumbfounded. He contemplated the beautiful city. He'd spent a considerable amount of time studying maps to find a place where he knew he and Erika would find nothing. The Bragadin Palace. Frescoes on the walls and ceilings in every room. Ideal for wasting precious hours looking, believing, hoping. But he'd made it all up. Once Goebbels had revealed the fact that Hitler would be coming to Venice, he had had no choice—he'd created a false lead to bring them all here.

"So, where is the relic?" asked Laure.

Tristan smiled.

The swastika had indeed stayed briefly in Crete, and the soldier-monk Amalrich had left a trail of clues. But someone else had found it before them. Someone who had changed the face of the world but remained perfectly unknown to it. Lanz, the man who created Hitler.

"It's somewhere no one will ever go looking for it. On the Führer's lapel."

53

The Cinema Palace, Lido Island, Venice
December 1941

The final measures of the *Tannhäuser* overture detonated in a hail of brass and strings. With beads of sweat pearling on his forehead, the conductor waved his baton in the air one last time, his hands trembling.

Thunderous applause echoed off the concrete walls of the great hall at the Cinema Palace. This home to the Venice Film Festival and its artistic high-society evenings had been built a year before war had broken out, and it embodied the new Italy. A country of virile, triumphant, monolithic modernism, free of old-fashioned flourishes. A sharp contrast to the venerable Venetian palaces built under the doges' rule, which were seen by the fascists as stone sentinels of an excessively refined and decadent past.

But this time, the cheering wasn't for movie stars. All eyes were on the two dictators sitting in the front row. Mussolini stood first, joining in the crowd's ovation. He adopted his favourite posture— tense features, raised chin, imperious gaze. To convey his satisfaction, the Duce nodded his bald head, which shone like a snooker ball in the light from overhead. As if he had conducted the orchestra himself. Hitler stood in turn. He had been transformed by the performance. His eyes sparkled. Wagner always made him happy, whatever the circumstances.

The most powerful man in Europe and his Italian counterpart—who was convinced he was just as important—shook hands and turned towards the audience. As usual, the Duce was overly effusive, his smile much too warm to be sincere. But that didn't bother the leader of the Third Reich. They had spent two hours discussing things, and the Italian had been more than accommodating about the Führer's requests.

More Italian troops in Russia, granted. More Italian troops to support the Afrika Korps in Libya, granted. Pressure Pope Pius XII to silence a handful of uncooperative German bishops, granted. Toughen anti-Semitic laws in Italy, granted. Mussolini hadn't really had a choice. Hitler had saved him from humiliation following his disastrous invasion of Greece. Kept at bay by the descendants of Sparta and Athens, the Italians had been relieved to receive German reinforcements—over half a million soldiers, a thousand tanks, and hundreds of planes. The Battle of Greece had been a resounding victory for Hitler and a moral defeat for Mussolini. The balance of power between the two dictators had definitively shifted, to the detriment of the Duce.

Sitting in the fourth row, Tristan and Erika applauded as well. The head of the Ahnenerbe leaned in and whispered in the Frenchman's ear, "I don't know why, but I feel like your applause lacks sincerity."

"Not at all. I thoroughly enjoyed the concert. As for the rest . . ."

"I guessed as much. Did your stroll through the city help revive your powers of deduction?"

"Yes, it did me a lot of good."

She gave him a strange look. "I'm delighted to hear it. The power of Venice is surprising. Perhaps we should sneak out to get back to the Bragadin Palace?"

Tristan shook his head. "Not right away. I've been granted the immense honour of an opportunity to get closer to your Führer. I'd like to take advantage of it."

Goebbels appeared on the stage, where he enthusiastically shook hands with the conductor. The Minister of Propaganda basked in his triumph. Hitler's quick visit to Venice was a total success. He took the microphone from the musician. The audience grew quiet.

"How pleasant to be here in the temple of the famous Venice Film Festival, where our beloved Leni Riefenstahl's *Olympia* won the award for Best Film," he said with a smile. Then he turned to the dictators. "*Mein Führer*, Duce, I know that you don't want to give any official speeches. I just wanted to thank you for taking some of your precious time to attend this modest evening held in your honour. We know how hard you work to lead us to victory. I wish resounding success to the Axis Powers and invite you to enjoy the buffet in the next room."

Applause rang out again. The Dwarf cast a suspicious glance in Himmler's direction. He knew the head of the SS had had a long meeting with the Führer and was terribly jealous of their time together. But tonight, the Reichsführer was on the sidelines; it was Goebbels's turn to shine. As the audience worked its way towards the neighbouring room, Count Di Stella approached Goebbels.

"Thank you for your tribute, Doctor," said the Italian. "I have a burning question, though. Why did you invite the Vienna Philharmonic instead of the Berlin Philharmonic?"

"The Führer was born in Austria and discovered Wagner in that delightful city. Plus, sixty of the orchestra's one hundred and twenty-three members belong to the National Socialist party—it's a record. And a source of great pride for our Aryan culture. Music is a fabulous instrument for guiding the masses."

"Is it?"

"Of course. Did you know that I'm currently imposing a new tuning frequency throughout Europe for all classical music? We've replaced the former norm—432 Hz—with a new one at 440 Hz, which has long been the German standard."

"Why is that?"

"Studies at our research institute, the Ahnenerbe, have shown that this frequency encourages discipline. Music penetrates the deepest folds of the brain and modulates its activity."

"I didn't know," said the Count simply, nodding to hide his scepticism. "And why didn't you invite the Führer's favourite conductor, Furtwängler?"

Goebbels's face darkened. "Don't throw salt in the wound! The maestro cancelled at the last minute, officially due to a cold. But I don't believe it for a second. I have doubts about his devotion to the party. I'm convinced he didn't want to appear alongside the Duce and the Führer."

"But he gave such an extraordinary concert last year, which Hitler attended."

"Yes, but I learned afterward that he intervened quietly in favour of Jewish musicians. Oh, he's a clever one, but I'll catch him. I plan to organize a concert for our Führer's birthday next year. I'll inform Furtwängler far ahead of time, so he won't be able to pull out. And he won't be able to fall ill either—I'll have my personal doctor take care of him. So, if he refuses, he'll go straight to a camp!"

A waiter passed between them with a tray full of champagne flutes. Goebbels took one as the Count watched the attendees navigating the buffet.

"Congratulations, in any case, for choosing Venice over Rome or Milan," said the aristocrat. "All of the city's fascist aristocrats are honoured."

An SS officer came over to them. Tall and thin with strange eyes, he seemed a bit too sure of himself.

"Ah Heydrich, Himmler's trusty bloodhound," offered Goebbels. "Did you enjoy the concert?"

The head of the Gestapo was at least a head taller than the Minister of Propaganda. He gave the Dwarf an icy glare.

"A real delight, except for the strings, which lacked subtlety, in my opinion."

"Oh yes, I'd forgotten that in addition to your work as a devoted police officer, you're also a violinist. Let me introduce Count Di Stella, who helped me organize this event."

"We've already met," replied the aristocrat.

The SS officer bowed slightly.

"Dr. Goebbels, maybe you forgot that I oversee the Führer's safety. I went over the list of guests and staff with the Count. And we spent over an hour inspecting the surroundings together."

"I'm already bored with this conversation," said Goebbels with an ostentatious yawn. "I'd rather talk about culture than lowly police work. Please excuse me, Count. I must say hello to a friend."

And with that, the master of propaganda was gone. He hurried over to Erika, who was chatting with Tristan.

"Erika von Essling, save me!" said Goebbels as he elegantly planted a kiss on her hand.

"From whom, my dear Doctor?"

"From that sinister individual," replied Goebbels, with a disdainful glance at Heydrich. "As soon as he shows up anywhere, it feels like he's about to arrest everyone. Himmler chose him well."

Erika introduced Tristan. "I'm sure you'll prefer the conversation of my French colleague, Tristan Marcas. A leading archaeologist and art historian."

"I like the French, though their blood isn't as pure as I would like. I hope you're not Jewish at least, Herr Marcas?"

Tristan shook hands with the Minister of Propaganda, repressing a smile. With his dark, slicked-back hair, the Dwarf wasn't exactly the embodiment of the Aryan ideal. "I don't think so, but who really knows? It's hard to tell."

"What do you mean?"

"Sometimes you meet Germans, pure Aryans, who are short with dark hair, and other times you meet Jews who are as blond as freshly harvested wheat and as athletic as Greek statues. It's hard to keep up. My scientific mind prefers archaeology to racial biology."

Erika gave her lover a dirty look. Goebbels stood up straight in his platform shoes like a flustered rooster. "I suppose that's French humour?"

"Not at all," lied Tristan. "I greatly admire your Führer. I'm terribly impressed by all that he's accomplished. When you think of the millions of impoverished, humiliated Germans after your defeat in 1918, all those poor people in rags, without jobs, all those desperate, bitter people . . ."

"All right, that's enough, Tristan," Erika interrupted, annoyed. "What's your point?"

"It's incredible, the way he turned penniless hordes into disciplined conquerors in boots and helmets. You'll notice I didn't say 'obedient'. An amazing feat. The same goes for the Duce. We haven't been so lucky in France. That must be why we took such a beating. Thank goodness our venerable Maréchal opened the door to collaboration. Maybe we'll succeed in imitating you. Though I'm sure we won't do any of it as well as you, of course."

Goebbels agreed. He seemed not to notice the Frenchman's irony.

"Your words speak to my heart, Herr Marcas. If I may say so, Pétain lacks something crucial: divinity!"

"That's an intriguing thought."

"Open your eyes! Hitler and Mussolini are no longer men; they're gods! They are feared and worshipped by millions of men and women. Their power is limitless. They impose their will on entire peoples. Nazism and Fascism are both avatars of pagan religions. They're the gods of a new era. Women faint when the Führer or the Duce looks at them. And I have played a major role in their deification. Propaganda is a kind of priesthood of mass adoration."

"And all this time I thought your strength lay in your Panzers and Messerschmitts."

"Such an easy mistake! Industrial feats are not everything," replied Goebbels in an exalted tone. "You French believe too much in reason. You lost the mystique of an anointed leader with the decapitation of Louis XVI. The Enlightenment perverted your people, cutting them off from a physical and spiritual bond with a supreme leader. It's more than a cult of personality, it's worship. Worship that pushes people to sacrifice their lives for their god."

Suddenly they heard breaking glass at the other end of the room. Shouts rang out, then a scream.

It was Hitler.

54

The Cinema Palace, Lido Island, Venice
December 1941

The waitress looked terrified. Her grey tray lay on the marble floor, surrounded by shards of glass. Seemingly hypnotized by the scarlet wine stain on his lapel, Adolf Hitler finally looked up, his features tense and determined, as if he were ready to crush anything in his path.

The room had gone silent and all eyes were on the German leader. On Heydrich's orders, two SS men appeared and grabbed the young woman by the arms, as if she'd tried to assassinate their Führer.

Mussolini broke the silence by hurling a string of insults at the distraught woman. She stuttered excuses, but her voice was so shaky that they were inaudible.

Count Di Stella intervened. "I apologize for this *imbecille*'s clumsiness," he said. "She's my cook's sister."

Mussolini puffed up his chest. "It wouldn't change anything, even if she were your daughter! I'll have her shot."

"Please, she's only a child. It was just an accident," he pleaded. Then he turned to Hitler and spoke in German. "Führer, I beg of you, please show clemency. I know you care for our people."

Hitler's face relaxed ever so slightly as he whispered to his translator, who nodded and replied. "The Führer says it's forgotten. He would like someone to fetch a clean suit from his suite, since he can't possibly dine wearing this one. He says it would be ridiculous and rather sad to execute a beautiful Italian woman during his visit to Venice."

The entire audience broke into applause for Hitler's unexpected magnanimity.

"I'll send my men immediately," offered Mussolini. "Thank goodness the Count thought to have you stay at the Excelsior, just a few steps away."

Heydrich came over to the aristocrat, a thin smile on his angular face. "I'd like to interrogate that young woman, if you don't mind."

"Whatever for? It was just a clumsy mistake," replied the aristocrat.

"I'm simply following standard security protocol," said Heydrich. "Nothing . . . sinister." The way the German pronounced the last word froze Di Stella's blood in his veins.

Tristan and Erika had moved closer to the scene but were still some distance away. "Your Führer is shorter than I thought," whispered the Frenchman in the archaeologist's ear. "He wouldn't have been recruited by the SS . . ."

"Size isn't everything. He has an iron will," replied Erika.

"No doubt. If you don't mind, I need to go and powder my nose," he joked. "I'll meet you at the buffet."

He spun around and left the great hall, then made his way to the spot agreed with Laure—a broom cupboard on the first basement level, right next to the kitchens. The Frenchwoman was waiting for him, her back resting against a crate that the cooks used as a bin. She was wearing the blue uniform of the palace's cleaning staff.

"That outfit doesn't suit you at all. I liked that flattering dress you were wearing yesterday," he said with a crooked smile. "And the atmosphere here isn't anywhere near as romantic as Saint Mark's Campanile."

"I prefer this uniform to the revolting dress your SS lover is wearing."

"You really should get a sense of humour . . . So, we don't have much time, but it should be just enough. Hitler will be changing clothes in about fifteen minutes. Count Di Stella managed to get me a copy of the key to the room where he'll be. The Count will create a diversion while Hitler's putting on his new suit."

Laure grabbed Tristan's arm. "There's been a change of plans."

"What?"

"Fleming and his men are planting explosives in the second basement. Their orders are to kill Hitler and Mussolini."

"What? That's insane!"

"I only just found out. Now I understand why Churchill handed this mission to the navy."

Tristan placed his hands on her shoulders. "Take me to your boss! Now!"

"You're hurting me."

He let go.

"It's not far. Follow me," she said.

They took a service stairwell, jumping down the steps several at a time, then crossed a storeroom containing hundreds of boxes of film posters. Stars lay on the floor, covered in dust—Marlene Dietrich, Gary Cooper, Elisa Cegani, Vittorio De Sica, Greta Garbo . . . They had all come to Venice to promote their films before the war. Tristan stepped on a poster for *Jud Süss*, an anti-Semitic film produced by Goebbels, which had premiered at the Venice Film Festival in 1940.

"Faster, no one must notice I'm gone," he said.

They hurried down another staircase and found themselves in a huge crawl space with a ceiling so low they couldn't stand. At the far end, about a hundred meters away, the members of the commando unit were huddled around a supporting column. One of the men was carefully connecting a timer to a stack of dynamite sticks against the wall. He stood up and wiped his forehead.

"There, that's the last one. With all of the charges we've laid, there will be nothing left but dust and bones. It's enough dynamite to blow up an aircraft carrier. Captain, do you want to set the main timer? The other charges will be set off by the heat from the first explosion."

"Not right away," said Fleming. "I want to be certain Hitler is up there. Leave him enough time to change and return to the hall. He has an annoying gift for narrowly escaping the bombs people set for him."

"Have there been many tries?" asked one of the SAS men.

"Quite a few. And they've all failed because of a last-minute scheduling change. The last attempt was in 1939, at a brewery in Munich. Someone had set a monstrous bomb to explode during Hitler's speech. But he unexpectedly cut his talk short and went back to Berlin. He left the beerhall thirteen minutes before the explosion. Just thirteen minutes changed the course of history. I don't want to take that risk."

Tristan and Laure suddenly appeared in front of them. The sweating Frenchman looked like a jack that had just popped out of his box.

"What is this bloody bomb business?"

"Calm down, old chap," replied Fleming. "Prime Minister's orders. We're going to kill those bastards. It doesn't interfere with your mission. Just focus on getting your trinket—I'm afraid you won't have much time."

"You don't understand!" said Tristan, grabbing Fleming by the collar. "If your bombs go off before I get my hands on the relic, it won't do any good. I've been working on this operation for years! And Count Di Stella and that girl who spilled the wine on Hitler risked their lives today. Doesn't any of that matter to you?"

"It would be in your best interests to let go of me immediately! Assassinating Adolf and Benito is the priority, ahead of your . . . archaeological research. As for the Count, he knows about our ultimate goal. He'll get out in time."

"Do you really think the Germans and Italians will turn into obedient little lambs overnight? If Hitler dies, someone else will take his place. Göring or Himmler. Do you want the SS in charge in Berlin? And we won't even have the swastika on our side."

Fleming unholstered his gun and glued it to Tristan's forehead. "John Dee or Tristan Marcas or whatever your name is, you'd better go back upstairs. You're wasting time. Precious time."

"You don't realize what's at stake, you're an amateur!"

The commando leader cocked his pistol. "Do as I say, or I've got a bullet with your name on it in my Browning. Right between your eyes."

The men stared at each other until Laure intervened and lowered the barrel of the gun. "That's enough! You can work together. How much time do you need, Tristan?"

"I don't know. It depends on how long it takes the new suit to arrive. Half an hour, maybe."

Laure turned towards Fleming. "You can give him half an hour, Captain. Until Hitler's changed, he won't even be in the room."

"Fine, I'll give you half an hour," said Fleming. "As soon as I know the targets are in the room, I'll set the timer for ten minutes. Afterward, meet us at the boat to be exfiltrated. It will be docked across from the lifeguard station."

Tristan glared at him one last time, then turned to leave. Laure ran after him.

"You must have known when we met earlier," said the Frenchman as he picked up the pace.

"I couldn't believe it when Fleming told me. I doubt Malorley even knows. It explains why they put a Royal Navy man at the head of the commando unit."

"You're an excellent liar. You must have paid close attention in SOE training."

They emerged from the basement and ran up the stairs.

"Don't you trust anyone?"

"No, and you shouldn't either. It's why I'm still alive."

55

The Cinema Palace, Lido Island, Venice
December 1941

Leaving Laure behind, Tristan entered the reception room where caterers fussed around a buffet overflowing with delicacies. It seemed, however, that no one had warned the Italians that Hitler was a vegetarian, the Frenchman noticed. Despite his rising stress levels, Tristan was still able to observe, analyze, and find the irony in it all. This strength meant he always performed well under pressure. The décor was excessive and tasteless: all the walls were covered in alternating swastika and Italian fasces banners, and two huge portraits of the dictators were lit by torches. It was like something out of a bad film. He noticed Erika, just a few steps away, in discussion with Goebbels, and he swerved to avoid them. She nevertheless caught his eye, and her features hardened. Leaving her alone with the Dwarf was terribly rude. As he studied the different cocktail options, the Count discreetly beckoned to him.

"Where did you go?" asked Di Stella in a strained tone. "His fresh suit has just been delivered. Hitler will be going up to change any minute. And Heydrich is interrogating the waitress. If he resorts to torture, we'll have big problems . . ."

"I'm sorry, but I've just learned that Fleming is trying to blow up half of Lido Island."

"I know, but I can't do anything about it. It's up to you to get the relic before he does. Are you ready?"

"I have been for years . . ."

The Count looked at him in surprise. He knew why *he* was

fighting dictatorship, but what was in it for Tristan? Unfortunately, there was no time to ask.

"Listen closely," continued the Count. "Use the key I gave you to get into the bedroom on the first floor and wait there. I'll create a diversion on the second floor, drawing the butler out of Hitler's room. Right before," Di Stella lowered his voice, as if his own words frightened him. "Right before you climb the staircase to confront the lion . . ."

Tristan and the Count went their separate ways when Fleming entered the reception hall. Dressed in a pristine Wehrmacht captain's uniform, with a monocle glued to one eye, he looked like the real thing. A first-class Iron Cross shone brightly on his jacket. He clicked his heels, as expected, to salute all the superior officers he came across, then made his way towards the bar. As he sipped his champagne, he saw Count Di Stella and then John Dee leave. The naval officer preferred the code name to Tristan, which reminded him of Oscar Wilde. The novelist had chosen it as Dorian Gray's pseudonym during his romps through the rougher parts of London, so Fleming had a hard time associating it with the Frenchman. He also had a hard time understanding why Dee was willing to take such risks to get his hands on a bloody relic. When the admiral had summoned him to his office to explain the mission, he'd thought it was a joke. Putting together a commando mission in fascist Italy to collect a trinket—pure insanity! But then he realized it was only a pretext. Malorley and his men had been played. The Prime Minister himself had signed the execution order for his adversaries.

Fleming slowly scanned the room. He quickly spotted the famous Erika. Laure had described her several times. A frigid, blonde beauty. The archaeologist was deep in conversation with Goebbels. The Minister of Propaganda always found the most beautiful women at any party. But in this case, he was way out of his league. Fleming smiled to himself—the idea of the Dwarf's impending humiliation relieved some of the mounting pressure. He checked his watch. It had been fifteen minutes since the commando unit had left the basement. Laure and the others must already be aboard the motorboat docked on the far side of the building, ready to speed towards Poveglia and the submarine that would take them back to Malta. As for Fleming, he would return to England covered in glory—the man who killed Hitler and Mussolini! The naval officer in His Majesty's service who won the war for the free world!

Fleming was growing impatient. As soon as the Führer returned to the room, he'd go down to the basement and arm the bombs. He was about to change world history.

His inner excitement was becoming unbearable. Worse than a game of baccarat. To relax, he decided to serve himself a second glass of champagne. Alcohol had always had a positive effect on him.

When he turned around, he bumped into Reinhard Heydrich, whom he recognized immediately. There was a thick file on Himmler's second-in-command in the Naval Intelligence archives. With any luck, he'd be blown to bits along with his boss. The SS man looked him up and down, his eyes hovering over the Iron Cross, as if he found it gleamed too brightly. Fleming felt his heart race as he bowed politely. "Pardon me, Obergruppenführer."

"No trouble at all, Captain . . . ?"

"Drax. Hugo Drax. Of the Third Infantry Division," replied Fleming in perfect German. He couldn't thank his mother enough for making him spend his teenage summers in Goethe's homeland.

"You're a long way from your unit, Captain Drax. It's fighting in the Ukraine at the moment, if I'm not mistaken. Ousting Russian partisans east of Kiev, isn't it?"

"I've been in Berlin for seven months, Obergruppenführer," replied Fleming without skipping a beat.

"So, you're working at the Office of the General Staff as a liaison officer?"

"That's why I'm here, with Marshal Keitel's party."

Heydrich's eyes narrowed. Up close, there was something reptilian about his face.

"Really?" he asked coldly. "I don't remember seeing your name on the guest list. And I have an excellent memory."

56

The Cinema Palace, Lido Island, Venice
December 1941

Tristan had easily entered the luxurious room whose balcony looked out over the Lido's beach. In honour of the Führer's visit, the local authorities had lit up the coastline. Unfortunately for them, Hitler only had eyes for the mountains. There were no signs of anyone staying in the room, except for a lacy black nightgown on the sofa. Tristan smiled. The suite, which was supposed to welcome important guests, seemed to be used exclusively by the palace director's mistress. It made it easy for her to come and go unseen since her lover's room was just above, with a private staircase between them.

The Frenchman slowly climbed the steps, careful to make as little noise as possible. When he reached the door, he checked his watch. The Count would draw the butler away soon. The lion was there on the landing, on a 1940 Venice Film Festival poster. The winged beast from Saint Mark's Square roared from the top of a column set against a dark-blue background. It must have been a subtle message of virility for the women who entered the director's den.

Tristan glued his ear to the wooden door. The muffled but still instantly recognizable sound of a shower reached him on the landing. Suddenly, his heart began to race. Voices raised. Short, brutal bursts. Two different voices, but he recognized one of them. The leader of the Reich. The Frenchman realized that a single oak door separated him from the most evil man the world had ever known. The man who had plunged all of Europe into a sea of blood. Evil incarnate.

Tristan felt his hands begin to shake.

Not now . . .

It was silly, he knew, but Hitler's presence petrified him. He had been through so much over the past three years—prison, hunger, torture in Spain—and had escaped much more dangerous situations. He was constantly playing a deadly role as a double agent, but now he felt like a small child intimidated by an authoritarian adult. He was ashamed, but also too weak to act.

You're being ridiculous. Get hold of yourself!

He did his best to slow his breathing, then knelt down to look through the keyhole.

He couldn't see the dictator, just a blond SS officer meticulously brushing a brown jacket. Tristan frowned. Of course Hitler's butler was a member of the most feared Nazi order. That said, there was something comical about an SS officer handling such a banal domestic task. Tristan wondered if the man was a valet who had been handed an honorary SS uniform to keep up appearances, or if he really was one of Himmler's followers who devoted his time to ironing and polishing boots.

There was a discreet series of knocks on the main door to the suite. The butler put the jacket down on a chair and disappeared from Tristan's field of vision.

The Frenchman froze. The stained jacket was right in front of him on a chair. With the ancient swastika attached to the lapel.

This time his heart felt like it would beat right out of his chest.

The third relic was almost within reach. The swastika that Lanz, the mad monk, had given Hitler thirty years before. The source of all his power.

And he, Tristan, could change the course of history. Steal the dictator's talisman and definitively change the balance of power in favour of the free world.

Two swastikas for the Allies and only one for the Axis Powers.

He placed his ear back on the door and easily recognized Count Di Stella's melodious voice. He couldn't hear what they were saying, but a minute later the door closed, and the room was silent.

It was now or never.

Tristan inserted the key into the lock and carefully turned the knob. The door opened without a sound. He could hear that Hitler was still in the shower. The dictator's pores produced sweat and filled with impurities and waste, just like any other human's—but no soap could ever cleanse the filth produced in his mind.

The Frenchman moved cautiously into the room. The butler could return at any moment. Marcas imagined the worst—shouts, SS officers tackling him to the ground, Heydrich, torture, a painful death. He pushed the terrifying images out of his mind and neared the chair.

Calm down . . .

He grabbed the stained jacket and deftly severed the threads that fastened the gold swastika to a leather tab on the underside of the lapel. He took the relic in his left hand and held it up to the light.

At last!

The object seemed harmless enough. Nothing like the other two relics, from Montségur and Tibet, which were much bigger. How could a trinket like this have given Hitler so much power? Himmler had had it right in front of his nose for years, every time he crossed paths with his idol. How terribly ironic!

He watched the swastika glint in the light, which it seemed to absorb. Suddenly, it didn't look so ordinary anymore. It seemed to emit a strange pulse. Tristan's mind raced. Who had made it and the other three relics thousands of years ago? How had it gathered such power? And why? He felt an invisible light illuminate his palm. Maybe the swastika had chosen *him* to change the fate of the world.

As he lowered his hand, the sound of running water stopped. A hoarse voice emerged from the bathroom. "Karl, get my clothes ready."

Tristan turned towards the door. The monster was there, just on the other side. Naked and defenceless.

What if . . . ?

The Frenchman slipped his right hand under his jacket and tightened his fingers around the butt of his Luger. He could kill two birds with one stone. There was no need for the bombs and the bloody trail of innocent victims they would leave behind. All he had to do was go into the bathroom and aim at his target. He could savour the German's look of surprise, then his terror as he contemplated the dark barrel of the gun. He could bask in Hitler's fear. What would the frightened Führer look like? Would he beg for mercy? Throw himself at Tristan's feet? It didn't matter . . . Marcas would empty his clip between Hitler's pale eyes either way. For all of the innocent people murdered by his forces. Eight bullets would chop his brain to pieces, rip his flesh apart, and crush his bones. His face would become an unrecognizable mush, his body a naked corpse collapsed in the shower. A demeaning death.

Tristan took the safety off his pistol. It was too tempting. He would be the man who killed the monster. Humanity's saviour.

All he had to do was open the door to the bathroom. And fire.

But that would destroy any chance he might have of escaping with the relic.

The first shot would summon SS officers and the butler. He might be able to kill them, but he would probably be wounded as well. And there would be more, dozens of heavily armed men hunting him like a wild animal.

He would never manage to give the swastika to Laure or Fleming. Worse, the tyrant's successor would get his hands on the relic and they would be back at square one.

The dilemma consumed him.

Reason told him to execute the monster. The results were guaranteed. Hitler would be wiped from the face of the earth. But an inner voice urged him not to. The relic came first. It was more important than the tyrant's life or death.

Reason was his right hand, which held the gun.

Intuition was his left, which held the swastika.

He had to make the decision of a lifetime—kill Hitler or take the relic.

57

The Cinema Palace, Lido Island, Venice
December 1941

"How dare you question an officer's word. I'm a Wehrmacht captain, awarded the Iron Cross for my bravery on the eastern front. I'm afraid you can't say as much!"

Fleming didn't back down from the head of the Gestapo. Quite the contrary—he was playing to a tee the proud and arrogant German officer for whom the SS were just a bunch of vulgar, opportunistic street thugs. Though this was the first time he'd ever worn a monocle, it remained perfectly in place despite his pronounced facial expressions. There was little chance that his attitude would impress Heydrich, but it enhanced his credibility. When bluffing, it was always best to go all-in. And never break character. It was a question of self-control. Luckily, nights of playing baccarat in casinos had given him nerves of steel. But this time his life was on the line.

No one around them seemed to notice their confrontation. Everyone was focused on Goebbels, who was introducing his wife, Magda, to Mussolini. The smiling blonde Valkyrie seemed to have made a big impression on the Duce.

"Don't take it personally, Captain Drax," said Heydrich softly. "Your childish behaviour won't get you anywhere. Follow me."

Heydrich showed his cards—he unfastened his holster and placed his hand firmly on the grip of his pistol. "If it's an organizational error, I will apologize thoroughly. In fact, I love making mistakes . . . I rarely have the opportunity."

Though Fleming's face remained impassive, his mind was

feverish, as it was every time he had to choose a trump card. He could, of course, unholster his Walther PPK, tucked away at his right ankle, but Heydrich would shoot him before he could do anything with it. And he knew where—one bullet to the stomach, so he could still be interrogated. The Englishman rapidly scanned the room.

"Stop wasting my time," ordered the head of the Gestapo, placing his hand on Fleming's shoulder to urge him towards the door located between the two huge portraits of the dictators. "All of the exits are guarded."

The secret agent squinted. His adversary had a better hand. But he still had one trick up his sleeve—he could destabilize Heydrich and try to escape. Nevertheless, his chance of success was next to zero. The only remaining option was to go along and try to buy time. Maybe, if he was lucky, Tristan or the Count would come back into play.

Or maybe not. In which case, it was game over. Fleming ran his tongue over the hollow molar that contained the cyanide capsule. "After you, Obergruppenführer."

When they reached the corridor, two SS officers escorted Fleming and Heydrich under the watchful gaze of rows of cinema stars. Clark Gable, Katharine Hepburn and Vivien Leigh all graced the walls. To keep calm, Fleming convinced himself that his life wasn't in danger. He was surprised that the Italians had left these portraits of Hollywood actors on the walls. The Nazis despised American films, though people said Hitler had a soft spot for Chaplin's shorts, which he watched regularly in Berlin. The corridor seemed endless. The head of the Gestapo hadn't taken out his gun, but the Englishman was clearly his prisoner. For Fleming, it was like walking down death row.

"Where are we going?" he asked.

"To visit a charming, though clumsy, waitress. My men are interrogating her."

Fleming's face froze. Suddenly the sound of boots rang out at the other end of the corridor. A breathless junior officer appeared.

"Come quickly, Obergruppenführer!"

Heydrich tensed immediately. "I'm about to conduct an inter-rogation. Return to your post."

"We've just found a bomb in the basement! The Führer's life is in danger!"

Heydrich turned to Fleming and shouted to his guards, "Take him to where the girl is being held and interrogate him. Immediately. Keep going until he talks."

Two floors above, in evil's lair, Tristan was about to show his cards as well.

Just before he reached a decision, the door to the suite opened slightly. A man's shadow appeared on the floor. The butler would soon be back in the room.

An Italian voice reached Marcas from the corridor. "In Italy, we make apologizing a point of honour."

"I'm certain he'll gladly agree to speak to you when he comes back down," replied the butler.

Tristan uncocked his gun. It was too late to assassinate the dictator. Fate had decided for him. He placed the jacket back exactly where he had found it and slipped the relic into his pocket, then hurried through the door to the private staircase just as the SS man entered the Führer's room.

"Please tell him I'm one of his most fervent admirers," pleaded Di Stella, grabbing the butler by the arm.

"I will be sure to do that, Count. We'll see you later," concluded Hitler's man as he slammed the door in the aristocrat's face.

"What's going on, Karl?" asked the leader of the Reich.

"Nothing, *mein Führer*. It was Count Di Stella, who was desperate to present his apologies. These Italians stick to you like overcooked pasta!"

"Come now, Karl—they're our allies."

"Forgive me, *mein Führer*."

"Hand me my clothes."

Tristan's heart thundered against his ribcage as he rushed down the staircase. How long would it take for Hitler to realize his precious talisman was gone? But this was no time for questions. He ran across the room below, then into the deserted corridor and onto the stairs that led to the ground floor.

His anxiety had subsided, replaced with elation. He had the relic!

Now all he had to do was get it to Laure or Fleming, and go back to Erika as if nothing had happened. No one would suspect him—it was impeccable work. Luck had smiled on him once again. If the stars remained aligned, the swastika would reach England *and* Fleming would blow up his bombs and send Hitler and Mussolini to hell.

His mind was on fire. Everything he'd fought for was coming to a head. Fate had chosen to place him in the front row for these exceptional events.

This bombing would go down in history. For both sides. During his stay in Berlin, Tristan had seen first hand the hysterical enthusiasm that Hitler inspired in the German people. Even those with fine minds, like Erika, had succumbed to the swastika's evil spell. The entire country had given its body and soul to the madman. As Italy had to its Duce.

The death of the two dictators would unfurl a wave of joy in England, Russia, and all the occupied countries. And a wave of shock and anger in Germany and Italy.

This night would forever mark the memory of mankind.

For some, it would be the night when good triumphed.

For others, the night when evil claimed its victory.

As he reached the ground floor, a woman appeared at the bottom of the stairs. He slowed immediately.

It was Erika.

"Where were you?" she asked.

Tristan casually made his way down the last steps. "I got lost. They said the toilets were upstairs, but I never found them."

The archaeologist came closer, her voice strangely calm. "And I suppose your full bladder is why you were running down the stairs? Or maybe the Devil's on your tail?"

"He may well be."

"Stop lying," said the young woman, staring straight into his eyes.

58

Blood trickled down Captain Fleming's lower lip as he looked up.
They had tied him to a chair, and he could no longer count the
number of blows his face had taken. An inescapable tide of pain
was rising in him, but the hardest part to handle was the young
woman screaming and writhing on the floor, her hands raised to
protect her face. She had lost a lot of blood, especially from her
right eye socket. The waitress's eyeball lay on a table next to a
knife with a flat, dark blade—the standard SS model, engraved
with the motto *My honour is loyalty.*

Fleming had heard about the technique. During his training,
the Polish instructors had told them all about the Gestapo's creativity when it came to interrogations. Enucleation was one of their
trademarks. Everything was as they'd said, right down to the
presence of another tortured victim—a woman or child, prefer-
ably—to weaken the subject's mental stamina.

"What's your name? What is your mission?" asked one of the
three SS officers, his arms crossed over his chest. His expression
was neutral, almost polite, as if he were conducting an interview
rather than an interrogation.

"Hugo Drax. Captain Hugo Drax. I'm—"

Before he could finish his sentence, a fist hit his temple. Fleming
almost fell over, but one of the other men held the chair to the
floor.

"There is no Captain Drax on the lists. You're wasting our time.
The girl has already admitted she was paid to spill the tray on the

Führer. We'll have to try another technique to get you to open up." The SS officer picked up the knife and brought it to Fleming's face. "If your next answer doesn't suit me, I'll take out your eye. Like I did hers. Then the second. After that, we'll move on to another . . . more intimate part of your anatomy."

Fleming realized it was over. There was no way out. They would slice him to pieces until they got exactly what they wanted.

No one can resist torture. It's only a matter of time before you talk, the Poles used to say during his hands-on training as an interrogation victim. Even after a severe beating from the instructors, Fleming had been sure they were exaggerating. Now he knew that was not the case.

Another SS man held the Englishman's head in a vicelike grip. The tip of the knife slowly cut through the lower edge of his eyelid.

"All right! I'll talk," said Fleming. "But leave that poor girl alone. She has nothing to do with any of it."

"Okay, we'll leave her alone."

The third SS man took out his Luger and shot the waitress point blank in the head. Her body convulsed, then went limp, releasing a foul odour. Bits of pearl-coloured brain covered the wall.

"Your wish has been granted. No one will bother her now. We're listening."

Fleming barely managed to repress his urge to vomit. It was time to end this. To bow out of the game—at a loss. He would never be the man who killed Hitler. He would die miserable and alone, and no one would remember his name.

Just as he was about to bite down on the cyanide capsule, the door opened and a cleaning woman came in with a broom and bucket in hand. Despite the pain, Fleming almost laughed. Fate was really taking the mickey out of him this time. The previously tragic scene had just become ridiculous. He was about to die in front of the poor woman who would have to clean up his postmortem mess.

One of the SS goons turned and barked, "Get out!"

"I'm sorry . . ." said Laure as she dropped the bucket, unholstered her Browning, and unleashed death.

The German behind Fleming was the first to fall, his head atomized by the first wave of bullets. With her legs firmly planted, knees slightly bent, arms straight out, hands at eye level, and her face calm, Laure would have received top marks for her stance. She killed a second German before stepping forward and taking out the last SS man with a bullet to the spine. He wriggled like a snake on the floor before going still.

Laure untied Fleming. "You were in a rather tight spot, Captain. How does it feel to have been saved by a cleaning lady?"

"You disobeyed my orders. You were supposed to wait in the boat."

Laure helped him stand. "Really? No 'Thank you'? I stayed to ensure your safety . . . and Tristan's. The rest of the commando unit is waiting for us at the boat."

"I have to go. There might still be a way to set off the bombs," said Fleming as he grabbed a Luger off one of the dead Germans.

"We can't," replied Laure. "Access to the basement has been blocked off. Where's Tristan?"

They'd emerged into the corridor. Fleming hesitated before deciding on a direction.

"I don't know. I think he got your damn relic, but he'll be caught as well."

"We have to find him—"

"There's no time. All we can do is hurry to the meeting point and pray that Tristan meets us there. You're very impressive, Laure," he said as they fled. "What you did in there . . . I didn't think—"

Furious about leaving Tristan, the Frenchwoman replied, "That a woman could fight like a man and kill her adversaries? Well, if you get out of this alive, at least you'll have learned something useful."

At the bottom of the stairs, Tristan and Erika stood facing each other. The lovers knew they were now enemies.

"Let me go," said Tristan.

"No, I'll call the guards."

"You know you'd be sentencing me to death."

"What I know is that the Bragadin Palace was a ruse. You wanted to come to Venice, but you had other plans."

"Don't let your imagination run wild, Erika . . ."

"That's enough! Tell the truth. You've pretended to love me all this time to get what you wanted, haven't you?" she asked, her eyes suddenly softer.

He looked at her for a few seconds, then came close. It was time to take off the mask. It was bound to happen eventually. "I've been working for the British since the beginning. Now let me through."

"Never!" she replied. "You lied to me. You screwed me, in every sense of the word."

He grabbed her hands, but she jerked them away.

"I'm not a traitor like you!" she said. "I'm serving my country."

"No, you serve a monster. And you know it. You and your countrymen have put in power the most evil man the world has ever known. The swastika cannot fall into the hands of that madman and his followers. Don't side with them."

"I took an oath of loyalty, though I know that's a word you don't understand."

"Look deep into your heart, if you don't believe me. Do you really want the whole world to be subjected to the horrors of Nazism?"

"I may disapprove of certain things, but Germany is my home."

"Couldn't *I* be your home? Your future? You could change the course of history, Erika—you could end this war! All we have to do is get the relic to the Allies."

She was suddenly shaken. "You found it?"

"Yes, it's in my pocket."

Erika was shocked. "You're lying! As always! The relics from Tibet and Montségur were too big to fit in a pocket!"

Tristan shook his head and brandished the swastika. "This one is a miniature version, but it has the same powers. Hitler has worn it on his lapel for quite some time."

"But how . . . ?"

"Do you remember the old monk I went to see at Heiligenkreuz? His name was Lanz. He discovered the relic and gave it to Hitler, back when Hitler was no one. We all know what happened next."

"That's unbelievable!"

"Yes, and it's why I had to find an excuse to get close to the Führer. When Goebbels announced he would be visiting Venice, I created the perfect diversion: the Bragadin Palace. Now you know everything," he said, placing his hands gently on her shoulders. "Come with me. We can be clear of Venice in a few hours. You'll be granted asylum in England. Don't be an accomplice to the Nazis' horrors."

A single tear fell on the archaeologist's cheek. "I can't betray my country," she said.

"You're making the wrong choice, Erika."

He wanted to take her in his arms, but it was too late. He took a step back and looked around, trying to find an exit.

"You'll never leave here with the relic."

When he turned around, he saw Erika aiming a gun at him.

59

The lovers were in a stand-off.

"Don't make me shoot. Give me the relic and I'll let you go to your British friends."

Tristan shook his head. "I didn't risk my life for it to fall into the hands of your masters."

"Then I have no choice . . ."

Screams and shouts suddenly rang out. "A bomb! There's a bomb!"

A crowd of men in tuxedoes and dress uniforms and women in evening gowns flooded the corridor. Erika made the mistake of looking in their direction. Tristan seized the opportunity to hit her wrists, sending the gun to the ground. Furious, she jumped at him, but he dodged the blow. She rolled across the floor and hit her head on the wall.

A group of fleeing waiters pushed through the narrow space. Tristan threw himself over Erika to protect her. He checked the back of her head, but there was no blood. The archaeologist was in shock, but she hadn't passed out.

"I'm sorry, Erika," said Marcas. "I never wanted to hurt you."

"Don't leave me, please," she said, her voice hoarse.

He stood up and grabbed a passing waitress. "What's going on?" he asked.

"Let go of me! They said to evacuate—there are bombs in the basement!"

Tristan let her go. Fleming must have triggered the timer. He had to get out of there and make his way to the rendezvous point. The chaos would protect him.

At his feet, Erika tried to get up, but the herd of people rushing out the doors kept throwing her back against the wall. She would be trampled to death or blown to pieces in the explosion. He couldn't leave her there.

"Hang on to me," he urged as he grabbed the Luger. Erika wrapped her arms around his shoulders, letting her head rest on his neck.

"Stay with me, my love," she whispered.

They inched towards the exit in the general stampede. She held on tightly to Tristan, like a shipwreck victim clinging to a raft in a storm.

The doors to the palace had been knocked off their hinges by the panicked crowd. Once past them, Tristan and Erika found themselves on an esplanade that overlooked Lido Beach. A row of searchlights lit the landscape right up to the seashore, shining on a group of men and one woman. She screamed in despair, "Find the Führer, quickly!"

Tristan turned to see Goebbels and Magda surrounded by a group of SS officers, who were pushing guests out of the way to keep them safe.

"The Führer, where is the Führer? I must be by his side!" cried the Dwarf as he paced like a man possessed.

One of the officers grabbed him by the arm. "He is safe and sound, along with the Duce. You'll see him later. But first, I must evacuate you."

"No! I want to see him right away!"

The Frenchman walked on, placing Erika safely on a bench. She didn't want to let him go.

"Please . . ." she whispered.

He cut her off with a gentle kiss. "Goodbye," he said.

Tristan stood up and looked around to get his bearings. Where was the commando unit? Where was the dock by the lifeguard station?

★

The motorboat's dual engine purred quietly. Three of the commando members had gone on board to avoid being seen. Only Laure and Fleming remained on the dock with Count Di Stella, watching the evacuation of the palace through a pair of binoculars.

"It's utter chaos! Giuseppe's bomb warning worked—I hope it will give your agent the time he needs to join you. He'd better hurry!"

Fleming, whose face was still covered in blood, was angry. "You sabotaged my mission! I didn't have time to set the fuse!"

"We have an old Venetian proverb: 'Once the ship has sunk, everyone knows how it might have been saved.' There's no way you could have reached the basement."

"What if the waitress gave up your name under torture?" Laure asked the Italian aristocrat.

"Impossible. The man who hired her gave her a fake name. I really must get back to the officials, or my absence will raise suspicions." He continued, pointing to the boat: "The captain will take you directly out of the lagoon. You can't go through Poveglia anymore. The submarine will already be waiting for you at the rendezvous point, anyway."

He bowed to Laure. "I hope one day we'll meet again to celebrate the end of the war. You will be my special guest." Then he turned to Fleming. "Tell your superiors that neither King Victor Emmanuel III, nor the Grand Council of Fascism, will support Mussolini forever. The Italians don't want to be fighting this war."

"I will tell them, Count. Good luck to you."

They watched him walk away, his hands in his pockets as if out on a casual stroll. The picture of aristocratic indifference.

"What a man! I envy his courage," said Fleming.

The captain of the boat stuck his head out of the cockpit. "We have to go. On the radio they're saying patrols are moving to block all routes out of the lagoon."

"Not yet, we have to wait for Tristan," replied Laure as she studied the teeming swarm of guests on the beach.

The captain cursed, then added, "If you want to stay here and dance the tango with the SS, do as you please, but I'm leaving in three minutes. No later."

Tristan climbed down the wooden staircase that led to the beach, which was so brightly lit, it could have been midday. Men and women were standing around in groups as if watching a show, waiting to see when the monolithic palace would explode into the sky.

The Frenchman forced himself not to run, to avoid attracting attention. Armed Blackshirts and *carabinieri* dotted the sand. He walked around a row of pale-blue beach huts and caught sight of the lifeguard station not more than a hundred meters from where he stood. He instinctively clutched Hitler's swastika tighter.

Luck was on his side. He saw the dock on the right, and the motorboat waiting for him. He could see silhouettes on the deck. He thought one of them was Laure, but he couldn't be sure.

Just as he stepped onto the sand, a woman's voice rang out on the esplanade. "Stop that man!"

Tristan looked up to see Erika pointing an accusing finger in his direction.

"That man, there, in the grey suit!"

Tristan pretended he hadn't heard. People stared in surprise, but no one tried to stop him. His heart began to race. The dock was there, and the boat, its lights on. When he was only a few meters away, two Blackshirts blocked his path.

"Halt!"

Tristan stopped. "What's going on? Can't you see I'm a member of the German delegation?"

"Why is that woman up there saying we should stop you?" asked one of the fascists, his thin face hostile.

"It's nothing," lied Marcas. "We had a little disagreement. You know how it is with women. She's just learned about a recent indiscretion of mine . . ."

The shorter of the two men laughed, but the thin one remained wary. "I don't care about your love life. Show me your papers."

60

Tristan pulled a brown leather wallet out of his jacket and handed them a trifold card in German. The Blackshirts studied the photo ID carefully, noting the SS symbol, but still didn't seem inclined to let him through.

"Stop him! Stop him! He's a spy!"

Tristan turned around and saw Erika shouting as she made her way down the stairs. He had to do something, and fast. He pulled out his Luger and aimed at the two men. "Get down on the ground. Now."

The surprised fascists took a step back but didn't comply.

"This is your last chance. Get down!"

The shorter one did as he was told, but his colleague made the mistake of reaching for his gun. Tristan was faster. He fired two bullets at point-blank range. The fascist opened his eyes wide in disbelief, then collapsed face first onto the dock. The Frenchman hit the other man hard over the head with the gun's grip.

"He's a traitor! Don't let him go!" Erika was still shouting as she drew nearer.

Tristan stepped over the guards' bodies and ran for the boat. Only twenty more meters and he would be safe. In the distance, to the left, the beam of a searchlight was moving up the beach towards the boat. His heart pounded as he ran. He saw the sailors undocking the boat. Shots rang out behind him, but he didn't turn around. Every second counted.

★

From inside the boat's cockpit, the captain noticed the big yellow oval of the searchlight heading their way. "We've been spotted," he shouted in a panic. "Get on board, quick!"

The hull vibrated and the boat shifted as the engines revved.

"No!" shouted Laure, who could see Marcas's face now. "He can make it."

Fleming grabbed hold of the Frenchwoman to keep her from running to Tristan. "It's over, we're going. He won't make it."

She fought like a wild animal, and one of the other members of the commando unit hurried over to help Fleming. The two of them together managed to get her onto the deck. The engine roared and the motorboat backed away from the dock just as Tristan reached them.

Marcas could see Laure's face as she pounded on the glass of the cockpit with her fists.

It was over. There was only one option left.

The relic couldn't fall back into the hands of the Nazis. He took out the swastika and contemplated it for a moment, then threw it into the dark water. As far as possible.

The swastika drew an arc through the night air, then sank into the lagoon.

As for the boat, it had turned off its lights and melted into the darkness.

Strangely, Tristan felt at peace. His mission was over. So was his life.

The operation was a failure—the Germans would capture and torture him. Erika would testify against him, without the slightest regret. But he didn't hold that against her—it was just the way things were. He nevertheless felt he had accomplished his destiny. Others would continue the quest for the last relic.

The air was cool and the lapping of the water against the wooden posts of the dock was calming. The stars lined up perfectly in the sky. It was a good place to go.

He placed the barrel of the Luger under his chin. He'd heard that it guaranteed better results than the temple.

He closed his eyes.

He was leaving the darkness for the light.

Just as he was about to pull the trigger, a male voice spoke behind him. "Such poor taste. Saint Mark's Square is where people commit suicide, not Lido Beach."

Tristan turned around to see a man in the immaculate white uniform of a high-ranking fascist official. He smiled as he placed a cigarette in the corner of his mouth.

"I cleaned up your mess," said Count Di Stella.

"What do you mean?"

"The Blackshirt you knocked out is no longer of this world, and your German friend will need intensive care, or she'll die too."

Tristan lowered his gun. His chest tightened. "Erika . . ."

"I hope you won't hold it against me. A bullet to her head, but I was too far away. I'm a good shot, but you know how it is—perfection is always out of reach. Cigarette?"

The Frenchman put his Luger down on the dock. Fate was mocking him yet again. He felt like a leaf shed in autumn and carried off by the wind.

"You have a choice to make. I can hide you and have you exfiltrated, or you can choose to stay with your German friends. I can say I saw the British shoot the guards and your friend. No one will question my word, given my standing."

Tristan's mind churned. If Erika died, there would be no witnesses. He could continue his mission and maybe even get his hands on the fourth relic. If she survived and talked, though, that would be the end. There were too many uncertainties. His chances of survival were much greater if he fled. Only an idiot or a reckless fool would choose to stay.

The Count saw the doubt in Tristan's eyes. "Do you like Verdi, Signor Marcas, or whoever you are?"

"Yes, more than Wagner . . ."

"He composed the famous opera *La Forza del destino*. As I see it, men fall into two categories. There are those who follow their destiny, and those who create it. What kind of man are you?"

A blinding light landed on them as Tristan was about to reply. The spotlight flooded the dock and the surrounding sea. Shouts and barked orders grew nearer. Tristan blinked and took a long drag on his cigarette, then said clearly, "I make my own fate. Why don't we go and join the other guests from tonight's magnificent party?"

The game was back on.

"On the way, I'd like to check on the precision of your shot," continued Marcas.

The two men reached the beach, which was crawling with armed men. The Frenchman felt safe with the Count. No one dared approach them. In fascist Italy, submitting to those in uniform had become second nature. They took the same path Tristan had taken earlier, avoiding the group of people gathered around the two Blackshirts, and heading instead for the area where Erika had fallen.

As they got closer, Tristan could feel his determination waning. His brain wanted Erika dead, but his heart wanted her to survive.

A small crowd was standing around a deckchair that bore a woman's body. Tristan instantly recognized Erika's blonde hair. An SS officer was examining her head. One of the men turned around as Tristan and the Count approached.

It was Heydrich.

"Ah, there you are," said the head of the Gestapo. "Erika von Essling seems to have run into the British commando unit. Did you see her attackers?"

"No, I was with the Count. My God, what's happened?"

Heydrich held up his leather-gloved hand to prevent Tristan from getting closer to the body.

"That's strange, since you were seen with her in the palace. She looked unconscious."

"She was knocked over by the fleeing crowd," explained Tristan. "I set her down on a bench and ran to find a doctor."

"He did," added Count Di Stella. "He asked me to help, and I took him to the lifeguard post. Unfortunately, it was closed. How are the Führer and the Duce?"

"Safe and sound. The terrorists didn't have time to set off the bombs. I'm actively hunting their accomplices in this failed attack."

"I hope you'll hang them," lied the Count. "They nearly succeeded."

"Fate wouldn't allow it," replied Heydrich. "As always with the Führer."

Tristan tried to get around the head of the Gestapo. "Please let me through, I want to see her."

This time Heydrich stepped aside. "Oh, that's right—you were particularly taken with her . . ."

Tristan knelt next to the young woman's body, his heart pounding. A puddle of blood looked like a halo around her head.

"Don't worry," offered Himmler's right-hand man. "She's unconscious, but alive. She'll pull through. As for the Führer, he's completely unharmed."

61

The footman pushed open the door to the royal sitting room and let the Prime Minister through. Even for a regular like Churchill, this place, where so many politicians had seen their careers reach their zeniths, had a powerful atmosphere. It was also the only place in Britain where smoking was theoretically prohibited, given the sovereign's presence. Luckily, he enjoyed a personal dispensation. It could hardly bother the King, who was a compulsive smoker himself.

Churchill had never been fascinated by the royal family, but he knew that they were an integral part of British history. And King George VI's decision to stay in the palace, despite the Blitz, had galvanized the people behind the throne.

As he entered the room, the Prime Minister bowed to the King, who was standing in front of one of the light-filled full-length windows that looked out over Green Park. One thing that Churchill had always found impressive was the sovereign's desk. It was home to all the necessary instruments for his royal correspondence, which had remained largely unchanged for centuries: the seal, sticks of red wax, and—the only concession to modernity—a gold lighter to melt it.

"Please come in, Prime Minister," said George VI as he held out a firm hand. The thin, pale, yet regal-looking King was wearing his black admiral's uniform. In private, he preferred this more elegant attire to the army uniform he wore for public appearances. As Commander in Chief of the Armed Forces of the United

Kingdom and Canada—a title that was more honorary than operational—protocol dictated that he wear the uniform every day.

"Please sit down."

"Gladly, Your Majesty. My left knee has been playing up of late.
I suspect it might be a double agent on Hitler's payroll."

George VI smiled. He had learned to appreciate the Prime
Minister's sense of humour. Their personal relationship had
changed greatly since Churchill had become the head of the government on 10 May 1940—the very day Germany invaded much of
Western Europe. It was common knowledge that the King had not
wanted Churchill as Prime Minister, thinking him too fickle, unpredictable, and aggressive. What's more, the Bulldog had been a
fervent supporter of his brother, Edward VIII, whose short reign
had ended in forced abdication. But then a miracle had happened.
Churchill had inspired the British people with his energy and
leadership. The King himself had fallen under the spell of his
impetuous Prime Minister. Within eighteen months they had forged
an unbreakable alliance underpinned by deep-seated mutual
respect. Each week, the Prime Minister sent the King a comprehensive report, and they discussed it together over glasses of
twenty-year-old single malt.

"To your health, Prime Minister," said the King.

"Long live the King!" proclaimed Churchill.

George VI smiled again as he opened his gold cigarette case,
which bore the royal coats of arms. He took out a cigarette, which
featured a white filter bearing a crown. It was his twentieth of the
day. He had smoked like a chimney since he'd finally triumphed
over his stutter four years earlier.

"I won't offer you one, my dear Winston, since you have made
your preference quite clear."

"Cigars are much better for your health," replied Churchill as
he lit a Romeo y Julieta, then emptied his glass—his second of the
morning—in a single gulp, and let out a satisfied chuckle.

"You seem in good spirits, Prime Minister," said the King, who
had returned to the window to contemplate the park.

"For good reason, sir. The moustached dictator's offensive has halted outside of Moscow. Radio Berlin announces the city's fall daily, but the Germans aren't going anywhere. Pretty soon Hitler will begin imagining he's the victim of a Judeo-Masonic conspiracy by his own troops."

A ray of sunlight shone through the window, landing on the King's face. He crossed his arms and lowered his voice. "Speaking of conspiracies, Winston, I've had a look at your weekly review, and I have a few thoughts on Operation Doge in Venice."

"I imagined you would."

"You knew that I was hesitant about the assassinations of Hitler and Mussolini, even though our German adversary tried to have me and my family kidnapped."

"I take full responsibility for the operation's failure, but we had to try."

The King shook his head as he exhaled a tall column of white smoke. "Combining the assassinations with the primary objective of the mission—retrieving the third swastika—was a great risk. And as a result, Hitler and Mussolini are still alive and well, and the swastika is lost to us all, at the bottom of the Venetian lagoon."

Churchill remained impassive. He had expected the King's disappointment and reproach, but didn't let it preoccupy him. In the United Kingdom, the sovereign could share his opinion with the Prime Minister in private, but he had no real power over the way the country was managed. Or the war. Parliamentary monarchy ensured that the King was no more than a figure of moral authority. Nevertheless, Churchill greatly valued his relationship with George VI, whose popularity and prestige among the people was at an all-time high.

"May I speak freely, Your Majesty?" asked the Bulldog in a conciliatory tone.

"Of course. Our relationship is based on our shared candidness."

Churchill placed his palms flat on the table. "And our mutual trust," he said. "Earlier this year, you interceded personally to ensure I would help Commander Malorley search for these relics. I shared my scepticism with you but did as you asked. He led his first operation in Montségur and brought back the . . . object, and then I authorized him to create his own research department within the SOE. As promised."

"And I thank you for it. Did you notice that the Germans invaded Russia just after we recovered the second relic? It was a risky operation, but it opened a new front to the east, providing some much-needed relief for Britain."

"I hope you'll forgive me for seeing it as a mere coincidence, Your Majesty."

The King remained perfectly still. "Kings don't believe in coincidences, Winston."

Churchill gnawed on his cigar. "I am a profoundly rational person! You'll never get me to believe Hitler decided to attack Russia because of divine inspiration."

"I myself am a follower of reason, but that doesn't exclude the possibility of believing in God and his mysterious ways. There are powers out there that are beyond us."

"Your Majesty, please understand that I cannot conduct this war based on such assertions. That being said . . ."

"Yes?"

"I'm a pragmatic man, and if the quest for these supposedly magical relics can play a role in the outcome of the war, we might as well stack the odds in our favour."

George VI sat down facing his Prime Minister, a broad smile on his face.

"I'm very glad to hear that, Winston. There is still one more swastika to be found. Please give Commander Malorley all the necessary resources to continue his quest. Speaking of which, I know Aleister Crowley is now a member of his team. Keep an eye on that man. He's dangerous."

"Why?"

The King didn't answer. Churchill stifled his annoyance. He hated it when people kept things from him. "I'll take your silence as a reply, Your Majesty, but there is one question that I can't shake."

"The same one as usual, I suppose?"

"Yes. Why do you believe so firmly in the power of these objects?"

The King massaged the bridge of his nose. Churchill had noticed he did so when hesitating.

"I'm sorry, Winston. I can't tell you. At least, not for now."

"I must insist. I need something to strengthen my support for this . . . quest."

The King seemed to be thinking. He had inherited his father's marble features. He was a sphinx. After a moment, he spoke. "You're right. It must all be very strange to you, so I'll tell you what I can. My father, King George V, knew about the legend of the four swastikas. Like his father, and all of our ancestors who have sat on the throne. Every royal family in Europe knows about it."

"I don't know what to say, Your Majesty. That's . . . unbelievable!"

"The quest for these relics is hardly new. It began long ago, when royal dynasties became established in the West. And those who forgot about it didn't survive . . . That's all I can say for now," affirmed the King as he stood, signalling that the meeting was over. "I won't keep you any longer, Prime Minister. You must be terribly busy."

Churchill stood in turn, bowed respectfully, and shook the King's outstretched hand. He felt reassured by the sovereign's explanation, unbelievable though it might be. He was relieved that it wasn't simply a personal obsession—there had been cases of mental instability in the royal family before.

As Churchill was leaving, George VI's voice reached him. "I know you don't believe me, Winston, but you'll see. Hitler's loss of the swastika will provoke a major event in the days to come."

The Prime Minister froze.

"So, I'll give you a bit of advice, if I may," continued the King. "Find the last relic. It's the only way to escape the Apocalypse."

62

The building's neo-baroque façade looked out over the Thames.
Malorley stood in front of the window on the sixth and last floor,
watching the river's muddy waters flow past. No real Londoner
would ever dare dip even a toe in, for fear of catching a terrible
disease. The Blitz had destroyed a third of the city's sewer pipes,
so the public works department had been forced to install temporary collectors that dumped vast quantities of waste water directly
into the Thames.

The Commander closed the window and returned to his desk.
They'd moved into the new offices two days earlier, and he couldn't
stand the damp smell that filled the air, forcing him to open the
windows repeatedly. The Prime Minister had personally ordered
the move to this anonymous building. There was no sign—not at
the entrance nor upon exiting the lift. Nothing suggested that
Department S—an illegitimate offspring of the SOE—even existed.

S for swastika.

The quest had become a priority.

The Department occupied the entire top floor, but three-
quarters of the offices were still empty. The head of the SOE had
assured Malorley that reinforcements—occult specialists from
Naval Intelligence—would be arriving shortly. Department S was
now an invisible replica of the Ahnenerbe.

A red light flashed on his telephone. He picked up to hear his
secretary's grating voice. "Captain Fleming and Miss d'Estillac are
here."

"Send them in."

He sat back in his chair, a pensive look on his face. They'd just returned from their mission, and Fleming had already handed in a copy of the report he'd delivered to his superior at the Admiralty. As he'd read the account—unusually well written for that type of document—Malorley could feel the writer's bitterness about the outcome. For Fleming, though, only the failed assassination attempt mattered. The details about how they had lost the relic were an afterthought.

Malorley did not share the navy man's pessimism. The important thing was that the swastika hadn't fallen into the Germans' hands. But Ian Fleming couldn't have cared less about the relic and its hypothetical powers.

The door opened and the two secret agents stepped in. Malorley stood up to greet them. Laure looked troubled, and Fleming's face was bruised and swollen, as if he'd lost a boxing match.

"I'm glad to have you both back here safe and sound," he said amenably.

"Thank you, Commander," replied Fleming. "Do you have any questions about my report?"

"No," said Malorley, tapping his finger on the cover of the brown file. "I just wanted to see you. Of course, I'm sorry things didn't go according to plan. For you . . . or for us."

Fleming pretended not to grasp the allusion to the double mission. "As the mission leader, I would like to formally request that Laure, or Matilda here, be awarded the Military Medal. She was exceptionally brave. And, of course, another for Tristan Marcas . . ."

"I will back your request, which will undoubtedly be accepted," replied the Commander. Then he turned towards the Frenchwoman. "Unfortunately, Laure, you won't be able to wear it until the war is over. A disadvantage of belonging to the SOE."

The young woman looked coldly at Fleming, then focused her gaze on Malorley.

"I don't care about your trinkets. We abandoned Marcas on Lido Island. He doesn't need a medal! He needs our help to escape the Nazis, if he's even still alive."

Fleming's features hardened. "I stand by my decision. He is an invaluable agent, but we couldn't save him. I couldn't risk the lives of the rest of the commando."

Malorley realized just how much tension there was between the two agents. Their relationship had clearly deteriorated. It was a shame, but there would be no consequences. The mission was over, and Fleming would go back to Naval Intelligence, while Laure would continue her work with Department S.

"I agree with Captain Fleming, Laure. He made the right decision, given the circumstances. As for Tristan, we are going to try to save him." Malorley pulled out a pale-yellow file and placed it on top of the report. "Everything's in here. I shouldn't reveal anything yet, but we'll be launching the operation in just a few hours."

There was a number on the cover: *007*.

"I truly hope that man makes it out alive," replied Fleming, intrigued. "What's the significance of that number?"

"Curious, aren't you?"

"I like numbers. A hobby of mine . . . They're the secret language of the universe. Nothing mystical about that."

"The captain even explained to me that according to numerology, France will be liberated in 1944," Laure chimed in. "But I suspect he just wanted to cheer me up."

"So, why 007?"

"Just last week the administration asked us to begin assigning code numbers to active agents. I chose this one as a tribute to John Dee, one of Marcas's aliases."

"I don't understand," replied Fleming.

Malorley stood up and walked over to the bookcase, which covered most of one wall. A hundred rare books, including some printed before 1500, were carefully lined up on the shelves. He selected one with a damaged red binding and brought it back to his desk. He opened it to a page near the end. On the left page, an engraving depicted an elderly man with a thin beard. On the right, there was a text in Shakespearian English with illustrations of astrological signs.

"This is a work by the real John Dee. *The Five Books of Mystery*. And this is his portrait. The mathematician, astrologer, and alchemist was also, as you know, a spy for Queen Elizabeth I," explained Malorley as he placed his index finger at the bottom of the portrait. "Look here, just under Dee's neck. His symbolic signature. He signed all of his secret reports for the Queen this way: *007*. The double zero represents the Queen's eyes. For her eyes only. The seven, Dee's favourite number, symbolizes understanding. Like Tristan Marcas, he looked for the sacred swastikas. That's why I chose his name and his code."

Fleming smiled. "I'm not sure why, but *007* really does have a ring to it."

Malorley closed the book. "It's a bit odd that you focus on that, when I've just revealed that Dee was looking for the relics in the sixteenth century."

"Don't take this the wrong way," said the navy man as he stood, "but I don't believe in all that for a second. Hitler has lost his silly bauble, but nothing has happened yet."

"I hear you're a gambling man, Ian," said Malorley. "I bet you a case of my best whisky that something major will happen soon. Something in our favour."

"I accept," said Fleming. "Now, if you don't mind, sir, I'd best be going. I have a meeting at the Admiralty in an hour, and I don't want to be late."

"Of course, Captain."

Fleming bowed to Laure. "I hope that someday you'll forgive me for Venice. It was the only way . . ."

"If you say so," she replied coldly.

The Captain stepped out of the room, leaving Malorley alone with Laure.

"That Fleming is an interesting man," said the Commander. "His report was such a pleasure to read. He has a real gift for writing."

"Good for him. He and his pretty words can go to hell," answered Laure. "You said you had a plan to save Tristan?"

"Yes, I didn't want to get into it in front of Fleming. Better to keep this among us . . . and another Department S agent." He picked up his telephone again. "Crowley? Come to my office."

Then the Commander turned to Laure. "I kept busy while you were away. You remember Moira O'Connor, don't you? The owner of the Hellfire Club?"

"Of course, that awful redhead from the cemetery."

"We've managed to convince her that Crowley is a double agent. He's been feeding her information for her contacts in Berlin. And—"

There was a knock on the door. When it opened, the mage appeared. Laure hid her surprise at what she saw. He was no longer the eccentric man she had met before the mission. Crowley was wearing a classic grey three-piece suit with a red tie. With a pipe in his mouth, what little hair he had left carefully coiffed, and a calm look in his eyes, he could have been one of the honourable members of Malorley's club. It even looked like he'd lost a few pounds.

"Ah, Laure, I'm delighted to see you safe and sound," he said, kissing her hand. He sat down in the chair Fleming had occupied.

"I was just telling Laure about the information you're going to feed Miss O'Connor," said Malorley as he pulled a message on a piece of SOE letterhead out of the 007 file.

"Did the last message I gave Moira get results?" asked Crowley as he filled his pipe.

"Yes, the Nazi saboteurs packed their bags and disappeared the very next day. Which means they took the bait. Here's the new message we're supposedly sending to our agents in Germany. The Scarlet Fairy could inadvertently save our man. Take a look."

Laure and Crowley leaned in to read the text. *Operation Swastika 3 failed. Be ready to exfiltrate our agent, Erika von Essling. Eliminate the Frenchman.*

Laure smiled for the first time since she'd entered Malorley's office. "If they think this is real, Tristan might have a chance. But I wouldn't want to be in that woman's shoes. You realize she'll be handed over to the Gestapo, don't you? They'll torture her to death."

The head of Department S clasped his hands together on his desk as his expression darkened. "I am sorry for her, but if it means Tristan can get back in the game and continue the quest, I have no regrets. I'd light the fires of hell myself if it could help us win this war. Each camp has one relic now. The last one will determine our fate. I'd rather it ended up with us, on the side of good."

Crowley gently tapped his pipe against the ashtray on the desk. "Beautiful words, Commander, really! Good, evil, freedom . . ." said the mage ironically. "Do you really think those relics give power to whoever holds them?"

"I do now. And I'm not the only one."

Without warning, Crowley slammed his fist onto the table. Laure stared at him in surprise. An energy she'd never seen in him before had suddenly hardened Aleister's plump features. "You retrieved the relic from Montségur last June, and Hitler invaded Russia. A new front, what wonderful news! A bit of respite for Britain! The Nazi wolf left us alone, to sink his teeth into the Red bear. But at what cost? Hundreds of thousands of soldiers killed, alongside unprecedented civilian massacres."

Malorley remained silent. This was the first time he had ever seen Crowley so worked up.

"And now, with your message, you're sending another innocent person to her death. Yes, of course, she's German, our enemy, so what does it even matter in the giant abattoir that we call Europe? Your obsession with the swastikas is destroying the humanity in you."

"The sex-addict sorcerer is giving lessons in ethics? Now I've heard it all!" joked the Commander.

"You are so certain you're on the side of good that you have forgotten to ask the most important question."

"And what's that?"

Crowley studied Malorley, his eyes gleaming, almost hypnotic. Suddenly his voice filled the room. "What if the relics are instruments of evil?"

Epilogue

Soldier First Class Joseph Lockard yawned. His eyes burned from watching the radar screen for hours on end. He looked up at the clock on the wall. 7:03 a.m. Just half an hour to go until his shift was over. Afterward, he'd head to the base for some well-deserved rest. He looked out the window to see the rising sun over Opana Point. The only good thing about the night shift was enjoying this view of the first morning light.

He stretched, then went back to his screen.

Six bright-green spots suddenly appeared, as if by magic, on the top screen. Lockard immediately picked up the phone to call his superior officer. It was standard procedure.

"What's going on?" asked his boss in a sleepy voice.

"Lieutenant, I've got echoes on my screen."

"Are you sure it's not just clutter, like last time?"

"No, I don't think so."

"Okay, I'll be right there."

Three minutes later, Lieutenant Kermit A. Tyler strolled into the radar room in shorts and a white T-shirt. The officer leaned in to get a better look at the screen and scratched his chin.

"Don't worry about it. It's the B17 bomber squadron from San Diego. I got a memo about it last night. They're refuelling here on their way to the Philippines."

The number of spots on the radar screen kept growing.

"That's a lot of planes for just one squadron, Lieutenant. Could it be the Japanese?"

"Lockard, you need to get some rest. Japan is over six thousand kilometers away. They're not crazy enough to come here and attack us. And I seriously doubt they'd send their aircraft carriers all this way."

"So, we shouldn't sound the alarm?" asked the radar operator worriedly.

"Not for this. Last time, the Admiral told me off himself. I'm going back to bed. Wake me when your shift's over."

Lieutenant Tyler would go down in history as the most foolish officer in the history of the American navy. As he lay back down in his bed, a large fleet from the Empire of the Rising Sun was cruising just three hundred and seventy kilometers off the Hawaiian coast. Six aircraft carriers, two battleships, three cruisers, and nine destroyers had travelled thousands of kilometers undetected, to attack the Americans. Over three hundred bombers and fighters took off from the floating beasts, ready to rain death on their enemies.

Twenty-seven minutes after radar picked up their presence, the first Japanese plane flew low over the island's northern coast. It was a Zero reconnaissance plane, which encountered no resistance—because no one had sounded the alarm.

The pilot sent the agreed message to Vice Admiral Chuichi Nagumo: *Pearl Harbor is sleeping.*

Ten minutes later, all hell broke loose on the idyllic island where the American Pacific Fleet was based. The Japanese devastated Pearl Harbor, then left as quickly as they'd come.

The United States was wounded.

The next day—December 8, 1941—Congress ratified President Roosevelt's declaration of war. Japan had woken the sleeping giant. Britain and Russia were no longer alone.

They say that Prime Minister Winston Churchill kissed all of his staff members and opened his best bottle of whisky when he heard that Pearl Harbor had been attacked. In his memoirs, he wrote: "No American will think it wrong of me if I proclaim that to have the United States at our side was to me the greatest joy."

And the conflict became a World War.

Germany and Italy stood by Japan and declared war on the United States. The Axis Powers against the Allies. The dice had been cast. Two huge alliances would go head to head in a battle to the death for control of the world. Though the outcome of the war depended on the weapons and soldiers on the front lines, a few people on both sides knew that another war was being waged. A secret war in which each side possessed a sacred relic. A balance of power, for the time being.

The first was kept in the impregnable Wewelsburg Castle. The second was safely hidden in the United States.

Though the third lay at the bottom of the Venetian lagoon, there was a fourth . . .

The last swastika.

The one that would determine the fate of the world.

Acknowledgements

Thanks to the entire team at our publishing house, Jean-Claude Lattès, which has supported this project since its conception, and to all of the Hachette representatives, to whom our books owe so much.

GIACOMETTI
RAVENNE

Hellbound

Translated from the French by
Maren Baudet-Lackner

There is both creative and destructive energy in every animate and inanimate entity on earth. Light and darkness coexist side by side. The four relics are made up of this union of energies, whose power is so all-consuming and terrible that Christ himself averts his gaze in its presence.

Excerpt from the *Thule Borealis Kulten*

21 June 1942
From: SOE headquarters, Echelon E
To: The Prime Minister's Cabinet War Rooms
Classification: Top Secret, Level 5

Place found:
Yarlung Valley, Tibet: 29°21'26.7"N, 90°58'23.3"E
Montségur Castle, France: 42°52'32.1"N, 1°49'57.5"E
Heiligenkreuz Abbey, Austria: 48°03'23.2"N, 16°07'50.5"E

Last known location:
Wewelsburg Castle, Germany: 51°36'25.6"N, 8°39'04.9"E
MIT, United States: 42°21'36.6"N, 71°05'39.1"W
Venice, Italy: 45°24'17.9"N, 12°22'14.2"E

PROLOGUE

Ipatiev House, Yekaterinburg, Russia
July 17, 1918

It was a warm July night. An enchanted hiatus as rare as a bumper year here, at the foot of the Ural Mountains, the border between Europe and Asia, where summer lasts but the blink of an eye before the land is petrified in solid ice again.

A perfect night for drinking and laughing far from the log cabins and for falling asleep under the stars without the risk of catching pneumonia. And yet, in this July night, not a single soul was enjoying the balmy air in the streets of Yekaterinburg. Since the Revolution, they had all been living in permanent winter—huddled away behind locked doors. Out of fear. Fear of the communists who held the city, first and foremost. The region was nicknamed *Krasnyi Ural*—the red Urals—because of the local council's zeal when it came to mass extermination of the enemies of the people: the bourgeois, kulaks, and reactionaries of all stripes. Fear of the Whites, too. Of the heterogeneous army made up of imperial regiments loyal to the deposed tsar and hordes of Cossacks under the thumb of cruel and intrepid warlords. The Whites were emerging from the plains of Siberia in droves, getting ever closer to their goal. In a matter of days, they would reach the city.

Two rabid bears were ripping Russia to pieces. Red against White. A blind and ferocious fight which only one of them would survive.

"Comrade Evgueni, do you think they'll spare us if we fall into their hands?"

"The Cossacks will give no quarter. Pity is not one of the rare qualities displayed by Ataman Krasnov's white dogs. They'll cut you into such little pieces your own father won't recognize you. And all while you still breathe, of course."

Evgueni Berin, who had just spoken, wasn't yet thirty but spoke slowly, like an older man. His eyes were dull, faded by the horrors he had seen. The young soldier by his side seemed to be barely more than a boy. He was drowning in his oversized coat which had been mended in several places.

Sitting in the sentry box of the watchtower, the two men were sharing a half-spent cigarette with their feet up on the Maxim machine-gun's ammunition reserve. The weapon was trained on the shutters of Ipatiev House. The Ural council had transformed the opulent two-storey house nestled into a hillside on Voznessenski Street into a makeshift fortress. A tall wooden fence with two watchtowers surrounded the property. The windows had even been painted white to keep anyone from seeing inside. A Red Army detachment had been assigned to guard the house at all times. And as if that were not enough, a team of Cheka agents had arrived as reinforcements a week ago. The reason for this display of force was no secret. All of Yekaterinburg knew the identity of the family that had been sequestered at Ipatiev House since the end of April.

"To lull me to sleep, my mother used to tell me that whenever one of us dies, a new star is born," whispered the young man. "According to her, the Milky Way is a pearly fabric in which each star represents a soul."

"Tolia Kabanov, your mother is surely a good woman, but she's also a fool!" exclaimed Evgueni Berin as he slapped the other soldier on the back. "The people mustn't believe in such nonsense anymore. Souls, God, heaven . . . All invented to keep peasants and workers from rebelling. The only heaven there is, is the one we build here on earth." *If we manage to do so,* he thought to himself.

The Revolution was less than a year old and had so many enemies that not a single communist would have bet on its triumph any time soon. Broad swathes of territory were under the control of the White Army, quietly aided by the English and French, who were unhappy about the peace treaty signed between the Bolsheviks and the Germans.

Evgueni stubbed out the cigarette on the floor of the sentry box and checked his watch. It was time. He had been waiting for this moment for too long. An eternity. Thirteen years to be precise. Said to be one of the most feared Cheka officers, Evgueni Berin was proud to be an early convert to the Revolution—a soldier activist forged from the purest ideals of Bolshevism. Comrade Lenin had chosen him personally to relay what would happen here tonight within the walls of Ipatiev House. Evgueni had travelled nearly 2000 kilometers east from Moscow, on the Trans-Siberian Railway. It had been a long and difficult journey dotted with a seemingly endless number of stops between Nizhny Novgorod and Yekaterinburg.

Light escaped through the front door to the house as it opened slightly. Comrade Pavel Damov appeared with a wave. Evgueni despised the man. Damov was an unscrupulous brute. Unfortunately for Evgueni, he was also remarkably intelligent. Having successfully climbed the ranks during the Revolution, he had joined its most feared branch—the Cheka. It was there that he had earned the nickname Lord of Lead, during a crackdown on a monastery in Kostroma, on the banks of the Volga. On a whim, Damov had forced the monks to swallow molten lead before finishing them off with an axe. The exploit had earned him a promotion within the Cheka: in less than six months, he had become the official assassin of the regime's most vocal enemies. People whispered that he was corrupt to the core, but no one had ever proved it.

Evgueni stuck his fingers in his mouth to whistle at the lorry driver parked in the street. The old ZIS's engine coughed three times before roaring into life.

"I don't understand, comrade," said the young soldier, Kabanov. "This is the third night in a row you've asked Grigori to start up that heap and waste petrol idling there for fifteen minutes. You can hear it from the other end of the street. The neighbours complained yesterday."

"I'm delighted to hear it," replied Evgueni. "Stay at your post."

"Are you sure you don't want me to come with you?" the boy asked hopefully.

Evgueni studied him. How old was he—sixteen, seventeen, maybe? He may not live to see his next birthday. The latest reports of Red Army casualties were gruesome. No, Kabanov didn't need to see what was about to happen. "You better stay here and watch the stars," Evgueni replied firmly.

He climbed down from the watchtower and strode up to the heavy front door, which had been left wide open. A waft of sweat and tepid wine welcomed him. A seven-cartridge Mauser in hand, Lord of Lead stood flanked by a dozen men with Nagant revolvers. Half of them were Latvians—non-Russian allies to the Bolsheviks. Yakov Yurovsky, the commander sent by the Ural council, was also present.

"You're just in time, comrade," said Yurovsky with a tap on Evgueni's shoulder. "They're all gathered upstairs."

"We told them we were going to take their photograph in the cellar, to show the world they're still alive," chuckled Damov.

One of the Latvians raised his hand in annoyance. "It's the boy. He can't walk because of his illness."

"Have his father carry him," laughed Damov. "And don't bother me with such details again, do you hear?"

Evgueni followed Lord of Lead and Yurovsky down to the cellar. Their boots clicked on the stone steps. Twenty-three. There were twenty-three steps. Evgueni knew the number by heart, having run through the scene several times. He was no amateur.

Damov reached the cellar first. He was pleased to see his instructions had been followed to the letter. Wooden boards covered the back wall of the room, which was large enough to house a neighbourhood party committee. An out-of-place chandelier with teardrop beads shed a frigid light on the room.

"Even in their cellars, the bourgeois have to boast," he spat.

Evgueni had withdrawn into a dark corner for the best view of the room and its occupants. He watched as the council's representative stood in the middle of the cellar and took a crumpled piece of paper from his jacket. In a solemn voice, he read out the terse text that authorized their presence in the house on this night. No one had dared sign the official document.

The clicking of heels and clogs echoed in the stairwell. Evgueni stepped even further back into the darkness.

The servants came first. A valet, a chambermaid, a cook, and the family doctor. Their eyes darted fearfully around the room. Evgueni thought one was missing, but wasn't sure. Not that it mattered—the staff were not important.

The Chekists ushered them towards the far end of the cellar. "Stand against the wall. Slaves behind the masters, for the photograph," one of them ordered.

Then came softer steps. And whispering. Five women appeared in the dim glare. With weary faces and wild hair, they advanced in their thick grey dresses as if they were sleepwalking. The eldest, the mother, moved slowly, followed by her four distraught daughters. The ghostly figures seemed to be tied to one another by an invisible chain. A man appeared at the rear gazing affectionately at the child in his arms. A bushy moustache and full beard covered his hollow cheeks, while his oversized shirt only highlighted his thin frame.

"May we have chairs for my wife and son, please?" he asked hesitantly.

Lord of Lead grabbed him by the collar. "Do you really still think you're the master, Kolya?" he barked.

Commander Yurovsky intervened. "Let him have his chairs, comrade. We're not monsters . . ." He signalled to one of the Latvians, who pulled up two rickety chairs.

The mother sat down without a word as the father settled the boy. "Sit up straight, Aliocha," he said. "They're going to take our photograph. Look dignified." Then he turned to his daughters: "You too, remember who you are."

The group was finally ready. Masters and servants were perfectly lined up, awaiting the photographer.

An eerie silence filled the cellar.

From his spot near the stairs, Evgueni Berin studied every detail of the scene before his eyes. A long-forgotten feeling arose in him: pity. These men and women were flesh and blood, just like him.

Steadied by her older sister, one of the girls was desperately trying to stifle her sobs. The mother didn't seem to realise what was about to happen. Evgueni knew their names by heart. The four daughters were Olga, Tatiana, Maria, and Anastasia, and the mother Alexandra. As for the youngest, weakling son, his name was Alexei.

Evgueni felt his determination falter but knew he could not lose track of his goal. He had waited for this moment for too long. His hand closed around his little sister's silver necklace in his pocket. She had never taken it off in her lifetime.

At once, his courage returned. This was not a family like any other: the five women, the boy, and the man were the Romanovs. The imperial family that was part of a dynasty that had ruled the country with an iron fist for the past three centuries. The thin patriarch, who was trying to adopt a flattering pose in front of an imaginary camera, was Nicholas II, former Emperor of All Russia. But today, this man, who he hated more than anything else in the world, seemed about as fearsome as a famished old dog. Evgueni struggled to chase the image of the brave father from his mind. This was Nicholas the Bloody!

On a freezing night in 1905, at the Winter Palace in Saint Petersburg, this man's frail hands had ordered his troops to fire into a crowd of hundreds of poor, defenceless people.

Evgueni tightened his grip on the necklace. Natalia had just turned thirteen. In the early morning, he had found her dead body on the frozen square, her face appallingly disfigured by a sword.

Comrade Lenin was right. There must be no pity for the oppressors.

Damov's voice broke the silence. "Comrade Yurovsky, it's time to end this."

The commander walked over to the tsar and puffed up his chest. There were rules to be followed. "By ruling of the Court of Justice and the unanimous vote of the Ural council, you, Nikolai Romanov, your wife, and all your children, have been condemned to death. The sentence is to be carried out immediately."

The sound of the Nagant revolvers being cocked echoed through the room. There were panicked cries.

The tsar stood his ground and kept his head high. "This is not justice—this is murder," he said. "The murder of women and a child. You are evil incarnate. God and men will judge you for your crimes."

Evgueni came out into the light and walked over to the deposed emperor. Their faces were nearly touching. "You know a thing or two about murder, don't you, Nikolai?"

The former tsar shook his head. "I don't understand," he said.

"This is a waste of time," interrupted Yurovsky, coming over to join them, gun in hand.

Evgueni raised his hand and shot him an imperious look. He was Lenin's right hand and his authority was the law for everyone in the room. The commander retreated.

"Let me finish," ordered Evgueni. "Then you can do your duty." He turned back to Nicholas II. "My father and sister were protesting beneath the windows of your palace on the 9th of January 1905."

Nikolai went pale.

Evgueni continued, his voice tense. "Do you remember? All they wanted was a little bread and a few freedoms. My sister loved you. She said you were a good and generous ruler. There were many women and children among the protestors. Hundreds. Children the age of your own. And what did you do that night? Your dogs at their heels, your soldiers butchered them with their swords. People say they even laughed. When I reached the square in the early morning, I found my sister's dead body. My father had been disembowelled, bled like a pig for an Easter feast." Anger coursed through Evgueni's veins. "They say that the very same night, in the same palace, your wife and daughters were trying on fine gowns embroidered with pearls and emeralds that had arrived straight from Paris. And that you sat smoking a cigar as the carnage raged below."

"My God, no! I love my people far too much for that," said the tsar as he shook his head. "I never ordered that massacre. The general made the decision on his own. I ask God for forgiveness every single day."

"Well, that's lucky. You're about to be able to address him directly," replied Evgueni with a sign to Yurovsky.

"No, wait!" begged Nikolai. "Spare my wife and children. In exchange, I'll tell you an invaluable secret. A secret that will make you powerful men, more powerful even than Lenin and Trotsky."

Evgueni studied the former emperor. He was used to being lied to; it came with his job. But this man seemed sincere. "I'm listening," he said.

"Our dynasty has passed it on from generation to generation for centuries. It bestows wealth and power on us. At the beginning of the Revolution, I foolishly sent it away for safekeeping. I'll tell you where it is if you free my family."

Evgueni took out his pistol and glued it to Nicholas II's temple. "You are in no position to give orders, Nikolai. Tell me your secret."

"It's a relic. A sacred relic from the depths of time. It's—"

A gunshot rang out. The last tsar of Russia was unable to finish his sentence. He staggered as a red stain spread across his chest. Then he collapsed as his family and servants looked on in horror and began to scream again.

"A relic! What utter nonsense," exclaimed Lord of Lead over the top of his smoking gun. "Lenin says superstition muzzles—"

"I give the orders here!" shouted Evgueni.

"You came to watch. I came to execute them. Would you like me to report your counter-Revolutionary attitude?" scolded Damov. "Stand back before you get shot too."

Evgueni glanced discreetly at the commander and other executioners, who were staring at him. He knew those looks. The slightest hesitation on his part would be relayed to the authorities. He stepped towards the firing squad.

"All right, but spare the girls and the boy. They don't—"

"No room for bourgeois sentimentalism here!" shouted Lord of Lead as he brandished his Mauser. "Comrades, aim for the heart, like I taught you. Whatever you do, don't shoot them in the head—it's too messy."

The rifles and revolvers fired one after the other amid screams from the imperial family and their servants. One of the executioners ran out of bullets and resorted to his bayonet, which he plunged into the throat of the tsarevich as he crawled across the floor. The crown prince died with his head on his father's boots.

"You idiot!" shouted Yurovsky. "He'll bleed all over the place!"

The empress and one of her daughters seemed to still be alive. Damov leaned over the tsarina, who was writhing like an exposed earthworm. Red and green shimmers of light escaped from the bloody bodice of her dress. "Look at this! The bullets bounced off these gemstones sewn into their dresses." The Chekist grabbed two emeralds and a ruby from Alexandra's chest, then nonchalantly shot the nearest daughter, who was grasping for her mother, in the eye.

Evgueni was beginning to feel nauseous. The execution had turned into a bloodbath.

"Finish them off!" shouted Yurovsky "And take the bodies upstairs to the lorry."

"And then what?" asked Evgueni.

"We'll take them to Four Brothers Forest, about thirty kilometers from here. We'll burn them and dump them in a well. Make sure to state in your report that everything went to plan. The comrades fulfilled their revolutionary duties without hesitation."

The killers knelt over the bloody corpses to collect their jewels. Now all Evgueni wanted to do was murder *them*. They were just like the soldiers who had killed his father and sister.

"I will be sure to underscore your courage when faced with these women and the boy," he replied disdainfully. "And, Damov, you'll need to hand over all the jewels your men are so eagerly collecting. They are the property of the Revolution."

With that, Evgueni turned to leave. He was about to be sick. The revenge he had waited so long to claim had turned into an indescribable horror. The floor and wall were covered in a viscous mixture of flesh, blood, and urine. A foul smell wafted through the cellar, tormenting his feverish mind. This would be his final memory of the Romanovs.

When he stepped outside Ipatiev House, he took a deep breath of clean air and contemplated the night sky, where he was certain he could see new stars twinkling.

PART I

Success is not final; failure is not fatal. It is the courage to continue that counts.

Winston Churchill

I

The car glided slowly down a gravel road that looked like it hadn't been travelled for years. A grey, impenetrable wood stretched as far as the eye could see on either side. Tristan Marcas wondered if the region was truly inhabited; there was an occasional path breaking away from the road and disappearing into the trees, but he hadn't caught sight of any village rooftops or even a squat, isolated farm. When he looked carefully, Tristan could indeed see traces of human activity—bundles of branches tied together with brambles and a tree cut down with an axe and already covered in moss—but the place seemed abandoned.

Since they had left Königsberg, the road had wound deeper and deeper into this opaque forest that blanketed the land right up to the sea. Every now and again, Tristan had seen the uniformed chauffeur glance feverishly at the maps spread across the passenger seat as though he too had the dizzying and absurd impression that they were lost in an endless land.

"Are we far from the castle?" asked Tristan.

The driver took his time before answering. In the SS, it was always best to think long and hard before speaking. "I think it will take half an hour to reach the coast, then another solid hour before we arrive at the von Essling estate," he responded.

Tristan rolled down the window and stuck his head outside. High up over the road, the heavy branches formed a vault of leaves so thick he couldn't see the colour of the sky. But he could smell the salt in the sea breeze. The Baltic Sea was near. Given the dwindling distance to his destination, he decided to collect his thoughts.

He'd left on direct orders from Himmler himself. During the brief meeting the Reichsführer had granted Tristan, he'd made it clear that, with the United States now in the war and the intense fighting on the eastern front, the Ahnenerbe would need to take on new responsibilities. And Himmler wanted to know if Erika von Essling was fit to lead the institution, despite her injuries.

"Look," said the chauffeur.

The once-dense forest was growing sparser. Through the trees, Tristan could see light reflected off an immense grey surface. Twisted pines groaned in the wind. They were almost free. Suddenly, as they rounded a bend, the sea appeared. The endless grey expanse seemed to touch the heavy white clouds on the horizon.

The car came to a halt, and Tristan stepped out into the wind.

In an hour, he would see Erika and meet his fate.

Liebendorf
The von Essling estate

Erika von Essling had not been in her childhood room for years. When she had returned to the castle to recover, her family had chosen to place her in a different bedroom, to avoid confusing her. The doctors said she had amnesia, and that they mustn't strain her memory. What idiots! She remembered everything, from the first tooth she had lost and slipped under her pillow to her last torrid night with Tristan. The one thing she couldn't recall was what had really happened in Venice, the night of the meeting between Hitler and Mussolini. She had woken up at the hospital, her right temple mangled by a stray bullet. They told her she had been hit during a firefight between German soldiers and the English commando that had tried to assassinate the Führer, but she couldn't remember any of it. She had been trying in vain to piece things together ever since.

Erika opened the door and stepped in. The shutters were closed, but she didn't bother opening them. Ever since she had injured herself, bright light had been provoking dizzy spells, so she preferred to remain shrouded in darkness. And besides, she knew the view behind them by heart: a long hedge-lined drive that wound through the estate to the main gate. The gate Tristan would arrive at.

She lay down on the bed. It felt softer than it used to. Several blankets must have been layered on top to protect the mattress from damp. The walls were bare, except for one, which featured two photographs in glass frames. The first one, in sepia, depicted a woman wearing a sparkling gold diadem and countless necklaces. It was Sophia Schliemann, the wife of the archaeologist who had discovered the legendary ruins of Troy and Mycenae. Adorned like an idol, Sophia was wearing ancient jewellery her husband had unearthed. She had always fascinated Erika and had impacted her decision to become an archaeologist in a decisive way. The second picture was of a tanned, jovial man in his thirties. He stood in front of an ancient wall holding a pick. Hans had been her archaeology professor at university—and her first love. Full of nostalgia, she reached out to stroke the frame. What would he say if he knew she was running the Ahnenerbe? Erika still wondered how she had ended up leading it. She had gone from being a promising young archaeologist to a leading Reich scientist. How had she—a young woman from a good family—ended up scouring the globe for sacred swastikas, from Montségur in Spain, to Crete, and then Venice? The first time around she had been following the Reichsführer's orders, but what had prevented her from quitting after that?

The answer had a name: Tristan.

He was the reason she had continued with the quest. She got up from the bed and steadied herself against the wall. Once again, she felt dizzy. Where had he been when that bullet had nearly killed her in Venice? What had he been doing? Why hadn't he protected her? The memory of that night kept escaping her grasp. A memory she knew involved the man she loved.

The Baltic Sea

The road ran alongside a dune covered in wild grass. Tristan was leaning against the parked car. He closed his eyes to keep out the sand that was being blown about by the wind. Summer was an alien concept here. He pulled away from the car and ran towards the narrow path that led through the dune to the beach. The sand was littered with grey flotsam and empty shells. It was like crossing a crowded marine cemetery. He felt better once he reached the narrow strip of darker sand right by the water. As his feet sank into the wet ground, he finally felt like himself again. Deep down, he had always hated the ocean. The endless horizon was too much for mankind: its limitless space kindled the desire to go beyond what was possible. He was certain mad conquerors and insatiable dictators were once men who had spent too much time contemplating the sea. As for Tristan, he needed to feel his feet on the ground to think—now more than ever.

As the telephone didn't work well, the Frenchman had been writing to Erika since she had retreated to her family estate, but the young woman's replies had been terse and trivial and full of contradictions. Was her amnesia getting worse, or was she suspicious? Had she been more seriously injured than everyone had thought, or was she preparing her triumphant return, or even revenge? Tristan had grown wary. He did his best to be discreet and hadn't sent a single message to London since Venice, playing dead.

He turned around and headed back through the dune. In just an hour, he would come face to face with Erika and know where they stood. Either she remembered nothing, or she knew exactly who had tried to sink a bullet between her eyes.

In which case, he would be left with no choice.

Liebendorf
The von Essling estate

Broad steps led up to the castle, whose central building, framed by two smaller wings, looked out over the park. The forest reigned all around. The former hunting residence had belonged to the von Esslings for centuries. Erika's parents had renovated and added to the estate to make it a more comfortable summer residence for the family. But even so, despite the French doors and the colourful roof tiles, the castle remained austere.

Tristan couldn't help but frown as he got out of the car. The castle looked like a tomb waiting for winter to bury it in the snow.

Then Erika stepped out. Her hair, which she had neither cut nor plaited, hung down to her waist. She had lost a lot of weight. As he strode up the drive, Tristan wondered if he should kiss her. Over the course of their long separation, they had never mentioned their relationship. As she drew nearer, he noticed her face had grown nearly transparent. Only her eyes still seemed alive. She was wearing a pair of old boots over riding trousers that were too big for her. Her bust was invisible beneath a woollen shawl.

"Are you cold?" asked Tristan, reaching for her shoulder.

"It's always cold here, even in summer," replied Erika, quickly taking a step back.

She led him through some French doors straight into a vast sitting room with views over the drive. Out of the windows, Tristan could see smooth grey ponds reflecting the crowns of the surrounding trees.

Without so much as glancing at the view, Erika settled in an armchair near the fireplace. She held out her hands to warm them. "I'm still recuperating, but I want to get back to my post as soon as possible. What news do you have from the Ahnenerbe?"

Tristan noticed her tone grow more serious with every word. "Wolfram Sievers, a prehistorian, has been named interim director. He's managing daily affairs. Given the intensification of the war effort, most of the research programmes have been suspended," he explained.

"What about the quest for the swastika? There's only one left now."

Tristan walked towards the fire. He wasn't cold, but the glow of the flames in this huge, gloomy house felt reassuring. "As you know, we got all our information on the swastikas from the *Thule Borealis*," he said. "It led the Ahnenerbe to Tibet, Montségur, and then Crete. But there's nothing whatsoever about the location of the last relic."

"And yet the manuscript is perfectly clear about the fact that four swastikas were hidden," insisted Erika.

"Yes, but the book is incomplete. Either a part of it was cut out, or the author of the *Thule Borealis* didn't have time to finish it," explained Tristan.

Erika's face lit up; it was as though she suddenly had a new lease of life. "We must determine which of these hypotheses is correct. When you get back to Berlin, put together an interdisciplinary team including a philologist, to see if there are any linguistic clues that would indicate that the book is unfinished, as well as a paper specialist. They should be able to determine if one or more pages were removed by studying the manuscript closely."

"That's true," said Tristan with a nod. "But it would be even more useful to follow the *Thule*'s trail to the present day. We know it was written in an abbey in the Middle Ages, but where did it travel after that?"

The Frenchman stood up to study a display case at the far end of the room. Its shelves were filled with bronze torcs and fibulas, funerary urns, and a ceramic statue of an enigmatic character brandishing a mallet. Had these relics encouraged Erika to read archaeology?

"Weistort is the one who first found the *Thule Borealis*," explained Erika.

Tristan turned around abruptly. *Weistort, the former head of the Ahnenerbe, whose methods were often rather summary?* "Why have you never told me that before?" he asked.

Erika shrugged. "I only found out myself right before we left for Venice, through some of Weistort's unclassified documents.

He got the manuscript from a Jewish bookseller in Berlin in 1938."

"I doubt he purchased it . . ."

"That doesn't matter. But we need to find that bookseller."

"Do you really think Weistort let him live?" exclaimed Tristan.

"His family then. Maybe they know something," concluded Erika.

Tristan's eyes widened. "You want me to find a Jewish family in Nazi Germany in 1942? Where should I look first: the camps or the cemeteries?" he asked ironically.

"Why don't you tell me why you're really here instead," she replied drily.

"Himmler has plans to restructure the Ahnenerbe and wants to know if you're well enough to return."

"And he's asked you to assess my condition?"

Tristan kept quiet.

"With the exception of occasional dizzy spells, I'm feeling fine. But I would be even better if I knew what happened in Venice," she added sharply.

"You really don't remember anything?" Tristan asked, incredulous.

This time Erika didn't reply.

"You were hit by a stray bullet. A commando unit tried to—"

"I don't want the official story," she interrupted. "I've heard it a thousand times. I want your version. Where were you when I was shot?"

"Right next to you on the terrace at the Cinema Palace. That's where they evacuated the German delegation. Across from the beach," Tristan lied.

"And you didn't see anything?"

"I saw you fall. I hurried over to find your face covered in blood. Help arrived quickly."

"That's it?"

"Why would you imagine anything else?" asked Tristan, who was growing more agitated by the second. "Everyone tells the same story. There were dozens of witnesses."

"Well what if I remember something different?" asked Erika.

Tristan studied her face. Either she was bluffing, or a part of her memory had suddenly returned. But be that as it may, she clearly didn't trust him anymore. The risk had become too great. "Sometimes with amnesia," he explained, "false memories come in to fill the void."

"I didn't know you were a neurologist, too," she said with a smirk. "I can see you've done your research. Why?" she insisted.

Tristan looked through the French windows to the drive. He hadn't seen anyone on his way in. Not a single gardener or maid. Who lived in this castle with Erika?

"No answer? Do you think I'm crazy? Is that what you're going to tell Himmler?"

Through the open door, Tristan glanced at the oak staircase that led from the hallway to the second floor. The smell of turpentine wafted through the air: it had just been polished. Erika stood up and had to grab the armchair to steady herself.

"Why don't you go and lie down," Tristan suggested. "You're not feeling well. You need to rest. I'll go with you. Is your room upstairs?"

Just as he placed his hand on the Erika's shoulder, the sound of an engine came from the courtyard. Tristan looked out of the window to see two SS officers heading up the steps to the main entrance. A door slammed shut and the squeaking of boots could be heard in the hallway.

"Herr Marcas?" The officers stepped into the living room.

Tristan nodded.

"Come with us."